REASSIGNED

"You've got to help us," sa[...] a major terrorist operation[...]

"No offense, but all you have is an intercepted e-mail that could be about a bomb plot or the opening of a new pizza place," said Fisher. "I'd lean toward the pizza place myself."

"Jeez, Andy, if you don't help me I'll have to rely on the Defense Intelligence Agency."

"That's kind of an ugly threat, Macklin."

"What if I got you permanently assigned to Homeland Security? You'd love it over here. Get your own expense account, nice car. We have our pick of impounds. I can probably hook you up with a drug dealer's condo or something. You should see our office up in New York. Out in the suburbs, on the water. Tell you what—come by around noon tomorrow and I'll set up lunch with the big cheese himself."

"I have a question for you."

"Shoot."

"When you join Homeland Security, do they make you go through a behavior modification program to learn to call the boss 'big cheese'? Or do they do it with drugs?"

CYCLOPS ONE

"A complex and intricately plotted story that skillfully combines a military techno-thriller with a classic 'who-dunnit.'"

—Dale Brown

THREAT LEVEL
BLACK

JIM DeFELICE

POCKET **STAR** BOOKS
New York • London • Toronto • Sydney

This book is a work of fiction. Names, characters, places and inci-
dents are products of the author's imagination or are used fictitious-
ly. Any resemblance to actual events or locales or persons, living or
dead, is entirely coincidental.

An *Original* Publication of POCKET BOOKS

A Pocket Star Book published by
POCKET BOOKS, a division of Simon & Schuster, Inc.
1230 Avenue of the Americas, New York, NY 10020

Copyright © 2005 by Jim DeFelice

ISBN: 0-7434-6423-0

First Pocket Books printing March 2005

10   9   8   7   6   5   4   3   2   1

Cover design by Jae Song

Manufactured in the United States of America

For information regarding special discounts for bulk purchases,
please contact Simon & Schuster Special Sales at
1-800-456-6798 or business@simonandschuster.com

For the men and women in the FBI who bust it every day and end up dodging as much political BS as bullets.

PART ONE
Shut out the Lights

CHAPTER

1

The last light went off in Manhattan three seconds after the bomb blast.

Brooklyn, farther from the epicenter, flickered for another half-second. . . .

The D train had just entered the tunnel under the East River and slammed to a halt, sending its nearly one hundred passengers hurtling toward the front of the cars. The magnetic pulse that had exploded over the Con Ed power yard at the top of the island had wiped out more than just the power; all electrical devices within twenty-five miles stopped functioning—watches, radios, backup generators, old-fashioned fuses, computers, Walkmen, TV sets, electric toothbrushes, hair dryers, toasters, microwave ovens, fire alarms, security devices, video cameras, and children's toys died, their microchips fried. Transformers, regulators, transistors, capacitors—they were all cooked by the blast.

With the lights out in Manhattan, two cars ran through Times Square, crashing into the lobby of the Loup Theater, where a crowd had just gathered for the revival of *Cats*. Flight 704 from London managed to land on the darkened runway at Kennedy but then slid off the apron, just in time to witness the midair collision of two flights trying to land at nearby LaGuardia. The nearly sixty thousand people crowding into Yankee Stadium for the start of the World Series against the Braves began to riot as they rushed for the exits. A fire truck speeding to a car fire on the access ramp of the Brooklyn Bridge skidded out of control at the jammed intersection. Striking an obstruction, it went airborne, flying up and over the bridge into the dark water below. On the George Washington Bridge, a distracted driver swerved his SUV into a liquid propane truck, sending the truck crashing into a rail. The tank hit the metal obstruction at just the right angle to compress the tank sufficiently to make it explode, turning the exit for the West Side into a yawning gate of flames.

Over on the east side of the island, the tram to Roosevelt Island stopped over the river, perched exactly 250 feet above the water. A woman aboard the car pressed her face to the glass, awed by the sight of New York completely dark. A dark shadow looped toward her; she stared at it for a moment, wondering if it was a cloud or some avenging angel sent by God. In the next moment the shadow materialized into the underside of a traffic helicopter whose gauges and controls had been devastated by the blast. The skid of the helicopter pierced the glass of the gondola, spearing the woman and her nearby companion before tearing the tram and its assembly down into the water in a huge fireball. The flames landed squarely on the deck of the *Elflon Oil,* a barge en route to a new floating power station about a quarter-mile upriver. The barge began to sink at the rear, leaking its fuel out into the water. Miraculously, the helicopter did not set the oil on fire; that happened a few minutes later when gasoline leaking from a tanker ignited, heating the thin layer of fuel sufficiently to turn the river into a layer of red and yellow fingers grasping desperately at anything in reach.

Then things got really ugly. . . .

*   *   *

"Serves the bastards right for outlawing smoking," said Andy Fisher, turning away from the computer where the simulation was running.

"That help you?" asked the programmer.

"Only psychologically. I can't stand New York."

"Of course, that's only the first five minutes. It'll take at least three months to get replacement parts for that electric yard that was fried in the blast, and God knows what else. It won't be confined to New York, either. Remember the blackout in the summer of 2003? Spread from a few power lines in Ohio, right? Well, this thing will spread twenty times as far and at least as fast. And when the power goes out this time, it'll stay out, at least in New York. Because the E-bomb fries everything. You don't have a chance to pull the circuit breakers: They're all fried. Everything's fried. You know how long it'll take to get replacement parts?"

"Months."

"In some cases years. So you think: city without power for months? No lights, no elevators, no subways—"

"Yeah, but I'm sure there's plenty of downsides." Fisher took a last swig of the coffee—Chase & Sanborn, 2003, north side of the mountain—then went outside to have a cigarette. He was joined there half a smoke later by Michael Macklin, who headed the CERN–Homeland Security joint task force that had called Fisher in.

"What do you think?" Macklin asked.

Fisher shrugged. "You couldn't have worked Godzilla into the picture somehow?"

"He does Tokyo."

Fisher took a long drag on the cigarette, working it down toward his fingertips. Something about the air in suburban Virginia made cigarettes burn quicker. Fisher had a theory that the burn rate increased in inverse proportion to the distance from Washington, D.C., with the Capitol building the epicenter of inflammability. Undoubtedly there was a flatulence factor involved.

"So is this something we worry about, or what?" asked Macklin.

"Oh, you can always worry," said Fisher.

"Should we, though?"

Fisher took a last drag of his cigarette, then tossed it to the ground and took up another. Macklin had a kind of earnestness—grating, even under the best of circumstances, whatever those might be.

"Turning lights off in New York—not exactly the sort of thing that's going to piss off Middle America," said Fisher. "I know a bunch of ministers who might even get behind it."

"The DIA thinks it's a real threat," Macklin said.

"Well, there you go, then," said Fisher. "Obviously it's nothing to worry about."

"You're joking, right?" Macklin eyed his cigarette, but Fisher wasn't sharing, at least not with him: The head of Homeland Security had just suggested a five-cent tax on smokes to help pay for his department. "They say it's good intelligence. There are intercepts between this Muslim cell in Syria talking about power going out. Problem is, they're to a cell phone that no one's been able to find. But the DIA thinks it's good intelligence."

"They ever tell you they had bad intelligence?" asked Fisher.

Macklin shifted around nervously. "Should we go to an orange alert?"

"What color are we at now?"

"Yellow."

"You get a raise if the color changes?"

"No way."

"Sucky job. You should never have left the FBI, Mack. You wouldn't have had to worry about colors or the DIA. New York gets fried, it's somebody else's problem."

"Hey, come on, Andy, give me a break here. I didn't want to work for Homeland Security. Leah made me do it."

Leah was Macklin's wife. The pair had met while working together at the FBI several years before and, despite extensive counseling, had gotten married. From the moment he uttered the words "I do," Macklin's life had nosedived: The poor slob had given up smoking, cut back on coffee, and according to the latest rumors even enlisted in a health club.

"I'm sorry for you, Mack. I really am," said Fisher.

"So, can you help me out?" asked Macklin. "I need to make a recommendation to the big cheese in the morning."

Fisher shook his head. It was pitiful, really. In the old days, Macklin never would have called the boss—anyone, really—the "big cheese." Marriage really did screw people up.

"I asked Hunter to send you over because I figured you could help," added Macklin. "Come on, Andy. Help us out here. Help *me* out. For old times' sake."

"I *am* helping you," Fisher told Macklin.

"All you're doing is busting my chops."

"That's not help?" asked the FBI agent. He looked at his cigarette thoughtfully. Jack Hunter was executive assistant director for National Security/Special Projects, a kingdom within a kingdom within a broom closet at the FBI. He was also allegedly Fisher's boss. Hunter had in fact sent him over to talk to Macklin, but the executive assistant director—*ex-ass-dic* to people in the know—had specifically instructed Fisher to be not particularly useful.

Or, as Hunter put it, "If I wanted to help them, I'd send somebody else."

"Turning off the lights seems too simple," said Fisher. "All that's going to do is make people mad at Con Ed, the power company. That's not exactly a major accomplishment."

"It's not just turning off the lights," said Macklin. "An E-bomb—whether they explode it over New York or Tokyo or Des Moines or wherever—every electrical device within twenty-something miles goes out. It takes months to get everything back online."

"Yeah, I saw the show. Something else is up."

"Mayhem's not enough for you?"

"I like mayhem, personally. It's just not enough as a motivating factor."

"So, what's going on, then?"

Fisher sighed. "Jeez, Mack, do your own detective work. You used to work for the FBI, right?"

"Yeah, but I wasn't like you," said Macklin. "Come on, Andy. You're the hot-shot hound-dog snooping machine. You look at an airplane crash and you can figure out what the pilot had for lunch."

"Well, sure, if it's splattered on the windshield," said Fisher.

"I heard what you did with that Cyclops case."

Fisher shrugged. He'd just about single-handedly broken one of the most far-reaching, diabolical conspiracies ever to rack the American military and political establishments. The President had personally thanked him. Even better, Hunter had avoided him for forty-eight hours after the busts were made public.

That and five bucks would get him a pack of cigarettes. Two packs if he got it through his Indian friends online.

"You got to help us," said Macklin. "We could be facing a major terrorist operation here."

"No offense, but all you have to go on is a three-sentence report from the DIA and one intercepted e-mail that the NSA says could be either about an E-bomb plot or the opening of a new pizza restaurant. Not a hell of a lot to go on," said Fisher. "I will say one thing, though."

"What's that?"

"The kid who wrote that simulation program's got a real future. I like what he did with Yankee Stadium."

"Jeez, Andy, if you don't help me, I have to rely on the DIA."

"That's kind of an ugly threat, Mack."

"What if I asked Hunter to permanently assign you to Homeland Security? You'd love it over here. Get your own expense account, nice car. We have our pick of impounds. I can probably hook you up with a drug dealer's condo or something. You should see our office up in New York. Out in the suburbs, on the water. Tell you what: Come by around noon tomorrow and I'll set up lunch with the big cheese himself."

"I have a question for you."

"Shoot."

"When you join Homeland Security, do they make you go through a behavior modification program to learn to call the boss 'big cheese'? Or do they do it with drugs?"

"Shit, Andy." Macklin sighed. "Can I have a cigarette?"

Fisher reached into his jacket for the pack and shook one out. "You owe me a nickel."

CHAPTER

2

Dr. Park Syoun Ra-ha took a deep breath and rose from his workstation, trying to appear no more nervous than any other scientist might be when called to the director's office. The two men who had come to fetch him waited stiffly a short distance away—not out of respect but because the work done at Nyen Factory was top secret, and anyone who looked at the wrong computer screen might be accused of a crime. Inadvertent or not, merely gaining top secret information was punishable by death in North Korea. Disseminating it was a crime beyond all imagining, and giving it to the Americans must surely be ten times worse.

Park felt his fingers trembling as he followed the men into the hallway. The complex's name meant "kite," but that was a convenient cover, for the items constructed here were not a child's toys. The factory buildings nestled against a hillside north of Kujang hosted a weapons development facility that had few rivals in Asia. There were at least three different research areas, and most likely a full dozen; even Dr. Park wasn't sure how many there were. He was personally responsible for the creation of a weapon that could send a modern city back to the Stone Age in a heartbeat.

Dr. Park did not want to see that weapon used. He also had decided he must leave North Korea. He had combined these two goals and, after considerable debate, taken steps to fulfill them. But now as he walked to the director's office he worried that he had acted too rashly. He worried that he would forfeit his life in a most painful manner.

Worse, his attempt had been completely ignored by the Americans. He'd sent the e-mail nearly a week before. There had been no response.

Dr. Park could reconcile himself to that. But he had thought that if he were going to be caught, he would have been caught nearly right away. When no one sent for him by the end of the second day after he'd sent the message, he had concluded he was safe.

One of the guards stopped Dr. Park when they reached the director's outer office. He knocked on the door and went inside. When he did not immediately reappear, Dr. Park wondered whether this was a good or bad sign. If they thought he was a traitor, wouldn't they deal with him swiftly? But, on the other hand, where was the need to be swift? Letting him sweat out his guilt would be part of his punishment.

While death would naturally be the outcome, the end would not come swiftly. On the contrary, the process of punishment would be long and slow and painful. This went without saying. He had heard stories about cattle prods and special beatings, terrible things done to a man's privates.

The muscles in Dr. Park's thighs began to vibrate as he walked into the office. A pain began to grow at the back of his head on the right side, spreading quickly toward his eyes, pressing his skull the way a vise might.

"Dr. Park," said the director. "Welcome. You know General Kuong Ou?"

Dr. Park felt a shock in his chest that forced the air from his lungs. Kuong was the head of the Military Research Institute, the bureaucracy that ran this plant. He commanded an army division and was related to the Dear Leader, Kim Jong Il, North Korea's father and commander in chief. He was one of the most important people in North Korea.

Kuong's visit here had not been announced, and to find him in the corner of the director's office—what else could this mean but great, great distress for Dr. Park?

Horrible distress.

As the director began speaking, Dr. Park could think only of torture. The one happy thought that occurred to him was the fact that he had no family: His parents both had died some years before, and he had never found a wife. At least his humiliation and pain would belong only to him.

The director's words seemed more like stones than sounds, pelting the sides of his face, pummeling him without meaning.

Vacation.

Rest.

Moscow conference.

Reward.

What was he saying?

Kuong was smiling.

Smiling?

"Your unit has done brave work," said Kuong. "In the current situation, it is most admirable—beyond admirable."

Was this part of the torture: to tell him that he was being rewarded and then send him to prison?

But why so elaborate a ruse?

No, they were smiling. He was . . . free.

Free!

"Our Russian comrades are hosting a conference on power generation similar to the ones you've attended in China," added the director. "There's unlikely to be anything new there, but you will have to make a full report."

Dr. Park looked at the director and then at the general. He struggled to return their smiles.

"Enjoy yourself," said the director. He began telling him of the arrangement details: An aide would accompany him as a guide and translator. Though the director did not say so, the aide would actually be a minder from the security service, prepared to report him for any infraction and willing to kill him if necessary. But typically such men were corruptible; it was a question of finding their price.

Dr. Park had never been to Moscow.

There were trains, connections to other cities.

Or perhaps if he simply went to an embassy . . .

Yes.

Would the Americans take him? There had been no answer to his e-mail.

"You do want to go?" asked the director.

He made it sound as if Dr. Park had an option, which the scientist knew wasn't the case. In North Korea, even recreation was mandatory.

"You do want to go, don't you?" added the general when he did not respond immediately.

"Of course," Dr. Park said, bowing. "Of course. I welcome the opportunity."

"Good," said the director. "Very good."

Dr. Park smiled weakly, then left the office.

3

William Howe stared at the shadows on the ceiling, turning over on the thin mattress of the Hotel Imperium in Parkland, Virginia, just outside of Washington, D.C. He knew it wasn't quite five A.M., but he also knew it made no sense to lie here any longer. If by some miracle he managed to actually fall asleep, he would be woken by the alarm in an hour anyway. Early in his Air Force career, Howe had adopted a rule about sleep: If he couldn't get at least two hours, he wouldn't bother.

He got out of bed and went into the bathroom to shower and shave. Now that he thought about it, he'd made up that rule in college, which predated the Air Force. But he'd been in the service so long, everything in his life seemed to originate there.

Howe wasn't in the service any longer. Three months before, he'd turned down a promotion and a Pentagon posting, arranging instead to resign his commission. His decision had followed a wild sequence of events that had simultaneously made him a hero and left him disillusioned about everything from love to government.

Disillusioned. One of his commanders had used that word, trying to figure out why Howe—a full bird colonel—wanted to walk away from a career that could have led all the way to the chairman of Joint Chiefs of Staff.

Disillusioned. It was an interesting word, but Howe decided it wasn't exactly right. He wasn't disillusioned. Being disillusioned implied that he had been naive. William Howe, former fighter pilot, former project liaison officer of one of the most revolutionary war-fighting systems ever, had not been naive.

Trusting, perhaps. Too ready to assume that others held to the standards of honesty and duty and responsibility that he himself held dear. But not naive.

Burned.

That was a better word. He had been *burned*.

Howe pulled on the gray suit pants over his white shirt. So, if he'd been burned, why was he back in D.C.?

Because his mother had been excited by the fact that the national security advisor to the President of the United States had called her son not once but twice. And actually spent several minutes chatting with her.

Chatting was the word she had used.

The national security advisor to the President of the United States. We chatted for quite a while. A very, very nice man.

She had had the same tone in her voice nearly twenty years before, when he was a high school junior being courted by colleges offering athletic scholarships.

He looked at his reflection in the bathroom mirror and laughed at himself. At thirty-five, he might be a bit younger than some of the people he brushed shoulders with in Washington, but he wasn't going to pass for a high school kid anymore—though in some ways he felt like one again.

National Security Advisor Dr. Michael Blitz—and, to hear his mother tell it, the President himself—wanted Howe to take on a very important job. But what job that was hadn't been made clear. Howe figured it was as some sort of advisor to the President, a glorified pencil sharpener more for window dressing than anything else. He wasn't going to take it, but the truth was, he was getting bored hanging around his parents' house in rural Pennsylvania; he could do with the change of scenery. And sooner or later he did really have to decide what the hell it was that he was going to do when he grew up.

Howe laughed again. Then, remembering it was still god-awful early, he clamped his mouth shut, grabbed his suit jacket, and went down to see if he might find a place for breakfast.

CHAPTER
4

HELLO AMANDA

GOING TO MSCW. CAN YOU GET ME OUT? BEST CHANCE THURS. PLEASE! I HAVE INFORMATION.

--------------------------- Headers ---------------------------
Return-Path: <J.Smith@simon.com>
Received: from rly-xc04.mx.aol.com (rly-xc04.mail.aol.com [172.20.105.137]) by air-xc02.mail.aol.com (v93.12) with ESMTP id MAILINXC23-3f873ec520e528b; Fri, 7 March 2008 13:33:25 -0400
Received: from mail.simon.com (mail.simon.com [66.43.82.172]) by rly-xc04.mx.aol.com (v93.12) with ESMTP id MAILRELAYINXC48-e43ec520cf1bf; Fri, 7 March 2008 13:33:03 -0400
Received: from mdcms001.simon.com (ss-exch-smtp. simon.com [172.30.65.47]) by mail.simon.com (AIX4.3/8.9.3p2/8.9.3) with ESMTP id NAA96516 for <JD@aol.com>; Fri, 7 March 2008 13:37:33 -0400
Received: by mdcms001.chuster.com with Internet Mail Service (5.5.2653.19) id <K8SXA6FM>; Fri, 16 May 2008 13:33:03 -0400
Message-ID:
<A27A160FD659C648B8665DCD07B7C90A8488FE@MDC MS002>
MIME-Version: 1.0
X-Mailer: Internet Mail Service (5.5.2653.19)
Content-Type: multipart/alternative;
boundary="—_=_NextPart_001_01C31BD1.3326EE10"

5

The knock on the door had a familiar rap to it, the sort of hollow sound Death might make if he had a hangover.

"Fisher. I know you're in there," said a voice not unlike Death's own.

"He's not here," said the FBI agent.

"We need to talk."

"So talk, Kowalski. You're good at it."

"Face-to-face."

"This early in the morning? I don't know if my stomach can take it."

Fisher refilled his coffee and lit a fresh cigarette: no sense approaching a Defense Intelligence Agency agent unarmed, even one like Kowalski.

"Why the hell aren't you working up some plans to take over a minor country, like France or Germany?" he asked as he opened the door.

Kowalski stood in the hallway of Fisher's small apartment building, flanked by a pair of men Fisher didn't recognize. Their suits were pressed and their ties didn't clash: The DIA was recruiting a better class of people these days.

"You're dressed," said Kowalski.

"Sorry to spoil your thrills," said Fisher. He took a sip of coffee. "What happened? You took a wrong turn at Gomorrah and got lost?"

"Can we talk inside?"

Fisher stood back and let the three men enter the small studio apartment. When Kowalski was inside he turned to the other two men. "This is what working for the government will get you."

"If you're lucky," said Fisher.

"That coffee or motor oil you're drinking?" asked Kowalski.

"Both." Fisher turned to the two men Kowalski had brought with them. "You guys are DIA?"

"Yes, sir."

"I could tell from your haircuts."

"Don't mind Fisher. He comes off like a real jerk, but once you get to know him you'll see he's worse than he looks," said Kowalski. "Have some coffee, boys. Your widows will be well cared for, I promise."

"Don't want the full breakfast?" Fisher asked.

"We had breakfast on the way, sir," said the taller of the two men.

"Kowalski made you pay, right?"

"Uh, yes, sir."

"Same old Kowalski. You see his tie? Some of those stains are five years old."

"It's a design, Fisher. This is an expensive silk tie that my wife gave me for my birthday. I don't wear clip-ons like you."

Fisher considered demonstrating the disadvantages of Kowalski's sartorial preferences but decided the tactical advantage might come in handy if he had to choke him some day.

Kowalski put his head inside the small fridge at the side of the kitchenette. "You got stuff growing in here."

"Penicillin. Saves on doctor bills."

"God," said Kowalski as he adjusted his coffee. "This is almost drinkable."

"If I'd known you were coming I would've gone all the way."

Fisher walked into the other half of the apartment, pausing over a pair of card tables that served as his combination dresser and entertainment center. He took his watch, wallet, and Bureau credentials off the ancient Philco TV, then examined his gun, a .44 Magnum nearly as old as the black-and-white TV set and arguably only half as deadly.

"So, how much do you know about the E-bomb?" asked Kowalski.

"I don't know anything," said Fisher.

"I heard Macklin called you in to consult."

"He called me in to look at a computer video of New York City blowing up. He thought I'd be nostalgic," said Fisher.

"Homeland Security is peeing in their pants," said Kowalski. There was a note of triumph in his voice. "So you coming aboard or what?"

"I'm not doing anything unless they roll back the cigarette tax," said Fisher. "Why are you here?"

"Because we're the ones who came up with the intelligence on the E-bomb in the first place. Macklin didn't tell you I was the guy who figured it out?"

"No. But probably he had trouble putting your name and the word *intelligence* together in the same conversation."

"We're putting together a joint task force. Homeland Security. DIA. And you."

"Me?"

"We can use somebody for comic relief."

"I'm too old to run away and join the circus."

"Listen, Andy, this is going to develop into a big one. When we bust this, we'll be on *60 Minutes.*"

Fisher thought he detected a smirk from Kowalski's taller sidekick. There was hope for the country yet.

"You really do want to join up," added Kowalski. "I told Macklin it was a great idea. That's why I'm here."

Fisher took the cigarette butt down to the nub, then put it out in a glass of water in the pile of dirty dishes in the sink. Under ordinary circumstances he would have left it there, but since he had company he thought it best to keep up appearances: He leaned over to the nearby window and tossed the butt down into the alley.

"So? You in or out?" asked Kowalski.

"Boss promised me a nice Internet porn case if I show up for work before noon today."

"Internet porn? Come on. That's not your style. You're a high-tech guy. National security. Lives on the line. Not T & A."

"Nothing wrong with a little T & A now and again," observed Fisher.

"Seriously, Andy. Come on. Macklin wants you. I want you. We could use some help determining if this thing is real or not."

"No, thanks."

"Could be a career boost. Jump in pay—get you into some upscale digs."

"This place isn't upscale?" Fisher spread his hands around his domain. "Listen, I have to get going. Thanks for the wake-up call. But I got a question for you."

"Yeah?"

"A serious question."

"Shoot."

"How come you used the salad dressing instead of milk in your coffee?"

CHAPTER

6 Howe handed his entire wallet to the Secret Service agent, letting him examine his license even though his ID had been checked twice before and he already knew his name was on the list of visitors. He'd been to the West Wing of the White House only once before, and that time he had been accompanied by a high-ranking assistant to Blitz, Howard McIntyre, who'd smoothed him past all the security hoops and barriers. It was somewhat different this time around. To the men checking his ID he was just another name on the list. Howe thought he liked it that way.

The agent pointed at him and gestured to the side of the hallway. Howe stepped over to the wall, unsure of what was going on, but he wasn't being singled out for a search and there was nothing wrong with his credentials. A moment later a phalanx of dark-suited men appeared, leading the way for President Jack D'Amici and his entourage. Dr. Blitz was at President D'Amici's side, and the two men were engaged in a deep discussion. The secretaries of defense and state walked immediately behind, frowning deeply, while a handful of aides scurried behind, trying to keep up.

Deep furrows lined the President's forehead. The tips of his close-cropped hair were stained gray, and though his body was trim, even on the thin side, the flesh at the corners of his chin had begun to sag. He was perhaps two decades older than Howe, young for a president, though the office weighed on him as it weighed on every man.

Howe had met him after the recovery of Cyclops One, the airborne laser plane that had been hijacked and then recovered by a team Howe had led. The pilot had come away from the meeting disappointed; spending a few minutes alone with the President had punctured the larger-than-life fantasy he'd unknowingly had of the man. But now that he saw him in the hall, absorbed in thought, Howe felt a sensation of awe take hold. This was the President of the United States, the commander in chief, and if he wasn't larger than life—if he wasn't a god or even a demigod—he was nonetheless a man of uncommon ability and even greater responsibility.

President D'Amici shook his head at something Blitz said. As he did he turned toward Howe, catching a glimpse of him.

"Colonel Howe, how are you?" said the President, as matter-of-factly as if he saw Howe every day. Before Howe could actually say anything in response, D'Amici added, "Good, good," and walked on, not even breaking his stride. Blitz himself took no notice of Howe, not even pausing in his conversation.

"Hey, Colonel," said a tall black man peeling off from the back of the formation to pump Howe's hand.

"Tyler?"

"How the hell are you?" Major Kenal Tyler had been an Army Special Forces captain when he and Howe had met a few months before. Tyler had led a team that helped recover the Cyclops airborne laser weapon.

"You're in D.C. now?" asked Howe.

Tyler laughed. "Everybody's got to be somewhere. I'm on a special task force. Brain work. I'm attached to the Joint Chiefs staff, but I've been doing tons of work for the NSC. What are you doing these days?"

"Supposed to meet Dr. Blitz."

"Great. You going to work for him?"

Howe shrugged.

Tyler looked at him as if he expected an explanation. When Howe didn't offer one, the major suggested they have a drink sometime. "Where you staying?"

Howe told him the hotel. Tyler nodded—it wasn't clear to Howe whether he was truly interested in getting together or not—then ran off down the hall to catch up with the others.

If the Secret Service agent was impressed by the fact that Howe knew the President, it didn't show in his manner. He checked the ID again before letting Howe pass.

"Would you like some coffee, Colonel?" asked Mozelle Clarke, Blitz's administrative assistant, when he arrived in Blitz's office a few minutes later.

"Not really, thanks. I'm kind of coffeed out this morning."

"Mention that to Dr. Blitz," she said.

"Mention what?" said Blitz.

"That some people drink too much coffee."

"I give up coffee every few months," said Blitz, meeting him at the door. Blitz looked every bit the academic he had been before coming to work with the administration: His shirt was rumpled and his tie loose at the neck, while his glasses leaned so far off the edge of his nose it seemed impossible that they didn't fall. Books were stacked high around the office, and the titles that were visible included tomes on biblical studies, English literature, and French philosophy as well as world politics and military analysis.

"Against my better judgment," Blitz said, as if commenting on something he had said before.

"The coffee?" asked Howe, sitting down.

"Coffee? No. The arrangements. Keeping the contract agencies on. Privatization—between you and me—it's bullshit. Total, complete, utter bullshit. The military ought to be in control of its own fate. I don't buy all this outsourcing crap, even if it can be expedient."

Howe still wasn't sure what Blitz was talking about.

"But rearranging everything, between Congress, the budget fight—God help us if we had to raise taxes," said Blitz.

"Yes, sir," said Howe, falling back on the old military habit: When in doubt, salute.

"So we're stuck with it. But if someone gives you a lemon, my stepfather always said, make lemonade. And that's what I'd like to do."

"Excuse me, but I'm not really following," admitted Howe.

Blitz smiled and nodded, as if finally getting some inside joke. "National Aeronautics Development and Testing. We've gotten rid of Bonham—for a long time, I'd say. He's going to plead guilty. There won't be a trial."

Howe nodded. A retired Air Force general, Clayton Bonham had headed the National Aeronautics Development and Testing agency. Commonly abbreviated as NADT, the private company was responsible for developing and testing cutting-edge weapons for the military. Bonham had been in the middle of the conspiracy to hijack Cyclops, using it to cheat on the tests for an augmented ABM system.

Howe realized that he should feel some relief that there would be no trial, since he would undoubtedly have been a witness in the case. But he felt as if justice had been cheated. In his opinion, no jail sentence would sufficiently punish Bonham for what he had done: betraying his trust for money.

"But the company itself—its function developing and testing new weapons systems—it has too much potential in the present political and economic climate to just walk away from," continued Blitz. "Outsourcing and private industry sharing the risks—it's the way we'll be doing things for the next decade at least."

Howe detected a note of regret in Blitz's voice. Howe, though he had worked with NADT, agreed that outside contractors were gaining too much control over military projects. Originally conceived as a way to rein them in, NADT had helped encourage the trend. Set up as a government-sponsored company like Freddie Mac—the comparison had often been made—NADT had quickly set its own course. It now controlled or had a hand in nearly a hundred projects, including large ones like Cyclops and the Velociraptor, an improved version of the F/A-22 Raptor jet aircraft. While it wouldn't be fair to say that the agency controlled the Pentagon, it also wouldn't be accurate to say that the Pentagon controlled NADT. The company had far more say over individual projects than traditional contractors like Boeing ever dreamed of.

"If the structure has to remain, if outsourcing is still the order of the day," added Blitz, "then we have to make the best of it. It does present certain opportunities—advantages in terms of expediting things, making things work. Of course, there will be reforms. That's why it's important to get the right people—the absolutely right people—in place."

"Right," said Howe absently.

"Richard Nelson is set to be elected as the new chairman, probably by the beginning of next week. But we need a new president of the company, someone to take Bonham's place."

"Of course."

"Will you?"

"Will I give you recommendations?" asked Howe.

"No, I don't want recommendations." Blitz plucked at his goatee. It was blond, a shade lighter than the hair on the top of his head. "I want you to take the job. President of NADT. It's going to play an important role developing weapons, not just for the Air Force, but for all the services. I want you in charge."

"Me?"

"The President agrees. As a matter of fact, you could even say it was his idea."

Howe leaned back in the seat.

"There will be changes. There have to be changes," said Blitz. "You'd have the President's confidence and free rein to get things done. A mandate to get things done."

"I don't know," said Howe.

Blitz bent forward across the desk, his face intent.

"It would be an important opportunity for a man like you," said the national security advisor. "A good career move."

Howe started to say that he didn't have a career: The only thing he was thinking of doing, seriously, was hooking up with a friend of his who was building spec houses up in rural New York about fifty miles from where he'd grown up. But Blitz didn't wait for an answer.

"More than that, it will be a huge contribution to our country. Huge," he said. "And financially it would be well worth your while."

Howe said nothing.

"General Bonham's base salary was roughly half a million dollars," continued Blitz. "The entire compensation package would be somewhat complicated and would have to be negotiated."

Half a million dollars, thought Howe. The sum seemed incredible.

Am I worth that much?

What do they expect for that much money?

"I'm sure an equitable arrangement would be worked out. I understand you're not the sort of man who makes decisions based on money." Blitz got up. "Don't answer now. Think about it. Go out there—you've been there. Take a long tour. A few days. Think about it."

"Of course."

"Go over, talk to people, talk to Jack Myron on the Defense Committee, talk to everybody. Take a week to talk to different people. I'll arrange it—whoever you want. Mozelle will set it all up. Go over to the Pentagon, get with Admiral Christopher at the CIA. Go into it with your eyes open," said Blitz. "As a matter of fact, I gave Congressman Myron your phone number at the hotel and your home. I hope you don't mind."

"No, that's fine."

"Take some time and think," added Blitz. "But believe me, your country needs you."

CHAPTER

7

"DIA has the intercepts and some details about how an E-bomb would work, probably from one of their Middle East sources, maybe because someone here wanted to get an understanding of it," Fisher told Hunter in Hunter's FBI headquarters office. "That's the extent of it. They have Homeland Security so twisted in knots over it that they're putting together a joint task force. Macklin and Kowalski are going to work together."

"Where?"

"Not sure. Macklin mentioned New York, which seems to be where the terrorist cell was operating."

"You're sure they don't know about our guy?"

"I'm sure."

"How sure? Give me it on a scale of one to five."

Fisher shrugged. "I'm not good with numbers."

"They're trying to muscle into our case," said Hunter. "Those fucks. They want to take our deserter. Fuckheads."

Fisher generally approved of cussing in a man; it implied an appreciation for the finer things in life, like spit and horses that finished just out of the running. But from Hunter's mouth the words sounded as if they were being read from a dictionary.

"We have to bring this guy in," said Hunter. "We have to get him out of Korea."

"Okay," said Fisher.

"I want you to do it."

"Sure," said Fisher.

"Bring him in, we debrief him, go the whole nine yards. We need our own task force," added Hunter. "Yeah, that's what we need: a task force. Yeah. We'll get military people, CIA—the right CIA people. This is a big deal, Andrew. A very big deal."

Fisher didn't like the sound of that. Whenever Hunter used his first name—with or without expletives—trouble surely followed.

And as for working with the CIA . . .

"We really don't need a task force," he said. "Not yet. We have to make sure this guy is real. Then we can figure out how we're going to get him. If the CIA is involved, there are going to be meetings and written estimates, budget lines. . . ."

"You're in the big time now, Fisher. You have to think big. *Big.*"

"Can I smoke in here?"

Hunter blinked. "Are you out of your mind?"

"Just checking to see if it was you I was standing in front of."

"You fly out to—what was the name of that town in Arizona again?"

"Applegate."

"Yeah, right. Fly out to Applegate, meet the scientist, make contact, find out what we need. I'll get a task force going. What we'll do is, we'll get everyone who's not on the DIA–Homeland Security task force on our task force. Then we'll nail those bastards to the wall."

"Assuming this guy is for real," said Fisher. "Assuming he knows something about E-bombs. Assuming there's some sort of connection between North Korea and Middle Eastern terrorists who are so dumb even the DIA can stumble across them."

"Right," said Hunter. "Go for it."

"What?"

"The whole nine yards."

"Why not ten?" asked Fisher.

He made his escape while Hunter tried to come up with the answer.

CHAPTER

8

North Korean army general Kuong Ou had not begun his life as a superstitious man, nor was he presently given to omens or fortune-telling, except for this: He played *o-koan* every morning.

The ancient arrangement of dominoes—the Korean words, taken from the Chinese, meant "five gateways," a reference to famous battles fought by an ancient general—was a longtime habit. He had learned the skill as a babe, studying the meaning of the bone tablets. *O-koan* could be played as a game of solitaire, a mathematical puzzle to be worked out, but it was also an ancient way of predicting the future and seeing beyond the future to the world as it was, the cycle of endless rearrangement and sorrow. There were lessons in every piece and rule, most importantly this: The lowest tablets were the most powerful when combined. Even as general of an army division and the head of the North Korean Military Research Institute, Kuong Ou could not afford to forget that lesson.

Kuong held the pair—the two and four, the one and two, called *chi tsün*—in his hand, turning them over as he considered their relation to the event unfolding in the world around him. The regime was in collapse, army units openly rebelling. Even many of Kuong's men had deserted him, including his cousin Sang. Kuong had not heard from Kim Jong Il, the Korean ruler and his half-brother, in two weeks. He had begun to believe even that he was dead.

There were many plans to assassinate the leader. There were even plans to assassinate Kuong Ou. He had already killed the conspirators he was sure of, but to eliminate every possible enemy he would have had to kill the entire division he commanded, and half the leadership of the rest of the army and air force besides. And that didn't even include the silent traitors, those who told lies and claimed they could be counted on but who Kuong knew would vanish at the moment of need.

Kuong Ou had to publicly maintain his position and the regime. This was his duty, and to shirk it would bring dishonor much worse than death: Death was merely a stage in the cycle, whereas dishonor followed one through many cycles and could only be expunged with great exertion. On the other hand, he was not a fool: Given the choice, he preferred to live. He had made many plans to escape, holding them as contingencies against disaster.

One by one, they were disappearing. The easiest—escaping north to China or south to the so-called Republic—had been blocked long ago. The units on both borders had leaders who were his enemies, and even if he made it past them he would never be safe in either country, even for the short time he needed to get away from there.

But he would succeed. He would have revenge against the Americans who had placed his country, his leader, and himself in this predicament. The bones foretold it.

Kuong Ou scooped up the tablets and prepared to play another game.

9

Ten years before, Applegate, Arizona, had been a pristine patch of sand and tumbleweed populated only by the wind. Now it was a pristine patch of high-tech factories punctuated by macadam and people who smiled a lot, undoubtedly because they had just cashed their latest stock options. The factories had been built by a collection of new-wave defense contractors; as far as Fisher could tell from the backgrounder he'd been given, the companies specialized in making things that didn't actually work—and taking a very long time to prove it.

The airport terminal looked like a pair of trailers piled one on top of the other, with a few windows added for light and structural integrity. Fisher walked inside with the other dozen people from the airplane, noting the No Smoking signs and strategically placed ashtrays filled with pink-colored sand. This seemed to Fisher the work of a particularly perverse antismoking group: Not only did they want you not to smoke but they harassed you with Day-Glo colors.

Then again, it could be part of a guerrilla movement intent on undercutting the antis by mocking their weaponry. Or, worse, it occurred to Fisher that the sand might mask some nefarious incendiary device lurking just below the surface of ash. Deciding the matter needed more investigation, Fisher took out his cigarette pack and lit up, tossing a match into the tray to see if it was flammable.

"You can't smoke inside," whined someone behind him.

Fisher glanced left and right without finding the source of the voice.

"Fisher, right?"

Something bumped his elbow. Fisher looked down into the gnomelike face of a forty-year-old woman. The face was attached to a body that barely cleared his belt. Fisher was tall—a bit over six feet—but not *that* tall. This woman defined vertically challenged.

"I'm Fisher."

"Special Agent Katherine Mathers," said the woman, jabbing her hand toward his. "And you can't smoke in here."

"That's good to know," said Fisher. He took another drag. "Are we walking to where we're going, or is there a car?"

"I've heard about you," said Mathers. She frowned and headed across the reception area, all eight feet of it, toward the exit. Fisher caught up outside at the curb, where Mathers was waiting behind the wheel of a 1967 puke-green Ford Torino.

"Nice car," he said, getting in.

"Oldest Bu-car in existence," she said, using the accepted slang for a Bureau-issued vehicle. If she hadn't, he might have thought of asking to see her ID.

"No smoking," she told him.

"No?"

"No."

He was almost at the butt anyway, so Fisher rolled down his window and tossed it.

"You do that again and I'll have to bust you for littering," said Mathers. "We're very ecology-conscious here."

"I could tell from the car you were driving."

Mathers stomped on the gas pedal—or, rather, the three wooden blocks taped one atop another on the gas pedal. The Torino lurched away from the curb, smoke and grit flying.

"Can you see where you're going?" Fisher asked the other agent.

"I heard you were a wiseass."

"That's me."

"I can see fine," said Mathers, whose head would not have been visible from outside the car. "They brief you or what?"

"You got some guy who met some other guy who

knows someone who built an E-bomb for North Korea and wants asylum," said Fisher.

Mathers shook her head. "First of all, the guy's a gal."

"Okay."

"Second of all, the gal met the scientist himself, not someone else. There's only two players."

"That's a relief. I was afraid we'd have to use zone coverage. Now we can just go man-to-man."

"What are you going to do?" Mathers asked.

"After we stop for some coffee, I'm going to talk to the guy who's a gal," said Fisher. "And we'll take it from there."

"We don't have no fancy bullshit coffee here," said Mathers, in a tone that made Fisher forgive not only her driving but the business about smoking in the car. "Just stuff that'll burn a hole in your crankcase."

"The only kind I drink," said Fisher.

The e-mail that had brought Fisher to Applegate consisted of exactly two words:

OUT, PLEASE.

Attached was a technical diagram of an E-bomb—or, as the technical people preferred to call it, "an explosive device intended to render a disruptive magnetic pulse."

The e-mail had been sent to Amanda Kung. While Kung worked at a defense-related company, neither she nor the company had anything directly to do with E-bombs—or any weapons, for that matter. The company built UHF radios that could fit on pinheads, undoubtedly seeking to exploit the burgeoning market of seamstresses who needed walkie-talkies.

According to Mathers, the connection between Amanda and the Korean who had sent the e-mail was personal: They had met in China during a conference two years before and occasionally corresponded electronically.

"Love thing?" Fisher asked as they drove toward the complex on a road that might be charitably described as a succession of bumps interrupted by gullies. Fortunately, Fisher had equipped his coffee cup with a safety shield; when you found java this bad, you didn't want to spill a drop.

"Could be love. Probably just curiosity: how the other half lives, that kind of thing," said Mathers. "Typical flighty-scientist kind of thing. Women. You know what I mean."

"Sure."

"So, did you really commandeer a C-17 over the Pacific to make a bust?"

"Gross exaggeration," said Fisher. "I won the C-17 in a game of darts."

Mathers smiled. "You're an inspiration."

"Don't get giggly on me, Mathers."

She veered from the pothole-strewn highway onto what looked like a dust-swept field. The Torino growled as they took another turn, the engine chuttering while the air filter chewed on some pebbles.

And then, like a scene from a Charlton Heston movie, the dust cleared and a four-lane concrete road appeared. The Bu-car settled down as they approached the building where Amanda Kung worked, K-4 Electronics. A quartet of khaki-clad guards with German shepherds met their car. The two FBI agents were instructed to get out of the vehicle and the car was searched before being allowed to proceed. Inside the gate, they were met by a six-foot-five protosimian who pointed to a parking space and gave them coded tags to wear.

"Computer system figures out if you're inside and don't have a tag on," warned Mathers.

"What's it do, vaporize you?"

"Very possibly."

Inside the building, the agents were met by a personal minder, another large athletic type Fisher thought he might recognize from WFW reruns. He led them to a private room where Amanda Kung was waiting.

As a member of the high-tech community, the company had a certain image to maintain and therefore did not call the room a room but rather a "cell." It looked very much *like* a room, at least to Fisher, though the decoration was not in keeping with the ultra–high-tech style of the rest of the building. Twenty-feet-by-twenty-feet-square, it had thick red carpet, leather-upholstered furniture, wainscoted walls, and paintings of various dogs. Kung explained that this was because the firm had begun its existence by making special radio collars for an invisible K-9 fence before branching out into the more lucrative defense field.

There were a number of dog jokes attached to the explanation of the company's history. Fisher made it through the first—*We're the only business that succeeded after going to the dogs*—then decided to cut Kung off and ask if she could tell him about the Korean.

"I met Dr. Park two years ago at a conference in China," said Kung. Short and thin, Kung had the female dweeb look down, with thick glasses beneath uneven bangs. Her purple blouse hurt Fisher's eyes. "He is an engineer working on electrical generation projects."

"That's it?"

"That's what he told me. I got the idea that he might know more, because of the sessions he was at. And then I got that e-mail."

"Want to go to Korea?" asked Fisher.

"Korea?"

"North Korea. I have some frequent-flier miles to redeem. Supposed to be pretty nice in February. They put out fresh mud."

"I don't know." Kung looked at Mathers.

"You want to help your friend, don't you?" said Mathers, apparently ignoring the ESP signals Fisher had beamed into her brain.

"He's not really my friend," said Kung. "He's just an engineer I met."

"Well, he thinks of you as his friend," said Mathers, stubbornly impervious to mental suggestion.

Kung pursed her lips.

"You're not married, right?" asked Fisher.

Kung's lips turned white. "He's going to Moscow the day after tomorrow," she said.

"Moscow?" asked Fisher.

Kung unfolded a piece of paper and slid it across the table to Fisher. "This came this morning."

HELLO AMANDA

GOING TO MSCW. CAN YOU GET ME OUT? BEST CHANCE THURS. PLEASE I HAVE INFORMATION.

Fisher took the e-mail and looked at the header that showed the path the message had taken:

```
---------------------------- Headers ----------------------------
Return-Path: <J.Smith@simon.com>
Received: from rly-xc04.mx.aol.com (rly-xc04.mail.aol.com
[172.20.105.137]) by air-xc02.mail.aol.com (v93.12) with
ESMTP id MAILINXC23-3f873ec520e528b; Fri, 7 March
2008 13:33:25-0400
Received: from mail.simon.com (mail.simon.com
[66.43.82.172]) by rly-xc04.mx.aol.com (v93.12) with
ESMTP id MAILRELAYINXC48-e43ec520cf1bf; Fri, 7 March
2008 13:33:03-0400
Received: from mdcms001.simon.com (ss-exch-
smtp.simon.com [172.30.65.47])
by mail.simon.com (AIX4.3/8.9.3p2/8.9.3) with ESMTP id
NAA96516
for <JD@aol.com>; Fri, 7 March 2008 13:37:33 -0400
Received: by mdcms001.chuster.com with Internet Mail
Service (5.5.2653.19)
id <K8SXA6FM>; Fri, 16 May 2008 13:33:03 -0400
```

Message-ID:
<A27A160FD659C648B8665DCD07B7C90A8488FE@MDC
MS002>
MIME-Version: 1.0
X-Mailer: Internet Mail Service (5.5.2653.19)
Content-Type: multipartlalternative;
boundary="----_=_NextPart_001_01C31BD1.3326EE10"

There were various ways the actual route an e-mail took could be hidden, and the agent recognized one of the remailers as a kind of semianonymous clearinghouse in Asia that he'd seen in the course of another investigation.

"Can I keep this?" asked Fisher.

"Sure."

Fisher got up. "Well, think about going," he said.

"Where?"

"Korea," said Fisher.

"Why Korea if he's going to be in Moscow?" asked Mathers.

Fisher decided the time was right for the ultimate weapon and unleashed the double-dog–drop-dead stare. Mathers's breath caught in her chest and she swallowed whatever sentence had been lurking in her mouth.

"That's all you want to know?" asked Kung.

"Pretty much," said Fisher.

He stopped at the door. "I do have one other question," he said, reaching into his pocket. "Do you have a smoking area?"

"That was your entire interview?" asked Mathers as they walked back to the car.

"Yeah."

"I have to say, your interrogation style leaves a lot to be desired."

Fisher went around to the passenger's side, waiting while Mathers fiddled with the locks. The car was searched once again as they left. The search was thorough enough for Fisher to smoke two whole cigarettes and start on a third before having to get back in the car.

"I'd really appreciate it if you didn't smoke in the car," said Mathers. Her voice was so sincere that Fisher almost considered putting the cigarette out.

"Could you at least roll down the window?" asked Mathers.

Fisher could do that, and did.

"I shouldn't have criticized you," she said as they drove away. "I'm sorry."

"Not a problem."

"But if those were the only questions you were going to ask, why bother coming out here in the first place?" asked Mathers.

"Boss wanted me out of Washington," Fisher told her.

"You figured the people at the company are listening in," said Mathers a few miles later.

"I'm sure they were," said Fisher.

"You don't think you can trust them?"

"Haven't a clue."

"So, what do we do? Go to Moscow? Talk to her at home?"

"We find a place with really bad chili dogs and have some lunch," Fisher told her. "I haven't had a good case of heartburn in more than a week."

CHAPTER
10

Howe pushed himself down into the cockpit, listening as the NADT contract pilot gave him a few last-minute instructions on the Iron Hawk's handling. Jeff Storey, the other pilot, was a former Navy man under contract as a test jock; Howe had met him a few times before. Storey was going to fly wing in a second plane while Howe took the Iron Hawk for a short familiarization hop, part of the campaign arranged by Dr. Blitz to convince him to take the NADT director's job.

Howe had started early that morning with a tour of the headquarters building, where every single female employee appeared to have been instructed to wear the shortest dress imaginable. Following the flight, he would be taken to lunch at one of the area's best restaurants. A briefing on more NADT programs was planned for late afternoon, and then he was supposed to join two senators for dinner.

Howe was actually looking forward to the flight. His aircraft combined a host of different technologies that, apart from its aeronautical abilities, demonstrated what NADT could mean to the military. But he was interested primarily in feeling the strain of gravity against his chest, and the giddy rush that the experienced pilot still felt when he goosed the throttle. He hadn't been at the stick of a jet in months.

Howe's aircraft had ostensibly started its life as a McDonnell Douglas T-45, an extremely airworthy and capable aircraft used by the U.S. Navy as a jet trainer but versatile enough to serve as a multirole fighter for foreign air forces. NADT had taken the basic airframe and reworked it for its own purposes. Among the many obvious changes were longer wings shaped in a modified delta, forward winglets near the fuselage that helped maneuverability, and a reworked cockpit area. While the new cockpit allowed only one pilot, not the two common in a normal trainer, it included a "bathtub" of titanium and a carbon-fiber compound designed as a kind of bulletproof armor to protect the pilot. The idea was that the Iron Hawk would be especially survivable on a close–air-support mission, where it might come under ground fire while swooping down to support troops.

Less noticeable improvements included the more powerful engine, the large-capacity fuel tanks, and an improved radar/synthetic sight system called AMV.

AMV stood for *advanced military vision* and was at least potentially a quantum leap over normal radar. In its most basic modes, it combined phased-array, millimeter-wave, and microwave devices and input from multispectral and hyperspectal image sensors—optical, infrared, and near infrared viewers to synthesize a radar "picture." The combined sensors gave it a far wider detection span than what was possible with radars normally installed in tactical fighters; a B-2 bomber could be seen at about fifty miles. *Seen* was an appropriate word, because the technology that was used to integrate the sensors also allowed the computer to draw a three-dimensional picture of the detected object. In the Hawk, the image was presented on a flat, two-dimensional multicolor screen, but the system could be mated to a 3-D hologram display similar to that being developed for the F/A-22V.

AMV had several modes that would be familiar to any interceptor pilot since the advent of solid-state avionics. It could sweep a wide area, track particular planes while continuing to search for others, and target an aircraft at long and close range using all of its sensors. It included a system to "cue" a pilot in a dogfight, essentially telling him when to fire. But the radar capabilities also allowed synthetic close-up modes, useful for a number of applications. For example, an airplane suspected of smuggling large amounts of drugs or weapons could be "scanned" at about five miles. In layman's terms, the system provided a detailed "X-ray" of the interior. The computer interpreter attached to the system could assess what it was looking at quickly and then present the information to the pilot transparently. It not only could tell an F-15C from an F-15E but detail the target aircraft's fuel and ammunition states. AMV had potential for police uses as well: It could scan a smuggler's aircraft and detect bales of marijuana, for example.

Perhaps the real breakthrough was the size of the unit: It was small enough to be carried by the Hawk, which had given over part of its fuselage and undercarriage to the antenna pods and sensors, but otherwise still looked like the compact airframe it had begun life as.

There were still a number of bugs to work out. One of the most annoying was the failure of the software routines that filtered out things like birds at long distances; a single bird would occasionally blink onto the screen as a red triangle "unknown," staying there for a few seconds before the computer satisfied itself from the flight pattern that it was in fact a bird, rather than a cleverly disguised missile or aircraft. Nonetheless, AMV had major potential for the future.

The Iron Hawk itself was just a tester, but NADT was preparing to propose the plane as a lightweight attack aircraft, versatile enough to serve as a backup interceptor. In theory it could replace both the A-10A and F-16, with much of the toughness of the former and all of the adaptability of the latter. It could take off and land on short runways with a full load of bombs, withstand several direct hits by 23mm flak guns, pull 10 g's without coming apart, and accelerate to just over the speed of sound in a hairbreadth. As a dogfighter, it couldn't match the F/A-22 or even an F-15, but it cost considerably less. All of that made the aircraft exceptionally attractive.

But Howe wasn't here to evaluate the plane, just to get a look at NADT's toys.

Maybe *his* toys?

At a half-million dollars a year, he could afford his own plane. And a nice house, and nice vacations, and whatever the hell else he wanted.

"Bottom line, flies just like a T-45 with a full load of fuel," Storey told Howe. Storey was flying an identical plane. "Takes off smooth—you'll swear you were in a trainer. It's that easygoing. Very forgiving, very friendly. But it still goes like a champ."

Howe gave him a thumbs-up and began familiarizing himself with the cockpit. Despite the NADT upgrades, the basics were recognizable descendants of the Navy's Cockpit 21 program—a McDonnell Douglas designed arrangement that featured multifunction displays and a layout perfected during in the late 1980s and 1990s. Aside from some updated GPS and radio gear, the main improvements concerned the radar and weapons systems the Hawk was meant to test. He soon had Hawk One snugged and tiptoeing toward the flight line.

NADT leased space at Andrews Air Force Base in Maryland; the arrangement allowed it to make use of the finest facilities in the world. The Air Force also provided some of the security around its three hangars—though regular Air Force personnel were not admitted into the compound area, and in fact would have been subject to court-martial if they dared even approach the external fences. It was a sweetheart deal for NADT, demonstrating not only how important the private agency was but also showing the vast resources it could call on if necessary. The people maintaining the plane Howe sat in included veteran mechanics and other technical people who'd gained experience in the military, and the engineers who had actually designed the systems were available for consultation.

Besides the Hawks, two other NADT aircraft were housed here. Howe happened to be familiar with both. One was an F-15E that had been used to test some of the systems later installed in the F/A-22V Velociraptor. The other was a knockoff of the Russian Sukhoi S-37/B Berkut—a two-seat, next-generation version of the super plane built by NADT from specifications obtained by the CIA.

The S-37/B had been Howe's introduction to NADT; he'd come to the D.C. area on a special temporary duty assignment specifically to fly the aircraft. The project had been so secret that only two men had been trained to fly the aircraft, Howe and Tim Robinson.

Timmy had lost his life in the Cyclops project.

The Sukhoi sat under a tarp in the far corner of the

hangar, mostly forgotten now that its mission had been completed and it had yielded its data to the CIA and Air Force. Howe powered up and rolled away from the hangar.

"I'm not taking this job," he reminded himself as he waited for the tower to give him clearance. "It's not what I want to do. And besides, it's a desk job."

Although there were fringe benefits: He felt one of them as he accelerated into the sky.

"Hawk One, this is Two," said Storey as they tracked out into the small rectangle they'd been given to fly in. "I'd say you've flown before."

The two aircraft moved over the Atlantic, passing through a thick bank of clouds.

"Clear skies," remarked Storey as they burst above and ahead of the weather. It was as if the sun had disintegrated the curtain of clouds; the sky seemed so clear you could look up through the canopy and spot the angels polishing the stars.

Howe pushed his wing down and began a gentle bank, riding the Hawk southward in a lazy orbit. The stick responded easily, the aircraft eminently predictable despite all its mods and miles. One thing he had to give NADT: They knew what they were doing.

If he took the NADT post, he could do this whenever he wanted.

If he really wanted to fly, why had he left the Air Force in the first place?

Hell, he could find a job as a contract pilot somewhere. Anywhere, just about. Work as a test pilot.

Maybe that was the slot he should take at NADT, not boss man.

Turn down the chance to be rich?

Maybe the money had corrupted Bonham. Wasn't money the root of all evil? Or was it your own soul where the problem was?

Half a million bucks a year—more, potentially lots

more, when you threw in bonuses and stock options and all the perks. Maybe it was a drug you couldn't resist.

As they neared the end of the cleared range, Storey started talking up the plane, mentioning some of the improvements in engine technology. As a general theme, the engineers had substituted new materials for the traditional metals, seeking to make the power plants lighter and yet tougher at the same time. Howe knew the real question wasn't whether the materials were usable but rather whether it would be practical—as in affordable—to use them in full-scale production. Even the military had financial constraints, and just because you could make something smaller, faster, and lighter didn't mean it was cost-effective to do so.

Howe started a series of maneuvers, doing inverts and sharp cuts, rolling out and climbing, diving toward the ocean and whipping back upward, doing his best impression of a 1920s barnstormer. While admittedly the Hawk couldn't match those old biplanes for sheer warp-ability, it could slash around the sky fairly well. He managed some tight angles and high g's, felt the restraints press against his body and the blood rush from his head despite the best efforts of his flight suit.

The maneuvering forward airfoils and the variable-attack edges on the main wings gave the smallish Hawk some serious advantages in a close encounter with an enemy fighter. Howe found himself almost wistful for the days of cannon-punctuated furballs, close-in dogfights as much decided by the skill of the engineers who constructed the aircraft as the pilot himself. Today a dogfight would typically end without the planes even seeing each other; an American fighter pilot was equipped and trained to down his opponent before the enemy's radar even picked him up.

Forget the romance. There was no arguing against the idea of beyond-visual-range combat. The goal was to shoot down the enemy and live to tell about it, and a great deal of work had gone into making that happen.

Reality and fantasy veered in different directions. Reality: The NADT job would be a pain in the ass. He'd be a paper pusher. And maybe worse: They'd expect something for their half-million big ones.

"All right, Hawk Two, let's head back," said Howe.

"Roger that. I'll tell the folks back home to warm up the car."

As Storey clicked off, Howe caught part of a transmission from a ground controller querying a light aircraft back near the coast. It was flying toward a restricted area north of Washington, D.C. Something in the controller's tone caught Howe's attention; he glanced at the radar screen and located the plane about twenty-five miles to the southeast.

The plane failed to respond to the queries. About sixty seconds later a ground controller vectored an Air National Guard flight toward the aircraft to check it out. Howe called in to ask what was going on.

"NADT Test Flight One, we have an aircraft refusing to answer hails or directions at this time," snapped the controller.

"We'll check it out for you. We're closer than Guard Sixteen," he said, referring to the F-16 that had been vectored to check out the plane.

The controller hesitated but then acknowledged. Howe and Storey selected max thrust—the Hawks had no afterburners—and changed course for the intercept.

The small low-winged monoplane was flying a straight-on path toward the Capitol building. A bomb-laden plane on a suicide flight? Or a lost civilian with his radio out?

Howe's augmented radar system painted the light plane to his right as he approached. A new controller added data about the plane. The pilot was off his filed flight plan by several miles.

Howe and Storey tried hailing the pilot on the civilian frequencies and an emergency channel but got no response. In the meantime the Air National Guard F-16 was galloping toward them with orders authorizing the pilot to shoot down the plane.

As he cut the distance between them to under five miles, Howe flipped through the radar modes into Close Surveillance to scan the interior of the aircraft.

"NADT Hawk Flight One, advise your situation," said the Air National Guard pilot.

Howe told him he thought he could get a look at the cockpit.

"You're not going to make it in time," said the other pilot, who naturally assumed that Howe would have to fly alongside the other plane at very close range, matching his speed and altitude, to see what was going on.

A blue bar at the top of Howe's radar image screen alerted him that he was now close enough to get a good view of the plane. "Interior image," he told the computer. The two planes were still about two and a half miles apart.

The pilot was slumped over the control yoke. But there was another person in the plane.

An injured pilot and a hijacker? Or an injured pilot and a scared, nonpilot passenger.

The person in the first officer's seat was much smaller and moved around.

The rest of the plane appeared empty.

No bomb that the gear could see.

"Guard Sixteen, pilot of target plane appears unconscious. There's a passenger. Looks like a kid," added Howe. "He's light on fuel as well."

"How the hell do you know all that?" demanded the Guard pilot.

"NADT Flight to Guard Sixteen," said Howe, hoping his call sign would provide a clue, "I'm afraid I can't go into details. But I do know it."

There was a spar and a compartment behind the cockpit area painted solid by the AMV: The gear couldn't see inside. It was possible that it was a bomb.

"NADT Flight Hawk One, Hawk Two, Guard Sixteen,

we have additional data on the intercepted flight," said the ground controller before the F-16 jock could respond. "Pilot is a thirty-four-year-old male, one passenger, ten-year-old girl, his daughter."

"Shit," said Storey.

"All right, let's think on this a second," said Howe. "How many terrorists are going to take their daughters with them on their final flight?"

"How do we know that's really who they are?" responded Guard Sixteen.

"The person in the first officer's seat is pretty small," said Howe. "Yeah, it's definitely a girl. She's got long hair."

Howe slid closer, riding inside twenty yards, ten, worried that the turbulence off his aircraft might upset the plane. He didn't need the high-tech AMV system any more: He could see the girl pretty clearly through the large window in the relatively new plane. He tried to signal for her to speak, but she didn't seem to have a headset. He tried a few times to mime that she should take her father's, but he knew that wasn't likely to help much. Whatever happened in the movies, in real life the odds of talking a ten-year-old into a safe landing had to be a million to one.

"How much fuel does he have left?" Storey asked.

One of the ground controllers thought he was talking to him and replied that, if the flight plan was correct, he ought to be able to fly for another half hour or so. Howe thought the estimate fairly accurate based on the scan, though it was difficult to tell without more details about the airplane and its engine.

"That should take it out of the restricted area," said Storey.

"Then what happens?" said the ANG pilot.

"I think it's a Cirrus SR22," said Storey.

"And?"

"If that's a Cirrus SR22, it has a parachute," explained Storey. "All we have to do is get the kid to pull it when she's clear of the capital."

The controller confirmed that the plane was designed to carry a parachute—but added that there was no way to know if it had one.

"Where is it located?" asked Howe.

"Behind the cabin area," said Storey, describing the compartment.

"It's there," said Howe. "I say we give it a shot," said Howe. "Better than shooting down a ten-year-old kid over the Potomac."

"Stand by," said the ground controller.

The Capitol building loomed ahead. Two more interceptors were flying up from the southeast, along with a police helicopter.

"We have a company representative on the line," said the controller finally. "We think it might work. Can you hang with them?"

"Not a problem," replied Howe, exhaling slowly into his oxygen mask.

"Good advertisement for the I-MAN system," said Storey.

I-MAN was an emergency piloting system that would allow the controls for a private plane to be taken over in an emergency such as this. It was another NADT project. Until this moment he hadn't thought that much about it—and certainly hadn't seen it as important or even worthwhile.

But it might be. If he took the job, he could find out. He could help all sorts of people, not just the Air Force, not just the military. It was an important job.

Just not his.

"You have to get that passenger on the radio," said the controller, explaining that they would need to instruct her to kill the engine and then deploy the chute. Howe acknowledged, then closed in.

"Radio," he said, miming how she should take the headset from her father and put it on. It took several tries before she finally got it. But she still didn't acknowledge the broadcasts.

"Wave your hand if you hear us," said Howe.

She did.

"Okay, ground," said Howe. "For some reason she's not transmitting, but she can definitely hear. Do we have an easy place to land ahead somewhere?"

The controller mapped a spot in Virginia. They were a good ten minutes from it when the aircraft's engine began to cough. That at least solved one problem: They didn't have to tell her how to cut power.

Howe listened as the controller, speaking in what had to be the calmest voice he'd ever heard, told her to tug on the emergency handle. It took forty pounds of pressure to pull the lever; Howe watched anxiously as the girl pulled down with all her weight.

Nothing happened for a second. And then the panel at the rear of the cockpit seemed to mushroom upward. The parachute appeared as if it had come down from above, snagging the aircraft in a harness. The airplane slowed abruptly and Howe lost sight of it for a moment as he banked to the north. By the time he came around, the Cirrus was descending calmly toward the ground, more like a balloon than a skydiver. It landed against a patch of trees near a baseball field; a Coast Guard helicopter that had been scrambled as part of the rescue effort closed in.

"Time for lunch, Colonel," said Storey.

His flight suit was soaked. He'd been sweating his brains out, worried about the kid and her father.

"Colonel, we going home?" asked Storey. "We're, uh, getting low on fuel ourselves."

Howe glanced at his instruments and realized with a shock that he was already far into his fuel reserves; he had something on the order of ten minutes of flying time left.

"Roger that," Howe said, plotting the course to the airfield.

CHAPTER

11

Blitz dove into the e-mails on his desk, trying to clear away the most important business before his next round of meetings. But it was no use; he was about two messages deep when Mozelle buzzed with a call from the CIA deputy director of operations. The calls multiplied, and Blitz found his head swimming in a myriad of details and distractions.

Just a few months earlier the U.S. had forcibly prevented nuclear war from erupting between Pakistan and India. In the first wave of optimism after the trauma, commentators had hailed a new era of peace. Now things seemed as chaotic and volatile as ever. North Korea was Exhibit One: The supreme leader, Kim Jong Il, was reportedly sick and hadn't been seen for several days. Some intelligence reports claimed he had been poisoned; others noted that revolt was a common topic in army circles. Satellite data showed several different units on the move.

Blitz wanted more than regime change in North Korea. American interests in Asia ultimately depended on reunification. Not only was this the only way to effectively prevent war, it was the best short-term solution to growing Japanese restlessness about its constitutionally limited military establishment. Unlike some of his predecessors, Blitz realized that a rapidly rearming Japan presented a grave danger in Asia. China would have to react, and inevitably this would lead to further confrontation.

Blitz knew his goal; the difficulty was that it looked impossible to achieve, short of war. War in Korea would inevitably kill hundreds of thousands of civilians, even if the nuclear warheads the country was believed to have were not used.

While many worried about the nuclear weapons, ironically they were relatively easy to neutralize or at least target. Central Intelligence had confirmed that North Korea had two warheads loaded on Taepo-Dong 1 missiles that could hit Japan but that the CIA had concluded were currently aimed at South Korean targets. For the past eighteen months the country had been reprocessing uranium, or at least claiming that it was, turning it into bomb material. There was considerable debate about how much weapons-grade material the North Koreans had made, but the consensus was that the country probably had enough for four or six more weapons. Among the many reports on Blitz's desk was one updating the likelihood that these had been placed on the Taepo-Dong 2 two-stage missile, a long-range weapon theoretically capable of striking Alaska. The missile wasn't very accurate, but as the head of the Air Force pointed out, you didn't have to be very accurate with a nuclear warhead.

All of the missile sites, along with potential bomb storage areas and a number of "hot spots" where sensor readings indicated uranium was present in some form, were under constant surveillance and could be destroyed within roughly twenty minutes—less time than it would take the Koreans to prepare the missiles for launch. If the North Koreans tried to go nuclear, Blitz was fairly confident that the threat could be met.

More problematic, though, were the massive number of rocket and artillery weapons aimed at South Korea. Two hundred and fifty 240mm rocket launchers were deployed by one unit alone, all aimed at Seoul from just north of the demilitarized zone. The total number of guns and rockets capable of killing people in the heavily populated area near South Korea's capital literally could not be counted but numbered well in the thousands. Many of these weapons could be reloaded and used several times within just a few minutes.

Those weapons, too, were targeted. Most would be wiped out quickly if the order to attack was given, but presumably by then the damage would be done.

The Koreans may have seen the weapons as a deterrent to American attack. In some ways, however, they were exactly the opposite: It made more sense to launch a preemptive strike if things looked dicey than to stand around waiting until Seoul was on fire. Logically, Blitz realized that this meant America should attack before the North Koreans had a chance to. But successfully navigating the postwar environment required "moral authority," which presumably would be lost if the U.S. struck first. Whether it made sense to or not.

"President's looking for you," said Mozelle, appearing over his desk between calls.

Blitz glanced at his watch. "I'm supposed to head up to NADT and have lunch with Bill Howe. What's up?"

Mozelle gave her eyes a little half-roll, which meant she had no idea. "FBI director just came over, along with Jack Hunter."

"Hunter? What the hell does *he* want?"

"President didn't say."

Blitz grunted. He left his assistant to deal with the phones and went down the hall to the President's office, where he found President D'Amici lining up a putt on the carpet. Charles Weber, the head of the FBI, sat at the side of the President's desk. Hunter, who was presently the third or fourth man in the agency, depending on how you interpreted the depth chart, sat beside him. Both men were dressed in identical brown suits; the cuffs of their pants were hiked just enough to reveal a line of skin above their argyle socks.

The President flicked his wrist and sent a ball shooting across the carpet into the plastic cup. A little flag shot up at the side and the ball spun back.

"Dr. Blitz—just the man I wanted to see," said the President, as if Blitz had wandered into the office by accident. He pointed his golf club at Weber. "Charlie, give the professor the lowdown."

"Actually, Jack's got a better handle on it."

"Three days ago," began Hunter in a voice that sounded as if it came from a TV commercial, "one of our field agents received a call from a young woman in Arizona. . . ."

Hunter continued, detailing a contact from a scientist in North Korea who wanted to defect. The situation would not have been particularly unique, except for the fact that the scientist had supplied a copy of plans for an E-bomb, a weapon North Korea was not known to possess. That, and the fact that the DIA had recently begun working on a case involving the potential threat of using such a device on a major East Coast city.

Blitz hunched down in his seat and scratched his goatee. "Are these two things related?" he asked.

"We're not sure," said Hunter. "We're still trying to flesh things out. The Korean is going to Moscow in two days. We want to try to contact him there."

Different experts had slightly different opinions on the potency of the weapon: One thought it would send a surge through all unprotected electrical devices within a five-mile radius, frying them for good. Another thought its potency would be limited to roughly a mile or so. The three other experts who'd been consulted were somewhere in between. All agreed that the explosion would almost certainly cause the Northeast's power grid to go down for several days, probably more.

"Best-case scenario, this is a real catastrophe," said Hunter. "Nothing like the August 2003 blackout. The surges in the system will wipe out at least some of the safeguards that have been put in place since then. Worst case I don't even want to speculate about."

Hunter had his own ax to grind here, Blitz realized; he was angling for the FBI director's job, which was due to open at the end of the year with his boss's planned retirement. Blitz didn't mind ambition, though it could be a powerful set of blinders when information was being conveyed.

"What does CIA think?" Blitz asked.

"I spoke to Anthony late yesterday," said Hunter, referring to the head of the CIA. "He thinks it's valid. We've sent one of our best people out to nose around, back up the field agent, Andy Fisher."

Blitz knew of Fisher from the NADT scandal. Though unorthodox, the agent was reliable.

"We'd like to grab this guy and bring him back," said Hunter.

Blitz stroked his chin. A Korean plot against the United States: That would clearly justify intervention, maybe even a preemptive strike.

Have the President go on television—no, have the *scientist* go on television.

Wouldn't work.

"We want to help this guy defect," repeated Hunter.

"What do you think, Professor?" asked the President. "Is it worth it?"

"Information on their weapons would certainly be useful," said Blitz. "But what about the DIA's angle? How would they get it here?"

"We don't know," said Hunter. "To be candid, from what we've seen, it's just pure speculation by the DIA and it's unrelated to this. But of course we should take it seriously."

"That's why I thought it best to bring it to the President's attention personally," said Weber.

The President took his putt. It hit the corner of the cup and bounced off to the left. He shook his head as he corralled the ball, then lined up another shot. "Why are they sending this scientist to Moscow?"

"It's about the only place in the world the Koreans are still welcome," said Hunter.

They should grab him, Blitz decided. The potential risk of such a weapon—even if it was only used in Korea—was great.

"I think we should move ahead," he told the others.

Hunter's face blanched. The President took another putt. It rimmed the cup, then sank down.

"Yes," said the President, shepherding the ball as it came back. "But this sounds more like the sort of thing the CIA ought to handle."

Hunter's face blanched.

"Of course, the FBI should remain involved. You've worked together before," added the President.

"Of course," said Weber. "We were going to suggest a joint operation."

Hunter asked who would be lead agency. It was a political faux pas: Had he not asked, he could have claimed sovereignty in any discussion with his CIA counterparts.

"If it's overseas, I'd prefer the CIA," said the President.

"Of course," said Weber quickly. Whatever he lacked in police abilities he made up for in political acumen. He rose from his chair, obviously intent on getting out before Hunter blundered further.

"Stay with me a second, Professor," the President told Blitz. "I have a few minutes before my next appointment, if John's timeline is right."

When the others were gone, the President asked Blitz if he thought the North Korean government would collapse soon.

"Hard to say," said Blitz. "It might fall apart tomorrow. Then again, no one thought Kim Jong Il would even last this long. We may be talking about this twenty years from now."

"You and I won't," said the President.

"We're ready for an attack if it comes," said Blitz.

"You're still in favor of a preemptive attack, aren't you?" said the President.

"That's not what I was in favor of," said Blitz.

"No?" The President took a shot and missed.

"It would solve certain problems, and create many others," said Blitz. "Ultimately it doesn't make sense."

"But if it did, it would save a lot of lives," said the President.

Blitz wasn't about to argue with that.

"Have you found a new head for NADT yet?" asked the President, picking up his golf ball and stowing his putter as he changed the subject.

"I'm still working on Colonel Howe. We're supposed to have lunch, actually." Blitz glanced at his watch, more for show than anything else: There was no way now that he'd make the appointment.

"Money not enough?"

"I think the money's part of the problem," said Blitz. "I think it may scare him."

"Tell him he deserves it. More than most of the fat cats running corporations around here who think they're God's gift to America."

"Nonetheless," said Blitz.

"He can always arrange to take the equivalent of his government salary."

Blitz frowned, even though he knew D'Amici was only joking. Right or wrong, financial compensation was one way defense contractors and Washington kept score; Howe had to have a salary commensurate with his responsibility or he wouldn't be taken seriously.

"Who's your backup?" asked the President.

"Trieste, I guess," said Blitz, mentioning a retired two-star Army general whose name had been floated around.

"*Not* my first choice," said the President. His tone made it clear Trieste wasn't even on the list of acceptable candidates.

"What about my former assistant, Howard McIntyre?"

"Way too young for that job," said the President.

"So is Howe."

"Howe has considerably more experience, and he's a hero," said the President. "And he's older than Howe— who is a good man, don't get me wrong."

"I'll keep working on Howe," said Blitz. "I haven't given up."

"You think you can control him?" asked the President.

"No," said Blitz. He didn't want to control Howe, necessarily, just steer NADT a little more toward the administration's agenda than in the past.

"Maybe you should take the job yourself," suggested the President.

That snake pit? Blitz knew he wouldn't last six months.

"I'm happy where I am," he said. "We need someone qualified and independent but who won't come with their own ax to grind—and won't be in the pocket of people looking to get rich. Howe's perfect."

"Be careful, Professor, you may get what you wish for," said the President.

CHAPTER

12

The fact that he was supposed to be Swedish rather than American didn't particularly bother Fisher; he'd always had vaguely Nordic ambitions despite his dark hair and lack of a sauna fetish. Nor did he worry that the few phrases of Swedish they'd given him to memorize were unpronounceable tongue twisters; Fisher figured that anyone he was likely to meet in Moscow would understand even less Swedish than he did. Not even the ridiculous nonstop hopscotching across Europe as he made his way to Russia threw him off his game. On the contrary, it gave Fisher a chance to sample terrible coffee in a succession of small airports, confirming his opinion that the java brewed at airport terminals belonged in a class all its own.

No, the real problem with his cover were the European cigarettes he was forced to smoke for authenticity. He'd settled on some British smokes as being the closest thing to real tobacco he could find. But for all their storied contributions to civilization, the English had yet to come up with a smokable cigarette.

Worse, the damn things were filtered.

On the other hand, smoking was permitted and seemingly mandatory throughout much of Russia; he'd even been able to light up on the airplane into Vnukovo Airport outside of Moscow without anyone looking cross-eyed at him. It seemed particularly ironic that the country that had given the world gulags, mass murder, and fermented potato juice had such an enlightened attitude toward cigarettes. Fisher was sure this was a good omen for the country's future and even thought about the possibility of buying a retirement home here. The fact that he couldn't speak the language was surely a plus, since it would spare him from knowing what was going on around him—one of the prime benefits of living in a foreign country.

The CIA officer who had assumed control of the operation, Hans Madison, met him in the terminal. Vnukovo was southwest of Moscow and used mostly for regional flights. While it was watched by the FSB, one of the internal security agencies that had succeeded the KGB, the Russians felt that any spy forced to use it must be pretty low on the feeding chain and therefore of less interest than the big shots who flew directly into the main airport, Sheremetyevo-2. This meant that the FSB put its own second- and third-stringers here. Within a few minutes of arriving, Fisher and the CIA officer in charge of the operation—he introduced himself as Hans Madison, a name so goofy Fisher thought it might be real—were free of their shadow and riding in a bus toward the city. The bus was more like a six-wheel minivan with a trailer welded to the body; it was operated by a brand-new company capitalizing on the inefficiencies of the existing public transport system by inventing its own. Capitalizing on government inefficiency was a growth industry in Russia, but then again, the same might be said for just about anywhere in the world.

"Our man arrived last night. He's staying at a youth hostel," said Madison as they rode.

"Youth hostel?"

"Cleared it out for the conference. They're putting up foreign scientists from North Korea and China there. Rest have to stay in real hotels."

Amanda Kung's flight was supposed to arrive at Sheremetyevo-2, within a few hours. Kung had agreed to come to Moscow and let the scientist contact her. For some inexplicable reason she'd insisted on having Mathers as her FBI bodyguard. Mathers had been equipped with a cover claiming she worked with Kung as a junior engineer and had come to take notes.

"We've already bugged the conference rooms," said Madison, continuing to lay out the operation. "You'll be inside with two other agents. A little tricky to wire everybody, so we'll have to go silent com. We have some small radio units, but they're very short-range. You'll have to back up with sat phones. The phones are encrypted, but the Russkies will know you're using them, so obviously that's a last resort. What do you know about power companies and electrical generation?"

"They turn off the lights if you don't pay the bill on time," said Fisher.

"Guess that will have to do," said Madison. "We have a portfolio for you as a Swedish electricity minister."

"Cattle prod come with the job?"

"Not this time around," said Madison.

13

Dr. Park made his morning ablution to his ancestors, trusting himself today especially to the memory of his great-grandfather, who had told him stories about fighting against the Japanese. A more objective observer might have questioned whether his great-grandfather had personally been involved in the battles he spoke of, but Dr. Park accepted them uncritically. His great-grandfather was for him a warrior, and he needed that quality now.

The American had sent word that she would attend the conference. His salvation was at hand, if he was brave enough to seize the opportunity.

Dr. Park dressed quietly. Chin Yop, the minder sent to accompany him through Moscow, snored loudly in the bunk a few feet away. It occurred to Dr. Park that he might take this chance to simply run for freedom: go out on the street and find a cab, then take it to the American embassy. But he didn't know Russian, and even his English was halting. Besides, there were undoubtedly others watching him besides the mild-mannered man who had accompanied him from P'yŏngyang, Russians as well as Koreans.

"Trust us," the American had said in her message.

It was his only option. Dr. Park finished dressing, then woke his minder, telling him he was going to the day room for breakfast.

14

There was black, and there was black. And then there was the blackness of Russian coffee, a shade beyond the naked oblivion beloved of philosophers from Plato to Sartre. Plato had his cave, Nietzsche had his superman; Fisher had his coffee.

It occurred to Fisher that the great German philosopher Immanuel Kant could not have been a true coffee drinker; he was too much of an idealist. Or, rather, given his syncretistic leanings, he would have been the sort who added milk and sugar, botching the whole operation and skewing his view of the universe in the process.

Coffee like this—strong, black, so full of caffeine that the surface buzzed—this sort of coffee was the reason Russia had produced musicians and writers rather than philosophers and poets; the liquid was as thick as sandpaper, scrubbing away the ethereal coatings of your esophagus, a region much given to philosophical thoughts. And the heartburn that would surely follow tended to wipe out lyrical expression.

Fisher, never much for poetry or philosophy, decided he would have to drink more of this on a regular basis. Maybe he could get his local Dunkin' Donuts to import it.

The FBI agent achieved these insights while sitting at the back of Assembly Room Two in Meeting Hall Pavilion A, Government Facility Conference Buildings, Moscow, listening as an engineer sang the seemingly unlimited praises of microcurrents. Fisher was sitting two rows behind Kung and Mathers, who were themselves two rows behind the Korean subject, who had come with his minder and sat in what appeared to be rapt attention, though his dossier said he spoke little English, the language of the presentation.

There were another dozen people in the room, including one Russian agent and one of the CIA backup team members. Fisher had also spotted a Chinese conferee sipping coffee with cream; this was a dead giveaway that the man was either an intelligence agent or a German philosopher trying to reform.

The speaker droned on in an English that came from somewhere between London and Düsseldorf. Apparently there was a brave new world lurking in the circuits powering modern life; Fisher didn't understand most of what the man said, but it did give him a new respect for his cordless shaver.

He remained in his seat as the session broke up, watching Dr. Park up close for the first time. Thirties, no family to speak of, the man was a mid-level drone in the Korean scientific community. As far as that went, he had a relatively sheltered life; in that society he would even be considered privileged.

So why did he want to defect? Beyond the obvious appeal of apple pie and Chevrolets?

Fisher got up as Kung and her gnomish bodyguard passed by his seat. Mathers wagged a finger at him as if they were in junior high; Fisher set his glare on stun and fended her off.

Outside, the hallway was crowded with scientists, engineers, and spooks assigned to make sure they didn't make off with too many doughnuts. Fisher sifted to the far end of the snack table, making like he was checking the program listing.

Fisher had emphasized the importance to Kung—and to the gnome—of letting Dr. Park come to her. So far she was sticking to the program, nibbling on cookies with Mathers at one end of the long table while Dr. Park stood almost motionless on the other. A Finnish engineer came up to the two women and started talking about alternating current, obviously some sort of codeword for threesomes involving short people.

Fisher slid through the crowd and got closer to Dr. Park. He had a minder and a shadow: The shadow had registered as a scientist from China, but Madison ID'd him as a Korean agent. A pair of Koreans from the embassy were watching outside in a car.

A lot of company for a mid-level scientist, unless they suspected he wanted to defect. But if that were the case, wouldn't they have stopped him from attending the conference in the first place?

Fisher watched as Kung and the gnome walked off toward the next session. Dr. Park moved in the opposite direction.

Where were the professional matchmakers when you needed them?

"From Swiss National Electric?" asked a cheery balding man, glancing at Fisher's name tag. His accent was very British, and his name tag revealed that he worked for the London Power Company.

"Sweden," said Fisher. He mimicked the man's accent and threw a lisp in as a bonus, though it was a lot to weigh on a single word.

"Spent time in the States?"

"Too much," said Fisher.

"Many issues there, I suppose."

"It all comes down to too many volts," said Fisher, shambling after Dr. Park.

Miss Kung was plumper than he remembered, and a little older. Still, she had an exotic air about her. Her smile was not quite Korean, but it warmed the room nonetheless.

Dr. Park had not realized until he saw her at the conference that he was attracted to her in a romantic way. Perhaps he had not been until that moment.

He knew she was some sort of spy. The Americans routinely sent their agents across the world to enmesh unsuspecting males; he'd learned that as a child at school. They were devious, but that was one of the things that made dealing with them attractive.

As he walked toward the conference room, Dr. Park realized with great disappointment that Miss Kung was not attending this session. He could not change his own plans, however, without arousing the suspicion of Chin Yop.

A tall European with an absentminded, arrogant air bumped into him just outside the door. The man managed to knock the packet of handouts Dr. Park was carrying from his hand onto the floor.

"Pardon, pardon," said the man, bending and helping pick them up.

Dr. Park stood motionless as the man handed him the folder.

Was there a message in the papers he handed back?

Chin Yop grabbed the folder.

"Sorry," said the man who'd bumped into him.

Dr. Park wanted to run away: He thought of jumping on the man, grabbing his chest, demanding help.

But he wasn't even an American. All that would accomplish would be to expose himself and his plans. He would be dragged away, taken back home to Korea, shot.

They wouldn't bother taking him home. He would be shot in Russia, left in an alley for the dogs to eat.

"You—cigarettes? Have some?" asked the European in broken English.

Dr. Park couldn't get his mouth to speak.

"Cigs?" repeated the man. He took a pack out and held it in Chin Yop's face. He said something in a foreign language that Dr. Park didn't understand, then repeated it in English. "Where I can get more?"

Confused, the minder shook his head.

The European turned to Dr. Park. "You?"

Dr. Park managed to shake his head.

"No smoke?" said the European. He turned back to Chin Yop, said something indecipherable, then switched to English. "I can tell you smoke. Where do you get your cigs?"

The minder glanced at Dr. Park. "Is he crazy or what?" he said in Korean.

Dr. Park shrugged. Chin Yop did, in fact, smoke: He

had a box of Marlboros that he had picked up near the hostel in his pocket.

"Cigarettes? You smoke American?" asked the European, pointing at the box.

Chin Yop nodded hesitantly.

"Can I have one?" said the European, pointing at the minder's pack. "Two of mine for one of yours."

Chin Yop held up his hands, not understanding or at least pretending that he didn't.

Dr. Park explained in Korean, then added that he ought to hold out for three at least.

"Three?" said the European when the trade was offered. But he made the deal, trading his entire pack for three Marlboros. He lit up immediately.

"Where?" he asked as he exhaled. "Buy them? Where did you find them? American, right? I didn't know you could get them here."

"Should I tell him where I got them?" Chin Yop asked Dr. Park as he deciphered the question.

Dr. Park shrugged. Cigarettes were available throughout the city, though they had bought theirs from a black-market vendor near the hostel at a considerable discount.

Was this man really a Russian policeman, checking on them?

"You tell him," said Chin Yop.

"Me?"

"Yes."

"But I don't know."

"You're the senior man. Go ahead, it will seem odd if you don't reply."

Dr. Park looked at the European and then at his minder. Probably the minder was simply worried about his English, but perhaps this was part of an elaborate trap: Dr. Park would be arrested for buying forbidden items, then thrown into a Russian jail.

"Is he a policeman?" asked Dr. Park in Korean.

"You think so?" answered Chin Yop. "No. Too confused. Look, he's a geek like you."

"Maybe it's a trick."

The minder looked at the European and laughed.

If it was a trick, Dr. Park decided, the minder wasn't in on it.

"Go ahead and tell him," said Chin Yop. "He's harmless. A nicotine addict."

Dr. Park had trouble smiling, still unsure if he would be arrested for answering.

"I have heard that you can get them near Kolomev Street," said Dr. Park, naming the street where their hostel was located. He had to repeat it twice before the foreigner understood.

"Oh." The man nodded. "I heard there are shops in Arbatskaya."

Dr. Park felt the blood leave his head as he finally understood who the man was and what he was doing. The Americans were quite clever after all.

CHAPTER
15

After the excitement of the Hawk flight, Howe found the rest of his week rather mundane. The girl in the aircraft was okay—physically, at least: Her father had had a heart attack and died as she watched. Howe, who had lost his own father when he was young, knew she would never truly get over that.

He had missed lunch with Blitz and they kept missing each other as they tried to reschedule, but otherwise he got the full-court treatment, VIPs at every meal. He phoned home once and sometimes twice a day, talking to his mom and occasionally his younger sister, who lived nearby and stopped by the house every so often. They were terribly impressed.

So was his friend Jimmy Bozzone, who kept calling him a big-shot muckety-muck and asking if he'd be able to get him tickets to all the sporting events now.

"What would that do for you, Jimmy?" asked Howe as Jimmy ragged him that night after dinner.

"Well, like, you know, you talk to the powers that be and get an executive box and I come along as your aide-de-campo."

"Campo?"

"Whatever. As long as I get a free beer. Listen, they're having the Final Four down in New York City this month. Get us some tickets."

"Right." Howe shook his head and lay back on the bed. He yawned.

"Sorry if I'm keeping you up," said Jimmy.

"All this wining and dining is hard work." Howe hadn't told Jimmy how much money was involved. He knew if he did, Jimmy would yell at him, call him a fool for even hesitating.

Would he, though? Jimmy valued his independence, and that was something you couldn't really put a price tag on. As head of the NADT, Howe would be answering to all sorts of people at the Pentagon, the White House, Congress. He'd have to deal with contractors, blue suits, Navy people, the GAO—everyone in the world.

That was why they would pay so much money.

"You watching Syracuse?" asked Jimmy. "They're ahead."

"I may turn on the TV just to see them get their asses kicked," Howe told him.

"Screw yourself. And don't forget, I want tickets to the finals at Madison Square Garden."

They were having the Final Four championship games at the Garden this year, the first time ever. Jimmy had gone to Penn State but had inexplicably seized on Syracuse as a team to root for after moving to New York State a decade or so before. Howe had no doubt that he would try and scalp tickets at Madison Square Garden if the Orangemen somehow made it to the play-offs. Tickets would go for thousands, he thought; everybody was making a big deal out of the fact that they were at the Garden.

"Ain't gonna happen," said Howe.

"We'll see," said Jimmy.

After he hung up, he flipped on the basketball game, a first rounder in the NCAA finals. Syracuse *was* comfortably ahead, but they were only playing Marist, which had managed somehow to draw the last bid of the tourney. With Syracuse up by twenty after one period, the game was pretty boring. He was just about to click off the set when the phone rang; thinking it was Jimmy calling back to rub in the game details, he hesitated but then picked up the phone.

"Hello?"

"Colonel Howe," said a female voice, "stand by, please, for Dr. Blitz."

"Colonel," said Blitz, coming on the line before Howe could even answer. "Sorry we've been missing each other. A lot of stuff going on over here. I know it's getting late and I won't keep you. How about we have dinner next Tuesday night?" suggested Blitz. "My wife loves to cook."

"I wasn't planning on staying in town quite that long," said Howe. "I was hoping to leave Saturday."

"I'm afraid I have to go to Camp David for the weekend with the President." Blitz paused. "Why don't you come along?"

"I don't think so," said Howe.

"No, no, you really should: A lot of the important people you'll be working with will be there."

Howe smiled at the way Blitz had made it sound as if he'd decided to take the job.

"I think I'll pass on the weekend, if that's okay. Thanks, though."

"Well, let's set up that dinner, then. And I think the President will want to talk to you as well."

Howe sighed. They really *did* want him to take the goddamn job, didn't they?

Maybe he wanted it as well. Because really, if he didn't, wouldn't he have gone home already?

"So I can mark you down for dinner Tuesday?" asked Blitz. "Come over to my office in the afternoon—four, say. This way the President can drop by and say hi."

Howe barely got "Well . . ." out of his mouth when Blitz started talking again.

"I understand your hesitation," said Blitz, in a voice that suggested the opposite. "At least let the board of directors make a formal offer," insisted Blitz. "We'll have lunch Monday. Come over to my office. In the meantime, use that limo. Go out. Have fun. Even if you don't take the job."

The national security advisor paused and said something to someone else in his office. "Maybe you should have your mom come down from Pennsylvania. Show her Washington," he said when he came back on the line.

"My mother's sixty-eight."

"Colonel, you really ought to relax for the next few days, just give yourself some time to think. Enjoy it—like a little minivacation. You've dedicated your life to your country, and you've made huge contributions. This is just a little bit of payback."

"I'll see you for lunch. I have to be honest, though: I'm leaning against the job. Very much against."

"We'll talk Monday," said Blitz. "Wait until Monday."

CHAPTER

16

Fisher was now officially played and had to stay in the background as the operation proceeded. Unfortunately, he couldn't just disappear; one more lecture on joules and he would stick his fingers into the nearest light socket. So he feigned gastric distress and made a show of heading quickly to the men's room, where he hung out for a while, smoking the cigarettes he'd traded for and listening to the attendant harangue customers for greenbacks instead of rubles. A few strategic groans kept him from being bothered, and when he finally emerged, the attendant steered well clear of him. Fisher made his way back to his hotel three blocks away; Madison flagged him down in a small Toyota.

"Nobody followed you," the CIA officer told him. "You must've put on some act."

"Looking stupid just comes naturally to some of us."

They headed toward Arbatskaya, an area west of the Kremlin that once had a vaguely bohemian flavor and lately had become something of a tourist trap. Kung and the gnome were already en route, driven by a CIA operative disguised as a taxi driver; Madison would "deploy" them once Dr. Park arrived in the area.

If he arrived in the area.

"Your partner's bugged, so we'll hear what happens."

"Who's my partner?" objected Fisher.

"What's-her-name—the short one. Mathers."

"The gnome is not my partner," said Fisher.

"Will he show up?" asked Madison.

"Got me," said Fisher. "His minder will, though. I just about cleaned him out of smokes."

Dr. Park walked past the shop, his heart thumping. Moscow was supposedly undergoing a very warm winter, but he felt like ice, even inside his warm parka. It had not been difficult to persuade Chin Yop to come here; he mentioned that he had eaten in the area during his one previous trip to Moscow and that it was very inexpensive. Chin Yop was undoubtedly being paid an allowance, and thus any savings on meals would go into his pocket.

Were the Americans following? How would they approach him? When? What would they do to Chin Yop?

Dr. Park tried to clear the questions from his mind. If they were following him—and they *must* be following him, he decided—then they would make contact at a time and place of their choosing, a time they felt was safe for everyone. He had to trust that they would handle the business appropriately: They had done well so far.

Dr. Park let his companion choose the restaurant, a small basement café at the foot of a large brick building that held apartments. The man who greeted them at the door spoke English in such a heavy accent that Dr. Park could not make it out. They found a seat in toward the back and managed to pick out items that seemed benign from the menu. In truth, anything they ate here would be exotic; Dr. Park's diet consisted mostly of rice and bits of vegetable or, on occasion, fish. From the looks of his thin wrists and neck, Chin Yop did not fare much better.

"Oh, hello!" said a woman in English from across the room.

Dr. Park looked up. Ms. Kung and another woman were making their way across the room. Chin Yop had a strained look on his face.

"Mr. Chin," said the shorter woman, bowing her head toward Dr. Park's minder. "And your friend?"

Dr. Park introduced himself. The short woman said that her name was Ms. Mathers and she remembered the pair from the conference. Chin Yop smiled faintly, then said to Dr. Park in Korean that the taller woman was quite beautiful.

Dr. Park seized the chance to look directly at Ms. Kung. She was, he agreed, most beautiful.

"Mine," insisted Chin Yop.

Dr. Park turned to him in surprise.

"Don't be a prude," insisted the minder, pushing his chair back and insisting in his poor English that the two women join them.

Dr. Park did not know what to do. His minder's instructions would undoubtedly have been explicit: Such contacts should be kept to a minimum; certainly dinner would violate that edict.

A test?

Dr. Park could smell her perfume. What if the minder wanted to defect as well?

Perhaps he had his own plan.

Or perhaps he knew that Ms. Kung was here to contact him.

"I think perhaps we might eat alone," suggested Dr. Park in Korean. Chin ignored him, talking with the women, asking them about America.

America!

Surely this was a trap. Dr. Park sat silently as the others ordered. When the food arrived he tried to eat slowly, but he could not: He was too hungry. He quickly cleaned his plate, then sat while the others laughed and talked.

"What the hell is she trying to do, pick up the security agent?" Madison asked Fisher. "She's all giggly."

Fisher shrugged. "Probably she gets that way when she's nervous."

"Why would she be nervous?"

Not only could they hear the entire exchange via Mathers's bug, but two of Madison's team members had slipped in with a small video spy cam and were sitting at the next table. The cam was embedded in a brooch on the female op's blouse and provided a fish-eyed view of the room, fed onto a laptop in Madison's Toyota.

The Koreans' own trail team sat in a Russian car half a block away, just barely in view of the entrance. A scan had shown that they were not using any bugging devices—probably, said

Madison, because they couldn't afford them. There didn't appear to be any other minders or Russian agents nearby.

Mathers suggested vodka. Fisher rued his decision not to object to her joining the operation.

The four of them drank and ate for more than an hour. Dr. Park was clearly uncomfortable at the start; he became more so as the time went on. He looked the part of a defector: nervous and antsy. But he also looked like a typical North Korean scientist anxious because his minder was clearly breaking the rules. Paranoia was the one behavior in Korea that didn't attract attention.

Finally, Chin Yop got up to go to the restroom. Dr. Park said something to him as he pushed away the chair.

"Don't leave me alone with these women," whispered the CIA translator from the team van, two blocks away.

Chin Yop said something in return; Fisher assumed it was a lewd suggestion, because the translator, a woman, didn't immediately supply the line.

"All right," said Madison, pointing to the screen. "Let's do it."

"No. I think we ought to wait," said Fisher.

"What?"

"I think we ought to wait."

"Screw that," said Madison. He brought his arm to his mouth and spoke into his mike. "Go," he told his people.

Fisher shook his head.

The CIA officer with the brooch said "Good evening" in Russian—the words sounded a bit like "Duh breeze there"—giving the signal to exit. Mathers jumped to her feet and grabbed Dr. Park. He pushed her away but got up, starting to walk toward the back. The other CIA agent inside the restaurant loomed at the left, corralling him. One of the patrons yelled something.

Then both the audio and visual feeds died.

"Shit," said Fisher, jumping from the car.

*　　*　　*

Dr. Park felt his head spin as the man pushed him toward the door.

The Americans were trying to help him escape—surely they were trying to help him escape. But the woman and the man who had approached him had spoken Russian. Where were they taking him?

Dr. Park took a step toward the back when the man from the other table grabbed him. He whispered something that Dr. Park didn't understand.

He thought it was Russian, yet it seemed almost Korean.

Dr. Park was being pushed toward the front. He tried to grab Ms. Kung, but she was sliding away, running toward the exit.

What was going on?

The door flew open. Dr. Park tried to push against the large man but it was no use; he felt himself thrown out into the street.

"*Nyet*," he said, the only Russian he knew. "No! Help!" he shouted in Korean.

Where were the Americans?

"Come with us," said the short woman, Mathers.

She was speaking English.

Suddenly, Dr. Park understood: They were *all* Americans. He started to run.

A police car sped around the corner. Two men got out and began shouting, reaching for their weapons. Dr. Park threw himself to the ground.

Fisher got to the corner just as a pair of Russian police cars, one marked, one unmarked, arrived. Two policemen were in the street, guns drawn.

The American FBI agent pulled out the Beretta that Madison had supplied. As the Russian police grabbed at Kung, Fisher fired, making sure he hit the man square in the chest, where he was protected by his bulletproof vest.

The other policeman fired back, missing. The CIA

backup team finally got its act together, firing a barrage of tear-gas canisters that sent the policemen retreating across the street. Fisher, choking, grabbed Kung and dragged her away, then went back for Dr. Park. His eyes blurred with the gas; he grabbed a figure in front of him and pulled backward, his whole body burning with the thick gas. His eyes clamped themselves shut.

"Go, let's go!" Madison shouted.

Fisher managed to crack open one eye and saw that he'd taken Mathers, not the Korean scientist. Cursing, he let go of her and started back toward the restaurant.

Madison grabbed him. "No! The police are coming," he shouted. "We have to leave. Now!"

Fisher hesitated just long enough to hear a fresh hail of bullets hitting the concrete a few yards away.

"All right," he said, heading back around the corner where a van was waiting, eyes and nose raw with the gas.

"You okay?" asked Madison as they sped away.

"Yeah," said Fisher. "But I really hate tearjerkers."

PART TWO
Tacit Ivan

CHAPTER

1

Faud Daraghmeh closed the book and got up from the small table where he had been reading. He could hear his landlady's television downstairs as he went to the kitchen. The old woman would be dozing in her chair by now, no doubt dreaming of the grandchildren she never saw. She talked of them often to him, with the fondness that he thought his great-aunt must use when she spoke of him.

It was a weakness, one of many. Faud took the teapot from the stove and began to fill it. The imam had warned him; the worst temptations were the subtle ones, the almost silent callings of slothfulness and indecision.

But his path was set. He had completed the most difficult job more than a month earlier. Now he only waited for the next set of instructions. Whatever they were, he would be ready. Faith must win out over temptation.

He turned off the water and placed the teapot on the stove.

CHAPTER

2

In the aftermath of an operation, there are always several perspectives on its conduct and outcome. Often there is an inverse relationship between proximity to the operation and the opinion thereof: While those who had been at the scene might consider that things had gone decently under the circumstances, those several times removed might opine that *lousy* was a more appropriate adjective.

And then there was the opinion of Fisher's boss.

"A fiasco. Utter and complete."

"I wouldn't call it utter," said Fisher, speaking from the protection of the American embassy in Ukraine, where he'd been spirited after the fallout from the operation.

"What would you call it?"

"Something other than utter. I've never really understood what *utter* meant."

"You're a screwup, Fisher. Whatever you touch screws up. You're lucky the ambassador got you out of Moscow; I'd drop a dime on you myself."

Fisher hadn't heard the expression *drop a dime* since his days as a nugget agent investigating the Mob. It had a nostalgic feel which he couldn't help but admire.

According to both the NSA and the CIA, the Russians believed that they had broken up a robbery by a group of *mafiya*, a story supported by the versions of the incident supplied by Dr. Park and his security agent bodyguard. The Korean government had apparently accepted that explanation. But Fisher wasn't about to point that out to Hunter, who clearly wasn't in the mood to accept anything short of ritual suicide as an apology for the mission's failure. For some reason known only to Hunter, the fact that the CIA had taken over the project failed to mollify him; he considered a screwup a screwup. Fisher thought this an unusually altruistic opinion for one so committed to advancing in government service.

"You're off the case, Fisher," said Hunter.

"What a shock," said Fisher.

"I'm not putting up with your sarcastic back talk any longer."

"Does that mean I can hang up?"

Hunter was silent. Fisher thought he heard him murmuring to himself. It sounded as if he was counting to ten, though Fisher knew for a fact that Hunter couldn't count that high.

"Homeland Security has requested you be assigned to them," said Hunter finally. "I'm granting their request."

"What?"

"Work with Macklin on his task force."

"Are you kidding?"

"I don't kid, Fisher."

"Where exactly am I supposed to report?"

"Macklin is up in New York somewhere. Use your alleged detecting skills and find him," said Hunter. "I swear, Fisher, if it were up to me, you'd be on a Coast Guard cutter in the Bering Strait, guarding icebergs."

Roughly twenty hours later Fisher arrived at National Airport in Washington, D.C., bedraggled, grouchy, and in need of a shave—pretty much top form for any special agent. Technically he was off duty, en route to the special Homeland Security–DIA task force in the New York Metropolitan area. But Justice took no holiday. So he wasn't surprised to find her screaming when he walked through the lobby at National Airport.

"Fisher. FBI," he said, flashing his credentials at the two airport cops holding Justice by the arms. "What's up?"

"We caught her smoking," said one of the officers. "Then she went ballistic."

"I did not. You grabbed me—"

Fisher pointed at her. "You got cigarettes?"

"That's a federal offense?"

"As a matter of fact, it is," said Fisher. He turned to locals. "You have an interview room, right?"

"Well, uh, yeah, but usually we just give a citation and confiscate the smokes." He held up an entire carton of cigarettes.

"I'll take them as evidence," said Fisher. He recalled now that the interview room was down the corridor behind the plain white door marked Private to his right, and took a step toward it.

"I'm not going with you," said the woman.

Fisher turned and looked at her. He knew her type well; all he had to do was squint slightly and hold up the carton of Salem Lights—no accounting for taste in a felon—and she shut up. The airport cops, however, began burbling about procedures.

"Not a problem. It's my case," said Fisher as he nudged the suspect along, heading down the corridor and into the interview room.

Where he pulled out a chair, sat down, and lit up one of his own cigarettes.

"You really have to watch yourself," he told Justice, whose full name was Maureen Justice and whom Fisher knew, albeit vaguely, as the traffic helicopter pilot for WKDC, a local AM radio station. "Salem Lights? People have been shot for less."

"At National Airport?"

"Damn straight. I mean, granted, most of the people around here who have guns are federal employees, so odds are that they wouldn't hit you even if they emptied their magazines, but you never know."

"I'll keep that in mind," said Maureen. She took the carton and removed the top pack, which she'd opened earlier. "I owe you one, huh?"

"Big time," said Fisher. "And don't think I won't collect."

"Anytime, Andy," she said, blowing a perfect circle into the air. "Anytime."

3

Blitz had somehow managed to forget that he had invited Howe to have lunch with him Monday until the Secret Service people called up to his office. He decided to have him come up, even though going out for lunch would be impossible: The NSC had scheduled a meeting on Korea at one, and he was supposed to go over to the Intelligence Council immediately afterward. And he was just about to take part in a phone conference with the head of the CIA and the field agent who had managed to botch the snatch of the E-bomb scientist in Moscow.

In fact, he was deep in conversation with the CIA people when Howe walked into the office.

"Sit, sit," he told him, waving him into a nearby chair as he listened to a report of the botched mission. "Mozelle will have something sent in."

Howe shrugged and sat down.

"He was attending the sort of conferences that you would attend if you were interested in disabling electrical systems on a wide-scale basis," said Madison, the CIA officer in charge of the operation. He'd been asked whether the scientist was really in a position to know about E-bombs. "We have some blanks on his background, but he could have helped design a weapon. Whether he would know about its distribution or not is an open question. And we haven't turned up anything on delivery systems related to this."

One of the CIA desk officers picked up Madison's thread, recounting NSA intercepts related to the scientist. The North Koreans had accepted the Russian explanation that a rogue *mafiya* group had tried to hold up the foreigners and the local *militsiya* had saved the day, thanks to a phone tip from the restaurant, which the Korean bodyguard claimed to have made but which the U.S. had been unable to trace. Nonetheless, there were sure to be repercussions for the scientist as well as the security people.

"What about the DIA reports?" asked Blitz. "Do we have anything new?"

He glanced over at Howe on the chair nearby. The colonel was wearing the same suit he'd worn the week before. More than likely it was the only suit he owned.

"We're working on a new batch of intercepts," one of the NSA people said over the conference line. "We should have them in time for the afternoon NSC session."

"But we're agreed there's a threat?" said Blitz.

"There is a threat. The question is how severe."

"Where would they use the weapon?" he asked.

"Drop it over Seoul and the place goes dark for six months," said one of the CIA experts.

"And if they can smuggle it over here?" asked Blitz.

"Same thing. But we have nothing to indicate that they have, beyond the DIA's suspicions."

Blitz frowned and leaned back in the seat.

Howe shifted uneasily, waiting for Blitz to get off the phone and consciously willing himself not to listen to the conversation.

He'd made up his mind Sunday that he wasn't taking the job. And it had nothing to do with the money.

He'd taken a long walk around the National Mall on Saturday. Nearly deserted because of the late-winter cold, it had helped remind him of the importance of what happened in Washington. The memorials to Lincoln and Jefferson, the stark Washington Monument, the FDR Memorial, the sleek sadness of the Vietnam Veterans Memorial—duty had a somber weight here, an importance beyond the lunches and VIP tours.

Standing in front of the Reflecting Pool, gazing at the Lincoln Memorial, he had asked himself why he was hesitating to make a decision. Ordinarily he made decisions quickly and firmly. It was partly natural inclination, partly training as a pilot. You set your course and then proceeded.

And yet, he had hesitated over this. He had to admit it: Even though he knew he didn't want the job, the lure of the money and the trappings of power were enticing.

As was the sense of duty.

Howe watched Blitz on the phone. The national security advisor alternated between frowning and nodding his head, until finally he signed off from the conversation.

"Very well," said Blitz. "Get back to me then."

Blitz swiveled around and slapped the button on the panel behind his desk, killing the connection. Then he jumped up and extended his hand to Howe. The effect was comical, and Howe felt himself smiling despite his best effort to maintain a serious demeanor.

"How are you, Colonel? Have a good weekend?"

"It's been fine," said Howe. "How about yourself?"

"Going crazy," said Blitz. "Korea has us shaking our heads. One second it looks as if it's going to implode; the next it seems ready to launch World War III. We're trying to stay on top of the situation." He paused, and Howe thought he had decided he'd said too much. But then he continued: "The question is how much risk to take in retrieving information. How to make it proportional to the payoff."

"Sure," said Howe, though he didn't understand precisely what Blitz was referring to.

"Colonel Howe," boomed the President's voice from the open doorway. "Take the job yet?"

Howe felt the blood rush from his head as he jumped to his feet. President D'Amici took his discomfort in stride, patting the side of his arm and then pointing with his other hand at Blitz.

"Listen, Professor, I want a briefing on that incident in Moscow," the President said.

"From me or Anthony?"

"Just you," said the President. "Before our other meetings."

"Not a problem."

"I have to go," said the President as one of his aides appeared in the doorway behind him. "We'll talk. Good to see you, Colonel."

Howe nodded, then turned back to Blitz.

"That was completely off the record," said Blitz.

Howe, who had no idea what it was anyway, nodded. "I've come to a decision about NADT. I'm not going to take the job. Thanks for the offer, though."

Blitz's expression went from serious to pained. "Don't make a final decision yet. Wait to hear from the board of directors. They haven't even made you an offer."

"It's okay. My mind's made up." Howe suddenly felt tremendously relieved. "You know what, I don't really feel like lunch. Is that all right? I'm not insulting you or anything?"

"Well, no—uh."

"Thanks. Thanks a lot," said Howe, and pulled his suit jacket forward on his shoulders and walked from the room.

"Damn it," said Blitz after Howe was gone.

As he sat down the phone buzzed; he looked at the handset a second, then picked it up.

It was the CIA director again.

"Charlie Weber and Jack Hunter are here with a new e-mail from the Korean scientist," Anthony told Blitz. "You're going to want to see it."

CHAPTER

4

Dr. Park had not been able to eat since coming back from Moscow, nor had he slept. The hours stretched forward like the sheet of a bed pulled taut, then tauter still. He began to hear buzzing in his ear; he thought he heard whisperings behind his back.

And yet, the director and higher authorities seemed to have accepted the Russian explanation for the incident: that it was a robbery or perhaps intended kidnapping. Dr. Park had agreed with Chin Yop's version of the attack, which had the security agent fending off several thugs before the police arrived. The men who questioned him seemed skeptical, but Dr. Park stuck to the story, as Chin Yop had advised. To change it would only guarantee disaster.

When he returned to work, no one questioned him and, surprisingly, the director did not send for him. But this provided no relief for Dr. Park. On the contrary, his dread grew. His breath shortened. His palms were so sweaty that he could not hold a pencil, and his fingers jittered when he tapped at the keyboard of his computer. He saw shadows at the periphery of his vision. They disappeared when he turned his head, only to return when he looked straight ahead.

There were moments when Dr. Park managed to step back from himself, or at least from his fears; he wondered when he had become such a different person, wondered at why he had risked so much to get away in the first place. And then inevitably he would answer to himself that he hadn't risked anything at all: His life here had always been forfeit. The few luxuries he enjoyed—a better bed than most, a better roof, certainly more food—those were the Great Leader's luxuries, and could be taken away at his pleasure.

Dr. Park knew that the regime was dying; he could see the signs of chaos slowly building around him. Soldiers on the street did not answer the commands of their superiors; this fact in itself was a shock, nearly outside the realm of possibilities, yet it was happening all the time.

When the regime fell, so would he. The only hope was to escape to the foreigners.

That was logical, and logic was supposed to be a scientist's solace. And yet, these thoughts did not comfort him;

fear and dread grew until at every sound he could not think, at every question from a coworker he nearly confessed to his treason.

And so when the director sent for him he felt relieved. Finally he would find resolution. He did not welcome death, much less the torture he assumed would proceed it. But he hated the anxiety roiling inside him even more. He got up and followed the messenger, walking quickly through the black tunnel that surrounded him.

"You are here," said the director as he was shown inside.

Dr. Park bent his head. He began to tremble, for though he welcomed resolution he was not a brave man.

"Well, after the excitement in Moscow, I am glad to see that you are in good health," said the director.

He kept his head bowed. It was possible that he would be shot in the lot outside. This had happened some years before to an engineer, or at least was rumored to have occurred; Dr. Park himself had not seen it.

Would the bullets hurt his head, or would death come so quickly that he would not feel it?

A tingling sensation flared at the base of Dr. Park's shoulders, spreading upward like the licking flames from the bottom of a pile of leaves. He closed his eyes, and for a moment he thought he could feel the bullets that would kill him, striking at the very center of his skull.

"The camp at Dae Ring Son is a good one, though bare," said the director. "There are not many troops there, no more than a dozen at this time of year. But your needs will be met and the tests will not last long. . . ."

What exactly was the director saying?

Dr. Park could not hear the words through the cloud of pain and fear covering his head.

Tests?

Dae Ring Son? That was a small camp near an abandoned airfield to the north, not a prison.

"You will leave immediately?" said the director. He phrased it as a question.

Slowly, Dr. Park forced his eyes open.

His treachery had not been discovered.

His treachery would *never* be discovered.

"Dr. Park? Are you all right?"

"Yes, sir," he managed. "Of course. I can leave at whatever instant is desirable."

The director smiled indulgently. "Go and gather your things. A driver will accompany you. You are our representative. Remember, your behavior is our honor."

"Yes, sir. Yes, sir." Dr. Park bowed deeply.

"You honored us in Moscow," the director added.

"I did my best."

Dr. Park could manage to push nothing else from his mouth, and instead retreated from the office.

CHAPTER

5

"The NSA has a good read on the e-mails," CIA director Jack Anthony told the President. "We've verified that Dr. Park is at the complex. It's possible that there is a bomb there, or at the airfield two miles away. Getting him and the weapon would be an intelligence bonanza."

"It would be an important break," said Thomas Brukowski, the Homeland Security secretary. "Because, from the intelligence we've been getting on this E-bomb plot, something's going to shake out within a week to ten days."

Blitz closed his eyes. Brukowski was always saying that something was always going to "shake out" within a week to ten days. Blitz had seen the same intelligence that he had, and the prediction was absolutely not justified. In fact, the DIA and Homeland Security team investigating it had been spinning its wheels for more than a week without coming up with anything new.

Now that he had been belatedly informed of the scientist

and his offer to deliver an E-bomb—the latest promise—Brukowski naturally assumed that North Korea was the source of the weapon his people were hunting for. He was by far the most gung-ho member of the cabinet, which the President had gathered to discuss the National Security Council's unanimous vote that the scientist be "rescued."

"I don't think that scientist is worth the risk involved in trying to get him out," said Myron Pierce, the secretary of defense. "Too many lives would be on the line, and the potential for blowback is just too huge over there right now."

"We have a plan that minimizes the risk," said Anthony. "We may need some logistical backing, but it would be minimal. We'd use two CIA paramilitary agents, with some Special Forces backup. That's it."

"Korea is way too volatile," said Pierce.

"I concur," said Wordsworth Cook, the secretary of state. "We can't do anything to upset the Korean teeter-totter."

"What did you have in mind, Jack?" Blitz prompted, trying to get off the negative track.

"Infiltration from the coast. If we could deposit them via a submarine . . ."

Pierce scowled. "They'll be picked up before they get a mile from the coast."

"We have infiltrated agents before," said Anthony. "The only downside is how long it will take them to get to the target area. I'd prefer using an airdrop, but, given the defenses, it doesn't seem practical."

"And how do they get out?" asked Pierce.

"They march back to the coast."

"You think the scientist can walk that far?"

"No way of knowing unless we try."

While Blitz was tentatively backing Anthony's plan as a fallback, he preferred a more direct approach and had already put some feelers out to the military command responsible for Special Operations, as well as to some of the staff people who worked for the Joint Chiefs of Staff. He saw his opportunity now to push for a more aggressive plan.

"The location in Korea makes the planning problematic," Blitz admitted, rising from his chair and leaning over the large table in the cabinet room. He glanced to his right, looking at D'Amici. The President wore his best poker face. "But the time sensitivity argues for an aggressive plan."

"What time sensitivity?" said Pierce. "There's no imminent threat here. This is just one more weapon—which they may not even have."

"The situation in North Korea is deteriorating rapidly," said Blitz.

"If we start a war, it'll deteriorate even faster."

"I'm not advocating a preemptive strike, or anything of that nature," said Blitz.

"There are time constraints on our side," said Brukowski. "They've given the weapon to terrorists. I'm sure of it."

Pierce gave Brukowski a contemptuous scowl, then asked Blitz, "You buy the contention that the weapon has been smuggled into the U.S.?"

"I don't know," said Blitz, hedging; he actually didn't. "The situation in Korea is such that a well-designed operation, be it Special Forces or CIA, should be able to retrieve our scientist. I think it would be worth the risk. The North Koreans have been making outrageous claims about intrusions by our forces for months without basis; even if they see something now, who will believe them?"

"The Japanese," said Cook.

"Special Operations can put something together," said General Grant Richards, the head of the Joint Chiefs of Staff. "It would make sense."

"Helicopters, even Ospreys, aren't going to make it over the border from the south, given their present alert status," said Pierce. "And they'd be pushing beyond their range. If we put an aircraft carrier or an assault ship—hell, even a destroyer—close to the Korean coast, the Chinese are going to be upset."

"And we shouldn't be upset that the Koreans are building terrorist weapons and giving them to murderers?" said Brukowski.

"My point is, a large operation is going to be noticed," said Pierce. "Whatever you do. You use a ship to get close to the coast and use Ospreys or helicopters to land at the complex where he is, or you send a C-130 to the airfield. Either way, you'll be seen. This is North Korea we're talking about. There are only a limited number of ways to get by their radars and air defenses, and each one of them is very risky. As for getting a bomb out, forget it: It's a pipe dream. I bet this guy isn't even real."

"I think the situation calls for finesse," said Anthony. "I have a plan drawn up. I only need minimal help."

"If he's worth getting, we're going to have to take some risks," said Blitz.

"Let's see what those risks are," said the President. "Draw up some plans. I want to see your option, and I want to see what the Army thinks. By tonight."

"You want to review the plans yourself?" Blitz asked. While he wanted it to proceed, he understood the need for the President to stand aloof in case something went wrong.

"I want to see the outlines, not all of the specifics," said the President. "I don't need to know how many gallons of fuel we're using or how many clips of ammunition we're carrying. In the end I'm going to get blamed no matter what happens," he added. "I might as well deserve some of it."

6

Seeing New York City from the air always filled Fisher with a certain indescribable sensation. Fortunately, he had come prepared, and so, with the help of four or five industrial-strength antacids and an Alka-Seltzer tablet he found in the seat cushion, the FBI agent made it off the plane in reasonably good shape. He was just starting to feel the light tingle of a nascent nicotine fit when he spotted Karl Grinberg of the New York office prowling the JFK reception hall. Fearing the worst, he turned right, hoping to make his escape—only to run into Kowalski's extended arms.

"You better let me go or read me my rights," said Fisher.

"Even with jet lag, you're a pistol," said Kowalski.

"I don't have jet lag. I need a cigarette," said Fisher, edging toward the door.

"Fisher. Your boss wants to talk to you," said Grinberg, marching up.

"Which boss?" tried Fisher, though he knew it was no use.

"Hunter."

"I work for Homeland Security now."

"Yeah," said Kowalski. "He's going to swab the deck on a Coast Guard cutter."

"You better stay away from their recruiters, Kowalski," Fisher said. "I hear they have a tugboat shortage."

"Yuk, yuk, yuk. Come on. Make your call and let's get going."

"You came for me?"

"That and the pizza. Macklin says it's good here."

"One question, Fisher," said Hunter when Fisher called him from Grinberg's car.

"Thanks for the warning."

"Is the scientist legitimate?"

"What do you mean?"

"Was this scientist real?"

"Seemed to be breathing."

"You know what I mean," said Hunter. "Were they trying to snatch our gal, or was this guy really trying to defect?"

"I didn't get a chance to ask."

"No screwing around here, Fisher. The President wants to know."

"I'm not sure," said Fisher. "If I didn't think he was real, I wouldn't have gone in the first place." He blew a smoke ring toward the car dashboard.

"People's lives are on the line here," said Hunter. "And my reputation."

"Is that another question?"

"I'm asking you again: Was he real?"

"I think so. But maybe you ought to tell me what answer you want so I get it right."

Hunter hung up.

CHAPTER
7

HELLO AMANDA

I ASK AGAIN FOR HELP. AT LEAST ONE WEAPON SOLD. I HAVE INFORMATION.

PLEASE.

ANSWER.

------------------------- Headers -------------------------
Return-Path: <J.Smith@simon.com>
Received: from rly-xc04.mx.aol.com (rly-xc04.mail.aol.com
[172.20.105.137]) by air-xc02.mail.aol.com (v93.12) with
ESMTP id MAILINXC23-3f873ec520e528b; 2008 13:33:25 -
0400

Received: from mail.simon.com (mail.simon.com
[66.43.82.172]) by rly-xc04.mx.aol.com (v93.12) with
ESMTP id MAILRELAYINXC48-e43ec520cf1bf; F2008
13:33:03 -0400
  Received: from mdcms001.simon.com (ss-exch-
  smtp.simon.com [172.30.65.47])
  by mail.simon.com (AIX4.$\frac{3}{8}$.9.3p2/8.9.3) with ESMTP id
  NAA96516
  for <JD@aol.com>; 12 March 2003 13:37:33 -0400
  Received: by mdcms001.chuster.com with Internet Mail
  Service (5.5.2653.19)
  id <K8SXA6FM>; Sun, 16 March 2003 13:33:03-0400
Message-ID:
<A27A160FD659C648B8665DCD07B7C90A8488FE@MDC
MS002>
MIME-Version: 1.0
X-Mailer: Internet Mail Service (5.5.2653.19)
Content-Type: multipart/alternative;
  boundary="——_=_NextPart_001_01C31BD1.3326EE10"

CHAPTER

8

Howe celebrated his decision by walking against a brisk late-winter wind to Washington's Chinatown section and having lunch. He even gamely tried eating with chopsticks, though he soon gave that up in favor of tried-and-true Western utensils. After lunch he headed back across the mall to the Smithsonian National Air and Space Museum, studying the World War I–era aircraft and just wandering in general through the vast halls of the museum. A new computer simulation booth had been set up, allowing visitors to practice their skill in simulated World War II dogfights. Howe blasted a Focke-Wulf 190 out of the sky with a Hurricane—no mean feat—but had a much harder time against the V-1 buzz bombs, pilotless terror weapons used by Germany at the end of the war. The trick was to fly next to them, then tip them off course with your wing. Howe gave up his spot to a twelve-year-old after several unsuccessful tries; the kid upended the V-1 on the first try.

The visit to aviation's past made him feel as if he had let go of his own, and he arrived back at his hotel in good spirits, deciding to have one last meal in town at an expensive restaurant before leaving in the morning. He got into the elevator and held it open for a young mother and her child; the doors had nearly closed when a man in a blue pin-striped suit stuck his hand in, leveraging them back. The man leaned over and punched the button for Howe's floor—seventeen—even though it was lit.

The child in the elevator looked to be about two. Spit dribbled from his mouth. As his mother bent to wipe it, Howe noticed she wasn't wearing a wedding ring. For a moment he fantasized about striking up a conversation and inviting her to dinner.

The elevator stopped before he could think of anything to say. Howe reached to hold the door open for her; his gallantry earned him a smile from the woman, but he remained tongue-tied as the doors closed.

"Pretty," said the other man.

"Oh, yeah," said Howe.

"Instant family, though. Not for you."

Howe turned to him.

"My name is Jake Elder. I'm with the Pentagon," said the man. "Some people with the chief of staff want to talk to you about an aircraft you're familiar with, and they sent me to get you."

"What aircraft?" said Howe.

"Actually, I don't know," said Elder. "I think the nature of what they want to talk to you about requires compartmentalization. An Army major by the name of Tyler sent me," added Elder. "He said you'd know him."

The door to the elevator opened on Howe's floor. Neither man moved to get out.

"He also said to make sure you knew this was strictly voluntary," said Elder.

"All right," Howe said. "Take me to him."

Tyler met him in the Pentagon lobby, zipping him through security and filling him in as they walked upstairs to a suite of planning rooms.

"We were talking about Korea and your name came up," said the major. "I thought I'd take a chance that you were still around."

"I haven't been in Korea since I was a lieutenant," said Howe.

"It wasn't really about your experience there."

Tyler explained that he was working with a task force developing plans to target various North Korean advanced-weapons development sites in case of a war, facilities that might be difficult to bomb or worthy of study before being destroyed. The task force included CIA, DIA, and intelligence people.

"We've been asked to set up something special," added Tyler. "Something a little complicated, and we have to put a plan together pretty quick."

"I'll help if I can," said Howe.

A group of planners and intelligence experts, some in military uniform and some in civilian dress, were working in a large conference room Tyler led him to. Most had laptops open and sat around a pair of large round conference tables pushed awkwardly together, a large map at the center. The map was of North Korea. There were satellite photos and diagrams of a small airstrip known as Pong Yan and an adjacent installation.

"We want to pick someone up from this base," said Tyler. "It's in the northwest, fairly isolated, but a good distance from the coast."

"And where does Cyclops come in?" asked Howe.

"Cyclops?"

"The airborne laser. That's why I'm here, right? Because I helped develop it?"

"Not exactly," said Tyler. "Let me explain."

Their "target" was currently at the base, but had said he could make it to the airstrip. Two plans had been worked out. Both involved infiltrating Special Operations forces into the area. The first called for a force of two A teams—twenty-four men—to land at a point roughly fifty miles to the northwest. They would proceed overland—basically across mountains—meet the man at a prearranged spot near the camp, and then go back. The drawback was the fifty-mile trip: It was anything but an easy march, and while the soldiers could be expected to make it, the target was unlikely to be in very good shape.

"We'd probably end up carrying him out on a litter," said Tyler, still speaking as if he led a Special Forces A team, which as a major he would not.

"Why don't you use the airstrip?" asked Howe.

"That would be easier, but the goal is to make the rescue completely covert," Tyler explained. He pointed at the map. "We don't want the Koreans to know anything. And the problem here is that there are radars in this area that would catch anything approaching, and a barracks here and here. They would hear an aircraft or a helicopter."

And possibly shoot it down, Howe realized, though Tyler didn't say that.

"What about a Korean plane?" asked Howe.

"That's plan two," said Tyler. "Though there are some problems with it."

Problem one was the fact that Korean aircraft were always strictly accounted for, and one suddenly appearing overhead would instantly arouse suspicions. Problem two was that the field at Pong Yan was short, which limited the aircraft that could land—and, more importantly, take off—there. What they needed was an airplane that belonged there, with reasonable range to get in and out while still operating on a short strip. At the same time it would be nice if it had decent speed and maybe the ability to defend itself against Korean SAMs and MiGs.

"Like a Korean cross between an MC-130 and an F-22," said one of the civilian analysts.

"If you find a plane like that," said Howe, "let me know."

"Actually, NADT has something that might be useful," said the man. "And it happens to look like a Russian aircraft that's been operating over the country."

The Berkut, thought Howe, finally understanding why they had called him.

"We'd still have people on the ground," Tyler told him. "The team would go in and be prepared to secure the area if anything went wrong."

"I don't know if that plane can land there," said Howe, leaning over the satellite photo.

"The engineers say it can."

"NADT made it available?" Howe asked.

"That won't be a problem," said one of the civilians.

The Berkut was the NADT-built S-37/B, the two-seat American version of the Russian-made S-37 Sukhoi Howe had seen tarped in the hangar the other day. The American knockoff had several advantages over the real S-37, most notably in its payload and range, which could be extended with fuel tanks and an in-air refueling. Even so, the craft would have just enough fuel to make it from Japan, touch down, and then get out over the Sea of Japan for a refuel.

It had some drawbacks compared to the real thing, which was still in development. The American S-37/B was fitted with a Russian 30mm GSh-301 cannon, the same weapon used in the Sukhoi Su-27 series the original type was based on. This was a decent weapon, though of use only in a very short-range engagement. Because it had been built primarily to gain information about the Russian model's capabilities, the NADT plane had only two working hard points, or spots where missiles or bombs could be attached. These points had also been plumbed for drop tanks—and would have to be used to complete the mission. Which meant it would be flying for a long time over hostile territory without much of a defense.

Howe suggested a pair of F/A-22Vs as long-range, stealthy escorts. While an excellent idea in theory, there were only three Velociraptors in existence and all were currently involved in a suspended NADT test program in Montana; obtaining the planes and making sure they were ready would take more than a week. A squadron of regular F/A-22s were envisioned as standby escorts, operating off the coast and only getting involved if needed. The planners believed—and Howe agreed—that the Berkut would have a better chance of reaching its target area and returning undetected if it flew alone; even if it was seen, the initial reaction would be that it was a Russian aircraft, and radio transmissions could be made to reinforce that. The Raptors, while stealthy, were not quite invisible, and some of the long-range radars the North Koreans used had a reasonable chance of finding them.

"We know it's a long shot," said Tyler. "The question is, is it possible?"

Howe folded his arms, realizing that the real question wasn't whether it could be done or not: It could be. The question was whether he would do it. There were no other American pilots familiar with the plane. It would take several weeks to find another pilot and then train him to fly the aircraft.

"I can do it," he said. "When do we go?"

Tyler smiled. "Choice isn't ours, Colonel. We have to take the plan over to the White House in an hour and a half."

"Well, let's work out the details, then," said Howe, pulling out a chair and sitting down.

9

The evidence fit on a single sheet of lined yellow paper: two calls from a cell phone in New York City to New York addresses, and an e-mail message that, when decrypted, read: *Friends in NY Thursday.* Both the cell phone and the e-mail account had been paid with a credit card associated with a member of a terrorist group called Caliph's Sons, one of nearly a hundred on the CIA and FBI watch lists. The check used to pay for the credit card was drawn on a bank account that had paid for another e-mail account, this one with two messages about the potency of E-bombs. The messages were in clear text but were vaguely worded, with no indication that the sender or recipient had access to such a weapon. There was as yet no connection to North Korea.

As for Caliph's Sons, little was known about the group beyond its name and the fact that one of its members had blown himself up accidentally in Queens six months before, and that the same man had used the Internet to find out information about high-power microwave (HPM) bombs: weapons that attacked gigahertz-band frequencies, commonly known as E-bombs.

"So, what do you think?" asked Macklin.

"You got the case nailed here, Michael, I have to say."

"Come on, Fisher. Be serious."

Fisher looked over at Macklin. The task force had set up its headquarters in Scramdale-on-Hudson, roughly twenty minutes by train from midtown Manhattan. The compound had been seized from a drug dealer some months before; it included a six-car garage, heated swimming pool, and access to the Hudson River over the nearby railroad tracks, no doubt convenient for disposing of troublesome business associates. The heart of the operation was a low-slung contemporary house with more bathrooms than bedrooms. Most of its furniture was still in the house, including the 1970s-style waterbed in the master bedroom suite. Apparently the dealers had had a thing about animal skins: The couch and chairs in the living room were made of stretched tiger fur, a bearskin rug sat between them, and what looked like a gutted ocelot gazed from the wall opposite the fireplace. If the drug charges didn't hold, the U.S. attorney could easily obtain a conviction for poaching.

"Maybe a sauna will help you think," suggested Macklin. "Want me to stoke it up?"

"As a general rule, I try to sweat as little as possible, especially when I'm working." Fisher stood up and walked over to the massive fieldstone fireplace, squatting down to sit on the slate ledge in front of the hearth. He shook a Camel out and contemplated it, considering the alignment of the tobacco.

"You've staked out the places where the calls were received?" he asked.

"Around the clock."

"You couldn't run down the address on the e-mail?"

"Only that it was sent from overseas."

Fisher turned the cigarette over in his hand. Who was the first person to figure out that you could use a machine to pack tobacco? he wondered. Truly he had made a valuable contribution to the human race, and yet, he had been forgotten.

The way of the world.

"This reminds me of that case we had in Detroit that time," said Macklin. "Where we tapped the phone to find that kidnapped girl. Remember? We tracked those two bozos who were AWOL from the Army?"

Fisher lit up. "The mother killed the girl, Michael. How is this like that?"

"It just reminds me of that."

"Let's go see where that cell call was made from."

"I told you, it's, like, a ten-block radius at least," said Macklin.

"Good. There ought to be a decent place to get coffee in there somewhere."

CHAPTER

10

The FBI sent the new e-mail directly to Blitz, and he was just reading it when Hunter called to tell him about it. Blitz thanked him, then sat back at his desk, pondering the meaning of the short message.

Clearly, the scientist was getting antsy. Clearly, he had to be retrieved. But even Blitz was starting to worry now about the state of the country he was in. The latest estimate reported several army units in open rebellion.

Blitz had seen the Pentagon proposals for the operation. The planners clearly favored Force One, which called for an MC-130s to land at the airfield and secure it while another dropped several A teams into the camp a few miles away. There they would retrieve the scientist, by force if necessary.

The alternative, called Tacit Ivan, was admittedly more imaginative and was much more likely to remain secret. It was, however, even more risky, calling for a jet with minimal weapons to fly to the air base while the Korean scientist proceeded there on his own. The only man available to fly the plane, it appeared, was Colonel William Howe.

Reason enough in Blitz's mind to kill it.

"President is calling for you," said Mozelle, appearing over Blitz's computer. "Everyone else is in the cabinet room already."

Blitz looked up at his assistant. She had a strained look on her face.

"What?" he asked.

"That tie really doesn't go with that jacket," she said.

★   ★   ★

Tyler felt sweat creeping down the joints of his fingers to his palms as he stood against the wall in the Oval Office.

I'm nervous, he thought to himself. *Wow.*

And he was. Tyler had seen combat both with the Rangers and Special Forces. As far as he could remember, his hands had never sweat on him.

That was different somehow—which was odd really, because no matter what happened here, he wasn't going to get shot at, let alone killed.

On the other hand, that *was* the President of the United States sitting a few feet away, joking with the secretary of defense about college basketball.

The President of the United States.

Tyler looked around the room, trying to memorize the scene: It was part of history, and he was right in the middle of it.

He was also the only black man in the room, he realized.

"Sorry I'm late," said Blitz, coming in. The national security advisor seemed to wear a perpetual frown above his thin goatee; occasionally he tried to smile, which made his expression appear ten times grimmer.

"Now that we're here, let's have a brief summary of the plans," said President D'Amici, leaning back in his chair. "Pentagon first."

Colonel Victor Thos, who headed the special targeting task force, ran down the highlights of the plans with the help of a PowerPoint presentation. Force One, which had several options, was by far the preferred plan, and this came through in the presentation. Thos also outlined a more conventional plan with a force to knock out the radars and take over Pong Yan, the airfield near the camp.

"If we do that, we'll start a war with them," said Blitz. "If we can't do this covertly, we can't do it. Period."

Thos grimaced and then outlined Tacit Ivan, the plan

involving the Berkut. For some reason the plan sounded much more reasonable now than it had earlier when they'd gone over the presentation, though Tyler decided he still preferred Force One.

"I have one question," said the President when he finished. "Would you put your life on the line for any of these plans?"

"Yes, sir, I would," snapped Tyler.

The words had come out automatically, and Tyler realized belatedly that the President had actually asked the question of Thos. All eyes in the room stared at him.

"Excuse me," he said.

"That's quite all right," said the President. He turned to Thos. "I assume you feel the same way."

"Absolutely."

"Well, of course," said Blitz. "That's not the question."

Tyler knew from the meetings he had observed that the President didn't mind candid exchanges and even arguments, but Blitz seemed almost belligerent. The national security advisor began arguing about the need for alacrity—he used the word several times—because of the deteriorating situation. To Tyler, it seemed as if he was criticizing the plan.

"We can have people on the ground there within twenty-four hours," Tyler said finally when Thos didn't speak up in its defense. "I guarantee it."

The secretary of defense and the head of the Joint Chiefs of Staff glared at him. Tyler felt his jaw set; what the hell did they expect? Of course the job could be done. Otherwise they wouldn't have brought it here.

"Are you volunteering to take command of the mission, Ken?" asked the President.

Was he?

"Sir, I would in a heartbeat. Absolutely. I want to lead it."

The President smiled. Tyler sensed that he was coming off like some sort of cowboy gunslinger, which to him was the exact opposite of what he felt: He was here as a professional with a carefully considered, albeit risky, lineup of plans. He wouldn't have proposed them if he didn't believe in them.

Were the others testing him? Thos started to say something—either to change the subject or perhaps point out that the unit officers would be expected to command and would be more than qualified to do so—but the President raised his hand.

"I think Major Tyler would be an excellent choice. I have full confidence in him. And in Colonel Howe. I want a plan that has a chance to remain covert but can move ahead quicker than the CIA plan. That's Tacit Ivan. Get it under way immediately."

CHAPTER

11

"You figure terrorists are big on irony?" asked Fisher.

"How so?"

"Battery Park. Energy. E-bomb. Get it?"

Macklin's blank stare went well with his haircut, which looked as if it had started as a fade and veered toward Mohawk. Fisher walked past the museum building out toward the edge of the water. On a clear day you could see the Statue of Liberty from there—but this wasn't a clear day. A low bank of clouds loomed beyond the thin mist, and the sky above furled with an impending snowstorm.

Though the more optimistic weathermen were calling for sleet.

"You think he called from the middle of Battery Park?" asked Macklin.

"We sure it's a 'he'?" asked Fisher. The cell tower that had picked up the call was located on the top of a nearby building, but the fog was so thick Fisher couldn't see it.

"Good point."

"No other call, huh?"

"None," said Macklin.

"Why do you figure that is?"

"Reprogrammed it or used a different cell phone."

"Could be." Fisher turned around and looked out at the water. "Maybe he threw it in the water."

"You want to drag the harbor?"

"Even *I'm* not that crazy," said Fisher.

"They use the phones once or twice, they reprogram the chips," said Macklin. "I was at a seminar a few weeks back explaining how it's done. So you think he was in the park?" added the Homeland Security agent.

"Maybe," said Fisher. "Or on the water."

"What, swimming?"

"Could have been in a boat."

"Well, sure," said Macklin.

A ferry loomed in the distance. There were ferry slips at the very southern tip of the island; you could get to the Statue of Liberty and Ellis Island as well as Staten Island.

"Should we look for a boat?" asked Macklin.

"Probably not."

"Did they case out the Statue of Liberty, maybe?"

"Could be."

" 'Could be'?" said Macklin.

"Could be a lot of things, Michael. That's the problem."

"Well, what the hell are we looking for?" asked Macklin.

"Damned if I know," said Fisher. "But a good cup of coffee would sure hit the spot."

"We have to figure this out, Andy. We have to. America's counting on us."

The wind was too strong for Fisher to risk rolling his eyes. Instead he asked, "Where are those apartments?"

"One's in Washington Heights, the other's in Queens. They're under surveillance."

"Okay," said Fisher, starting to his left.

"Where are we going?"

"To get some coffee."

"Andy—"

"Then we're going to take a subway ride."

CHAPTER

12

"You can't command the force," Colonel Thos told Tyler as they walked downstairs.

"The President told me to do it," replied Tyler.

"He didn't tell you to go on the mission."

As originally drawn up, the ground commander would be an A Team captain working with men already in Korea and the Asia theater. Tyler interpreted the President's order to mean that he should go along personally and the captain would answer to him. Thos pointed out that the President hadn't specifically said that. Not only would it be contrary to normal procedure, from a logistical point of view, getting from Washington to Korea in time to be on the raid would be extremely difficult.

Tyler wasn't going to argue with Thos. As far as he was concerned, the President's order meant that he was to be there himself personally. Period.

Period.

Tyler replayed the meeting in his mind. Some of the others were looking at him with contempt, but the President hadn't. The President—his eyes had said something to him.

I need someone I can trust. Can I trust you?

There was no way Tyler was backing out. And screw anybody who suggested he do so.

If he were white, no one would say anything, Tyler thought.

That wasn't fair, not really, and certainly not in Thos's case. The colonel was from a mixed background himself: Malaysian as well as European. His argument was based on command structure and the normal rules and procedures the Army followed.

But it did make sense for Tyler to take command of the mission. He sure as hell had the experience and expertise: He'd only recently been an A Team captain and had been in Korea; he undoubtedly knew many of the men who would be on the mission. He had planned it and so knew the details intimately. He knew Howe as well. The only problem was getting over to Korea.

"Look, Tyler, you'll never make it in time," said Thos as they reached their car.

"I will," said Tyler. "And I think we can shave twenty-four hours off the timetable. You have to let me go, Vic. You owe it to me."

"I owe it to you? Bullshit on that." Thos frowned. "That's not the way it works."

"Well, it should be," said Tyler. "And I'm going whether you like it or not. The President told me to."

CHAPTER

13

Howe had been around enough military planners to realize that the Berkut plan was being developed as the weak sister to make the other options look better. Still, he agreed to hang around Washington, D.C., just in case the President green-lighted the operation. And so he found himself back at the hotel with nothing to do except sit in his hotel room and watch the last of the first-round games of the NCAAs. It was Auburn against St. John's, and for some reason he found himself rooting for Auburn, which of course was a mistake. While St. John's was no power-house, it had Auburn put away by halftime, and a few minutes into the second half Howe decided he'd go out for a walk.

It was warm for March, and Howe found he didn't need to zip his jacket.

He'd volunteered for the mission without question. More than that, he wanted to do it.

Maybe leaving the Air Force had been the wrong thing to do. But if he were still in the Air Force, he'd be queuing up for a general's slot down at the Pentagon, kissing as many butts as he could find.

An exaggeration. And surely he'd have a choice of commands. His star was rising. *Had been* rising.

Not that Howe didn't have detractors. He'd been having an affair with a woman who was known to be a traitor, and there were undoubtedly rumors about that.

More than an affair: She'd been the love of his life. What did that say about his judgment?

A few kids were taking advantage of the almost springlike weather to cut school and ride their skateboards down the back steps of an office building. Howe stopped and watched them through a chain-link fence as they tried to ride down the railing. Neither of the kids made it without falling as he watched, and while they were wearing helmets and pads, the lumps had to hurt. But they kept bounding up from the ground, eager to try again.

As Howe walked back to the hotel, he decided that he'd call Tyler and tell him he was heading home. It was time to get on with the next part of his life, move on.

But Elder, the Pentagon messenger, was waiting for him in the lobby, holding his suitcase.

"I took the liberty of settling your bill," he said. "I hope you don't mind. They're pretty anxious to have you get to Andrews as soon as possible."

CHAPTER

14

You could take the 1 or 9 subway up the west side of Manhattan from Battery Park to Washington Heights, and get out two blocks from the apartment the DIA and Homeland Security task force was watching. *What an endorsement for mass transit,* thought Fisher. *Even the terrorists take the train.*

During the American Revolution, Washington Heights had been the site of a needless fiasco for the American rebels, and its history had gone downhill from there. It never was much of an area for farming, and after it was developed it quickly became choked with refugees from less fortunate areas of the city, who found the cold-water walk-ups somewhat more hospitable than the crammed tenements farther downtown. There were a few upward bumps of progress here; for a few weeks during the 1940s, it was even considered a nice place to live, a way station to the greener pastures of suburban New Jersey across the way. Urban renewal and the construction of the highway network related to the George Washington Bridge, along with the grand plans of Robert Moses, razed some of the worst buildings in the early sixties, replacing them with structures whose main asset was their height. In the course of time, Irish immigrants were replaced by Puerto Rican immigrants who were replaced by Caribbean immigrants. Crack replaced bootleg whiskey.

In sum, it was exactly the sort of New York community Fisher felt at home in. But it didn't give him much of a grip on the terrorists.

"Corner apartment—there," said an NYPD officer named Paesano tasked to the team keeping the place under surveillance. The city had supplied about a dozen officers and support personnel to help with the nitty-gritty work. "Couple of ragheads have the lease, but there's at least five people live there."

" 'Ragheads'?" said Macklin.

"We're among friends, right?" said the cop, who was in plainclothes. They had taken an apartment above a store across the street from the three-story building the call had been made to. "They worship, if you can call it that, at a storefront mosque down the street. Got this imam in there who rolls his eyes backwards in his head and says 'kill the infidels.' "

" 'The only good infidel is a dead infidel,' " said Fisher.

"Yeah, except *we're* the infidels," said Paesano.

They'd passed the mosque on the way up; it looked more like the abandoned five-and-dime it had been than a house of worship. Metal grates and thick plywood covered all but one of the large plate-glass window areas, and the surviving glass was covered with advertisements and handbills. A piece of cardboard in the corner gave a lecture schedule; anyone interested in services was presumed to know when they were. According to the surveillance team, there were two guards at all times just inside the doorway.

"Theory is, these guys are connected with the mosque. They worship there. Two of 'em have jobs at that shoe store on the corner," continued the cop.

He was a smoker, but he preferred Newport menthols, which to Fisher made no sense at all. Why screw up good tobacco with a candy flavor? You wanted mint, buy some Tic Tacs.

"Maybe it's a front or something, but they do business," said the cop, referring to the shoe store. "We sent somebody in to check it out. They have used shoes and repairs. One of the DIA guys bugged the place."

"What'd they find?" asked Fisher.

"That it's hard to get EE width."

"Usual DIA efficiency," said Fisher. "Probably reviewing it at the Pentagon right now."

"I heard that, Andy," said Kowalski from the hallway. He and one of his lackeys came into the room.

"Good to see you, too, Kowalski."

"Yeah, I'm real emotional about it. But at least you're on the right team now. Maybe later on you can tell us how you screwed up in Moscow," added the DIA agent, never one to miss a chance to twist the knife.

"It was easy," said Fisher. "I just asked myself what you would do in my situation."

"As I was saying," continued Paesano, "ragheads stay in during the day, most days. They're all there now."

"Fire escape's clear," said Fisher.

"That significant?" asked the cop.

"Only if there's a fire." Fisher pushed the window open, trying to escape the odor of cat piss that had been left by the last tenants. The odor of rotten eggs and overcooked cabbage wafted into the room. It was a decided improvement.

"You shouldn't make yourself conspicuous," said Macklin.

"You think a bunch of white guys wearing suits in this neighborhood isn't conspicuous?" asked Fisher. He leaned out the window, casing the block. It seemed neatly divided between the man selling crack from the back of an old Toyota at the corner on the left and the two Rastafarians selling loose joints on the right. The Jamaicans seemed to be in a time warp: Most of the dealing in this area had been taken over by Nigerians long before.

"We have a warrant, and we have backup manpower," said Kowalski. "We can go in whenever we want."

"How about now?" asked Fisher.

"You think it's worth raiding the place?" asked Macklin.

"No," said Fisher. "But at least if you raid it you can close down this surveillance operation. Then Paesano can get the cat smell out of his clothes."

"Amen to that," said the cop.

*　　*　　*

It took several hours to set up the operation; in the meantime, Fisher and one of the city cops went down to the shoe store. The owner of the store spoke Spanish with a Puerto Rican accent, which gave him away as a long-time resident of the area. He was also nearly blind and partly deaf, though he did give Fisher a good deal on a new heel.

The shoe was fixed just in time for the FBI agent to join in the raid, which began with two large police vans from the city's emergency response unit blocking off the street. As they moved in, members from the SWAT team tossed military-style flash-bang grenades into the apartment window, then blew in through the windows and front door.

"Too bad we couldn't have been with the first wave," said Fisher wistfully as he walked up the steps with Paesano after the apartment had been secured. "I always wanted to do a Tarzan swing into a New York City apartment."

"Maybe next time," said the cop.

"Sure you don't want a Camel?" asked Fisher.

"No, thanks."

Cat piss seemed to be the odor du jour; it was stronger here than across the street. But at least in the Arabs' apartment it mixed with the scent of strong coffee and human excrement—the latter undoubtedly caused by the SWAT team's sudden arrival. Among those joining in the operation were two members of an Immigration and Naturalization Service task force: Three of the four men here had student visas that had expired.

There was a small amount of pot in one of the two rooms used as bedrooms. While under ordinary circumstances it might have drawn the equivalent of a parking ticket, the marijuana inspired creative thinking on the part of Paesano, who found grounds for a dozen related charges. Just the processing alone could keep them tied down for weeks.

The men were led downstairs under heavy guard; in the meantime, Macklin's people had begun interviewing neighbors for information.

"Nice computers," said Paesano.

And they were: three brand new Dells, all lined up on the kitchen table. Wires snaked off the cracked Formica top of the table across a chair to a router; there was a DSL modem strapped to a shelf on the wall where a phone had once hung.

"Hey, don't touch!" shouted Macklin as Fisher went to tap one of the keyboards. "They may have them rigged to erase the contents of the drives, or maybe explode."

"You think?"

"Fisher!"

"I'm just seeing what they were doing before the screen savers went on," said Fisher. "Relax."

One of the computers had not been on. The second had a word processing program active; it looked as though the user had been typing a letter home to Mom.

The third had a game called Red Rogue on the screen. A terrorist with a gas mask pointed a souped-up Mac 11 point-blank at the viewer.

"Computer guy is on his way," said Macklin. "We'll have everything analyzed. Don't screw with it."

"We'll wrap all this stuff up, get the crime scene guys in, dust around for prints," added Kowalski. "Very good operation. Very good."

"Why would you dust for prints?" asked Fisher.

"We don't know who else might have been here."

"You've had the apartment under surveillance for almost a week," said Fisher. "You know who was here."

"Yeah, but I want to dot all the *i*'s and cross all the *t*'s. Right, Macklin?"

The Homeland Security agent nodded but then looked at Fisher. "Don't we?"

"Sure." Fisher lit a fresh cigarette. If they wanted to waste their time, who was he to argue? Besides, crime scene guys usually got paid by the hour, and most of them could probably use the overtime.

There was a pile of computer games on the floor. Fisher bent to examine the boxes.

"Have these computer games checked out, too," he said, "since you're dusting for prints. Then give them to geeks and see if anything else is on them."

"Think there's something there?" asked Macklin.

"Probably not," said Fisher. "But they're bootlegs. I just want to make sure that's all they are."

"How do you know they're bootlegs?" asked Kowalski.

"No holograms," said Fisher, pointing at the boxes. "You know. Those shiny things."

"I know what a hologram is," said Kowalski.

"They could have messages, right? I've heard of that," said Macklin.

"Yeah," said Kowalski. "We'll ship them over to the NSA, get them decoded."

Fisher squatted down in front of the screen, examining Red Rogue. "One thing I always wondered . . ."

"What's that?" asked Macklin.

"Why would someone put a high-power scope on an Ingram Mac 11? I mean, isn't that kind of beside the point?"

CHAPTER

15

Just over twenty-four hours had passed since the President had set the plan in motion. In that time, the situation in North Korea had deteriorated to the point that neither the CIA nor South Korean intelligence knew where Kim Jong Il or his family were. Two armored units, each with about two dozen tanks, were guarding roads to the capital, though it was not clear who beyond themselves they were loyal to.

American troops were now on high alert, not just in Korea, but throughout the world. Two aircraft carriers and their assorted escorts were offshore, and two more were quietly but quickly steaming toward the peninsula. No less than six submarines with Tomahawk missiles and several surface ships were prepared to launch against North Korean targets on the President's command. The Air Force had round-the-clock patrols and a host of contingency plans: With a single word from the President, an attack could be launched that would make the opening salvos of Gulf War II look like nothing more than a few rounds of target practice.

President D'Amici had ruled out the use of nuclear weapons, even as a retaliatory measure. He saw no point: America's awesome conventional capacity could level the country, and nuclear weapons would only complicate the aftermath, endangering the Americans and South Koreans who by necessity would have to pick up the pieces.

"If Truman didn't use them, I'm not going to," the President told Blitz as they strode downstairs to the White House situation room, actually a suite of rooms with secure links and access to intelligence gathering around the globe.

Under other circumstances Blitz might have asked the President if he thought Truman should have used the weapons. But this was not the time for what-if scenarios.

The demise of the North Korean dictatorship—however much that was a good thing for the world—meant considerable uncertainty and danger for the South Koreans, the Japanese, and the Americans. Blitz was overwhelmed with estimates, questions, reports, bulletins: Tacit Ivan seemed almost small potatoes in the context of the situation.

Almost.

Homeland Security, the FBI, and local police had raided a New York City apartment the day before, following up leads on the E-bomb situation. The raid had not yielded anything beyond what the specially prepared eyes-only summary declared "potential leads." But the NSA had picked up several offshore cell phone conversations over the past ten days that used the words *black out.* One of the interceptions had been traced to a phone connected to a credit card believed to be used by Caliph's Sons. The information remained maddeningly vague, the connections convoluted, and the evidence elusive. True intelligence analysis required time and perspective; neither was available nor likely to be in the coming days.

When they reached the wood-paneled conference room at the heart of the suite, the President walked over to a cluster of Air Force officers to discuss the latest target list that had been developed for the B-2 bombers stationed in South Korea. The Air Force was shuttling bombers into the air around the clock to maintain coverage of critical targets. The two warheads that the American forces knew about were triple-targeted; both of those weapons would be destroyed within ten minutes of the President's direct and specific order to do so. Cruise missiles and air-to-ground weapons aboard other fighters would be aimed at nearly one hundred additional top-priority sites, including the suspected additional nuclear warhead missile sites. Missiles that managed to get off despite this would be handled by one of two airborne laser Cyclops aircraft, one over South Korea and one off the coast. An additional line of Patriot antimissile and aircraft batteries protected Seoul.

Twenty minutes for everything to be hit, one of the intelligence officers had said to Blitz. Minuscule in the history of warfare; an eternity if you were in the enemy's crosshairs.

The President hunched over the shoulder of one of the military analysts going over the latest satellite photos showing North Korean troop movements. There were positive signs: One division near the border seemed to have

mutinied and its vehicles were heading away from the demilitarized zone. They could see men following on the
roads in the dust, and the sharpest-eyed analysts said a few
had thrown away their guns.

"So, Professor, do we move ahead with Tacit Ivan or
not?" asked the President.

"Yes, of course," said Blitz. He put more confidence in
his voice than he felt; somehow the atmosphere of the Pentagon always did that to him.

"Even in the face of a coup and mutiny?"

"That's the best argument to proceed," said Blitz.

"I agree."

The President's face changed momentarily, the heavy
mask of responsibility melting. He smiled in a way that reminded Blitz of their much earlier days, ancient history
now, spent discussing geopolitics in the dark days after
Vietnam. Oddly, he could no longer remember the sub-
stance of the talks, but he could remember where they'd
taken place: several watching the Orioles, a whole host in
Syracuse, where the President spent a brief period as a
college professor before running for Congress.

"You're worried about Howe," said the President.

"Yes, of course."

"There's no question he's the right man for the job,"
said the President. "It comes down to the people on the
line. He's the right man."

"I don't disagree," said Blitz.

"Besides, this will remind him of how important duty is."

"What do you mean?"

"He'll take your job," said the President.

"That's the least of my worries right now."

The smile flickered as the mask of command once
more took over the President's face. "Are we set, then?"

"Everything's in place," said Blitz. He looked across the
room to Colonel Thos and nodded.

"They're waiting to hear from you at the Pentagon, Mr.
President," said Thos.

16

The MC-130 banked hard to the right, its wingtips coming within a few meters of the hillside. Turbulence off the rift in the earth pushed the aircraft downward, threatening disaster; the pilot had only a few feet to work with as he slipped the big four-engined craft through a hole in the North Korean air defenses. All the high-tech radar detectors and GPS locators in the world couldn't overcome the basic laws of gravity and motion, and as the Hercules came through the narrow mountain pass the success of the mission and the lives of two dozen passengers and crew came down to the reflexes of the man at the helm, a veteran Air Force pilot who had passed up a parcel of supposedly better assignments to stay with the Herky birds and the Special Operations soldiers who relied on them.

Back in the cargo hold of the plane, Tyler waited with his team members as the plane stuttered over the terrain. He checked his watch. They had about ten more minutes of flying time before they would reach the drop zone. He knew from experience those would be among the longest minutes of his life.

And the shortest.

He'd been right to insist on the assignment, and lucky to get it.

Of course, if they augered in right now, he'd be neither. The plane's nose bucked downward and the entire craft seemed to shift to the right, leaving Tyler temporarily hovering in space. His momentum caught up with that of the plane's a second later, and he felt his boots slap against the metal decking. His stomach sloshed up somewhere around his gallbladder, then pressed against his lungs.

He'd made the right choice. Definitely.

"Almost there!" he shouted confidently to the rest of the team. "Almost there."

* * *

The canopy exploded above him, its cells ripped open by the rushing wind. Tyler fought not so much to control the parachute but to control himself: He had a tendency to pull too sharply on the steering togs.

He could see the others nearby. Good chutes.

He wanted the ground but couldn't see it. He waited, the hardest thing.

Where the hell was it?

The plane had to crisscross back overhead, flying an extremely narrow corridor where the North Koreans couldn't find it on radar. A mile either way and not only would it be shot down but Duke and the twenty-two people who'd come out with him would be hung out to dry.

So where the hell was the ground already?

Tyler saw shadows and braced himself, trying simultaneously to relax and brace for the landing at the same time.

It didn't come. It wouldn't.

Too fucking long. A lot of guys wanted the jump to go on forever, or so they said; he was always anxious for it to end.

He was off balance now, unsure what the hell was going on.

More shadows. He braced again.

Nothing.

And then the ruck thumped behind him. His right leg touched down a millisecond before the left; he screwed it up, lost his balance, fell to the right instead of walking off like a champ. If this were a training film he'd be the shitful example, tumbling onto the ground, the idiot who did everything wrong, got his head messed up, doubted the equipment, dragged along on the ground as the chute inflated with the wind.

His fingers fumbled against the restraint snaps.

He was eating dirt. His face bashed against the rocks.

Three months in Washington and I'm this far out of it?

Tyler ignored the bumps and bruises, rolling up his chute and trying to hide the damage to his ego.

The team leaders quickly gathered their men together. Besides eighteen Army Special Forces soldiers—one and a half A teams—they'd taken along two Air Force air commandos with special training so they could refuel the aircraft if necessary. They also had two CIA people with them, a female officer and a native Korean agent, who could provide assistance as well. The agent had some familiarity with the terrain and would be useful in case things went very wrong; had the CIA version of the plan been approved, they'd have been here alone.

Tyler wasn't the only one who had trouble landing. One of the soldiers had broken his arm but insisted he could travel. Tyler's first call was whether to let him or not.

An easy call: The man could still walk.

"You're with us," said the major. "All right, let's move out."

He checked his AK-47. The team had been equipped with Korean weapons and uniforms; most of the men had Asian backgrounds and they might be able to at least temporarily fool an enemy patrol.

Temporarily.

"Let's go, let's go," repeated Tyler. "We have twenty miles to travel tonight."

CHAPTER
17

HELLO AMANDA

RECEIVED YOUR INSTRUCTIONS. THANK YOU! I WILL GO TO THE AIRFIELD EVERY NIGHT STARTING TONIGHT.

STILL NOT BEING GUARDED.

I HAVE PRAYED TO BE DELIVERED. I LONG TO LIVE IN FREEDOM. GOD BLESS YOU FOR YOUR HELP.

--------------------------- Headers ---------------------------

Return-Path: <J.Smith@simon.com>

Received: from rly-xc04.mx.aol.com (rly-xc04.mail.aol.com [172.20.105.137]) by air-xc02.mail.aol.com (v93.12) with ESMTP id MAILINXC23-3f873ec520e528b; Wed, 19 March 2008 13:33:25-0400

Received: from mail.simon.com (mail.simon.com [66.43.82.172]) by rly-xc04.mx.aol.com (v93.12) with ESMTP id MAILRELAYINXC48-e43ec520cf1bf; March 2008 13:33:03 -0400

Received: from mdcms001.simon.com (ss-exch-smtp.simon.com [172.30.65.47])

   by mail.simon.com (AIX4.3/8.9.3p2/8.9.3) with ESMTP id NAA96516

   for <JD@aol.com>; March 2008 13:37:33 -0400

Received: by mdcms001.chuster.com with Internet Mail Service (5.5.2653.19)

   id <K8SXA6FM>; May 2008 13:33:03 -0400

Message-ID:

<A27A160FD659C648B8665DCD07B7C90A8488FE@MDCMS002>

 MIME-Version: 1.0

X-Mailer: Internet Mail Service (5.5.2653.19)

Content-Type: multipart/alternative;

   boundary="——_=_NextPart_001_01C31BD1.3326EE10"

CHAPTER

18

From the outside, the Berkut looked like a Sukhoi with its wings on backward.

From the inside, it felt like a splinter that could change directions in the wink of God's eye.

The other man who had flown the plane compared it to a lighter, longer F/A-18; one of the engineers who'd been in the backseat thought it closer to an ancient F-104 Starfighter that could maneuver like an A-10A Warthog. Howe had flown the F/A-18 only once (it was a Navy plane) and had never sat in the cockpit of the Starfighter, which was retired long before he had joined the service. He'd also never flown an A-10A. His main comparison was therefore the heavily modified F-16 that he'd used to familiarize himself with the Berkut before strapping himself inside; the S-37/B was slightly faster and so twisty that it was easy for the plane to get ahead of the pilot during high-g maneuvers, becoming essentially uncontrollable. The nose of the plane had a tendency to shoot up during a hard turn, and despite all of the engineering it remained at least theoretically possible to jam the Berkut so tightly at high speed that the divergent forces of lift, gravity, and momentum would snap off the forward winglets.

Master those forces, however, and the plane form had a great deal of potential. The Russians were trying to sell their version, somewhat tamed down, as a multitasking fighter-bomber. As a ground-pounder the plane carried more armor—*a lot* more armor—which not only increased its survivability but took just enough of the maneuverability away to make it safer to fly.

Though much less fun.

Howe wasn't particularly concerned with the fun factor or even his version's ultramaneuverability as he took off from Misawa Air Base in northern Japan. As the crow flew, he was roughly eight hundred miles from his destination, but he wasn't a crow and he wasn't going in a straight line. After a refuel over the Sea of Japan and a rendezvous with a pair of flight groups providing cover in case anyone was tracking him, Howe would tuck toward the waves and begin his weave over the border of Russia and down into North Korea. His flight path led through a poorly covered defense zone, well north of a cluster of radar units that would be scanning for an American intrusion. Flying along the northern border of the country, he would have to watch for Chinese as well as Korean air patrols, but this ought to be relatively easy, as neither country was in the habit of flying many nighttime sorties in the vicinity. Once past the border town of Hyesan, he would cut southwest through Yanggang Province for about fifty miles before zagging through the hills and landing at the air base.

Ten minutes before he touched down, Howe would make a transmission in Russian indicating that he was experiencing engine problems. The SF team on the ground would hear the broadcast and relay a go/no-go via the satellite communications system to a mission coordinator orbiting far off the coast in an RC-135.

There were three options, the call to be made by the ground team, which by now should be ringing the airfield and observing the nearby camp where the scientist was staying.

The first plan, and the preferred option, had Howe landing and taxiing to the far end of the runway. The scientist would be waiting. Howe would help him aboard and then take off. They would fly out to the Sea of Japan, where he would meet a refueling jet. The Special Forces troops, meanwhile, would proceed back to a landing area near where they had parachuted; a pair of Ospreys would sneak through the radar-free corridor and pick them up two nights later. This was the preferred plan, and they would use it if the scientist left the camp where he was staying and went to the airport, as he had agreed to do via coded e-mail.

Option two called for the Special Forces unit to attack the camp, locate the scientist, and proceed with him to the airfield. Howe would take off with the scientist; the SF team would then either make their way to the place they'd been dropped or go via a second route to the coast.

Option three also called for an attack on the camp but involved a rescue package of MC-130s landing at the air base after Howe took off. In that case Howe would peel off west, covered by the escorts that came north with the cargo craft, and head to a South Korean base.

In the pilot's opinion, the choice was only between one and three: Shoot up anything on the ground and there was no way they were going to sneak out of North Korea.

The Berkut would be visible on radar for about two minutes before he landed and after he took off, but in his opinion the real hassle was his fuel management, which was going to be tighter than tight. The refueling option at the base had been discarded because the scientist warned there was no source of jet fuel there.

Howe checked his fuel state against the matrix and notes he'd prepared on his flight board. He seemed to be doing slightly better than anticipated, consuming less fuel than he'd used getting across the United States. The specially built GE engines were considerably more efficient than the Russian Saturn Al-31Fs, standard equipment on the Su-27. (Contrary to published reports, the Sukhoi's power plants were used rather than Aviadvigatel D30- F6s from the MiG-31 Foxhound.) Still, there was no confusing the Berkut with the F/A-22V, which could fly halfway around the world and back on a tank of gas. The plane's thin wings might help maneuvering, but they left little space for jet fuel. The fuselage on the American plane was actually a little bigger than the Russian model and added a bit more capacity, but the plane's ferry range only topped two thousand miles with a good tailwind. So refueling was a necessity.

Howe's tanker was an ancient beast, a military version of Boeing's venerable 707 that lumbered ahead, director lights glowing like the sign on a 7-Eleven as Howe ambled in for a Big Gulp. The Berkut's fly-by-wire yoke—like the F-16 and F/A-22, it was a sidestick, mounted at the side of the pilot's seat—sat easy in his hand as he moved into position behind the flying gas station. A pair of F-15s checked in over the horizon, playing their role in the elaborate game of cat and mouse concocted to keep Howe's mission from being known.

"Ivan One, you read us?"

"Roger that, Rogue Flight."

"Juice up and let's have at it," said the F-15 pilot.

Under other circumstances, the jocks might have exchanged some good-natured banter, but the normally loquacious Eagle pilots were under instructions to keep radio traffic to a minimum. The situation in Korea had the Eagles' unit at its highest alert, and even though the men didn't know what Howe's mission was, they surely guessed at his destination.

Even with all that, the flight leader couldn't resist a whistle when he spotted Howe's plane in the last rays of sunlight as he climbed through thirty thousand feet.

"At you," said Howe, initiating the mock encounter. He put the plane on its wing as the F-15s crisscrossed above him, one pursuing while the other orbited west. The brief tangle was over inside of two minutes—about as long as a real furball might have lasted. The two F-15s rocketed back and forth as Howe hit the deck outside of easy radar coverage. Within a few minutes they were headed toward Misawa Air Base. Their radio calls now referred to three flights, as would the landing instructions.

A flight of F/A-22s made a radio call to an AWACS. Orbiting to the south of Howe's course about seventy-five miles from the Korean coast, the interceptors were both decoys and emergency guard dogs: They and an AWACS plane operating to the east would watch for North Korean fighter action and would sprint to Howe's aid if necessary.

Howe, meanwhile, had nosed down below one hundred feet, clipping along close enough to sniff the foam from the waves. He checked his fuel—still doing good—checked the rest of his instruments, studied the radar warning receiver or RWR, reviewed his course. Everything was in the green.

Nothing to do now but fly into the gathering darkness. And so he did.

Thirty-two minutes later Howe slid over the Russian coast, ducking past the blunt fingers of an early-warning radar and pushing into North Korean territory. While most of the North Korean radar system was aimed at Seoul and the coast, there were radars and some SAMs here and they couldn't be ignored. Howe's course had been painstakingly worked out to run through the gaps, but he had to fly very low, hiding the sharp corners of his aircraft in the clutter of radar returns thrown off by the ground. While Howe's plane carried electronic counter-measures that could confuse the radars, using the jammers would be like turning a flashlight on in a darkened room: The Koreans would know he was there. And so he threaded a crooked needle as he flew, staying low and near mountainsides. The need to follow a precise course and the danger that he was in were a blessing in a way: They focused his thoughts entirely on his ship and what was around him. While immensely fatiguing, in another way the sheer concentration and immersion in what he was doing relaxed him. His muscles moved in an unconscious way, his eyes gathering data without conscious thought, his body and soul funneled into the moment. Waypoint after waypoint, Howe moved inextricably toward his goal. Nothing outside of the tense cocoon of his plane and the surrounding defenses disturbed him; the world consisted only of the Berkut and the people who would destroy it if they could.

And then he was fifty miles from his destination, just under ten minutes from putting down.

Howe checked the radio unit and broadcast the Russian message, which had been prerecorded on a special CD. Then he turned up the volume and double-checked that the radio was locked into the command frequency, ready to receive the signal on what to do.

19

Dr. Park got up from the chair and went to the window, bending his head to look up at the sky past the nearby mountainside. A few faint stars glimmered in the darkness; he thought of the folktale about the cowherd and the weaver, the constellations separated by a father's jealousy.

Why was he here? The unit Dr. Park had been told he would help had not arrived; in fact, there were no more than a dozen men all told, if that. The camp seemed as forlorn as any Dr. Park had ever seen. The airfield a few miles away where the tests were supposed to be held was emptier still, abandoned for months if not years. The open hangar at the far end of the runway area held two small aircraft, the remains of a UAV project that until now Dr. Park had only heard rumors about, but the crews who cared for the planes, as well as the men who had developed them, were absent. The other buildings there were falling in on themselves.

The buildings here were not much better. The rooms in his small bungalow smelled of mildew. A cook made meals only once a day; the rest of the time Dr. Park had to forage for food in the large kitchen in the administrative building, apparently as the others did. The few men he had contact with were young soldiers who answered questions with shrugs.

Had he been sent here as punishment for Moscow?

He did not think this could be so, for surely punishment would be more severe. It seemed more that he had simply been forgotten. He was free to wander back and forth and spend his hours playing one-man Ping-Pong against the folded side of a game table. A soldier or two was never far away—one had gone with him to the airfield the other day, and down the road for a walk the day before—but none ever stopped him.

Most likely the situation was a product of the growing

disarray in the country, the confusion between different branches and departments. Even in this isolated place Dr. Park saw it: A dignitary had arrived yesterday and yet received no official greeting; his car had swung in the gate and gone up to the main administration building, and if the man had even gotten out, let alone taken a tour of the place, Dr. Park did not know about it.

Dr. Park decided he would take a walk. He began thinking of the folktale again, the cleverness of coming up with an earthly story to explain the movement of the heavens. Dr. Park had always been interested in the stars; he saw it as an extension of his interest in science and math. He had vaguely hoped that if he was successful in leaving for America, he would be able to pursue those interests somehow. Perhaps there was a space project he might be assigned to, or some department dealing with the study of the stars. But the failure in Moscow—his own failure, he knew—had sealed his fate. He would live out his days as an engineer for the state, as preordained.

He walked around the perimeter of the camp, admiring the stars. Tomorrow he would find the camp director or someone else in authority and make inquiries, he decided. If he was not needed, perhaps it would be possible to visit his mother's cousin in Dao; she was his last claim on family, though it was doubtful she even knew that he was there.

Dr. Park took one last look at the stars before going back inside his hut. Now he thought about his grandmother when she had told him the folktale of the stars that could meet only once a year. He felt again her warm embrace, the only memory he had now of the day his mother and father died together.

The memory lingered as he crossed the threshold of the hut. It stayed with him even as the thick blade of a hatchet smacked into the back corner of his skull, sending the life from his body.

CHAPTER

20

Tyler leaned across the rock, training the nightscope on the runway. The airfield was practically unguarded, with only two men watching the road at the south. It seemed to have been used as a storage area but had been abandoned sometime before. The army camp where their contact was living was two miles away. At one time a cross between an army base and a factory, it, too, seemed almost abandoned: There were skeleton posts around the perimeter, with no more than a dozen guards. A three-man team had already scouted it; they had a way in if their man didn't show. Another team was sitting near the field itself, ready to intervene if the pilot needed help.

The communications man tapped him. Tyler cupped his hand over his ear and then clicked into the circuit, talking into the miniature boom mike that extended near his collar.

"*Etha bleekah*," he said. It was a transliteration of *Это близко*, Russian for *It's nearby*. While the odds against the radio signal being intercepted were practically nil, they had decided to use Russian code words unless there was a problem. The phrase was arbitrary, intended to tell the controller that everything was clear but that the Korean had not yet arrived.

"*Da*," responded the controller. *Yes*.

Howe was on schedule. All they needed was their package.

The communications man tapped him, then held up two fingers.

Team Two had the Korean in sight.

Tyler moved across the rise to a spot overlooking the road, careful not to stand upright where he would risk being silhouetted in the moonlight.

The man was alone, riding a bike.

He went back to the communications sergeant, who was

handling the team's twenty-pound radio, a modern version of the Raytheon AN/PSC-5(V). The radioman could select satellite, line- of-sight, UHF, and VHF frequencies.

"*Eh-ehta harasho,*" Tyler said into the mike, stuttering as he tried to pronounce the words *Зто хорошо: It's all right, we're cool, let's kick butt, let's go, let's go, let's go.*

He pulled off his headset, straining to hear the hum of a jet in the distance.

CHAPTER

21

Howe stood on the brakes as he touched down, the aircraft like a fully loaded tractor-trailer trying to grab the last spot in the Wal-Mart parking lot fresh off the Interstate. Short-landing characteristics were one thing; fitting yourself onto a postage stamp was something else again. The aircraft drifted to the right as he rode down the hard-packed runway; he pushed his whole body gently as he worked the stick, centering the aircraft with as much an act of will as muscle. Shadows flicked across his path; the g forces pinning him back to the seat suddenly eased, and one of the hangar buildings loomed on the left.

And then he saw the battery-powered lights the Air Force special operators had set to mark the edge of the runway.

He was in.

In.

Howe had just enough room and momentum to turn the S-37/B around at the end of the runway. As he did so, he popped the double canopy open and stared back at the shadows near the buildings. The lights told him that the air commandos and their Army brethren were all around him; all he had to do was sit and wait.

He had a pistol in his survival vest. He reached for it, pulling it out: It was a Makarov, in keeping with his cover, bulky and somewhat awkward, especially compared to his service Beretta, but it was reassuring nonetheless. He put the gun into his lap, holding it there, not wanting to scare the Korean off but not wanting to be caught unarmed either.

Belatedly, Howe pushed the timer button on his wristwatch, counting down his idle time. The buzzer would ring after ten minutes, but he'd already decided he would wait now as long as it took.

Four minutes had drained from the face of the clock when a figure appeared less than ten yards from the front of the plane. He had a gun in his hand; Howe involuntarily winced, bringing his own pistol up.

"American?" shouted the figure.

He ran to the side of the plane as Howe got out of the cockpit. The gun he held was a pistol—a revolver, Howe thought, from the shadow of the long barrel.

"American?" the man repeated. The accent had the hip-hop sound of a native Asian speaker, where tonal variations played an important role in meaning. "American?"

He pointed the pistol at Howe. Howe realized he was pointing back.

They had not set a password: How many jets would be appearing at this base; how many lone men would just happen to be close to it?

"American?" asked the man again.

"Yeah," said Howe.

By now the Korean was looking for a handhold. Howe reached down and pulled the man onto the front winglet. The Korean threw a small bag into the backseat, then reached to climb in.

"The bomb," yelled Howe. "Is the bomb here?"

"No bomb," shouted the Korean.

"Where is it?"

The man said something, but between the sound of the jet engines beneath them and the man's accent, it was impossible to understand.

"Snap on your restraints," said Howe. The Korean fumbled with the helmet; Howe pushed it over his ears, then made the connections. He checked the seat restraints and started back for his cockpit when he thought of something else.

"Your gun," he told the Korean, though there was no way the man could hear with the helmet on.

Howe reached over and grabbed for it; the man slapped his hand on Howe's.

"No," said Howe, shaking his head. "I get it."

The Korean didn't let go. Howe reached and took his own weapon; he thought of threatening the Korean but then thought of something better: He threw it down toward the ground.

Finally the Korean let go of his hand. Howe tossed the weapon down.

"Let's get the hell out of here," he said, going forward and climbing in.

CHAPTER
22

Tyler saw the vehicle before anyone else did.

"Take him," he said over the discrete-burst short-range com system that connected him with the men guarding the approach.

As he gave the order, the jet engines kicked up several notches on the field below, the plane roaring from the runway.

Belatedly, Tyler realized he had made a mistake. The truck was too far away to see the plane.

"Wait!" he yelled.

But it was too late: A Russian-made RPG grenade fired by one of his men blew through the windshield of the truck and exploded. A second later the rest of the team peppered its occupants with fire from their AK-47s.

"Shit," said Tyler.

"Major?" asked the warrant officer in charge of the team that had just destroyed the truck.

"My fuckup," said Tyler. "Make sure they're dead, then let's see what we can do about getting rid of the truck."

CHAPTER

23

Like the Russian design it had been based on, the S-37/B had special rough-field grates that helped keep debris and other nasties from shredding the engines on take-off. Something big cracked against one of them as the Berkut built speed; Howe felt the shock but pressed on, committed to taking off both by momentum and situation. He had his nose up but his wheels still on the ground: Airspeed wasn't building quite as fast as he expected. Something rumbled to his right and he held on, more Newton's passenger than his own.

The Berkut stuttered, then lifted freely.

He cleaned his gear and felt another rumble.

He was losing the right engine.

Howe's hands flew around the cockpit even as his mind sorted out the situation. Something had smacked against one of the louvers and sent bits of metal or debris into the right power plant. It couldn't have been much—the engine still *wanted* to work—but he could see the oil pressure shooting toward red and the power plant's output sliding.

Like most jets, the Berkut had been designed to operate on one engine, and now that he was off the field with a relatively light load, he'd dodged the worst of the situation. Even so, flying with one engine meant changing his flight plan. The nap-of-the-earth route out required good reserve thrust; there were several points where he'd have to pull the nose up and make like a pole vaulter, squeaking over obstacles, just not doable on one engine.

He could go directly south, but that path bordered on suicide. Better to take it higher and round off some of the edges. He had the Russian ID gear, darkness, and, if all else failed, the cannon.

"Ivan to Sky," he said over the satcom system connecting him to the mission coordinator in the RC-135 over the Sea of Japan. "I have a situation."

"Sky," acknowledged the coordinator, asking Howe to detail his problem.

"Down to one engine. Am proceeding."

"Copy that. You're on one engine."

"I'll run as close to the course as possible," added Howe.

The controller didn't answer right away.

"Sky?"

"Roger, we copy. Godspeed."

Howe thought of his passenger in the backseat. He flipped the interphone circuit on.

"We have a slight complication," said Howe, pausing, as he worried that Dr. Park might not speak English well enough to understand what he said. "We're down to one engine."

"I understand," replied the Korean.

His voice was so calm that Howe was sure the man didn't know what he had said, but Howe let it go. He banked gently to the north, moving his stick gingerly as he came onto the course bearing. He did an instrument check, then broke out his paper maps and began working out his alterations to the course.

One of Fisher's ideas in raiding the Washington Heights apartment was that if it was connected to a terrorist operation, even tangentially, hitting it might shake up everyone else connected to it and get them to do something stupid. Given that they had a whole net of wiretaps working and another apartment under surveillance, the idea was not without merit. While Fisher was not by nature an optimist, he did hope that the suspect in the other apartment—home at the time—might lead them to something that would, if not blow open the case, at least crack it a bit.

The problem with that theory, however, was that it required the team watching the apartment and the suspect not to lose track of the man. Which they promptly did within five minutes of his leaving the apartment an hour after the raid. He'd gone down to park near the Triborough Bridge, headed for the drug dealers who held market on the street nearby, then jumped into a small motorboat tied up on the rocks below. The boat had, of course, disappeared.

"Shoulda shot him," said Fisher when Macklin related the story. "Don't you teach these guys anything?"

They kept the surveillance teams on the apartment, waiting to see if their man, Faud Daraghmeh, returned. Fisher in the meantime sorted through various leads and made the rounds of the borough's coffee shops. He did better with the latter than the former, finding a Greek place just a few blocks from the surveillance post that managed to impart a burned taste even to the first drop of liquid from the pot. As for Caliph's Sons, the arrest of the men in the first apartment led to a variety of leads, none of which had panned out. Fisher wasn't sure whether this was because the DIA had been charged with running them down, though he had his suspicions.

The command post for the surveillance operation was a second-story office up the street from the apartment, located over a twenty-four-hour Laundromat. The machines rumbled constantly, and the place was so hot that one of the detectives assigned to the post theorized that the dryers were being vented through some hidden mechanism directly into the office.

A bank of televisions fed by video cams showed every possible approach to the apartment; in addition, a small radar unit and two bugs gave the detectives and agents a full picture of what was happening inside.

Which was nothing.

Fisher surveyed the feeds for a few minutes, then picked up the latest intelligence summary on the case, which ran down intercepts the NSA had made with any possible connection. That, too, was a blank, with the only mention of a blackout coming in a conversation that clearly had to do with basketball coverage.

"You missed the morning quarterback session," said Macklin, showing up with a bag of doughnuts around eleven. "Hunter was asking for you."

"Use any four-letter words?"

"Many." Macklin ripped open his bag and spread it over the table at the center of the room. "I'm thinking of pulling the plug on the surveillance. I have warrants so we can go search the place. What do you think?"

Fisher took two of the doughnuts from the table. "I think it's time to find out how good a cup of coffee Mrs. DeGarmo makes."

"DeGarmo? The landlady?"

"Yeah," said Fisher. He checked his watch. "Maybe if we stay long enough, she'll invite us for lunch. Plate of cold spaghetti would really hit the spot."

"Who's there?"

"Andy Fisher."

"Who's Andy Fisher?"

"FBI."

"Who? The plumber?"

"Yeah. You have a leaky faucet?"

The doorknob turned and the heavy door creaked open. Fisher saw a pair of eyes peering at him about chest high.

"You're a plumber?" she asked.

"FBI." He showed her his Bureau "creds," a small laminated ID card.

Mrs. DeGarmo squinted at it. In the right light, the picture looked a bit like that of a dead rat.

In bad light, it was the spitting image of one.

"Where's your tools, if you're a plumber?"

"I have to look at the leak first," said Fisher.

"Okay," said the woman, pulling the door open.

Lillian DeGarmo was ninety if a day. Her biceps sagged beneath her print housedress and her upper body pitched toward the floor. She tottered slightly as she walked but soon reached the kitchen, which lay just beyond the long entry hall.

"Sauce smells good," said Fisher.

"The faucet's in the bathroom, around the corner," said the old lady, pointing to the doorway at the other end of the small kitchen.

"Actually, I'm here for something else," said Fisher. "I'm an FBI agent. Say, is that coffee warm?"

"You want coffee?"

"Well, I have doughnuts," said Fisher, pulling the doughnuts from his pocket.

"Oh, I can't," said Mrs. DeGarmo. "The doctor said they're bad for my diabetes."

"Doctors. Probably told you not to smoke, right?"

She pursed her lips for a moment.

"I hate doctors," said Fisher, pulling out his cigarettes.

"Me too," said Mrs. DeGarmo, grabbing the pack.

By the second cigarette Mrs. DeGarmo had told Fisher all she knew about her tenant. Faud Daraghmeh went to

St. John's University, where he was a prelaw student. He claimed to be Egyptian—he was actually from Yemen, according to the Immigration and Naturalization Service— and greatly admired the United States. Until a few days ago he had kept a very strict schedule, always in by nine o'clock and always in bed before the eleven o'clock news, which Mrs. DeGarmo watched religiously. He got up within a few minutes of eight o'clock every morning—during the *Today* show—and left by noon, before the afternoon soaps (she called them her "stories") came on.

"You can hear him above the TV?" Fisher asked.

"Big feet," said the old lady, waving her hand. "More coffee?"

"Sure," said Fisher. "So a couple of days ago he just stopped coming home, huh?"

"Sometimes he goes away, but usually he tells me when he'll be back. 'Mrs. D,' he says, 'I go to see friend in Florida.' "

"Florida?"

"I think he said that."

"He said that this time?"

"No. Other times. This time, eh . . . *ragazzi.*"

Technically the word *ragazzi* meant "boys," though coming from the old Italian lady the word implied much more.

"He's a nice boy," added Mrs. DeGarmo quickly. "He's not in trouble, I hope."

"Might be," said Fisher.

"He's very nice. He helped me out."

"How?"

"Little jobs. He could fix things. You want lunch? I have sauce on the stove: Have a little spaghetti."

"Spaghetti's good," said Fisher.

Mrs. DeGarmo made her way to a pantry at the end of the hallway in the back where she kept extra groceries. The groceries were on a small bookcase in the hall; the pantry itself was occupied strictly by grocery bags. If there was ever a shortage, she could supply the city for months.

"Look at that," she said, pointing to the floor as she took the box of Ronzoni.

"What?"

"The rats are back," she said.

"Rats?" asked Fisher. "Rodent rats?"

"They always come back. This time at least they stayed away for weeks."

"Good exterminator's hard to find," said Fisher, helping himself to another cup of coffee as they returned to the kitchen.

"Faud knows how to chase them away," said the landlady, checking on her large pot of water.

"Really?" said Fisher.

"Oh, yes. He was very good at that. He was a very good boy."

"He put out traps?"

"No. Fumigate."

"Fumigate?"

"Very stinky. We had to go outside the whole day. He sealed it off. Smelled like Clorox when he was done, but there were no rats."

"Sealed what off?"

"Downstairs. Two times, he did it."

"Two times?"

"He was a very good boy."

"Mind if take a look?" asked Fisher.

"First you have something to eat. Then you fix the faucet," said Mrs. DeGarmo. "Then you take a look."

"Can't argue with that," said Fisher, twirling his spaghetti.

25

Howe was fifty miles from the coast when the radar warning receiver buzzed, picking up the two MiGs flying almost directly at him from the east at 25,000 feet. They were less than fifteen miles away, which would put them overhead in roughly sixty seconds. He pushed lower to the mountains, sliding down through 10,000 feet in hopes of avoiding their radar.

He thought he'd slid by when the RWR came up again; he'd strayed close to a ground radar. Howe held to his course anyway. There was another radar to the north closer to the coast, and maneuvering away from one would expose him to the other. The MiGs or at least their radars had disappeared.

Four minutes to the coast, then another five minutes before he'd be far enough away that nothing could stop him.

A flight of F/A-22s would be on station by now, off the coast to the south. If they scrambled north, they'd meet him over the coast, or just off it.

So, really, he only had to make it though four minutes. Two hundred and forty seconds.

Long seconds.

He got a blip: the MiGs.

Howe glanced down at the map he'd unfolded across his lap and leg. He could cut farther north and hope to avoid the MiGs by legging into Russian territory, but that would take him farther from the F/A-22s presumably scrambling to his aid. It also would stretch his fuel further and leave him vulnerable to the Russians, who surely would be interested in a plane that looked like one of theirs.

He looked up at the black night in front of his cockpit, calculating which way to push his luck. There was chatter on the frequencies used by the Korean air force.

"Ivan, be advised a second flight of MiGs scrambling

from Ŏrang to check unknown contact in your vicinity," warned the mission coordinator in Sky. "We're tracking them now. They're going to be in your face in zero-two minutes. SAMs are coming up."

"Ivan," acknowledged Howe, his grip tightening on the sidestick.

"Another flight: You're being targeted!"

The words were drowned out by the blare of the radar warning receiver, whose fervent bleat indicated that an air-to-air radar had just locked its grip on him.

CHAPTER

26

The first bulletin took Blitz by surprise. He was actually staring at a feed from a U-2 flying near the Korean DMZ, and as the screen changed he didn't immediately understand what he was seeing.

"They're going to war!" exclaimed one of the officers standing nearby him in the situation room. "Oh, my God."

Everyone around them jumped to their feet. The screens flashed. People started to shout.

Calmly, Blitz turned to his military aide. "Get the President on the line. Now."

CHAPTER

27

In the end the best they could do was push the wrecked vehicle into a ravine about fifty feet below the road. They took the two men they'd killed and carried them with them for a few miles before burying them in the rocks at a pass in the hills.

You screwed up, a voice told Tyler as he set out just ahead of the tailgunners. *You gave the order too soon.*

The muscles in his chest tightened; they felt like bands of steel clamping him together, slightly swelled like ice cramping against the sides of a hose. He concentrated on his job, on his situation, on his men, but still the muscles in his chest failed to relax.

They had to retrace part of their path, coming in on the route they had taken. Though risky by its nature—at least in theory someone who was trailing them would have the route covered—it had seemed the only way when they were laying out the plan back in D.C. Tyler had gone over it again before they kicked off; it was the only way to get across the mountains in that area while avoiding settlements and completely impassable terrain.

He second-guessed himself now, arguing that he should go a different way. Sweat poured from his neck as he walked, and by the time he finally reached the turnoff to the path beyond the pass, Tyler felt a wave of relief.

It was short-lived. They were just starting down the hill when the com system crackled with a warning: three vehicles approaching.

Silently the soldiers moved off the road.

"We can take them," said Warrant Officer Chris Litchfield, who was fifty yards ahead on the other side of the road.

"No," said Tyler.

Litchfield didn't reply. The first of the trucks came into view. It was a large canvas-backed six-wheeler, probably older than its driver. The other two were close behind; none of the three trucks had their lights on.

Tyler watched through his night optical device, or NOD, as the trucks stopped. Men began piling out of the backs of all three. They were chattering. A dozen or so went to the side of the road, climbed down a short way.

It was a piss stop, nothing more. Just a stop so a few soldiers could relieve themselves midway through a long journey.

Of all the luck.

Tyler saw what would happen a few seconds before it did.

"Get the lead truck," he managed to say before the first Korean shouted that there was someone on the hill.

CHAPTER
28

The RWR screamed at Howe as he threw the Berkut into a hard turn, trying to beam the interceptor's radar. It was too late; the Korean had launched a pair of radar-guided missiles at him.

The weapons were R-77 air-to-air missiles, known to NATO as AA-12 Adders and sometimes called AM-RAAMSKIs. The Russian-made air-to-air missiles were roughly comparable to American AIM-120 AMRAAMs.

Howe hit his electronic countermeasures, or ECMs, jinking back hard and then pushing the plane through a mountain pass that loomed to his left. It was a good move: Not only did he lose the missiles but the MiG that had launched them continued on its course blithely, flying away from him. But Howe was in no position to gloat: He had two more MiGs coming hot and heavy in his face.

Had he been sitting in an F/A-22 or an F-15 Eagle, both aircraft would be dead meat: He'd punch-button the bastards to death with a pair of AMRAAMs without losing a breath. But he wasn't. He had only the cannon and its 150 shells. And he had only one engine to work with.

Three minutes to the coast. One hundred and eighty seconds.

Howe leaned the plane on its right wing, ducking through a second break in the mountains. He had someone on his tail; he sensed it before the RWR began shouting that a fresh radar was trying to lock him down.

The S-37/B had a small stock of chaff, metal shards

that confused radars and made it hard to target an aircraft. As the MiG fired its weapons, Howe unleashed his tinsel and tossed the Berkut wildly left and right in a series of zigs and zags that were nearly as disorienting to him as to the weapons tracking him. Struggling to keep his head clear, he got a fresh warning— another MiG, this one coming from the south—and jagged back to the north.

One of the missiles exploded a half-mile away, its proximity fuse confused all to hell by his zigzags. It was one of the most beautiful sights Howe had ever seen.

"Missiles in the air!" warned Sky.

Jeez, no shit, thought Howe.

Howe yanked the stick and tried to head east, stomping on the throttle as he temporarily forgot he was on one engine. The Berkut didn't complain, but she also didn't move any faster.

Meanwhile an SA-2 battery began tracking him near the coast. The high-altitude, long-range missiles would be more an annoyance than anything else.

The Russian-made S-300s were another matter. Only a few months old, the missiles could be considered knockoffs of the American Patriot. A battery of four sat between him and the sea.

And their radar had just turned on, trying to track him.

One hundred and twenty seconds.

A mountain peak looked ahead. Howe pulled hard on his stick, just barely clearing the rocks. As he rose, his radar caught two contacts flying about three miles ahead. His first thought was that they were the F/A-22s, come to rescue him, but within a few seconds their speed gave them away as MiGs.

The enemy planes were not quite on a parallel course, seemingly unaware of where he was—or at least their radars hadn't locked onto his plane. He could swing behind them as they passed, then shoot them down.

One at least.

But that wasn't his job. His mission was to get his passenger out in one piece. Stopping to take potshots was more than foolish: It was a dereliction of duty.

Howe let them go, tucking south. He could see the glow of a city to his right, knew from the shadows that the water was just the head.

A launch warning: S-300s in the air.

He gave up the last of his chaff, hit the ECMs, and waited.

One of the missiles fell off but another dogged him. Howe started a turn south, desperate to do something.

The sky flashed above him. The missile had missed by a good distance.

A Korean MiG came up off the deck, then another: The two planes had been waiting for him out over the sea.

He cleared the coast at just over 5,000 feet.

Another pair of MiGs were running down at him from the north. They may have been the planes from before, since they didn't seem to be carrying radar missiles. In any event they were trying to close, either for a shot with a short-range heat seeker or their cannon.

There was no question of running away. Howe jerked hard to the left, then back. The red oval of a fighter jet appeared ahead.

He pushed down on the trigger. The Russian cannon spit its big slugs out. A dozen, two dozen, hit the plane. The rear of the MiG—it turned out to be an older MiG-21, scrambled without missiles—caught fire and then unfolded, a yawning mouth of death. Howe pushed right, trying to get his gun on the flight leader, but as he did, tracer rounds flashed across his windscreen: The MiG was on his tail.

Howe tucked downward momentarily, half-rolling his wings and then cutting back, making the slinky Berkut into a skyborne corkscrew. The maneuvers were far tighter than anything the MiG—a decent knife fighter itself—could manage, and within a few seconds the plane appeared above and then beyond his canopy. The MiG driver pushed right, but Howe wasn't about to let him turn inside him; he stayed glued to his tail.

If the North Korean had just put the pedal to the metal, he probably could have escaped. But he didn't realize Howe was working with only one leg, and as he cut back to the left in a kind of modified scissors escape, the American pilot laid on the trigger. His first shots flew wide right, but he stayed with it, nudging his nose and the stream of bullets into the starboard wing of the enemy fighter. Something flashed, and then his target disappeared.

"You going to leave some for the rest of us?" asked one of the F/A-22 pilots, finally reaching the area.

"Only if I have to," he answered.

"Ivan, be advised Koreans are turning south. You're clear. You're clear."

"Ivan acknowledges," said Howe. "Bring that tanker up. I'm getting mighty thirsty."

CHAPTER
29

The Korean troops were caught completely by surprise; the Americans destroyed their lead and rear trucks before the enemy could organize their return fire. But there were at least a dozen men in each vehicle, and two-thirds of Tyler's people were spread out along the road well beyond the trucks, not in a position to attack.

Tyler saw two Koreans advancing with rifles and immediately shot both, catching them mid-body with bursts from his AK-47. He jumped up and ran to the roadway, covering another member of the team who was firing at the men near the last intact truck. Something hit the vehicle and it exploded, flames bursting skyward in a bright arc of yellow and orange. The light silhouetted four Korean soldiers; by the time Tyler turned his gun on them the other SF soldier had gunned them down.

Tyler ran to a large rock at the right side of the road, sweeping the ditch with gunfire and then jumping down. The position allowed him to cover the road ahead of the convoy and gave him an angle on the trucks as well. The Koreans, meanwhile, were shouting in confusion. They knew there were soldiers around them but they weren't sure where exactly the enemy was; their return fire was disorganized, but it *was* return fire. A heavier weapon began firing from near the wrecked lead truck, set up by two or three of the Koreans and hidden from Tyler's side.

We should have taken them out when they were on the road ahead, Tyler thought to himself as he took out a Russian-made antipersonnel grenade. *I fucked up again.*

He pulled the pin and did a half step, whipping the grenade as if it were a baseball at the side of the truck. The grenade exploded with a loud echo because of the hills, but the machine gun continued to fire. Cursing, Tyler reached for another grenade and was just rising when another grenade, thrown by someone else from his patrol, exploded by the truck. He ducked down, then realized he'd already pulled the pin. He threw the grenade anyway, and this time saw it land behind the cab—or thought he saw it, because as it fell he tossed himself down for cover, and besides, everything around him was a blur. A stream of bullets ripped across the road in front of him, and the major found himself eating dirt, unsure for a moment where his rifle was, even though it was in his hand. Someone screamed something in English that he couldn't understand. Tyler began crawling forward along the trench, parallel to the road. A flare went up—obviously from the Koreans—and a fusillade of bullets rained on the three trucks, which were now mere wrecks.

"All right," said Tyler over his com system, "I'm in the ditch. I'm in the ditch on the south side of the road. Let's get positions. Sound off."

He got a garbled reply. Tyler leaned across the dirt, trying to puzzle out how many Koreans were left and where they were. When he couldn't see any soldiers who were still firing, he started to crawl up from the ditch. The two men he'd shot earlier were sprawled nearby, their uniforms thick with blood. Only one man had a rifle; Tyler kicked it back toward the ditch, then continued toward the trucks. Something moved at the far end; Tyler saw the squat figure raise his weapon at him and fired a burst. The man crumpled downward, a house whose foundation had evaporated.

"All right, all right," he heard someone say. The gunfight was over. "All right, all right."

He turned around, not realizing at first that he had been the one who'd spoken.

There was no way to hide this, and Tyler didn't bother. His immediate concern was two casualties. One of the men had been shot in the shoulder; the wound was relatively light and the sergeant joked about having had bee stings that hurt more. Tyler appreciated the lie.

The other man had been shot through the face and was dead. The A team captain took his shirt off and wrapped it around the dead man's face; Tyler thought he should have been the one to do this.

"We'll take him out with us," he said softly. One of the others had already begun to set up a litter.

Warrant Officer Litchfield looked at him but said nothing. He didn't have to.

Tyler's orders dictated that he call in about the firefight. The reply was brief: *Proceed to Pickup Zone 1 as planned.*

They did.

30

"Where are we landing?" asked his passenger about twenty minutes out of Japan.

"Misawa," said Howe. The Korean had been so quiet, he'd almost forgotten about him.

Almost.

"Misawa. I thought it might be there. Or Okinawa."

"Okinawa's a bit far for us," said Howe.

"Misawa will do very well."

Howe laughed. The Korean didn't know what he was in for. A team of debriefers was undoubtedly waiting on the tarmac, anxious to get at Dr. Park. He was going to be a very popular man for the next few days, and probably a good many months after that.

With the island in sight, Howe fought off his fatigue by concentrating on the plane. It had performed extremely well, one more example of the value of NADT and its diverse expertise. The organization *was* important.

So, did that mean he should take the job after all?

The strip came up wide and fat, his approach a gentle, easy glide that contrasted starkly with his landing in Korea. Howe felt his tires hit the concrete, the plane settling around him like a tired horse falling from its gallop after a hard run around the track.

It wasn't quite home, but it would do for now.

He trundled off the runway and was met by an SUV with a blue flashing light. He popped open the canopy and breathed the fresh air, following the truck as it led him away from the main area of the airport, past a pair of hangars isolated from the others to a wide expanse of concrete near a perimeter fence. It was obviously meant as a security precaution, but there were no support vehicles in sight, not even a tractor to haul him into one of the hangars. Howe wasn't exactly in a position to argue, though, and hell, he just wanted to get to bed.

Howe powered down. Two men, both in Japanese Self-Defense Force uniforms, got out of the SUV and trotted toward the plane. Until now, this had been a U.S.-only project, but they were in Japan and the Japanese tended to be slightly touchy over protocol. Lights approached in the distance: Obviously the U.S. Air Force team was uncharacteristically running a little behind the timetable.

Something popped behind him, an engine or something. He couldn't hear well with his gear on.

"All right, my friend, taxi ride is over," Howe said, removing his helmet and starting to push up from the ejection seat.

As he did, something smacked him hard on the side of the head. He caught a glimpse of a shadowy reflection in the right display. then blacked out.

PART THREE
Case Closed

CHAPTER

1

Blitz couldn't stop himself.

"How? How?" he demanded, pacing back and forth in the secure communications center below the Pentagon. "How?"

"I sure as shit would like to know that myself," said Pierce.

Actually, they had just been told how it had happened—or rather, the sequence of events that had followed Howe's landing at Misawa in northern Japan. According to the colonel who had made the report, a dozen men—obviously North Koreans—had infiltrated the base sometime after the Berkut had taken off. Wearing Japanese uniforms, they had killed the two American crewmen assigned to ride out to the Berkut when it landed and had taken over their truck. They had then diverted Howe to the abandoned area, where they knocked him out and spirited his passenger away. The Japanese unit tasked as escorts had been delayed, apparently with false orders. As it was, an American backup team had narrowly missed grabbing the scientist—or whoever he was—and may have saved Howe's life.

Had the Koreans somehow learned of the operation and then managed to thwart it? Japan was said to be filled with North Korean spies, but it didn't seem possible.

Blitz thought there was a more logical if equally outrageous explanation: The operation had been planned to get the passenger out of Korea. There were sketchy reports of intrusions at other bases and airfields as well, and while the information was vague, he thought this meant that the North Korean had tried to cover as many contingencies as he could without knowing all of the details of the operation. He must be fairly important, obviously, and thought that he would be recognized once in American custody. But who the S-37/B had transported remained a mystery.

In the meantime, the situation in Korea had dramatically changed. There had been a coup, and apparently in mistaken and unordered retaliation—or at least there was no intelligence indicating that orders had been given—two artillery units had fired on Seoul.

The American reaction had been swift and fierce. Within a few minutes ninety percent of the artillery tubes in the DMZ area had been bombed, shelled, or hit by missiles. The North Korean warheads had been destroyed by B-2s, and a phalanx of Tomahawk cruise missiles had destroyed command centers, barracks, and weapons depots deep inside the country.

And last but certainly not least, a Cyclops airborne laser had wiped out a medium-range intercontinental missile that had managed to get off the ground from a heretofore unknown base, blasting it out of the sky as it headed toward Japan.

It had not yet been determined whether the missile was armed with a nuclear weapon or not. It was irrelevant, in Blitz's mind: just so much more piling on in the geopolitical calculus.

American troops had taken over two military airports in

the southern portion of the country. The President had ordered the Joint Chiefs to proceed with a plan dubbed Righteous Force, cooperating with the South Koreans to secure the area near the DMZ and protect South Korea from further attack. In the meantime two different North Korean army commanders had proclaimed that they were in control of their capital. Depending on the report, North Korea's dear leader Kim Jong Il had either been killed, fled the country, or was fighting back from one of three strongholds.

Blitz stared at a computer screen, where a fresh casualty report had just been flashed up. Three thousand South Koreans had died and about twice that number had been injured.

Could that number be true? It was a ridiculously small price to pay—absurdly small.

The first reports were always wrong, he told himself. The first rumors from the field at Manassas proclaimed a great Union victory. But with a relatively low number of casualties—horrible as any deaths were—the U.S. might yet achieve the goals Blitz and the President envisioned without the catastrophe that everyone, Blitz included, had feared.

Should he be happy? Their hands were tied; they'd had no choice but to respond. The fact that the plan had gone off so well—assuming the reports were true, assuming there weren't other surprises—that *was* cause for celebration. Serious cause.

And yet, it felt sacrilegious. He wasn't a warmonger— the opposite in fact. He hated it. But ironically that made it necessary, at least in some circumstances.

"Sir, did you want to send a message regarding Colonel Howe before you left for the White House?" asked an Army captain. The young man had been tapped as a liaison to keep Blitz up-to-date.

"Just that I hope he's all right," Blitz told him. He turned to the defense secretary. "Myron, are you coming?"

"Yes," said the secretary of defense. "I don't know how you manage it, Professor."

" 'Manage it?' "

"To come out smelling like a rose when the rest of the world goes to shit."

CHAPTER

2

The Japanese doctor was speaking English, but Howe couldn't understand a word.

"I'm okay," he said. "Really. Except for my ego."

The doctor patted the back of his own skull and repeated what he said earlier: This time Howe caught the words *concussion* and *rest* and what he thought was *observation*. The man's English was actually quite good, but between his accent and the pounding pain in Howe's head he couldn't process it.

"I will rest," he told the doctor, standing unsteadily. "Honest. I will."

The physician frowned and shook his head. Howe took a few steps from the bed, pulling back the white curtain that separated the area from the rest of the small emergency-room suite. The doctor told him to wait. Howe waved his hand no but then saw that the physician was holding out a small envelope of pills; Howe took them, though he didn't know what they were.

His eyes hurt with the hard white glare of the lights as he walked toward the double doors at the end of the curtained corridor. Howe had no idea where he was, either in the hospital or even Japan. He pushed through the door, wondering if he was supposed to sign some sort of form or other paperwork and maybe pay. He had a credit card in his wallet and wondered if that would be good enough—and even if it was, whether his credit line would cover whatever his treatment cost was.

There was a desk just ahead, and beyond it a set of glass doors that led outside. He decided his best bet was to keep his head down and simply walk out and keep going until he was clearly beyond the hospital's care, then try to find a taxi or something back to the airport where he'd landed. But before he reached the doors a group of men in business suits poured into the passage.

"Colonel Howe, you're all right?" asked a short, bald man.

Howe stopped; the accent was American.

"Yeah."

"I'm Pete McCormack. I'm with the embassy. We'd like to talk to you about what happened."

"I think I'm supposed to check in with someone," said Howe.

"That would be us," said one of the others. Tall and thin, the man's cheeks were so hollow, he looked more like a corpse than a live person.

"We're in touch with Dr. Blitz," said the first man. "And General Jacobs."

Jacobs was the Air Force commander who had made the arrangements for refueling and looking after the S-37/B. On paper he would appear to be Howe's boss, though he was actually working for USSOCCOM, the special operations command.

"We want to debrief you," added the man. "We want to know what happened."

"Yeah, me too," said Howe. "You guys got a car?"

CHAPTER

3

In an inspired if somewhat misguided bid at camouflage, the task force's chemical surveillance truck had been painted to look like an exterminator's vehicle, complete with a giant mouse cowering from a man wearing a respirator. Fisher thought Kowalski had posed for both images, though the mask made it difficult to tell.

"You're a barrel of fucking laughs," said the DIA agent, who was wearing a hazmat suit and standing in Mrs. De-Garmo's kitchen. Two specially trained investigators were downstairs going over the basement with chemical detection gear. Two others were working upstairs in Faud Daraghmeh's apartment.

"Listen, if you're not going to do anything, why don't you go and start interviewing some of the neighbors," suggested Kowalski.

"Waste of time," said Fisher. He got up and poured himself another cup of coffee.

"How do you know it's a waste of time?" asked Kowalski. Fisher shrugged.

"You ought to be wearing a suit," said Kowalski.

"I *am* wearing a suit," said Fisher.

"You know what I mean." He began fiddling with the respirator unit.

"This is one hundred percent natural fibers," said Fisher, pulling at his sleeve. "Protects against anything. I could pour this cup of coffee on the pants and never even feel it."

"Go right ahead," said Kowalski.

He was just pulling on the mask when one of the two men who'd been upstairs came down through the front hallway.

"Nothin'," said the expert.

"Shit," said Kowalski.

"What'd you expect?" asked Fisher.

"What'd I expect? You're the one who called the team in. Jesus, Fisher."

Expecting Kowalski to process more than one piece of information at a time clearly violated the principle of chemical osmosis.

"Well, let me take a look," Fisher told him, starting for the hallway.

"Don't screw up the place. We need photos first," said the DIA agent.

"What for, a spread in *House and Garden?*"

Fisher found the other investigator in the bathroom, where he was reinstalling the trap under the sink.

"I'll be out of here in a minute," the man told Fisher.

"Take your time," the FBI agent told him. He went to the medicine cabinet. Mrs. DeGarmo's tenant was a Gillette man and preferred Bayer over the generic brands. Faud Daraghmeh couldn't seem to settle on an allergy medicine, however: He had a dozen, from generic store brands to Sudafed. No prescription medicines, though. And nothing more revealing.

"They find anything in the basement?" the investigator asked as Fisher closed the medicine cabinet.

"Not that I heard. How about you?"

"Used ammonia to clean."

"That mean anything?"

"Not particularly. I did think of one thing."

"What's that?" asked Fisher.

"He didn't brush his teeth."

"Maybe he just took his toothbrush," said Fisher. He went back to the medicine cabinet. "He shaved."

"Yeah?"

"You found hairs around?"

"Oh, yeah."

The bedroom had a small, single bed with a pair of sheets and a thin blanket. A small desk and chair were the only other pieces of furniture; the drawers were empty except for a paperback dictionary. The closet had a few shirts and pants in it, and two suits that looked as if they'd come from a thrift shop. There were no papers that Fisher could find in any of them.

"Damn it, Fisher. I told you we want to photograph the place," said Kowalski. He was still wearing his suit but carried the respirator and face shield in his hand. "And we're going to dust for fingerprints. Don't touch anything."

Fisher resisted the temptation to smear the doorknobs

and walked back out through the apartment. The living room furniture—it was included in the $1,093 a month rent, according to Mrs. DeGarmo—consisted of a pre–World War II couch, a marble coffee table that had once moved around on miniature wheels but was now propped off the floor with matchbooks, and a two-year-old thirty-two-inch Sony television. The lab people had taken the cushions off the sofa: The foam in them was so old it was degenerating into formaldehyde.

A phone line ran along the front wall. It had been cut open, slit as if for a splice, though Fisher couldn't see any or a box for an outlet. He bent down to the floor, looking at the line.

"What are you doing?" Kowalski asked.

"Matchbooks," said the agent, pointing to them.

"Clues, huh?" Kowalski scowled. He went to the coffee table and lifted it. "Sucker's heavy."

"I'll bet," said Fisher, standing up.

"Jesus, Fisher, aren't you grabbing the matchbooks?"

"Nah."

"But you just said they were important."

"No, I just pointed them out. Once upon a time, the person who lived here smoked. Or had access to a smoker."

Kowalski pushed the coffee table a few inches from its spot and put it down with a thud. He picked up the matchbooks, which bore Marlboro logos.

"So he was a smoker," said the DIA agent triumphantly. "All scumbags are."

"Those are the landlady's," said Fisher. "And they're at least five years old. Why do you think he shaved?"

The men working in the basement had several possible hits on two small saucers that had been placed near the boiler.

"Something like strychnine, probably," one of the men told Fisher after they'd finished going over the place.

"*Like* strychnine."

"We're going to have to do tests back at the lab. But it makes sense. Rat poison. She had a rat problem, right? Or mice."

"So you don't really know what it was?"

"Not until the tests."

"And you checked the sink?" asked Fisher.

"Cleaned thoroughly. Bleach."

"Bleach?"

The expert pointed to a set of bottles under the large tub. "It all checks out. Clorox. We'll double-check."

Fisher walked to the back of the long, narrow room; there was an outside door leading to a small garden courtyard. A crime scene technician was just setting up to see if he could get prints from the door and doorknob.

"Mind if I go outside?"

"Hang on a second," said the man.

Fisher stepped to the side, looking at the shelves of stacked flowerpots. There was a bag on the floor of potting soil.

"You check the dirt?" he asked the chemical expert.

"Yeah. It's dirt."

Fisher looked at the bag. Unlike the pots, it was very new.

"Could you use the dirt for lab work?" he asked the expert.

"Nah."

Fisher took the bag with him outside. While there had obviously been a garden here once, it was now overgrown with weeds. He emptied the bag of dirt on the small strip of concrete once used as a patio next to the house.

"Whatcha looking for?" Macklin asked, coming out from the basement.

"Here he is, the Homeland Security commander himself," said Fisher, "come to oversee the troops."

"So, what are you doing?"

"I always like to find the dirt in a case," said Fisher. He

looked for something to sift through the soil with, but there was nothing nearby. He went back inside to the shelves where the pots were; an old watering can with tools sat on the floor. It was dark in the corner; he brought the tools out with him and sifted through the dirt with a small hand cultivator, a three-pronged tool that looked a bit like a cross between a miniature rake and a claw.

"Something?" asked Macklin.

"Nada," said Fisher. He started to toss the cultivator back into the can, then got another idea and dumped it out on the ground.

In the pile of shovels and sticks lay two new and loaded autoinjectors.

"Now, those are worth dusting," said Fisher, pointing to them. "And then we have to figure out what they are."

CHAPTER

4

Kuong asked himself the question over and over: Why had his second pistol misfired when he tried to kill the pilot in Japan?

Kuong thought of the moment again and again as he traveled in the hold of the cargo plane to his next stop in the Philippines. It haunted him, as all his faults haunted him, mocking him again and again even as he vowed to correct it.

Had he lost his nerve? He remembered pulling the trigger twice, then looking at the gun, then firing again.

He remembered it but he couldn't trust the memory. Why would his pistol misfire?

If the American had not thought to make him get rid of his first gun, he would not have needed his backup weapon. That was cleverness on his enemy's part. And yet, Kuong had foreseen that possibility, and prepared for it.

Had Fate played a hand? Was it mere bad luck—or

something beyond? He could think of no other pistol failing him, at least not a gun that he had cleaned and loaded himself. He had used the weapon a short time before to dispatch the traitor, Dr. Park. Surely it could not have broken or even fouled in the meantime.

Fate, then. Luck: the other man's. There was nothing to be done about that. Or rather, there was nothing that could have been done at that moment. The man himself would have to be dealt with. To leave a witness—even one who was in the dark about what had taken place—was very dangerous.

Kuong knew the man's name: Colonel William Howe. He could not be difficult to find, especially in Japan or South Korea. And there were friends in America who could find him as well.

The Muslims could not be trusted with it. They were allies of convenience, and he could not even be sure if they would strike at the proper moment as planned in New York. Their strike would be welcome, but their real use was the money they had paid for the gas. He would not have dealt with them otherwise, and had risked much by simply allowing them to suggest a date and time.

Kuong could take his time. Clearly, Howe did not suspect who he was, and it was unlikely that he had seen the shed or realized what was kept there. The hangar with the two craft would have been obliterated by now in any event, and from past experience Kuong knew that the Americans were too arrogant to decipher the many hints they had of the threat.

He would be patient, as he had been with the traitor. He had been stunned two months before when his aides had brought the e-mail to his attention. The precautions against stealing information from the factory were many, and Kuong had to admit he thought it impossible at first; he did not know Dr. Park personally but it seemed inconceivable that anyone who worked at the factory would betray his country and the Dear Leader in such a way.

Obviously the man had been tempted by sex and money, the great vices of the Americans.

Kuong's first impulse had been to kill the scientist with his own hands. But then his more contemplative nature took over: He realized he might be able to use the scientist to mislead the Americans. He might allow the scientist to pass more information to them that would make them think the weapon wouldn't work.

And then, with the government collapsing and his avenues of escape closing down, he had an even better idea—more brilliant, more delicious. He had sent Dr. Park to Moscow to add to his legitimacy, intending to have the kidnapping foiled exactly as it had been. Dr. Park—actually, the general himself, with the help of one of his security aides and another scientist—would then send new documents claiming he was angry and had no hope of defecting any longer. But the deteriorating situation in North Korea, and the Americans' own lust for a traitor, had convinced him to take a chance on using them to get out. Ironically the Americans could accomplish what he could not; he was too well known and disliked by his own country's army as well as the South Koreans to slip by them. Only the arrogant Americans would assume they were too clever to be fooled.

Kuong had a packet of documents with him: the false ones prepared about the E-bomb, and a story that he was Dr. Park's coworker prepared in case his identity had been challenged at the airstrip. But they weren't necessary.

The *o-koan* had predicted they wouldn't be. The bones had told him that morning luck would come to him . . . if he could be patient.

It had taken considerable time to punish the scientist for his treachery, but Kuong's patience had been richly rewarded, not merely with the moment of triumph he felt when he personally killed the pathetic little man, but with this escape. Kuong had used his enemies' own cleverness against them for a rich triumph. Now he must be patient once more. He would have his revenge against the Americans for destroying his country. And he would remove Howe, the only man who remained alive who might be able to give him away.

It would not be long to wait.

CHAPTER

5

Howe settled his hands on the ends of the chair's arms, intending to pull himself upright, but somehow he felt too exhausted even to move. He had now told the story of his trip in and out of Korea four times, most recently during a conference call with Dr. Blitz and the defense secretary. He was tired and his head hurt.

But he also realized he was lucky. He could have been killed.

Why hadn't he?

The CIA agents who had debriefed him had several theories. One was that his passenger felt grateful for his rescue. It was possible, too, that the approach of the small American team and the Japanese security people had scared the men on the ground, or at least encouraged them to move quickly.

Or maybe he was just lucky.

"Colonel, the ambassador wanted to talk with you," said a young woman.

Howe had been introduced to her earlier but couldn't remember her name or position now, beyond the fact that she was a member of the embassy staff. Howe pushed out of the chair and her followed down the hallway, his feet sinking deep into the carpet as he walked.

The ambassador was a holdover from the last administration, a political appointee who had turned out to be an extremely popular figure in Asia as well as Japan. A touch of gray at the temples gave his severe face a dignified air;

his Montana accent had a slow, dignified beat. He came out from behind his desk as Howe was shown into his study. He clasped Howe's hand firmly, then gestured for him to sit in one of the armchairs at the side of the room.

"Colonel Howe, thank you for seeing me. I know you've been through a great deal."

"Sure," said Howe.

"North Korea is falling apart at the seams. More to the point, it *has* fallen apart."

"Yes, sir," said Howe.

"Do you have any idea who your passenger was?"

"No," said Howe.

The ambassador nodded. He was in shirtsleeves, but his tie was tight at his collar.

"I have a theory," said the ambassador. He took a long pause between each sentence, as if waiting for the words to line up in his mouth. "I believe it was a high-ranking North Korean. That's not much of a guess. I think it was one of Kim Jong Il's sons, or some other close relative."

"Why would he need me to help him escape?"

"Because, with only a few exceptions, he's hated worse than his father. The units that began the mutiny offered a reward for his capture. And he can't be located."

"What about the E-bomb?"

"I think it was merely a ruse to get us interested," said the ambassador. "If they had that sort of weapon, they would have used it—or *tried* to use it, rather, against Seoul."

Howe agreed, but when he started to nod, his head pounded.

"The Japanese police are searching throughout the country for your passenger." The ambassador rose, indicating the interview was over. "The situation is very delicate."

Howe got up slowly. It sounded to him as if the ambassador was hinting that he shouldn't talk about what had happened, but if so, such hints were unnecessary. Even if

Howe hadn't been naturally inclined to keep his mouth shut, the incident didn't make him look particularly good.

"You know, I saw some aircraft in that hangar near the end of the strip where I turned around," said Howe.

"MiGs?"

"No, they were pretty small. UAVs, I think. Or maybe ultralights."

"You think that is significant?"

"I don't know, really."

"We'll arrange for a flight back to the States," said the ambassador, gently touching Howe's arm.

"Actually, I have my own plane to look after," said Howe. "What I need is a ride back to the airport. The S-37 is an NADT asset."

"Yes, of course," said the ambassador. "You've done a very good job, Colonel," he added. "A very good job."

Howe nodded, though he didn't agree.

It was only in the car on the way back to the airport that Howe realized what he'd said—or rather, what he'd thought.

His asset. He wanted the NADT job. Not for the money or the power, but because it was where he belonged. He had the ability to do it, and the will to do it right.

And it was his duty to do it. Or at least to try.

CHAPTER

6

Blitz could hear the buzz of the press corps in the East Room of the White House down the hall. The President stood next to Blitz, going over the most recent bulletins and handing each page back as he did. The press conference was already running about three minutes late, but that made it early by President D'Amici's standards.

The President's press adviser had suggested something less formal, perhaps remarks off-the-cuff as he boarded *Marine One,* the helicopter that flew him around the country. But the President sensed this was a historical moment, and he wanted to use the White House setting to emphasize not only its importance but the fact that America was in control of the situation.

And it was. Almost.

The North Korean army had collapsed. While on paper it was one of the most ferocious fighting forces in the world, the reality had proven considerably different. As American and Korean troops came across the border following the missile launches and artillery strikes, most of the soldiers had fled. Roughly a dozen strongholds remained in North Korean hands, as did the capital and the area close to the Chinese border. But not even the most optimistic Pentagon scenario envisioned such a swift collapse. The remaining units were dangerous, surely, but negotiations were already under way with most of them for a peaceful surrender. The real problem now was to plan for the peace.

The President handed Blitz the last page, then checked his hair in a mirror held by one of his aides.

"Last thoughts?" the President asked Blitz.

"Only that we can't trust the Chinese."

"Agreed. But they seem to have been taken by surprise."

"That's why we can't trust them."

The Chinese had moved two fresh divisions to the border area, saying that they were to help with refugees. There were refugees; nonetheless, the troops and China in general had to be watched very carefully. The President planned on mentioning their involvement as peace brokers in the speech, praising their cooperation and mentioning his three phone calls with the country's leaders.

"What was the latest with Colonel Howe and the E-bomb

plot?" asked the President as one of his aides appeared in the hall, gesturing that all was ready.

"Still trying to figure out who we helped escape," said Blitz. "The ambassador thinks it was one of Kim Jong Il's sons."

"A very good guess."

"I think it's Paektu," said Blitz, meaning the number two man in the security police agency, Hwang Paektu Jang. "He's the sort who would think this up."

"Hopefully we'll find him soon."

Blitz didn't answer. With that well-thought-out a plot, he felt it unlikely.

The national security advisor listened to the President's opening remarks from the hallway. He had to give D'Amici credit: The President managed to communicate his personal vision in a speech meant for the masses. Blitz knew that D'Amici's model for the presidency was Eisenhower, but in his ability to speak he was closer to Reagan, though D'Amici lacked the folksy, casual touch Reagan could muster without any apparent effort.

Historically, however, D'Amici's vision seemed more like a blend of Teddy Roosevelt with some Woodrow Wilson thrown in, assuming one could remove some of the naiveté from Wilson's vision of world peace.

That was probably a bum rap on Wilson, Blitz thought; Wilson's private papers showed he was hardly naive, and while he'd been snookered in Europe, it would have been difficult if not impossible to get the French to do the right thing after the bloodbath of World War I anyway.

And to be honest, it only became apparent what the right thing was long after that indecisive war.

There were no real parallels, Blitz thought as the President summed up and started taking questions. They were in completely new territory.

Someone grabbed Blitz's shoulder. He turned around

and found the press secretary, who seemed nearly out of breath.

"The AP is reporting that P'yŏngyang has been declared an open city," he told Blitz. "The war is over."

"Now comes the hard part," said Blitz, walking out to tell the President personally.

CHAPTER
7

"Atropine mixed with oximes. Classic antidote for sarin gas," said Macklin.

"But no trace of sarin in the basement on anything," said Kowalski.

"Maybe they were neat," said Fisher.

"Or maybe they never brought it there," said Macklin.

"No, they must have," said Fisher. "The landlady smelled something."

"Sarin would have made her pretty sick," said Kowalski. He got up from the table and began pacing at the back of the room.

"She smelled the bleach, most likely," said Fisher. "He used it to clean up any traces of the chemicals."

"That's going pretty far," said Kowalski. "Not to mention that there might have been a reaction."

"But there wasn't," said Fisher.

"We've looked at his phone records," said Macklin. "He only made a few calls."

Fisher leaned his head back on the chair. Sarin gas—of which there was as yet no real evidence—represented a serious left turn in the investigation. But left turns were often useful. If you kept turning right, you would end up in the same place you started.

"The landlady's phone—did you check that?" he asked.

"The landlady?"

"Maybe he cut into her line," said Fisher. "There's

probably some sort of connection to the Internet, something along those lines."

"Subpoenaing the landlady's records isn't going to make us look very good," said Macklin.

"She'll give them voluntarily," said Fisher. "Just tell her we're looking for a billing error and rave about her sauce."

Macklin frowned.

"The problem is, we're not getting any closer to the E-bomb," said Kowalski. "This is just a diversion."

"Maybe there *is* no E-bomb," said Macklin. "That's the latest thinking from the CIA."

"They don't know what they're talking about," said Kowalski. "They're covering their butts because they blew it so badly on Korea. They didn't realize the country was going to collapse the way it did."

"What do you think, Andy?" asked Macklin. "Connected to the E-bomb case, or a red herring?"

"Definitely not a red herring," said Fisher.

"So, what is it?"

"Damned if I know."

"We got to break this," said Macklin.

"I agree," said Kowalski.

"I guess it's time for desperate measures," said Fisher.

"What are they?" asked Macklin as he got up out of his chair.

"Time to get a full night's sleep," said Fisher.

As a general rule, sleep didn't particularly agree with Fisher, nor had it ever led directly to any particular insight, much less helped solve a case. But during the eight hours he stayed away, the others followed up a number of possible leads, including Mrs. DeGarmo's phone bills.

There were calls to an Internet provider, and Macklin was now following up with a subpoena to see if they could come up with data on the account. The intelligence wizards had their fingers dancing on the computer keyboards, trying to pull up data from a myriad of sources.

Fisher stuck to the old-fashioned methods. He signed out the soil bag—just the bag, not the dirt—from one of the heated garages that was serving as the task force's evidence locker. Then he took Metro North to Grand Central and hopped the subway to Queens, walking to the apartment from Grand Street before exploring the neighborhood back around Steinway. It took three tries before he found what he was looking for: a hardware store that sold Agfarma potting soil.

"I'm looking for someone who bought a bag of potting soil probably about two months back," said Fisher. The store owner listened as he described Faud Daraghmeh, Mrs. DeGarmo's tenant.

The store owner shrugged, as Fisher knew he would.

"This guy would have bought a whole bunch of Clorox bottles, probably at the same time," the FBI agent told him.

"Like a dozen?"

"About that," said Fisher.

"That I remember. He cleaned me out."

"How did he carry them?"

"Had one of those two-wheel folding carts. You know the kind? Made two trips."

"You wouldn't have a name, would you?"

"You don't have to give a name to buy bleach."

"Maybe he used a credit card," suggested Fisher.

The man went to his computer. His inventory program allowed him to search transactions, and he was able to come up with the date of the purchase: February 23. But apparently he had paid cash.

"There's a couple of other times—twice, actually—when someone bought a lot of bleach," said the store owner. "One of them is a credit card. Both in February."

Fisher took the account number and the dates. There was nothing to tie the credit card transaction to Faud, however, which meant getting a subpoena to check that credit card account was highly unlikely. He walked back to the apartment, hoping inspiration would strike him somewhere on the way.

As usual, it didn't.

Mrs. DeGarmo had gone to stay with her granddaughter on Long Island. Fisher went first to the detail watching the house from a car across the street and asked for the key and a volunteer.

"Volunteer for what?"

"I want to look for a receipt in some bags," he told them.

The other detective, who obviously hadn't seen Mrs. DeGarmo's pantry, got out of the car.

"Jesus," said the man when he opened the pantry door. "You sure there's not a body in here?"

"If there is, it's not our case," said Fisher. He went upstairs and was still studying Faud's closets when the detective came up with a collection of receipts. Unfortunately, they didn't include any of the transactions involving bleach.

But there was one with the same credit card number.

"Thin," said Macklin when Fisher showed it to him and laid out the logic.

"Come on. I've built whole cases out of weaker links. All we need here is a subpoena."

"I don't know, Andy. You sure this isn't the landlady's credit card?"

Fisher had naturally checked that first but let the potential slight to his common sense pass without comment.

"Your theory is that he used the credit card twice?" said Macklin.

"My theory is he used it more than twice," said Fisher. "Otherwise it wouldn't be worth checking."

As it turned out, the credit card had only been used four other times: once more at the hardware store to buy twenty-eight dollars' worth of mouse poison, once at a nearby florist to buy a forty-eight-dollar bouquet, and twice for cash advances at an ATM.

Much more interestingly, the account had been stopped as the result of an investigation into identity theft by the FBI.

Fisher got a list of other account numbers and transactions and gave it to Macklin, who passed it over to the task force members tracking down the other credit card data. If time allowed, they'd try and run down everyone who had used a phony card.

That looked to be quite some time. There were over a thousand accounts.

"Maybe if we just look at the purchases in New York City," suggested Fisher.

"That's still three hundred cards," said Macklin. "We'll check them all if we have to, but it's going to take forever."

Macklin's office at the former drug dealers' home had been one of the bedrooms. It was more than big, probably twice the size of Hunter's back at FBI headquarters. The only problem was that the drug lords who'd owned the place had, for reasons best guessed at, covered the ceiling with mirrored panels, and Macklin hadn't gotten around to taking them down. It was difficult to resist the temptation to watch Macklin's reflection as he spoke; he'd begun to develop a bald spot, and it wrinkled whenever he opened his mouth.

Fisher saw the reflection of his own watch in the mirror. It was after four o'clock.

"I have to get going," he said.

"Where to?" asked Macklin.

"Buy some flowers."

Steve's Florist was located four blocks from Mrs. De-Garmo's building in a short row of buildings that seemed to be waiting for a demolition crew. The stores themselves, however, seemed busy, and inside the florist shop Fisher found himself at the back of a chaotic line. He drifted toward the back, watching the two clerks as they checked people out and occasionally dashed from the register to the refrigerated area where the flowers were kept. One was a middle-aged woman with bright orange hair and a miniskirt that stopped well above the thigh; the other was a twenty-something male whose white button-down shirt failed to hide a torso's worth of tattoos. A third man was working in the back, loading up a van for deliveries; he left before Fisher got a look at him.

Fisher got the middle-aged woman.

"So, is Steve around?" Fisher asked.

"Steve?"

"The owner. It's Steve's Florist?"

"There is no Steve," said the woman. "The owner's name is Rose. She's only in Monday mornings. I'm the manager."

Explaining that he was with the FBI, Fisher laid a copy of the receipt and an artist's sketch of Faud on the counter. The information meant about as much to them as Macklin's pool on the Final Four meant to Fisher.

"He lived a couple of blocks away," said Fisher.

"There are a lot of Arab men in the neighborhood," said the woman, whose name tag read Mira. There was a note of challenge in her voice, as if she expected Fisher to flay his suspect when he caught him.

He wasn't normally the flaying type, but nonetheless liked to keep his options open.

"I'm not really looking for other Arab men," Fisher told her. "Just him."

"Maybe Harry knows him," said the young man. His name tag said his name was Pietro, though the kid looked Scandinavian, even with his tattoos.

"Who's Harry?" asked Fisher.

"Works here on Sundays," said Pietro. He took the receipt and looked at it. "Yup: Look. This was a Sunday."

"Harry around?" Fisher said.

"It's not Sunday," said Mira.

"How old is he?"

"Thirty-five, forty," said Pietro.

"What's his last name?"

"Spageas or something like that," said Pietro. "Something Greek."

That narrowed it down to three-quarters of the residents of Astoria.

"You have an address or a phone number for him?"

Mira shook her head. Pietro just shrugged. Fisher rubbed his eyes, trying to focus on the paper tacked to the bulletin board behind the counter. But he was standing too far away to see if Harry's name was listed there.

"So, what would my friend have bought for $48.50?" asked Fisher.

Pietro thought it was probably a small grave bouquet, though the price didn't quite work out right. Mira had no opinion.

"If you see Faud again," said Fisher finally, "have him call me." He slid a business card with a special sat phone number onto the counter, even though he was pretty sure it would be thrown into the garbage after he left.

He was wrong about that. Mira ripped it in half before he made it to the door.

CHAPTER

8

The first thing Howe did when he got back to the D.C. area was check into an inexpensive hotel and sleep.

When he woke up eight hours later, it was a little past four A.M. He decided he would call Blitz and leave a message on his voice mail telling him that he had changed his mind and that, if the job was still open at NADT, he wanted it.

Much to his surprise, Blitz picked up the phone himself.

"Dr Blitz?"

"Who is this?"

"Bill Howe."

"Colonel. How are you? Are you all right?" Blitz's voice was tired and a little hoarse.

"Yes, sir. A little, uh, embarrassed."

"Nonsense. We're the ones who messed up: There should have been more people at the airport. Due to the circumstances in Korea—well, I don't want to make excuses."

"Is that job at NADT still open?"

Blitz didn't answer.

It's all right, Howe thought to himself. *My own fault.*

"It absolutely is," said Blitz, his words practically gushing. "You've changed your mind?"

"If that's acceptable."

"Of course it is. That's great. That's great. Where are you?"

"Actually, I'm not far from Andrews, in a motel."

"Can you come over to my office? There are a couple of hurdles—just little egos to gratify, really. But believe me, this is great. Really, really great."

"I'll be over as soon as I shave, sir."

If he'd been less tired, Blitz might have jumped up and done a little war whoop when he hung up the phone. Instead he merely got up and went over to the credenza where he had placed his coffee earlier. A full NSC meeting had been scheduled for seven A.M., and he needed to have a good handle on his recommendations for an interim North Korean government by then. Iraq stood as an important example: You had to get *way* out ahead of the curve on this, take advantage of the initial confusion and elation, and make the hard choices. The public would follow.

He was also supposed to talk about Israel and the Palestinians, whose latest peace talks had stalled.

His life lately seemed the embodiment of the ancient curse: May you live in exciting times.

He took his coffee mug and went to see if he could find any drinkable coffee down the hall.

Though it was ostensibly several hours before "regular" government business began, Howe found a good number of staffers on duty when he arrived at the West Wing. Security certainly hadn't been relaxed because of the hour: He was wanded and had his iris scanned for ID even though one of the men at the post recognized him. Upstairs he found Blitz sitting at his desk amid a variety of papers and reports.

"Colonel, thank you for coming over," said Blitz, who practically jumped from his chair to shake his hand. "You're making the right decision."

"Thanks," said Howe, sitting.

"I'd offer you coffee, but the only place to get it is down the hall in the chief of staff's office. They make it pretty strong."

"I don't really want any, thanks," said Howe.

"I haven't had much sleep. I'm sorry if I look a little beat."

Howe shrugged.

"I've made a list of people whom you'll want to talk to," continued Blitz, digging through the papers on his desk. He came up with a yellow pad. "Wait until after twelve, though. I'll have spoken to a few myself by then, and the word will be around."

Blitz continued talking, digressing into the legal separation between NADT and the government, a matter he had already gone over at least once before and a subject that Howe himself already knew. But the national security advisor's words had a certain momentum to them once he got going; it was difficult to stop him, even as he reviewed basic history. The arrangement was meant to help expedite the development and testing of cutting-edge weapons; while it had started out for only one project—a high-energy-beam weapon known as a rail gun that, ironically, had been abandoned—the previous administration had found NADT extremely useful for a wide range of projects and encouraged its continued existence. Under unique legislation, the President of the United States could select three of the private company's seven board members. Those three votes could be counted on for Howe, and Blitz had already sounded out three of the other four board members; all would back Howe gladly.

"I'm sure it will go fine, Dr. Blitz," Howe managed finally. "I know you're busy—"

"Yes," said Blitz. "Why don't you tell me about North Korea? I've seen the report, but I would like to hear it from you."

Howe summarized what had happened. Once again he remembered and mentioned the small aircraft, which he thought were UAVs.

"I'm not really sure I'm following you there," said Blitz. "UAVs?"

"Unmanned aerial vehicles, like Predator and Global Hawk," said Howe. "No report that I've seen says that North Korea had them."

"I see."

"These were fairly big. They'd have a good-sized payload. You might target them," said Howe.

"I'm sure they've been targeted," said the national security advisor.

"Well, good, then," said Howe, not quite sure that Blitz understood. But obviously the man had a lot of things on his mind.

"Check with me at the end of the week. In the meantime you ought to find a house or something to rent."

Howe realized he hadn't even thought of that. He shook Blitz's hand again, then left to find some breakfast.

9

It wasn't as if Tyler had disgraced himself. On the contrary, the ground part of the mission had gone off as well as could be expected given the circumstances, and certainly there was nothing to be ashamed of. But he couldn't get the feeling of failure to leave him. It felt like a heavy, oppressive thing, a monster sitting on his shoulder.

Tyler and his team had been picked up by Osprey as planned and flown to Kunsan Air Base, also known as K-8, near the western coast of the country well south of Seoul. But rather than the rest they expected, the soldiers were all ordered back to their parent units, which were preparing for a mission to look for refugees from the dictatorship near the Chinese border. Tyler was asked to join an evaluation team being put together by the Pentagon and the CIA; its primary task was to prepare estimates on the capacity of any insurgent groups to mount an offensive within a six-to-eighteen-month time frame.

He had to find his own transportation to a highly classified facility near Wonjun in central South Korea. Distancewise it wasn't that far, but the entire country was under what amounted to a lockdown because of the war. Just finding a car and getting gasoline into it was a major endeavor.

The Korea Joint-Mission Evaluation Group had space in a bunkered facility originally built as a backup command center by the CIA but occupied most recently by the South Korean army. It was therefore in scrupulously good repair and so clean that, before descending the double-wide concrete steps that led from the main entrance to the work areas downstairs, Tyler felt obliged to knock the dirt from the sides of his shoes. The masonry walls gleamed, and a visitor might be forgiven for thinking that he or she was descending into a chip fabrication plant or high-tech lab where clean suits and respirators were de rigueur.

Security was being provided by the U.S. Army, and the MPs made everyone show ID and submit to a weapons and bug search. Handguns had to be stowed in a locker under the security team's control.

Cleared through, Tyler walked down the hallway and turned to the right, descending another set of stairs before reaching a ramp that opened into the operating center. Within a few hours he found himself sitting at terminals in a computer center, tied into various secure information networks so he could update himself on the situation in the North.

Inevitably, doubt about the mission began to haunt him as the hours went on, second and third guesses about his actions and then not even his actions but what he might have done in other circumstances, all seemingly designed by his conscience to convince him he was a failure. It was stupid and ridiculous, but he couldn't get rid of the voice that nagged at him, calling him a failure.

Tyler read an account of a fierce tank battle about ten miles beyond the DMZ that had taken place on the first night of the war; a squad of American soldiers had become separated from the main body and found themselves confronting a Type 63 light tank. The men calmly and efficiently called in an A-10A, which within a few minutes (eight according to the report) obliterated the tank with its 30mm cannon. Tyler saw himself in the situation and began wondering if he would have handled it as smoothly.

Any objective observer would have laughed at such a ridiculous question. Of course he would have, if he hadn't found a way to deal with the tank himself. He'd proven himself under fire countless times. Yet, he couldn't seem to convince himself.

Tyler worked his way through a number of assessments, doing his best to focus on his task. By the time of his group meeting at three, he had a good enough handle on the situation to know where he had to look to get the data he needed. Arriving early for the session, Tyler sat and filled two pages of a yellow pad with questions that would be important to answer; he was starting on a third when the head of the group, a CIA officer named Clarissa Moore, came in with most of the rest of the members. There were several new faces, including a member of the Joint Chiefs of Staff J-5 planning department and an Air Force historian who had been added to provide a broad context to the situation. The historian was dressed in civilian clothes and Tyler gathered that he was a retired colonel; his name was George Somers and he certainly looked the part of a historian, with white beard and hair around his balding head, and a heavy tweed sports coat even though it was quite warm in the bunker.

Moore made the introductions and then briefly summarized the situation in North and South Korea, along with some of the developments in nearby countries including Japan and China. She then turned to the group's latest instructions from Washington. The NSC had asked them to prepare a report no later than the end of the week—and to base that report on "firsthand inspection of the situation on the ground."

"Basically, they want to see the dirt under our fingernails," said Moore.

She tapped her right hand on the conference table. Her own nails were clipped so tightly, there was no chance of any dirt hiding there. The CIA officer was about forty, with a trim body but a face that showed her experience. She wore no jewelry save for a simple set of earrings that peeked out amid the lower strands of her hair.

"So we need to put an itinerary together," she said, "determine where we have to go, what we have to see, people to talk to. A lot of this will be the obvious, of course. And then I'll need a small group of volunteers and someone to coordinate."

"It's pretty early to be going north," said Colonel Yorn, an Army officer with extensive experience in both intelligence and artillery. "The situation there is hardly stable. I doubt there's much to be gained from seeing it up close."

"Should we discuss this?" asked Moore.

"I'd just like to hear the argument in favor of going up there," said Yorn. "We'll simply be diverting resources and attention from people who probably already have their hands full. It's not a question of safety," he added. "It's a question of usefulness."

"Tyler?" asked Moore.

"I'll go," he said.

"That wasn't quite the question," said Moore. "Will we get useful information?"

Tyler's thoughts wouldn't focus. He wasn't an intelligence expert and wanted to say that; on the other hand he understood the importance of actually being on the ground so you knew what was going on.

"It makes sense to see what we see," he managed finally.

"I agree with the major that it would be worthwhile," said Somers, sitting next to him. "Colonel, you're right that it's pretty chaotic up there right now. But I'd like face-to-face time with some of the soldiers on the scene. Not just the commanders, mind you: You can't get an accurate assessment from just the officers. No offense."

"It is a point," admitted Yorn.

They discussed it awhile more. Tyler didn't take part in the discussion. It seemed moot with Washington pushing it, but as a screw-up he really didn't feel he had anything to add. When the debate ended, the consensus was that the trip would be more useful than not. Moore turned to him.

"Would you coordinate the trip?"

"Of course," he said, without hesitation.

10

Howe bought the newspaper but found the classifieds useless for finding an apartment. The listings were sparse near NADT's Virginia headquarters, and it occurred to Howe that he wasn't even sure what he could afford. General Bonham had lived in a gated condo community with its own security people; did he need a place like that?

He decided he would ask around the NADT campus to see if anyone had any ideas, and a little past nine A.M. he was about a mile from NADT when he spotted a small real estate office set back on a hill off the county highway that led to the campus. The building itself was an old Victorian-style farmhouse similar to the one where his mother lived, though in much better shape. Howe pulled up the long, winding driveway and parked in the gravel lot off the macadam. Inside he found a receptionist who bore an uncanny resemblance to his hometown librarian, complete with pink-rimmed bifocals and tightly wound curls.

"Yes, dear?" asked the receptionist.

"I'm looking to rent either an apartment or a condo," he said.

Before she could answer, the phone rang. Howe stepped back from the desk, his gaze wandering to the left side of the foyer. An old-fashioned steam radiator stood in front of the wainscoting, its thick gold paint glowing. The woodwork behind it had several sets of reveals as the panels stepped back to the wall. Whoever had restored the house had done a painstaking job; all of the original details shone through. Howe thought of his friend Jimmy's business and felt a stab of guilt, as if his decision to take the NADT job meant he was letting him down.

"Are you being helped?"

Howe turned and found himself staring at a woman about thirty years old. She wore a black sleeveless top and a matching skirt that came nearly to her knees; her light-brown hair had a gentle wave in it as it fell just behind her shoulders. She had a few freckles on her face, which was one of those that seemed naturally inclined toward smiles rather than frowns. Her eyes were blue, and she raised the brows as she waited for him to answer the question.

Howe found himself suddenly tongue-tied.

"I, uh, I'm looking for an apartment or a condo, I guess. Something not that big."

"Married?"

When Howe didn't answer right away, the woman smiled and held her hand out to him. "I'm not trying to pick you up," she told him. "Just find out how big a place you need."

"No, I know. I'm not." Howe stifled a sudden urge to smack himself on the side of the head. "I'm single," he added, still fumbling to explain. "I've just taken a government job, actually; it's a job with a company that does a lot of work for the government, but it's not actually a government agency per se."

"Per se?" Where the hell did that come from, he asked himself.

"I'm Alice Kauss," said the woman, holding out her hand. It felt warm and slender in his, yet the grip was firm. "Come on into my office and let me take down some information. Then we'll see what we can come up with."

She spun on her heels and walked into what would have been the parlor area when the house was first built. Howe followed across the parquet floor to a sleek metal desk that sat before a covered fireplace toward the back. Somehow the ultracontemporary furnishings looked perfectly at home in the old-fashioned setting.

Not that Howe was able to pay much attention to his surroundings. As they worked through the basic questions, he tried desperately hard not to stare at Alice's cleavage and found himself folding his arms over his own chest.

"How much?" she asked.

"I'm sorry?" His eyes met hers. The blue irises glimmered in the light from the halogen on the desktop.

"Your price range?"

"I'm not sure," he admitted.

Howe realized he had to do some more thinking before he was ready to rent a place, but now that he was here he couldn't just get up and walk out.

"Well, how much do you make?"

He smiled at her.

"We haven't settled on a salary yet," he said.

Alice put down her pen. "So you're more in the exploratory mode right now," she said.

"Yeah. I—listen, I do need a place. I'm just not sure exactly what I need. It shouldn't be too expensive or that big, but on the other hand, I mean—"

"You don't want to live in a slum."

"Right."

"And you want to rent or buy?"

"Rent. I think."

There were people in the front hallway. Alice's phone buzzed but she didn't answer it.

"I have an idea, William."

"You can call me Bill, really."

"Bill." There was that smile again, this time full force—not phony, and definitely disarming. "I have a closing in about fifteen minutes. I think that's them out there, a little early. And then I have a full slate for the rest of the day. But if you come back around four-thirty, say, I can take you to a few condos and you can get an idea of the market. If you can afford it, you'll probably do a lot better buying. What do you think?"

"Of buying? I don't know. I guess."

"Because of the market. But we can talk about it."

"Great," he said, standing. "Real great."

NADT had been envisioned more as a think tank than a weapons development company, and those roots showed in its headquarters buildings. The ultramodern buildings were located well back from the road behind manicured lawns and gardens. A range of security sensors, from cameras to motion detectors, maintained constant surveillance of the grounds, but to the naked eye the place seemed deserted until you passed a row of evergreens a few hundred feet off the road. At that point a pair of security guards and the small kiosk appeared a few feet ahead.

Howe had been told that devices were planted in the roadway a bit farther along that could paralyze car engines with an electromagnetic pulse, and he had seen firsthand some of the weaponry the NADT security force had at its disposal. But for all that, the guards appeared almost nonchalant, unfailingly courteous, and friendly; indeed, they were tested and graded on these qualities, with the overall goal of presenting an image to the world—or, more specifically, visiting politicians and high-ranking military people—of absolute self-confidence and efficiency.

Unfortunately, that image had been largely that: an image. The security staff had not exactly covered itself with glory in the Cyclops One fiasco. While the problems at NADT had been caused by Bonham and some of the investors, not the security people or the engineers and scientists and grunts who did the real work, one of his first tasks would be to determine if anyone else should be sacked because of it.

A difficult task. Just about everyone he knew here was dedicated and hardworking, serious and proud of the job they did. A lot were ex–military people, though of course that wasn't a carte blanche endorsement, either.

"Colonel, good morning," said Nancy Meile, meeting him just as the two gate men cleared him and his vehicle to proceed. Meile, about forty and a former partner in a private security firm, was the security director. "Rumor true? You're taking the job?"

"A few hurdles left," he said.

"I hope you take it."

"Why?"

The question seemed to take her by surprise, and she didn't answer right away. "I think you'll do a good job."

As an officer advanced through the ranks of the military, he or she couldn't help but become aware of the various political games that were played. For Howe, the gamesmanship was a severe negative: In his opinion it detracted not just from the mission he and his comrades had to accomplish, but from the bedrock duty and loyalty to one's oath and the country itself. The relative lack of games in the development projects he'd gotten involved in with NADT, as a matter of fact, was one of the attractions.

As head of NADT he'd have to devote considerable energy to playing those political games. But not with his staff.

"I wasn't fishing for a compliment," he told Meile. "I want simply to understand what needs to be done."

His words felt a bit too stiff in his mouth, but he at least got the thought across; he could see it register on her face.

"I'd be happy to talk with you at length when you think it's appropriate," she said.

"I'll take you up on that," said Howe, putting the car in gear.

He drove to the main building, a low-slung, modernist affair whose main floor served merely as a reception and processing center for the offices located in the bunkered floors below. Because of its unique relationship to the government, NADT was considered a possible target for a hostile government, and the protections against attack and, perhaps more importantly, spying were diverse. A copper sheath surrounded the different sections, rendering eavesdropping devices useless. Sixty feet of earth and concrete would keep any but the most powerful American bunker-buster bomb from damaging the heart of the complex.

The vice president for operations was a cherubic man

named Clyde Delano; he had worked for various government agencies under both Republican and Democratic administrations for close to thirty years before coming to NADT. A chemist by training, the years had magnified his academic demeanor. As he took Howe on a tour to meet some of the scientific and research staffers, he launched into a discussion of World War I, apparently because he'd been rereading Keegan's history of the war over breakfast. He asked Howe what he thought would have happened to Europe if America had not entered the conflict but remained neutral.

"Never really gave it much thought," said Howe.

"Very different world," said Delano. "Maybe Germany wins. Maybe the stalemate goes on for a decade."

Howe tried changing the subject—he wanted to know what Delano thought needed to be done at NADT—but the vice president for operations simply demurred, claiming he hadn't given it much thought. Howe found a similar reluctance to speak freely among the upper-level scientists he met, who failed to loosen up even over lunch in the company cafeteria, a facility that would rival many a D.C.-area restaurant. Meals here were free, a perk that helped compensate for the long hours and stringent security measures and discouraged people from taking off-campus breaks.

After lunch, Howe went over to the president's office, which had been vacant since the disgrace of General Bonham. All of Bonham's personal belongings had been removed, leaving the shelves and desk bare; the only things that remained were a few yellow pads and an old-fashioned Rolodex phone directory. Howe idly flipped through the directory: There was his name, along with a long list of contact numbers and addresses.

He took out the list of phone numbers Dr. Blitz had recommended he call. But instead of picking up the phone, he found himself thinking about Delano, who had functioned as Bonham's second-in-command. Clearly they were not going to be a good match; he needed someone else to take his place, someone he could trust.

Bringing someone else in from the Air Force would send the wrong signal, he thought; and besides, he wanted someone with better contacts with the administration and Congress, his weaknesses; someone in the service wasn't likely to have them.

He thought of Harold McIntyre, the former NSC assistant for technology, whom he'd worked with before. Though McIntyre could be a bit of a playboy and partyer, he had a good feel for who was who among the contractors and his standing with the administration was impeccable. He also liked Howe—not surprising, since Howe had led the mission that rescued him from India after war broke out there. McIntyre had left government following that incident, and that was a complication: Howe thought he might have had some sort of emotional collapse because of the stress he'd undergone.

McIntyre's name was in Bonham's directory, with his phone number listed. Howe picked up the phone, hesitated a moment, then punched in the numbers.

An answering machine picked up.

"This is McIntyre. Leave a message."

"Mr. McIntyre. Bill Howe here. How are you? Listen, I've been offered a job and, uh, well, I wanted to—"

The line clicked and a tone sounded.

"Colonel Howe?" said a distant voice.

"That you, Mac?"

"Yes, sir. How are you?"

There was a slight tremor in his voice, the sort of quality a freshly minted lieutenant might betray when he chanced to come face-to-face with the base commander. Very unlike McIntyre, Howe thought, though it was definitely him.

"I'm fine. How are you?"

"Not that well, actually." McIntyre laughed. "I, uh . . . well, they have me on Paxil."

"That a painkiller?"

McIntyre laughed again. It was a light, self-deprecating laugh. "Antidepressant. Supposedly, I have some sort of, uh, like, uh . . ."

"Delayed stress?"

"Yeah, something like that. Combined with depression."

Howe tapped on the desktop. He didn't want to subject the poor guy to more pressure.

"I heard you were up for that job over at NADT," said McIntyre. "Bonham's job. Head of the whole shebang."

"That's right," Howe told him.

"You ought to take it," said McIntyre.

"That's the reason I'm calling," said Howe. "I'm trying to get opinions on the place."

"Colonel, I'll give you a whole rundown if you want. Anything you're looking for. I owe you."

"You don't owe me, Mac."

"Yes, sir, I do."

McIntyre spoke as if he were a junior officer, though during McIntyre's time in the government—which was only a few months ago, after all—he'd been the one with more authority. He would be absolutely loyal if he took the job. But Howe couldn't offer him the post; the poor guy would feel obligated to take it, and then he'd fall apart.

Still, Howe could pick his brain.

"Maybe you could give me some background," said Howe. "Informally."

"You bet. When? Now? This afternoon?"

"I'm kind of tied up today. How about tomorrow— lunch, maybe?"

"You got it, sir. You got it."

They made an appointment for noon at an out-of-the-way Italian restaurant near McIntyre's condo.

"What do you think of this Korea thing?" asked McIntyre.

"You're following it?" asked Howe.

"Oh, yeah." He laughed again. "I get a kick out of some of these commentators. CNN even called me."

"You went on TV?"

McIntyre's laughter roiled into something almost vicious. "No way."

"Let me ask you something," said Howe. "Do the North Koreans have UAVs?"

"UAVS? I don't think so. I mean . . . well, in theory you can use just about anything as a UAV. Crop duster even. I forget the last assessments. You talk to Thompson over at the CIA?"

"Actually, no."

"They have the last force estimate. He'd know because he would've worked on it. He's the guy to ask. Why?"

"Just curious."

"Dalton would have a handle on the technology if you're looking to get up-to-date on UAVs in general," said McIntyre. He was referring to the head of NADT's technical aviation section, Mark Dalton. "I'd talk to him."

"You sure they were robot planes?" the scientist asked when Howe described what he'd seen. "In *North* Korea?"

"Pretty sure. There were no cockpits, and the fuselages were fairly narrow."

Howe took the small pad of Post-it notes from the top of Dalton's computer screen and sketched out the craft. It had gull wings that extended well to the rear.

Dalton shook his head. "You sure?"

"Yup."

"Like that or like this?" He took the pen and modified the wings, making them droop more in the rear.

"Might have been like that, yeah. That's what attracted my attention."

Dalton went online and pulled up some schematics of American projects. Howe thought he saw some similarities with a Boeing project dubbed Bird of Prey that had flown in the mid-1990s. It was a manned, jet-propelled craft that tested a variety of capabilities.

"But not an exact match," said Dalton.

"No."

"How big were they?"

"I don't know." Howe didn't feel he could tell Dalton everything—like the fact that he'd been in an airplane when he'd seen them.

"Well, let's think about this. You saw two abreast in a hangar. How big was the hangar?"

"It was small, designed for a small plane, maybe an early-generation MiG. There was some space on either side and between the planes."

Dalton estimated that the aircraft might have a wingspan from ten to fifteen feet; by contrast a MiG-21, itself relatively small, would span about twenty-three and a half feet. Payload, range, speed, and other capabilities would depend on any number of factors, but Dalton envisioned a several-hundred-mile range with good endurance.

"Low radar profile," said Dalton, explaining that between the plane's small size and angles, it would probably produce a radar cross section down toward 6- or 7/10,000 of a square inch. That was not quite as good as the best American stealthy designs, but it was extremely small, and a good deal smaller than the early F-117A, which had a cross section of approximately 8/10 of a square inch on normal radar, about that of a very small bird.

"Pretty capable aircraft, if they have them. No match for a manned fighter," said Dalton, "but potentially capable."

"What would you use it for?"

"Reconnaissance. Stealthy attack. Hell, put a bomb in it and you have a long-range cruise missile."

"Thanks," Howe told the scientist.

11

The credit card Fisher had found had been used for cash advances from several ATMs in Queens, running through the daily limit of five hundred dollars with a series of small withdrawals. With no other leads, Fisher spent nearly an entire day looking at where they were, trying to find a common link. He decided that they were all within six or seven blocks of R train stops, though what that meant if anything was difficult to say.

On the other hand, there was a significant correlation with decent coffee places; while such a fact could not be undervalued in terms of its contributions toward solving a crime, it was not, in Fisher's experience, of much use in the courtroom.

"So he probably doesn't have access to a car, but he's being supplied with credit cards," said Macklin after Fisher returned to the compound and they marked out the ATMs on a large map of the city. "He's trying to disguise where he is, so he makes withdrawals from all over the place. He has the antidote for Sarin poisoning in his basement, where he's obviously playing chemist, though we're not sure why. He buys a lot of Clorox: That eliminates biological traces, you know. If he was playing with some sort of bacteria, that would kill it."

"It also cleans the toilet and whitens underwear," said Fisher. "There's a problem with connecting Faud to these ATM withdrawals."

"What's that?"

"They were made when he should have been at school."

"You don't think he had perfect attendance, do you?"

Fisher went to the computer where the task force's information was fed. An investigator had spoken to his teachers and yes, Faud Daraghmeh had decent attendance. They hadn't asked about particular dates. Fisher scrolled about halfway through the interview notes when he realized he'd missed the obvious.

"The card and the money were delivered by the guy who made the cell calls," Fisher told Macklin. "Look at the dates. They're the same."

"So?"

"How long would five hundred dollars last in New York?"

Macklin shrugged. "Twenty minutes, if you spent it right."

Fisher pulled up Faud's and then Mrs. DeGarmo's phone records—they'd gone to the phone company and gotten incoming as well as outgoing—and tried to find a pattern. A number repeated every few weeks, but to the landlady's phone.

"We check these all out?" Fisher asked Macklin.

"Not enough time to look at her numbers yet."

Fisher called the number, even though he figured it would be a relative. But the call wouldn't go through. When they checked it, the number turned out to belong to a telephone booth near the subway station near the Washington Heights apartment.

So the courier would call—preferably though not always from the phone booth—before going to Queens. The calls were always around four in the afternoon, after Faud got home and while Mrs. DeGarmo was watching the last of her "stories" before making dinner, at least as she had described her day to Fisher. Something had caused him to deviate from that schedule once—the time they had been able to trace originally—but this was the more usual routine.

"You think he answered them in his apartment?" Macklin asked.

"You're starting to get ahold of this investigating thing," Fisher told him. "Let's look at some more phone numbers, okay?"

*   *   *

The phone booth was in Staten Island, within walking distance of the ferry but not in the station. Four calls had been made on the same day as the calls to the Astoria apartment, though roughly three hours before those.

"So your theory is, he calls ahead to make sure his people are there, then comes along?" said Macklin as they walked from the booth to a nearby pizza joint for dinner.

"Probably that's just a signal for them to meet him somewhere. If you're just going to show up at the apartment, why call ahead?" said Fisher.

"He's a courier, then."

"Maybe, or maybe more important than that," said Fisher. "He got off the ferry that one day the cell phone calls were made. The question is, why was he in Staten Island? But then again, that is one of the great unanswerable questions of all time."

After two slices of killer anchovy pizza, Fisher and Macklin took a walk, crisscrossing an area roughly eight blocks from the phone booth, looking for anything the courier or whoever had made the calls had been interested in. The area was half-commercial and half-residential, and while not the busiest in the city there were plenty of people on the streets. They didn't see any mosques.

While Staten Island was part of New York City, physically it was much closer to New Jersey, which loomed to the west and north and was visible over many of the buildings they passed. Three roadways connected to New Jersey; the only way to the rest of the city was either by the ferry or the Verrazano-Narrows Bridge, which led to Brooklyn.

"Boat," said Fisher.

"Boat?"

"It's easier to get here by boat than by car."

"Okay. How does that help us?"

"It doesn't," said Fisher.

"A lot of docks and slips and stuff back that way, the other side of Front and Bay Streets."

"Yeah," said Fisher, changing direction.

"Where we going?"

"Get some smokes. And a map of the train line."

"There's a train on Staten Island?"

The Staten Island train line ran down the eastern side of the island, from St. George to Tottenville. It ran far less often than the subways did, however. It connected to the ferry stop, and Fisher saw that it was unlikely their man had taken the train: With one exception, he made his phone calls before the train arrived at the terminal.

The bus system, on the other hand, was extensive; the possibilities led almost literally all over the island. So Fisher returned by necessity to his first theory: that the courier had made the call after walking from the area on foot.

"We're not getting anywhere," said Macklin after they walked around a bit more.

Fisher did what he always did when he couldn't figure something out: He lit a cigarette.

Actually, he did that when he could figure something out too.

"It's okay, Andy. You can't break every case, and you can't always be right. Staten Island's just a red herring," said Macklin.

Fisher took a long draw and wondered if Camel had altered its blend, or if cigarettes just tasted different on Staten Island.

"Even the best gumshoe comes up dry sometimes," added Macklin. "Let's head back."

Fisher, starting to feel cold, agreed. They were waiting for the ferry when Macklin's cell phone rang.

"Going to take us a while to get there," Fisher heard Macklin say after he answered.

Then he added, "Oh."

"What's the deal?" asked Fisher.

"It was Kowalski. They tracked one of the calls to a warehouse and they want to put a team together to raid it."

"Where is it?"

"Three blocks from the pizza parlor."

CHAPTER
12

"The granite counter is a dead giveaway," said Alice, swinging her hand across the room. "When you see it in an ad, it means the place is going for over three thousand a month. But it also tells you you'll get other amenities, like the whirlpool, which isn't always mentioned."

"Like a code, huh?" asked Howe, following her as she walked through the large kitchen into a much larger dining room. She led him back out into the hallway, showing off the unit's third bathroom. A chandelier strung with crystal beads hung down in the center at about eye level in front of the mirror. It was so bright that Howe had to look away when Alice turned the light on.

"They'd have to fix that," she said.

"Make it less bright?"

"No, raise it. It's down to make it easier for cleaning."

"A lot of places have chandeliers in the bathroom?"

"It's a half-bath," she said, as if that were an explanation.

Howe gave a mumbled "Mmmph."

"Five-five a month," she said, leading him back to the living room.

"As in five thousand five hundred?" he asked.

She nodded. "They might come down a little."

Howe and the real estate agent had spent the past three hours working their way up the price chain. While he had some rough ideas now of what things cost, in truth he was no closer to knowing what sort of place he wanted to live in.

Except that this wasn't it.

"I don't know about this place," he said.

"Well, is the price range okay?"

It seemed outrageously high, but everything did. Using the base salary figures that Blitz and the others were throwing around, though, he could easily afford it. But did he want a place with a crystal chandelier in the bathroom?

"It's not so much the price as—"

"It's too ostentatious," she said, finishing his sentence.

"Yeah. I'm not that formal. I've spent most of my time in the military, and, uh, not that I don't appreciate nice houses or anything . . ." he said, flustered again. "What kind of place would *you* live in? This?"

"Here?" She laughed. "I couldn't afford this."

"Let's say you could. Where would you live?"

"Tell you what, I'm hungry," she said. "Let's get something to eat and we'll think about it some more."

"Great," said Howe.

They were just getting out of her car when Howe's cell phone rang. He fumbled getting it out of his pocket, then thought maybe he shouldn't answer; this wouldn't be a good place to get into a discussion with a senator or one of the other influential people he'd called to sound out about the post. But habit and duty conspired to make him snap it open.

"Colonel, stand by for Dr. Blitz," said Blitz's assistant.

"I have to take this," Howe told Alice.

"I'll wait."

"It's kind of—"

"Your girlfriend?"

"No, I'm not— It's business."

She had a smirk on her face; Howe thought she hadn't believed what he'd said about it not being a girlfriend. "I'll be inside," she told him. Howe watched her walk away as Blitz came on the line.

"Sorry it took so long to get back to you, Colonel. What's up?"

"I've been talking to people about those UAVs I saw in Korea," said Howe. "I think they're significant."

"UAVs? What, at the base?"

"In the hangar there. I mentioned them. And they should be in the reports. I was talking to Mark Dalton over at NADT, and to Howard McIntyre."

"How is Mac?"

"I think he's fine."

"He's a good man. We have to get him back to work."

"I'd like to talk to the CIA about what I saw," said Howe. "According to Dalton, the aircraft would be pretty potent. And we don't seem to know about it."

"Tell you what, Colonel. There's an evaluation group at the Pentagon working with some of my staff and coordinating with the intelligence community. Why don't you talk directly to them. My assistant will make the arrangements. Have you spoken to Senator Elwell yet?"

"About this?"

"No, about NADT. You haven't changed your mind, have you?"

"No, sir."

"Good. Listen, I'm going to see Elwell tonight. I'll make sure he calls you tomorrow. Thanks."

Blitz snapped off the line.

CHAPTER
13

"You're just a guest, Fisher," said Kowalski. "If we want your advice, we'll ask for it."

"I'm just saying that the thing to do would be to wait and watch for a while, see who shows up," said Fisher "We don't have any other leads."

"We will once we're inside," said Kowalski.

"Maybe. Or maybe the place is rigged to blow up when someone walks in the front door."

"See, that's where we do things differently than the FBI," said Kowalski. "We're blowing a hole through the sidewall."

"*That's* different," said Fisher.

"We don't screw around."

"Kowalski's right, Andy," said Macklin. "We can't afford to sit on this. We have to find out what's inside."

"I'm not saying sit on it." Fisher wouldn't have liked to admit it, but he was a bit miffed at being called a guest. He prided himself on the fact that he hadn't been invited to anything since his best friend's bar mitzvah twenty years ago. "If you want to go in, go through that second-story window up there. Then you can check the place out, make sure there's no explosives, and get in through the doors."

"Take too much time," said Kowalski.

"You already know from the radar it's empty," said Fisher. The DIA people had brought in a radar unit that scanned the interior of the building. In addition, they used an infrared viewer and found nothing except for two cats. "And sneaking in would give you the option of setting up a sting."

"We can still set up a sting," said Kowalski. "And besides, the DIA doesn't sneak in anywhere. Neither does Homeland Defense. Right, Macklin?"

Macklin looked at Fisher, then back at Kowalski. "I guess you're right."

Sneaking in would have been difficult in any event, as the task force safety officer insisted that the first team in wear full protective gear, in case they actually found something. Fisher thought he detected a certain healthy skepticism in the officer's remarks, something he hadn't seen much of from the rest of the task force.

The special tactics people borrowed from New York City took out the door on the loading dock by shooting out the hinges with solid lead shot. Fisher had actually never seen this done and was kind of curious about it, but the protocol called for him to stay far away until the warehouse was actually secured unless he was willing to wear a hazmat suit himself. Since that would have made it difficult to smoke, he passed on the opportunity, contenting himself with watching the team from the video feed in the van. The door seemed to pop off the building, and the men disappeared inside. Ten minutes later it was all clear. Fisher got out of the van and walked the half-block to the place, arriving as the garage-style overhead door at the front of the building was rolled upward.

"There," said one of the men, pointing to a row of large canisters against the side wall. "That looks like it."

The tanks were the sort used to hold seltzer water in large soda fountain setups. Fisher walked over and started to inspect one; Macklin, who was wearing a respirator, grabbed him.

"Preliminary hit says they're filled with liquid sarin," said Macklin. "A lot worse than that coffee you're always drinking."

"Not necessarily," said Fisher, but he backed away anyway.

CHAPTER
14

"This is my dream place."

Alice opened the door and stepped through the landing. Howe followed. The living room to the left was open to the second story, with large windows covering two walls. The woodwork was stained a dark walnut that matched the inlaid pattern in the oak. He followed inside the kitchen—another granite counter—which looked into a breakfast nook and a family room. A large fireplace sat at the far end.

The wine they'd had over dinner, not to mention the conversation, had left him in a mellow mood. Howe followed her through the house: It was a house, not a condominium, and it was for sale, not rent. Her voice echoed through the empty room like faint music, luring him onward.

And her perfume. That, too, was light, almost a suggestion of a scent rather than the smell itself. A flower tickled by the wind.

God, Howe told himself, *let's not go overboard. She's just showing me apartments.*

And houses. One house. Her dream house.

There were four bedrooms upstairs.

"Master bedroom, kids' room, guest room," said Alice. "Assuming there's kids."

"A lot of rooms."

Jesus, what a dumb thing to say.

"What do you think? Isn't it great?" she said when they reached the downstairs landing.

"Yeah," he said. He didn't trust his tongue anymore.

"Want to know the price?"

Howe shrugged. "It's kind of big."

"He'll come down, I know."

He shrugged again.

"One point two."

"How much?"

"A million two hundred thousand. But he'll come down. He built it on spec." She flicked her hair back from her shoulder. "I don't represent him, so I can tell you this. I know he'd come down a lot."

"A million dollars. God."

"Payments would be about what the condo was. Less, depending on the down payment."

"I don't know if I have a down payment."

Alice made a face. "Your company could always loan you the money."

Howe didn't answer, though he realized she was probably right.

"Oh, I know, it's my dream not yours," she said, waving her hand at him. "I have to get back."

"Date?"

"Oh, God, no. I always stop by and see my dad on Wednesdays. Should we set up another appointment?"

"I'd like to."

"Tomorrow at four?"

"Tomorrow at four. Sounds good. Your office?"

"My office."

On the way back to the real estate parking lot where he'd left his car, Howe decided he wanted to kiss her. But somehow he couldn't find the right chance. He smiled, waved, and got into his car to drive back to his motel.

The light on Howe's phone blinked steadily as he came in, indicating he had a message. The motel's voice mail system was tricky to use, and Howe finally had to call down to the desk for help. The call was from a man who said he had some questions about something Howe had told a mutual friend. The man spoke so quickly on the phone that Howe had trouble making out the phone number he left, and couldn't entirely decipher his name; it sounded like "Woeful."

It was past nine o'clock. Howe thought he'd try the number anyway; maybe if the caller had an answering machine or voice mail he'd get at least an idea what this was about.

"Wu," said the voice on the other end of the line, picking up right after the first ring.

"This is Bill Howe."

"Colonel Howe, thank you for calling me back. Where are you now?"

Howe hesitated but then told him he was in his hotel.

"There's a diner about two miles down the highway if you take a right out of your driveway," said Wu. "Can you meet me there in half an hour?"

"What's this about?" said Howe.

"I'll have to talk to you in person."

"Does this have to do with NADT?"

"I have to talk to you in person," repeated Wu.

Howe thought back to his tour of the NADT scientific sections earlier that day, trying to connect the man's voice and name with a face. But there had been too many people he either didn't know at all or had met only once or twice.

"Half hour. Sure."

Wu hung up before Howe could ask how he would recognize him.

CHAPTER
15

It turned out to be surprisingly difficult for Tyler to arrange transportation across the Korean border. Inspection teams simply weren't afforded the priority that supplies and humanitarian aid were; what's more, the group's connection to the Pentagon seemed to work against it. When Tyler found four spaces on a Navy helicopter that had to stop nearby, he practically jumped up in glee, even though it would mean leaving behind half the team and all of the people they were taking for security. Tyler hustled to the airfield with Colonel Yorn, Somers, and a CIA paramilitary officer named Jake Dempsey. They just barely made the helicopter, and had to squeeze in amid extra medical supplies the corpsmen were transporting. Things were so tight that the pilot told them they were five pounds under their permitted takeoff weight.

"Good thing I didn't have much breakfast," said Somers.

The flight took several hours and was punctuated by a stop near the DMZ to refuel. No one spoke the whole way, and expressions grew more somber as they flew. Tyler had experienced this during combat: Even the most hardened veteran and shameless wiseass tended to focus on the job ahead as zero hour drew near. But to him, this was an easy gig; he hadn't even considered the possibility that they might be fired at.

And yet, that was a real danger. From birth, North Koreans had been taught to hate Americans, and while their army and government had collapsed, their hatred surely percolated just under the surface. Two American soldiers with M16s and grenade launchers patrolled near the runway as the helicopter put down. Seeing them reminded Tyler that they were deep in enemy territory and heavily outnumbered.

A pair of Hummers waited to take them to the forward headquarters of the division hosting them. Tyler got into one with Somers, listening as the historian talked with the driver and escort. Both men started out taciturn but within a few minutes Somers's easygoing style had them relaxed and, if not quite loquacious, at least speaking in sentences and paragraphs rather than single words.

"They're curious," said the corporal behind the wheel. "I get the feeling they think we have two heads and they're looking to see where we're hiding the other."

Tyler watched Somers as he carried on similar conversations with the staff at the headquarters and then later at their billet, a villa that had apparently been vacated by a high-ranking government official during the coup. While Tyler had initially wondered whether to take the older man along, he saw now it had been a good move. In just a few hours the historian had probably done the work of a dozen toiling analysts and poll takers, eliciting candid, off-the-cuff remarks. The consensus among American service people was clear: The North Koreans would be willing to go along with things for the short term at least, so long as there were reasonable measures to both keep them safe from retribution and to feed them.

"Hungriest people I ever saw," one of the lieutenants told them.

That seemed to be the bottom line, and Tyler made sure to repeat it several times during their conference call with Moore at the end of the day. After the call, he thought maybe that was his problem as well. A full meal, a bit of rest, and he'd be ready for whatever happened in the morning.

CHAPTER

16

Howe was on his second cup of coffee when the tall man stopped in front of his booth. His round, Asian face had been marked by a double scar along the right cheek, as if he'd been scratched there by a two-fingered claw.

"Are you Howe?" asked the man.

The question took him by surprise: If Wu worked for NADT, as he'd thought, he wouldn't need to ask. And Howe didn't remember meeting anyone with a scar so prominent on his face.

If he suggested they go anywhere, Howe told himself, he'd resist.

Wu slid into the booth. The waitress came right over and he ordered a decaf coffee. When she left, he reached into his pocket and took out a thin wallet.

"I'm with the CIA," said Wu, showing his credentials. "I'm sorry to make such a production out of this. I couldn't trust your phone at the motel, and I have to have the report together in a few hours."

"Which report?" asked Howe.

"Someone on the NSC staff mentioned that you saw UAVs on the airstrip in North Korea."

Howe nodded. Wu took out a small notepad. He'd written a brief summary of one of the reports Howe had made earlier. They went over it quickly.

"That's basically what I saw," said Howe when he finished. "I didn't get that close to them."

"But they were definitely there?"

"Yes, sir, they were."

Wu nodded. He waited as the waitress arrived with his coffee, then took a few sips before continuing.

"The Koreans aren't known to have any sort of craft like this," said Wu.

"So I've heard."

"You didn't take a picture or anything?"

Howe laughed. "I'm sorry. I don't know how much you know about what I was doing there and what happened."

"I had to ask."

"I'm sure of what I saw, but only of what I saw. Whether those aircraft were real airplanes, UAVs, whatever, I don't know. I talked to someone at NADT who made some guesses about how they'd be powered and that sort of thing. I can have him get in touch with you tomorrow."

"That's all right. I think really I have enough." Wu sipped his coffee. Obviously he had access to any number of experts. "One last question: Would you agree that these aircraft should be secured and examined?"

"Absolutely."

The CIA analyst nodded, then got up and reached into his pocket for his wallet.

"I got it," Howe told him. He stayed in the booth for a while, sipping his coffee and looking at a real estate magazine he'd grabbed on the way in. He left the waitress a nice tip and headed back to the motel.

CHAPTER

17

It was Thursday, and Blitz and the CIA director always met for breakfast. The Korean crisis didn't change that, but it did make them move up their schedule and change the location of their meeting: Blitz found himself walking up the path to the director's home at five in the morning, accompanied by an aide and two NSC security escorts, Army Delta troopers in plainclothes on special assignment. He was met at the door by one of the director's own security people. Inside the kitchen he found the director's wife, Jean, presiding over a pan of home fries and another of sausage.

"Well, if I had known we would have such a good cook on duty, I would ask to meet here more often," said Blitz.

Jean gave him a good-natured but tired smile, then asked what sort of omelet he wanted.

"I told you, load him up with cholesterol," said Jack Anthony, entering from upstairs. He smelled as if he'd just come from the shower, though he was fully dressed and looked considerably more awake than his wife.

"Would you like blue cheese and mushrooms?" asked Jean.

"That would be fantastic," said Blitz. He'd meant the compliment. This was shaping up as the best meal he'd had in weeks.

Blitz and Anthony had a very complicated relationship. Professionally, the men couldn't stand each other: They were bitter rivals for power and influence, and they had come to their positions by entirely different paths. Blitz had been in and out of government and academia, and while he was acknowledged as one of the country's foremost experts on international relations, he had been appointed largely because of his long-term relationship with the President. Anthony, on the other hand, had spent his entire adult life working for the government. Much of that experience had come at the CIA, but he had also worked for the NSA, the Pentagon, and briefly the State Department. He professed to be apolitical, though his congressional connections were strongest with members of the other party.

Personally, though, the two men got along very well. Not only were they baseball fanatics, they were both Yankee fans—a minority in Washington, D.C. Anthony had been a guest speaker for Blitz several times when Blitz was teaching, and had even informally reviewed one of Blitz's books before it was published, giving him a dozen pages of useful notes.

"Let's talk for a minute," said Jack, pointing Blitz toward the nearby family room. The oldest Anthony daughter lived nearby and had recently had a baby; a playpen was set up in the corner of the room. Blitz sat on the sofa next to it, listening as Anthony quickly ran down the important points in a CIA analysis of unaccounted-for North Korean weapons. The report would be delivered as an unofficial memorandum later that morning to the NSC, which would use it to make a recommendation on further Korean operations.

"We've now accounted for all but one hundred of the fuel tubes from the reactor," said the CIA head, focusing on the most important finding.

"A hundred? That's a hell of a lot to lose."

"We haven't lost them, we just haven't found them yet," said Anthony. "That's a big difference. We're not even one hundred percent sure they're gone."

The material had been at Yonbyon, the nuclear facility roughly sixty miles north of the capital. A large number of the fuel rods had been recovered or accounted for, but even a few dozen could present a serious threat. While processing their fuel into a bomb would probably be beyond the capabilities of all but a handful of governments, the material could be used in a so-called dirty weapon, spreading radioactive waste in a high-value site.

"These weren't used for another bomb?" Blitz asked.

"We haven't completely ruled that out," said Anthony. "But we have a handle on the bomb facilities and it seems unlikely."

"Accounting for the fuel tubes has to have the highest priority," said Blitz.

"Agreed."

They broke for breakfast, the conversation turning to the new grandchild. Jane stayed for a few minutes, then excused herself to go take a shower. When she was gone, Anthony and Blitz resumed their discussion of what to do next in North Korea. All of the ballistic missile sites had been secured, and separate teams had already completed preliminary reports on the technology. According to Anthony, there were no surprises: American intelligence had already done a decent job of psyching out the capabilities of the weapons.

The Koreans' small store of cruise missiles—primitive weapons based on a Russian antiship missile—were all accounted for. Several stores of chemical weapons that had not been listed on reports prior to the coup had been found. As of yet, records to check the inventories had not been located.

"What about the E-bomb?" Blitz asked.

Anthony shook his head. "Still looks like they snookered us on that. Two members of the Korean security police were arrested in Japan last night, and it's possible one of them was Colonel Howe's passenger."

"I doubt that," said Blitz. "Too low-level." His main candidate was the head of the DPRK intelligence, who had not been heard from since twelve hours before the coup. "Colonel Howe mentioned seeing some UAVs, or possible UAVs," added Blitz, remembering his conversation with Howe.

"One of our people checked into that. He's recommending a check at the site."

"As a CIA operation?"

"We don't have the resources at the moment," admitted Anthony.

"Perhaps we should run a military operation through the NSC," suggested Blitz.

"Might be an idea, if you can arrange it." Anthony took a sip of his coffee. "Is Howe going over to NADT?"

"He's the top candidate," said Blitz.

"I wonder if Howe is the right man for the job," said Anthony. "He's an outsider to Washington. And he was only a colonel."

"He's had a good deal of experience. He was responsible for the Velociraptors and has worked with NADT."

Blitz wondered if Anthony saw Howe as a potential political threat. The CIA did not deal with NADT on any sort of regular basis, but whoever took over as head of the agency would be at least a potential power in Washington.

"Is there something else about Colonel Howe I should know?" Blitz asked.

Anthony shrugged. "We're initiating an intelligence review in connection with the Korean operation."

"How does that affect him?"

"Just that he was part of it."

"He had nothing to do with the intelligence," said Blitz.

"It's odd that he was connected with that, and with a plot to steal one of America's most advanced weapons."

"He's not connected at all," said Blitz.

The matter was of more than passing importance, since it represented a potential scandal: He could just imagine what an unfriendly congressional committee would do with the information that the U.S. government had helped a Korean villain escape. Howe's involvement could be especially problematic; Blitz wondered whether his appointment should be delayed until they had captured the man.

The doorbell rang: Anthony's driver and aides had arrived. The conversation turned to more generic, benign matters. Blitz fretted about what to do. A review of the Korean matter could easily take months.

A way would have to be found to shortcut the process. In the meantime . . .

In the meantime?

One of the aides had the morning news summary with him, a compilation of important items prepared for the President and other top members of the administration. For a change, the item leading the roundup wasn't from Korea: A joint task force headed by Homeland Security and the DIA, with help from the New York City Police Department and a long list of others, had found a cache of sarin gas in a warehouse on Staten Island.

Anthony pointed out that the discovery had been made by the group originally put together to investigate the E-bomb rumor.

"So it wasn't a total waste after all," he said. "Keystone Kops stumbled onto the real thing."

Blitz made a mental note to call Jack Hunter at the FBI and congratulate him—and see whether the connection was just a coincidence as it appeared.

As the others went out to the car, Anthony held Blitz back for a second.

"About that review," said Anthony. "We've suspended security clearances for everyone involved."

"What?" said Blitz.

"It's routine."

"Like hell," said Blitz.

"Don't get mad, Professor. The review isn't going to take that long."

"Are you trying to torpedo Howe's appointment?"

"Absolutely not."

Blitz knew a lie when he heard one, but there was nothing he could do about it at the moment.

18

Fisher had a prime seat for the press conference: back near the coffee and doughnuts laid out for the media types. That meant he couldn't get a good view of Macklin and Kowalski as they smiled for the cameras: another plus.

It was a crowded podium. Besides Macklin and Kowalski, the city mayor, the police commissioner, the local federal attorney, the governor, and the district attorney from Staten Island were all on the stage at Gracie Mansion in Manhattan to announce the triumph. So much for setting up a sting.

They had, at least, made an arrest on the person who had leased the warehouse. He was an Egyptian émigré who'd been in America for four years. His name was Said Ahmet, and he claimed he had rented it to people who wanted to store auto parts. The story was so lame that Fisher was tempted to believe it. In the meantime, warrants had been arranged for several business associates of Ahmet, and city detectives were out looking for them. Faud, who had not been connected to the warehouse except by Fisher's roundabout logic, was now on a list of people to be apprehended but his name and description were not being released to the press.

If Fisher had had his way, nothing would be released to the press, and there would be no press conference at all. But at least the cheese blintzes were good.

"Andy, it's been great working with you," said Macklin after the TV cameras shut down.

"You going on vacation?"

"No. The case is closed."

"No it's not," said Fisher.

"Well, yeah, we have to wrap up loose ends and such. But Jeez, Fisher, don't you ever relax? We celebrate today, take off a long weekend, then come back and kick down doors Monday."

"Whose doors?"

"It's a figure of speech. Besides, you're out of here."

"How do you mean that?" asked Fisher, shaking out a fresh cigarette.

"Your assignment only lasted until we broke the case. I'm supposed to give you back to the Bureau as soon as I can. The case is closed. We'll be turning it all over to the U.S. attorney anyway and disbanding the task force. So thanks." He held out his hand.

"Who says we broke the case?"

Macklin just about crossed his eyes.

"We still don't understand the connection between the E-bomb and the sarin gas." Fisher hated stating the obvious, even to a fellow investigator, but there seemed no other choice.

"There is no connection. God, you're the guy who figured that out. You said—"

"That alone ought to be enough to bother you," said Fisher, walking away.

PART FOUR

Heroes and Other Players

CHAPTER

1

Tyler tapped the keys of his laptop, jotting the notes about the performance of the different weapons systems as the major assigned to brief him continued. Though he wasn't here to evaluate weapons or the unit's performance, Tyler let the officer vent. He was complaining about the failure of the coordinated information system that was supposed to provide battlefield commanders with coordinated real-time information from a variety of sources. Potentially revolutionary in design—in theory, the smallest fighting unit would have access to battlefield intelligence that only a few years before would have been hard to get at any level—the system was prone to failure. In place of real-time topographic maps with enemy positions, soldiers had found blue screens on the vehicle displays, laptops, and handheld computers they had carried into battle.

The NCOs were especially bitter, noted the major, as they'd been complaining for months about the systems. Tyler knew that while the sergeants generally ran the show, the upper-level people rarely paid enough attention to their advice. As a captain, he'd worked hard to be different; he knew a lot of other officers—this major undoubtedly was one—did, too, but the split between enlisted and officer was somehow ingrained in the culture.

Somers seemed amused by the failures of technology. He sat back on his metal folding chair, finger against his lip as he listened.

"The key point here," said the historian as the major's tirade finally ran out of steam, "is that your people found suitable work-arounds at the crisis point. Which to my mind illustrates their resourcefulness and training. It requires a supportive command structure as well. So, despite the technology screwups, once more the human factor came to the fore."

"Sure. Of course," said the major.

"The NCOs and the officers did well despite having one hand tied behind their backs with the technology screwups."

"And the men."

"Absolutely," said the officer.

Had the praise come from Tyler, it would have probably been dismissed as ass-kissing, or worse. But Somers made it sound more important and somehow more genuine. He was right, of course: The fact of the matter was that the Army had done well not because of its cutting-edge doodads—they'd screwed up—but because of its training and a command structure and culture that emphasized personal initiative in combat.

As they turned to the matter at hand, the major proved insightful and well connected; he picked up a phone and arranged a helicopter for a tour of several units to the east in the countryside.

"Did you butter him up on purpose?" Tyler asked Somers as they walked toward the chopper later.

"Butter him up?" Somers made a face. "Sometimes it's important to state the obvious. We lose track of it. This was the sort of advance that will be studied for a long time. Partly it succeeded because it was made against a demoralized, ill-equipped army that had no reason to fight. But such armies have surprised generals for centuries. Napoléon, Guderian, Burgoyne. Studying failure is instructive," added the historian as he pulled himself up into the Blackhawk. "The technology has to be straightened out. But we can't let the shortcomings obscure the successes."

Even from the helicopter, the poverty of the North Koreans was clear. Roads were rutted and empty, houses in the countryside were little more than shacks and often in disrepair. The country's abject state was almost a caricature. How, Tyler wondered, could a ruler so badly fail his people?

The translator, a South Korean on loan to the group, was somewhat prejudiced against the peasants they spoke to after putting down at a forward outpost. He shook his head as he explained that the people had no idea what they would eat when winter came.

"Ask if they have guns," said Tyler.

The translator practically rolled his eyes, but he asked. There had been rumors that the government had handed out weapons shortly before its fall, but these seemed false, at least here.

"We do not need guns, we need rice," said one old man when they asked.

They made four stops, spending much of the day talking to anyone they could find: American officers, sergeants, privates, and any North Korean brave enough to come near.

"They think of Americans as devils and look for your tails," said the translator at one point. He didn't seem to be joking.

"So?" asked Somers as they trudged toward their temporary headquarters at the end of the day. "What have we learned?"

Tyler smiled at the academic's pedantic style but played

along. "That North Korea is a hellhole and that we have to get these people food fast."

"And?"

"And what?"

"Can they mount a guerrilla campaign?"

"Some of the units are still intact. There are still weapons. But the population won't support it."

"I agree," said Somers. "What's really interesting, though, is the animosity between North and South," Somers continued. "You saw our translator, and the people's reactions to him. They thought he was arrogant."

"Sure," said Tyler.

"You don't think that's important?"

"Do you?" said Tyler.

"The friction is important," explained Somers. "I know you're here basically to see what the potential for resistance is from a military point of view, but the underlying realities are also important. Back home, people think that North and South want to be reunited. They think of Germany at the end of the Cold War. There is a lot of that, don't get me wrong. But there's also friction, as we've just seen. The North Koreans are looking at us with curiosity. They haven't formed real opinions yet. But they do know the South. Or at least they think they do. And vice versa."

"Okay," said Tyler, nodding.

Somers smiled. "It wouldn't be a minor matter to you if you were in charge of keeping the peace in a rural town. Think about it. For the most part you'd be relying on South Korean translators, and probably technical experts, to get the water running and electricity flowing. Could you trust what the translators were saying? Could you trust the people he spoke with to be open and honest?"

"Good points," said Tyler.

"I assume you were pointing out the obvious and not buttering me up."

Tyler laughed. As they turned toward the administrative building where they'd been assigned space, an MP came up in a Hummer.

"Major Tyler?"

"That's me."

"Sir, I need you to come to the secure communications center."

Tyler started to tell the soldier that he would be along after checking in with the rest of his group, which was waiting inside. But before he could say anything the MP added, "Major, you're wanted on the line to Washington immediately."

Tyler was surprised to find that the call wasn't from the Pentagon but rather an NSC staffer, who immediately began quizzing him about Tacit Ivan. The major answered the questions warily; he'd of course heard what had happened to Howe and was afraid that someone—maybe even Howe—was being set up as a sacrificial lamb for the failure of intelligence that had led to the botched mission. After a few routine questions about when they'd arrived there and how his men had infiltrated the field, the staffer began asking questions about the airstrip.

"Were you close enough to the field at Pong Yan to see into the hangar at the southeastern end?"

"Personally?" asked Tyler.

"Yes, sir."

"I couldn't see inside. But I didn't have an angle to look at it. I wasn't on the base."

"Who was?"

Tyler gave the names of the team that had infiltrated the abandoned base. The staffer then asked if Tyler had seen UAVs at the field, or heard about them.

"You mean, flying reconnaissance for us?" asked Tyler. "We were there by ourselves."

"No, sir, I mean based at the field. North Korean assets."

"Not that I know of."

"Yes, sir. Please hold the line."

Before Tyler could say anything, Dr. Blitz came on the line.

"Ken, how are you?"

"I'm very well, sir," he said cautiously.

"You saw no UAVs at the field?"

"No, sir."

"Are you in a position to get up there now?"

"I, uh, can be if you want me to."

"I do. Colonel Brott will get back to you with whatever orders you need. The sooner the better on this," added the national security advisor. "Tomorrow morning if not tonight."

"Yes, sir," said Tyler. "Right away."

"One other thing, Major. You enlisted Colonel Howe in the operation, didn't you? Initially," added Blitz.

"Yes, sir. He was the only person qualified to fly the aircraft. It was suggested by one of the CIA planners on the mission staff originally who'd been briefing the Russian flights; they had been touring the country the week before."

"Was he eager to go on the mission?"

"I think he wanted to do his duty. The, uh—to be candid, Tacit Ivan wasn't seen exactly as the first choice."

"Did Colonel Howe know that?"

"He might have figured it out."

"Did he push it?"

"No, sir. He just answered questions, that sort of thing. At one point I think he did volunteer to go—I mean, that was kind of implicit in his coming over, since he would have known that he was the only pilot available."

"But *you* suggested the mission."

"*We* suggested it to *him*, yes."

"Very good," said Blitz. "On this UAV project: You report directly to me. No one else is authorized to receive the information. Anything you need to do to accomplish the mission, anyone you want along—well, you know the drill. But otherwise strictly need-to-know. Strictly."

"Okay."

"Stand by for Colonel Brott."

CHAPTER

2

Andy Fisher believed strongly in the value of sharing intelligence with brother agencies. Especially when cooperation might lead to the rapid conclusion of a case.

"Great bagels on Fourteenth Street," he told Kowalski, dropping the bag on his desk at the Defense Intelligence Center in D.C. The DIA agent had returned to D.C. following the press conference announcing the sarin bust.

"Fisher, you got past security without being arrested? I can't believe it."

"Yeah, pretty slack. Hey, these are nice digs," he said, glancing around. "You'd never know it used to be a laundry room."

"What brings you here? You want to change careers and start working for the good guys for a change?"

"No, actually, I wanted to tell you that you were right."

"You know, we have a doctor on call," said Kowalski, a concerned look on his face. "He'll give you sedatives."

Fisher laughed.

"You really *are* sick, aren't you?" said Kowalski.

"Talk to me about the E-bomb intelligence. How good was it?"

Utterly confused, Kowalski got up and went to his door. When he had closed it, he returned to his desk and sat down. "You all right, Andy? You look a little . . . ragged."

"You mean that as a compliment?" asked Fisher, reaching into his pocket and taking out his cigarettes.

"You can't smoke in here."

Fisher put the pack away.

"I was kidding before, but now I know you're sick."

"So tell me about the weapon," said Fisher. "Why did we stop taking that seriously?"

"Everybody thinks it's smoke," said Kowalski. "It was part of a plan to get some big shot out of Korea before the shit hit the fan."

Fisher listened to the details of Tacit Ivan.

"After what happened to you in Moscow, everybody should have realized this was a setup," said Kowalski. "The whole deal. They showed you the real scientist, then pulled the switch in Korea."

"Maybe," said Fisher. "What about the bomb plans? Were they real or not?"

"Experts said they were. Sure."

"And we don't have the guy who sent them."

"Probably dead the second he got back to Korea from Russia."

Fisher settled back in the seat. Whoever Howe transported had figured out somehow that the scientist wanted to defect and had decided he might be a useful insurance policy in case he needed to get out. But that didn't mean that the E-bomb didn't exist. On the contrary, it argued that it did.

Unless the whole thing was a setup from the beginning, which was possible.

"If this guy has that much power, why doesn't he escape himself?" said Fisher. "Just get on the plane and go to Moscow instead of sending Dr. Park?"

"Because he's more afraid of his own people than us," said Kowalski. "They must hate him. And they'd recognize him. Besides, he's got too much to lose to just walk out. He only pulls the plug when the shit's hitting the fan."

Fisher reached for his cigarettes. "How do I go about finding Colonel Howe these days?"

CHAPTER 3

The ship appeared in the distance. It was a small tanker, riding low in the water as if carrying fuel, though as a man who had spent his whole life on land, Kuong did not appreciate this piece of deception.

What he did appreciate was the tarpaulin-covered deck amidships. His revenge.

The helicopter swooped lower, its skids within six feet of the deck at the stern. There was not enough space for it to land, but Kuong was prepared. He opened the door and stepped out, grasping the line at the side that had been prepared for him. He lowered himself slowly, using his feet rather than his hands to control the brief descent. As he reached the deck he handed his thick gloves to the crewman who had come to assist him, then turned and opened his arms to the captain, a childhood friend who was one of the few men in the world he would trust with his life.

The captain folded him against his chest, then turned and yelled an order.

The helicopter had begun to rise, starting away. There was a light swoosh nearby, a plume of smoke as the ship's crewman fired an antiair missile. A half-second later the shoulder-launched SAM struck the helicopter. Kuong turned to watch as the aircraft stuttered forward in the sky for a few meters before bowing down into the waves.

Things were proceeding very well indeed.

CHAPTER 4

The NADT security people looked embarrassed and even pained, but neither would budge nor say anything except that they were following their directions. Colonel Howe was not permitted in the facility.

"All right, get me Nancy Meile," Howe said finally, asking for the head of security.

"Sorry, sir, she's unavailable."

"She's not here, or she's not available?"

"Not available, sir."

Howe knew from experience that Meile generally did not schedule meetings after eight A.M., just so she could be available to the security details. Nonetheless, he asked for the shift supervisor. He was told the man was also unavailable.

"And my access is denied?"

"Your clearance expired." The guard twisted the screen around so Howe could see it from the car. The other man came over to the window and squatted down. "Sir, it's probably just a computer glitch, we know. But we can't let you past. It's the rules. It would be our jobs if we did. We're sorry. It's not like we don't know who you are."

The man rose. Howe knew the guards were just doing their duty—and that they were in no-win positions. They probably thought he'd have them fired when his appointment was made official.

On the other hand, they could also be fired immediately for letting him through now.

"All right," he said, stifling his anger, "I know it's nothing personal. Just do your jobs."

The guards nodded grimly as he backed up to turn around.

Howe's first call was to Delano, who apparently was in the same meeting as the security people. Howe didn't bother leaving a message.

He put in a call to Blitz and ended up talking to his assistant, who of course was sympathetic but had no idea what was up. She promised to have the national security advisor call, but warned him it might be a while: The Korea situation had made him even busier than normal.

Howe ended up at a diner, thinking things through.

Halfway through his first cup of coffee he decided it had to be just a computer glitch. He called Meile and left a message, asking her to get back to him; he did the same with Delano. The second cup of coffee made him suspicious once more and he made a call to a friend of his who worked in the Joint Chiefs of Staff J2 intelligence section and asked for some background on how the clearance system worked, explaining what had happened. His friend told him mistakes were certainly possible, though the circumstances seemed odd. The fact that he hadn't been notified argued for a mistake. But his friend had no way of finding out why the clearance had been cut, and he was too busy today to hunt around. Howe thanked him anyway. He was just hitting the End button on his cell phone when Andy Fisher came into the diner and walked over to his booth.

"Colonel Howe. How's the coffee?"

"Andy Fisher. What are you up to?"

"Looking for you," said the FBI agent, sliding into the booth.

"Excuse me, sir," said the waitress coming over. "You can't smoke in here."

"Don't those laws annoy you?" asked Fisher.

The waitress was unmoved. Fisher asked for a cup of coffee but made no sign of extinguishing the cigarette.

"You're looking for me?" Howe asked.

"All morning," said Fisher.

"What for?"

The waitress reappeared with two coffee cups: one filled with coffee, and one with water to extinguish the cigarette.

"I heard you took a trip overseas," said Fisher as the waitress walked away.

"I can't talk about that," said Howe.

"Sure you can. My clearance is higher than yours."

You don't know how true that is, thought Howe.

"Obviously, I already know about Korea," said Fisher.

Howe didn't answer.

"Look, Colonel, I can get the paperwork and the official orders to make you spill the beans if I have to, but what's the sense?" asked Fisher. "Making me spend the whole day chasing down my boss, the military liaison, the NSC people—you know how many cups of coffee that's going to take?"

"Let's go for a ride," Howe suggested. "We can't talk here."

It was the sort of deal Fisher appreciated: straightforward tit-for-tat, no strings. Howe would tell him everything he knew without making him go through the bureaucratic rigmarole to get proper authorization. In exchange, Fisher would use his wiles to find out who had pulled his clearance.

"It's not that I don't trust the people I'm asking already," Howe told him. "I just want to make sure."

"Oh, I get it," said Fisher, who was now curious himself to find out who was screwing Howe and why.

As it turned out, though, Howe's description of what had happened in Korea and Japan gave Fisher no more insight than what Kowalski had told him.

"Had to be somebody very, very important," said Fisher. "Close to the top. Somebody the military would know."

"A general or somebody?"

"At least." Fisher's list of missing North Korean leaders was extensive and started with Kim Jong Il himself.

"Thing that bugs me is why they didn't kill you when they had the chance," said Fisher. "He just knocked you out."

Howe shrugged. "I made him get rid of his gun."

"Probably had another one. Or he should have. Sets this up so carefully—probably covered a dozen bases with people—then doesn't kill you? You sure there isn't a deposit in a bank account somewhere I ought to know about?"

"Fuck you," said Howe.

"What did he hit you with?"

"I didn't see."

"What's the doctor say?"

"Something hard."

"Big or small?"

"Hard."

"Maybe it was a gun that couldn't fire," suggested Fisher. "It jammed or something. Maybe it was your lucky day."

"I guess."

Howe was the touchy type; the bank account question still bugged him. Most likely he thought his honor besmirched. *Tough to live like that around here,* thought Fisher, though it wasn't useful to point out.

"You don't believe in luck, Colonel?" Fisher asked.

"Not hardly."

"Luck is greatly undervalued in America. Except by people who play the lottery." Fisher took a puff of his cigarette. "I would lay money that they're looking for you now."

"Why?"

"Because you can identify who it was who got away."

"I can't," said Howe. "I've already looked at all sorts of pictures. The debriefers had me do that at the embassy."

"Yeah, but the bad guy doesn't know that. You being followed?"

Howe twisted his head to look. "Am I?"

"I don't think so. Let me off up there." He pointed to a convenience store just ahead.

"What about your car?"

"Ah, it's a Bureau car, don't worry about it," said Fisher. "You're not going back to the diner, are you?"

"I'll take you back if you want."

"Actually, I don't," said Fisher.

"Fine."

"Fine."

Howe stopped the car. Fisher dug into his pocket and pulled out a business card. "Day or night, you call me," he said, tapping his satellite phone. "This sucker always rings."

"You're going to keep your end of the bargain, right?"

"I will. One more favor," added Fisher.

"What?"

"You see my boss, don't give him the number. Okay? I'm pretty sure the paperwork on it got lost before it made his desk."

CHAPTER

5

Disaster had followed disaster. Providence had saved Faud from being arrested like the others, but the news of the raid on the warehouse in Staten Island shocked him. For surely the all-knowing God could have prevented such a catastrophe.

Blasphemy. It was a grave sin even to think that.

Faud knew sin. He knew sin very well. He was trying to redeem himself, purify his soul as it must be purified.

Was this God's way of testing him? Or was Faud's way to paradise being blocked by a devil?

Surely it was the latter. Faud heard it in the boasts on the TV in the corner of the store, the policemen bragging that they had stopped a "nefarious plot."

Nefarious. What precisely did that word mean?

"Terrible," said the woman behind the counter. Her skin was dark; she came from Pakistan. But he knew where she stood before she continued. "It shames us all. And makes it more difficult."

"Yes," Faud told her. He handed over a dollar for the newspaper. The system of passing messages was complicated: One paper would have a key or a clue referring to another. In this case he needed the *Times* to know which classified in the other to follow.

"What do you do?" demanded a voice behind him.

Faud froze. He was the only other person in the store, so it was clear he was being addressed.

Had they caught him too?

He turned slowly to face the person who had spoken. He saw with some relief that it was only the middle-aged black man who ran the store.

"What do you do?" asked the man again.

"I'm a student."

"I meant, what do you do about these terrible things?" said the man, shaking his head.

Faud nodded and started to leave.

"Wait!" said the woman at the counter.

Faud turned to her. Something in her eye showed him he had given himself away.

Fear had betrayed him. He was unworthy; his cowardice was shameful in the sight of angels.

"You forgot your change," she said.

He forced a smile, went back for the money. Hopefully this would end soon.

CHAPTER
6

Blitz rushed into his office, head tilted forward, walking so fast that he nearly bowled Mozelle over. As if the difficulties in Korea weren't enough, the Israelis had just launched a massive raid against Palestinian terror groups, rounding up more than a hundred leaders of Hamas. Under other circumstances Blitz might have applauded the move, but it came at a particularly bad time: The U.S. secretary of state was due in the region next week for the latest round of peace talks, and now there were sure to be reprisals and more unrest. Blitz's staff was already working on a paper listing potential fallout.

"Colonel Howe needs to talk to you," said Mozelle as she backed up to let him pass.

"God, I forgot all about him. Did John call about the CIA review?"

"He was going to e-mail you."

Blitz dropped into his chair behind his desk, grumbling to himself. He wasn't sure exactly what to tell Howe, but he couldn't let the poor guy hang out there, either.

"Coffee?" asked Mozelle. She'd already figured out the answer: A fresh cup was in her hand.

"Thanks."

"Where do you want to start?" she asked.

"Better get Howe on the line," he told her. "Might as well get that over with."

"Then you'll want to talk to Keiger at State."

"All right."

Blitz opened his e-mail queue and began going through his messages. He was about three e-mails in when Mozelle buzzed through, indicating Howe was on the line.

"Colonel, I'm sorry," said Blitz immediately, without waiting for Howe to say anything. "The CIA is throwing a roadblock up."

"That's why my clearance was pulled?"

"It'll be restored. They moved ahead before I could cut it off." Blitz had decided to simply have interim clearances posted through his office; he scanned the list of his e-mails to see if he had received confirmation that this would happen.

"What's going on?" Howe asked. "Am I being screwed here? Because if I'm being screwed, I don't want the job. The hell with it."

"Colonel . . . Bill. You have to calm down. This is unfortunately something that occasionally happens around here. I'll deal with it. I promise you, I'll deal with it. What happened was that the CIA launched a review, and as part of the standard practice, certain individuals who aren't under immediate control—say, a military person still working in a certain area—the clearance gets—"

"The CIA is screwing me?"

"It's not clear, precisely," said Blitz, who wasn't about to stick up for the agency. "On the one hand, the investigation has nothing to do with you. But on the other hand, they may be using it—*may*, I emphasize—they may just be trying to put pressure on. You're in a bit of a unique position. It's possible that they're looking for you to genuflect."

"You know what they can do with that."

Blitz drew a breath.

"Colonel, let me ask you a question," he said. "You knew nothing about the Korea operation until the Pentagon contacted you, correct?"

"That's a question?"

"Yes."

"I didn't know anything about it, no."

"And you've already told several people everything that happened."

"Absolutely."

"Then there's not going to be a problem. One of my aides will clear this up for you. As a matter of fact, it may already have been cleared up. In the meantime, you can just go about talking to the board members."

"How the hell am I supposed to do that?"

There were already two other lights lit on his phone, the next calls he had to make. Blitz decided to push on: Either Howe would stick with him or not. He couldn't afford any more time on this today.

"It's important that NADT be headed by someone with your experience and abilities," Blitz told him. "This isn't a roadblock, this is a pothole. Please don't get discouraged."

"Right." Howe hung up, clearly unhappy.

Blitz hit the Next button, moving ahead.

CHAPTER

7

Fisher had the cabdriver drop him off behind the department store that sat next to the diner. He waited for the cab to drive off, then went over to the Dumpster near the loading dock. The aroma mixed stale aftershave with week-old fish, and it got ten times worse when he opened the lid. But Fisher had given his nose for his country before; he took a step away, gulped semifresh air, then came back and began climbing up on the garbage bin.

"Yo, dude, what you up to?" said a store worker, appearing from the back.

"Stargazing," said Fisher, putting his hands on the roof and pulling himself up.

"Dude. Dude," said the store worker below as Fisher got up to the top. The roof was covered with tar, and Fisher realized he'd have to try vouchering the shoes on his expense account. But there was nothing to be done; he walked out to the end of the roof, peering over the side toward the parking lot where he'd left his car.

The car was there. If someone was watching it, they weren't being obvious about it.

"Yo, dude, you can't climb up on our roof, man," said the store employee, who'd climbed up after him.

"You don't think?" asked Fisher.

"What are you doing, dude?"

"FBI," Fisher said.

"Really. Like, whoa. Cool. You got, like, a badge?"

"Sure," said Fisher, without showing it to him. "I'm, like, with the roof-climbing division. We're checking to see if there have been any UFO landings here."

"No shit, whoa," said the kid. He turned his eyes toward the sky. "I think I saw a flying saucer the other week."

"You filed the report?"

"Wasn't me, dude."

Fisher went back to the spot where he'd climbed up.

"Hey, dude, I think I'm stuck in this tar."

"I'll send a helicopter."

On the ground, Fisher tracked around the back of the lot adjoining the diner, still looking to see if anyone was watching his car. Finally he went back inside, going up to the counter to order a takeout coffee. A man in the front booth near the window got up promptly and left; Fisher turned and watched him, trying to decide if he'd seen the man earlier or not. There was a problem in the kitchen about an order of hash browns after the eleven A.M. cutoff; by the time Fisher got his coffee, the man had driven off.

Fisher took a sip from his cup and surveyed the area. Either the surveillance operation on Howe was pretty good or it was nonexistent.

Or they had other places to watch.

Fisher went back inside to use the restroom, checking again to see if there were any obvious henchmen inside; henchmen, in his experience, were always obvious.

Outside, he went back to his car. He was just reaching for the door when he noticed there was something on the pavement underneath the back.

"Shit," he yelled as he threw himself down.

As he hit the ground the ground, the car exploded.

CHAPTER

8

Howe's conversation with Blitz had left him even more frustrated and angry. He drove around for a while, debating with himself whether to just go home and say, "The hell with everything."

This was exactly what he hated about Washington: bullshit political games. Why in the world did he think NADT would be different?

Belatedly, he remembered he'd told McIntyre to meet him for lunch. He made it to the restaurant only ten minutes late; McIntyre didn't appear concerned at all, and claimed he hadn't even noticed the time.

"Drinks?" asked the waitress.

"I'll have a beer," said Howe. It was clear he wasn't getting any real work done today.

"Not for me," said McIntyre. "Can't," he explained to Howe when she left.

McIntyre and Howe had not been close before Howe saved his life, but the former NSC aide was well known as an after-hours partyer, and the few times that Howe had lunch with him McIntyre had at least two drinks. He had also been more than a little full of himself, smarter than nearly everyone he dealt with and quick to admit it. But now he seemed humbled—not shattered so much as sobered.

"Are you really sick?" Howe asked.

"I was stressed. I'm dealing with it. I'm better than I was a few weeks ago, and I was better then than a few weeks earlier than that." He took a sip of his seltzer. "I don't know if there's an okay. I take an antidepressant, and I'm not supposed to drink alcohol, so I don't."

He shrugged.

"You were depressed?" asked Howe. "Like suicide?"

"No, it's more like being, I don't know . . . anxious? Super nervous? Like you have this adrenaline rush but no energy. And edgy." McIntyre shrugged again. "The doctor has all these metaphors. Basically, he calls it post-traumatic stress because of what happened in Kashmir. I killed somebody."

"You had to," said Howe.

"No. It was a mistake, what I'm talking about. It's not in the, uh, reports. It was a kid. I'd take it back but I can't." McIntyre took another sip of his soda. "You can't change things."

Howe saw no obvious signs of distress. If anything, the man sitting in the booth across from him seemed more analytical, more reasoned, than the one he'd known as a member of the NSC.

"You think you could hold down a job at NADT?" Howe asked.

"I don't know. I think so."

Howe looked up as the waitress arrived. He hadn't planned on offering McIntyre a position; he'd thought yesterday after talking to him that he wouldn't because of McIntyre's psychological stress or problems or whatever. But if Howe was going to take the job at NADT, he needed somebody exactly like him to help.

So he wasn't bailing out, then.

"What exactly are you thinking?" asked McIntyre.

Howe told him that he was looking for someone who would have a pretty high rank, preferably a vice president, who could deal with the political end of things.

"Me?"

"Is it the sort of thing you'd be interested in?" Howe asked.

"Well . . ."

McIntyre said nothing else for a while. Their sandwiches came; they ate in silence.

"I think the situation you were in, it was a tremendous jolt," said Howe. "I don't blame you for getting sick. I might have myself."

"No." McIntyre shook his head gently. "No. You and I are different. It's okay, you can say it."

"I don't know," said Howe honestly. "If uh, if I had to kill someone face-to-face—I don't know."

"Well, I didn't really have to kill him, did I? Because I screwed up."

Neither man spoke for several minutes.

"I think you can do the job," said Howe finally. "I think you'd do well."

"I might be able to do it, for you," said McIntyre. "For you. Because there would be a lot of people with their knives out. A lot."

"Like the CIA?" Howe explained that his clearance had been mysteriously pulled.

"Interesting," said McIntyre. "But . . . it might be just routine. Depends on who's running the investigation. Or it could be an excuse."

"How do you tell the difference?"

McIntyre smiled. "You can't."

"What's the best way to get it restored?"

"Well, if the professor says he's on it, he is," said McIntyre.

"He doesn't play politics?"

"Oh, he plays politics. He plays pretty damn hard. But if he says something like that, he means it. Besides, he sees you as one of his people."

"He does?"

"Sure. And there's a possibility this was aimed at him. All sorts of games go on, Colonel. You wouldn't believe."

"That's why I need somebody like yourself. You. Assuming I get the job."

"Blitz wants you. That should be enough. His stock is pretty high right now. And he's always been tight with the President. Have you talked about filling out the board?"

"No."

"There are a number of vacancies. You'd want some input."

"I haven't a clue who should be on it."

"People who like you." McIntyre laughed, but Howe could tell he was being serious.

"How do I get them on the board?"

"You *do* need me, don't you?" A little bit of the old McIntyre peeked through, a broad grin appearing on his face. Then the humbler version returned, his eyes cast toward the table. "I'll talk to some people for you and get the lay of the land."

"I'm taking you at your word that it wasn't you," Fisher told Jack Hunter as they surveyed the bombed-out hulk of the car.

"I'm glad you can laugh at a time like this," his boss told him. "I'm glad you can laugh."

"I ain't laughing," said Fisher.

The bomb had obliterated the car and shattered the windows of the diner. Two people inside had been cut by the glass, one severely. Fisher had lost his entire cup of coffee and crushed a half package of cigarettes. Otherwise he'd suffered only a few nicks and bruises.

"This is government property they destroyed," said Hunter. "This really pisses me off."

FBI agents and the local police were scouring the woods across the street and checking the surrounding area looking for evidence. Fisher theorized that someone had watched and waited for him to come out before pressing a remote control to detonate the bomb. Because of that, he couldn't be one hundred percent sure that the attempt was related to Howe or even the case he was working on: Too many people with access to explosives hated his guts.

But it seemed sensible to him to assume that it was related to Howe, and that the retired colonel was the real target; under that scenario he was a kind of consolation prize. Maybe the person watching thought he had spotted the bomb and worried that it might yield clues about his identity. Or maybe they just like to see things go boom.

"Look at this damage," Hunter practically moaned.

"Shame," said Fisher. "Less and less diners to go around."

The crime scene people had already set up shop, and now two in their white baggy suits asked Fisher and

Hunter to move off to the side so they could finish taking their samples.

"At least we know the E-bomb's real," said Fisher.

"How do you figure that?"

"Has to be."

"Don't give me that shit, Fisher. How do you figure that? Where's your proof? *This?*"

"I have to prove one and one is two?"

"By your math, one and one is a hundred and twenty-seven."

Fisher ignored the obvious reference to his expense chits.

"We have to get some security people on Howe," he told Hunter. He'd already tried calling the colonel's cell phone but it was apparently turned off.

"I'll talk to the White House about it," said Hunter.

"We don't have anybody we can send?"

"Jeez, Fisher, what the hell do you think? I have an army of people working for me?"

"Better do it quick," said Fisher. "If they were willing to blow me up, they must already have an idea where he is, or at least where he'll go."

CHAPTER
10

Howe started to drive back to his motel after lunch with McIntyre, but then realized that he was near the house Alice Kauss had called her dream home the night before. Recalling the conversation—and mostly recalling her—he turned down the street that led to it, turning to the right and then into the cul-de-sac where the house sat off to the side. He stopped the car and looked at it.

It wasn't a spectacular house. Oh, it was big—much bigger than anything he'd ever lived in—but it wasn't ostentatious: no elaborate drive, none of those really fancy pillars at the front, no copper on the roof. It was nice, definitely; the little porch at the front was just big enough for a small bench, a good place to read the paper on a Sunday morning, drinking a cup of coffee.

Not a bad life.

Over a million bucks, though? *Sheeeesh.*

Could he afford a place like this if he took the job?

Undoubtedly, but why would he want it? Alice had told him it was about 3,200 square feet. He'd be lost.

He drove around the cul-de-sac at the end of the block, then up and through the rest of the subdivision. Howe had grown up in a rural area, next to a farm. The word *subdivision* in his youth had a tinge to it; usually it meant a farmer had been forced to sell off his land to make ends meet. Things were changing now. The family farm was a thing of the past, even where he'd grown up. Soon it would all be subdivisions.

So, living in a condominium was better?

Howe hadn't heard back from Blitz or his aide about his security clearance, and figured that he might not for a few days. His best bet, he thought, was to get his personal affairs straightened out: find a place to stay, then go back home for a few days, visit with his relatives and friends. Once the job got going, who knew when he'd get a chance to get away again?

It was only two o'clock, but Howe was near the real estate office and decided he'd take a chance that she might be there. Her car wasn't in the lot, but he'd already driven up and decided he might as well go inside and see if she'd be back before four.

"I'm not sure," said the receptionist, peering at him from over her eyeglasses. "She didn't show up for work today, and she hasn't answered her phone. It's very unlike her."

"Where does she live?" he asked.

★   ★   ★

He drove by the apartment twice. Alice's car was in the lot. As far as he could see, there was no one watching it. He went back out onto the street and drove to a gas station nearby before trying her again.

The answering machine picked up on the second ring.

"It's Bill Howe again," he said. "I was wondering if maybe you'd want to push up our appointment this afternoon? But I guess you're not around."

He hit End, then called over to the motel to check for messages. Someone from the FBI had called; it wasn't Fisher but undoubtedly it was related to their talk. Howe took down the name and number but figured he'd talk to Fisher about it first. The only other call was from a newspaper reporter from his hometown, apparently referred by his mom.

He reached into his pocket for Fisher's card to call him. He thought about mentioning Alice and the fact that she wasn't around, then realized that would be silly.

Why did he think something had happened to her? More than likely she was inside sleeping, catching up after last night.

Or she was in there with someone else. But hadn't she been giving him the impression she was unattached?

Howe remembered her walk. Truth was, he was infatuated with her. She wasn't movie star beautiful but she was . . .

Beautiful.

And probably busy doing other stuff, attached, and interested in him only as a customer.

He put Fisher's card back in his pocket. He really didn't feel like talking to any more FBI agents today, not even Fisher. Howe glanced at the small notebook where he'd written the number of the journalist. The paper was a small weekly that occasionally ran man-in-the-news features on its front page. He wasn't much interested in being the subject of a story, but it was only fair that he call the guy back and tell him so.

He punched in the number and got a message that it had been disconnected. Thinking the hotel clerk had made a mistake, he called information and got the newspaper's number; it was nothing like the one that had been left.

The reporter who'd left the message didn't exist.

Confused, Howe considered calling his mother to see if she knew anything about the story, but then decided not to bother her. It was nearly three o'clock. He could fit in a few calls to the NADT backers before it was time to hook up with Alice.

CHAPTER

11

Daylight made a big difference.

In the dark, viewed through the night goggles and even in the starlight, Pong Yan had seemed about half the size of a small rural airport in America. In the early-morning light, as Tyler approached the strip where Howe's Berkut had landed and taken off, it looked more like a beat-up gas station with two sheds at the far side.

Tyler had found a team of Army Rangers as escorts, along with an Air Force officer he'd pressed into duty as a UAV expert. The man was actually a maintenance officer with a helicopter squadron who had only a passing knowledge of UAVs, but, as Tyler told him, just the fact that he could pick a UAV out of a lineup meant he had more experience than Tyler did. Tyler had also taken Somers along as a kind of all-around consultant; the old guy didn't know much about UAVs, but Tyler liked him and thought he might come in handy. Their job was pretty straightforward: go to the field, inspect the hangar, find the UAVs. If they existed, Tyler was to have them shipped back to the States for study. This mission took priority over the situation report, which Moore could handle without them in any event.

The two Air Force Pave Lows carrying the team circled the area once, the pilots and crewmen getting a feel for the situation. The helicopters were big green brutes armed with machine guns and able to lift vehicles a decent distance; they'd brought gear to attach to the UAVs with the idea that they would carry them sling-style to a large airstrip about seventy-five miles south, where a C-17 could be brought in to ferry them away.

Tyler leaned over the door gunner as the helicopter took a turn. The mountains had a dusty haze over them, a dull shimmer of dirt as if the despair that had settled over North Korea under its Communist rulers was finally being shaken off. The landscape itself was beautiful; from the air the hills and mountains beyond gave no hint of the hardship the people here had withstood for decades.

The helicopters settled down and Tyler climbed out, choking back the dust. The Rangers moved out quickly, fanning across the field to take positions. Tyler walked toward the hangars, then remembered Somers, turned back, and waited for the historian. For the first time since they'd met, he realized that Somers was actually quite short, perhaps five feet six or seven. Something in the older man's manner gave him a taller presence somehow—made him seem psychologically more commanding.

"That's what we're looking for?" asked Somers.

Two oddly shaped aircraft sat wingtip to wingtip in the open-faced hangar. The planes looked like something out of a sci-fi movie. Small—they were about the length of a pickup truck, and not all that much wider—they had no cockpits and short wings that angled up, almost as if they were origami gulls. Unpainted, their metal fuselages had sharp angles in the front, which melted into gradual curves about where the cockpit would normally be. Large, thick pipes sat at one side of the hangar, along with an array of what looked like large cans and tubing.

"That's it," said Tyler.

"These things fly?"

Their Air Force expert was bent over, trying to get a piece of dust from his eye. Somers took a step toward the hangar but Tyler stopped him.

"Might be booby-trapped," he told him.

"Nah."

"Let's get the experts to check it out," said Tyler, calling over to the Rangers' captain.

The planes had not been booby-trapped. According to the Air Force officer—who punctuated everything he said with a disclaimer that he was by no means an expert—the aircraft were surely robots but were missing key parts, starting with their engines. In fact, he wasn't entirely sure what sort of power plants they would have. Probably a jet, he thought, but the configuration at the rear might be able to fit a turboprop.

"Like I say, I'm no expert."

Tyler had brought along a digital camera and started snapping pictures. Meanwhile the helicopter crew sized up the aircraft for transport. They debated whether by removing their wings the aircraft would fit within the oversize helicopters, but that idea was soon vetoed; while they had equipment with them to cut off the wings, Tyler interpreted his orders to mean the UAVs should be returned intact if possible. The helicopter could lift 20,000 pounds, or roughly the equivalent of an empty F-16; the Korean UAV looked to be well within the parameters, though ultimately the only way to find out was to try it. Tyler decided they'd take a shot with only one of the craft; not only would that make transport safer and easier but it would leave another here in case something went wrong.

The Air Force crewmen, with help from the Rangers, pulled the UAV from the hangar, rolling it on its thin, tubular gear. The specialists trussed it with thick belts, arranging the sling to get the balance right. This took considerable time, and they knocked off for a bit, breaking with some MREs and some assorted candy bars before the helicopter pilots lifted the Pave Low up and hovered into position to hook up its cargo. Standing well off to the side as the specialists did their thing, Tyler thought the six-bladed helicopter was actually straining to stay down; her tail twisted upward slightly, as if she wanted to tell the men fussing below her to get out of the way and let her do her job.

And then the tail began rotating oddly, and the helicopter pushed hard right. Tyler stared at the big green bug, which looked as if it had been caught in a bizarre wind. He heard something crack: It was as if the sky above him was a large sheet of ice and snapped in two.

The helicopter fell off sideways, flames shooting from the area below the back of the engine, and he heard the explosion of a rocket-propelled grenade landing nearby.

"Take cover!" someone yelled, and he hit the dirt.

CHAPTER

12

Howe was sitting in Alice's office when his cell phone rang. Thinking she was calling him, he answered, only to find Fisher on the line.

"Half the FBI's looking for you," Fisher told him. "Where the hell are you?"

"I'm sitting in a real estate office, waiting for someone to show me some houses," said Howe. "She's late."

"Somebody's trying to kill you. They blew up my car at the diner."

"They're trying to kill me and they blew up *your* car?"

"I didn't say they were smart," answered Fisher. "Who's this girl you're supposed to meet? You know her?"

"She showed me some houses yesterday. And we had dinner."

"Give me her address," said Fisher.

"Why? You think she's been kidnapped?"

"I don't think anything. Just give me her address and the one where you are."

"You think they took her because they want me?" said Howe.

"I try not to think. It gets me in trouble," said Fisher. "Now give me the addresses."

Howe did.

"You stay where you are," Fisher told him.

"I want to wait in my car," said Howe. If someone was coming after him, he didn't want innocent people hurt. "If they really did kidnap her, what's going to happen?"

"They'll let you know they have her," Fisher said. "Look, you mind if I bring the FBI in on this? Kidnapping is kind of their area."

"You *are* the FBI."

"Yeah, but these guys are the real FBI agents. You'll see: fifties haircuts, Sears suits, whole deal. Listen, when you get called, the caller's going to tell you not to call the police, right? You don't pay any attention to that part. Okay?"

"I'm not stupid."

"That's good to know."

Howe sat in his car outside the real estate office, worried now and wondering what was going on. He thought of calling Fisher back for an explanation, and even brought the last-call menu up, but then didn't hit the Send button.

Most likely this was all going to turn out to be a product of overworked imaginations, of people getting tense when the best approach was just to lie back and see what happened.

Of course, if anybody was laid-back it was Fisher. If a

tornado was coming, the guy would light up a cigarette, then step to one side at the last minute.

A dark sedan made its way up the driveway finally. Howe got out of his car and walked over to it as it pulled to a stop.

"I'm Howe," he said, leaning down toward the passenger side as the door opened and a man in a suit got out.

"Into the car," said the man, pushing a pistol into his stomach.

As Howe hesitated, another man came out from around the other side. He saw a woman's arms, bound together, reaching from the back.

"Let her go," he said.

"Into the car," demanded the first man, this time putting the gun into his ribs. "Or I'll shoot you here."

CHAPTER

13

Fisher had Howe pegged as someone who didn't like to stay home when everyone else was out partying, so he wasn't particularly surprised when the FBI agents he'd sent scurrying up to him called back and said he was nowhere to be found.

"This is the girlfriend's address," Fisher told the agent. "Send somebody over there to check it out."

"Hey, listen, Andy, it's not like we got nothing better to do," said the agent, Pete McGovern. He was a nonsmoker but in every other way extremely dependable, the sort of guy who answered his phone on the first ring and paid off on poker debts. "Me and Christian over here have to finish checking on a whole shitload of references this afternoon."

"Which would you rather be doing," asked Fisher, "looking in some guy's bathroom window so Social Security can hire him to deny a widow's monthly check, or breaking the biggest national security case of your life-time?"

"Don't pull my pud, Andy."

"That's what I like about you, McGovern: You have a way with words."

"Where's the stinking address?" asked the agent. "And, for the record, these background checks were for the Department of Justice."

"Even more reason to blow them off."

The cell phone buzzed in Howe's pocket. The man sitting next to him turned and pointed his gun at his face.

"If I don't answer it, they'll get suspicious," he said.

"If you touch it, I'll shoot your head off," said the man.

Alice sat next to him in the back of the large Mercury, her hands bound and a scarf tied across her mouth. She looked angry, not afraid.

The men had put police-style handcuffs on Howe's wrists, but his hands were in front of him and he thought he might be able to grab the gun if he lunged. But the men in front also had weapons, and it seemed unlikely that he would be able to overcome all three men before one of them shot Alice.

He'd have a better chance once they stopped the car and they got out.

"What the hell is it you want, anyway?" Howe asked.

No one bothered to answer.

"Are you not telling me because you don't know?" he asked. "Or because you're stupid?"

"Just shut the fuck up, okay?" said the man on his right. He pushed the pistol against his head. "Because, really, the easiest thing to do would be to shoot you here."

"Franky," said the driver. "Not unless we have to."

Fisher pulled over to the side of the road to consult his map. As he pulled it out, his cell phone rang. It was McGovern.

"Apartment's empty. Door was unlocked. Sign of a struggle."

"Just like in the movies," said Fisher.

"We're going to need local help."

"Yeah, do it," said Fisher. "I got to keep this line clear."

He keyed off the call before McGovern could say anything else, then tried Howe again. Once more there was no answer. He went back to looking at the map. Of the hundreds of thousands of roads in the area, Howe could only be on ten thousand or so. Fisher lit a cigarette as he considered the mechanics of roadblocks. He flipped on the radio just in time to hear a traffic report from the WKDC traffic chopper. Fisher listened to smoking buddy Maureen Justice claim that traffic hadn't moved this smoothly since Madison's second administration.

Out of ideas, Fisher snapped off the radio and went to the pay phone to call McGovern.

"Local detectives sent some people right over," said McGovern. "They were real cooperative until they heard your name. What are you going to do now?"

"Wait for my phone to ring. If Howe calls we can track it down. I already have it set up."

"What if he doesn't call?"

"Then we move over to Plan B."

"What's that?"

"I'm not sure, but it involves spectacular detective work, a car chase, gunshots, and a hell of a lot of cigarettes smoked down to the nub."

Howe had to punch two keys on the cell phone to call the last number he had dialed; without taking the phone from his pocket it wouldn't be easy to find the buttons, let alone hit them in the proper order. And there was little chance of even getting the phone out without the thug next to him seeing.

The driver's comment earlier seemed to mean that they

were under instructions not to kill him. But it could also mean that he wanted to wait until they reached a place where it was more convenient.

They were moving along at a good clip on the highway, but there were enough cars nearby that someone might at least notice if the car veered suddenly, or even see bullets flying through the side glass.

Better to wait and see what developed.

CHAPTER

14

The world above Tyler's head shaded red, pulsing with the short, sharp breaths he took. He forced himself to look for Somers. Three breaths, four—he looked left, looked back right, finally saw the historian sprawled behind him.

God, I killed him.

Tyler scrambled over to him. Somers was breathing. As far as Tyler could tell, he hadn't been hurt, just lost his wind.

Gunfire popped nearby, the sound ricocheting off the nearby hills. The helicopter lay on its side fifty yards in front of him.

He was too scared to help the people stuck in it; too chicken.

Coward. Stinking coward.

Tyler leaned his head forward in the direction of the stricken aircraft. He felt as if something were holding him back, wind rushing against him. Voices screamed at him:

Coward.

Coward.

Something rippled across the metal of the helicopter. The front burst upward. Tyler couldn't process it: The big bird seemed to be moving on its own. Again the wind held him back and he pushed his head down, saw something in the metal: a hand. Part of the fuselage rippled from gunfire from a few hundred yards away.

Tyler jumped to his feet and ran to the chopper. A body sprawled against a spar just inside the open hatchway. Tyler leaned in and grabbed it. The metal beneath his chest gave way; he fell into the Pave Low in slow motion, the side of the helicopter squishing as if it were held up by Jell-O. Tyler started to choke and blinked his eyes, grabbed hold of something—body or metal, he couldn't even tell—and pulled.

"I'm okay. Get Chris."

Someone pushed through the twisted metal on his right. There was smoke, something brown in his face. Tyler leaned into the dark hole, knowing he wasn't coming out of here. He didn't want to; he wanted to get away from the voices persecuting him, wanted to just fall into this black hole. He was a coward and he wanted to just disappear, to be sucked into oblivion.

"Help," said someone.

"I'll help you," Tyler answered.

It seemed as if he were swimming, as if he were out on the river at night, under a bridge or a ledge, trapped as the current twisted around him.

"Out—we're getting out," he said, and there were raindrops now, the splatter of something against the surface of the water nearby.

He pulled and then pushed and could stand, and wasn't in the water anymore. And someone yelled, "Here," and the voice inside his head once more called him a coward. And then he saw that his hand was grabbing at a shirt. He stood and he pushed; he moved backward. Then he started to move forward.

"Come on," someone shouted. "You've got them all, come on. They're gunning for the helicopter."

Tyler threw himself backward, tumbling onto a sandy beach.

Not a beach: the strip, away from the downed helicopter, away.

The ground was farther than he'd thought it could be—so much farther. His head finally hit and the pain shot up against his mouth and then back to his ears and to his neck and down his spine, and he vibrated as he swam again, the voice calling him a coward over and over.

CHAPTER
15

They drove over a set of railroad tracks, down a road with weeds tall enough to flank the sides of the car. Howe saw two buildings ahead, metal warehouses with green and white walls. They hadn't been driving long enough to get out of Virginia, but where exactly they were he had no idea.

Howe looked at Alice. She blinked her eyes at him.

"Run," he mouthed silently.

She blinked again but didn't nod. The man in the front passenger seat got out of the car and walked around the front of the car.

Telling her to run was useless. Where would she go?

The door on her side opened. Howe grabbed her arms, holding her in the car.

"Let her go. You want me, right? Just let her go and we can work this out."

"Just shut up," said the man next to him. He opened his door and, as he was climbing out, gave Howe a sharp elbow in the side. Howe groaned and bent forward over Alice's lap; he felt her press down on top of him.

"Run as soon as you get a chance," he told her. "Just run."

Alice pushed her chin down into his back; if she said something, he couldn't hear.

If he was going to make the call, now was the time;

they couldn't see him. He reached into his pocket and slid out the phone, fingers jabbing the buttons. The man who had gotten out of the car reached back and pulled him out. Jerked upward, Howe dropped the cell phone near Alice's feet and stumbled out. He managed to fall down and rolled on the ground; he figured he might be able to overpower one of the goons if they got close enough.

But the men weren't that stupid. One squatted down in front of him, well out of reach, pointing his weapon at his face.

"You fuck with us, we shoot you and the lady. You want that?"

"I want you to let her go," said Howe.

One of the other men had come around on the other side of him and kicked him in the ribs.

"Just let her go," Howe groaned. "What do you need her for?"

The man kicked him again.

Fisher twisted the phone around so he could see the number as he hit the button to receive the call.

"Where are you?" he asked, but he got only a muffled reply. He pressed the phone to his ear, listening.

By the time the man grew tired of kicking him, Howe was writhing in pain. The kicker stooped down and picked him up, hauling him to his feet. Howe wobbled somewhat, moving forward unsteadily, trying simply to get his breath back. He couldn't seem to manage it, and though he willed his body to help, it just didn't seem able.

"Hey, this way," said one of the other goons.

"Let her go," muttered Howe.

"Tough guy, huh?" The man pushed him backward; Howe slipped and fell against the car.

"You know who I am?" Howe said.

The man laughed. "Like I give a fuck, right?"

He reached down and pulled Howe to his feet. Somewhere in the back of his head Howe heard a voice tell him to grab for the gun. This was certainly the right time for it: It loomed right in front of his stomach, angled away; it was far from a sure thing but it was a decent chance, maybe fifty-fifty. But his body wouldn't cooperate. His arms stayed frozen in front of him, weighed down by the handcuffs; his chest refused to supply the energy he needed, and the moment passed.

Alice was out of the car, being pushed toward the building. Howe finally willed himself toward her.

Slow, go as slow as you possibly can, he told himself.

But don't let them kill her.

CHAPTER
16 *Coward! Coward!*

"That was a brave thing you did, saving those kids in the helicopter," said Somers, helping Tyler up. "Foolhardy, but brave."

Tyler stared at him.

"Major?"

He turned around. The Ranger captain had a distressed look on his face.

"You okay, Major?" asked the captain.

"Yeah."

"We have two gunships inbound. We've chased the North Koreans out of their hide holes and have a pretty good idea where they were firing from. Mortar fire has stopped. We got their machine gun."

"Good work," managed Tyler.

"Everybody's okay," the Ranger commander added.

"Yeah, good," said Tyler. He frowned.

"I'm sorry, sir. I know we fucked up."

"What do you mean?" Tyler asked.

"We should have found those bastards before they fired."

"This is war," said Somers. "You can't see everything. The other side has a vote."

"That's right," said Tyler.

The Ranger captain had a pained expression on his face; he didn't believe him. Tyler grabbed his arm. "That's right. It's not your fault. If it's anybody's fault, it's my fault."

The man blinked, not understanding, then nodded.

"It's my fault," said Tyler.

"Thank you, sir," said the captain.

"No, I mean it."

"Yes, sir."

"Let me talk to the helicopter people and see if they can rig up another sling with the other UAV," Tyler said. "Get it the hell out of here before we're attacked again."

CHAPTER

17

Howe walked toward the warehouse, his heels kicking against pebbles and broken glass. A railroad track was embedded in the macadam; he stepped on the worn rail, sole scuffing. The gun was now a few feet away, on his left, behind him just enough so he couldn't see it without turning back to look at his captor. Another of the thugs pulled Alice ahead to the right, heading toward a door. The third was behind him somewhere—but where?

Rusted oil drums sat in a pile at the corner of the building; the other direction lay bare.

He could grab the gun, shoot the thug with Alice, take her around the side of the building.

Guy in the back would nail him, then her.

He turned right, trying to see. The low groan of the highway filtered past the buildings, making its way up the embankment. They were alone here, very alone. He heard a Cessna nearby and realized the civilian airport sat on the other side of the highway.

Someone would see them. Someone.

He heard a helicopter approaching.

"Move it." The thug on his left took a step forward and smacked him in the ribs with the blunt grip of the gun.

He can't shoot me that way, Howe realized, and in that second he sprang.

"There—go!" yelled Fisher into the headset. He grabbed at the door of the helicopter, pushing his elbow hard against it, only to have the wind slap him back into the seat.

"How close do you want to get?" asked Maureen Justice.

"Hit them!" Fisher undid his seat belt and leaned forward against the side of the forward panel of the traffic helicopter.

"Hit them? Andy, I don't owe you that much."

"You'll be able to broadcast it live. You'll be as famous as the helicopter pilot in the O.J. case." He pulled out his pistol.

"Hey, wait a second," she shouted. "You didn't say you were going to shoot somebody."

"I told you, it's national security."

"Andy!"

"Got to get their attention!" said Fisher, firing off two rounds from his revolver.

"Good, they're taking out guns! They're shooting at me!"

"Took 'em long enough. Come on, run 'em over."

"Jesus!"

Maureen swung the helicopter in an arc to the north, tilting wildly as she lurched away from the gunmen. Fisher was sure she'd seen much worse on her daily traffic reports, but there wasn't time to argue.

"Put me down on the roof!" he told her, whipping off the headset.

"The roof?"

Fisher hung on the helicopter door with one hand, belatedly realizing that the metal was thinner than it appeared. He swung his feet around, searching for the skids beneath. He looked down, saw gray concrete.

Between the wind and the engine noise there was no way the pilot could hear him, but Fisher knew that there were moments in every case when a strategic shout was your best and only option.

"The roof!" he yelled. "The roof!"

Ribs of white metal appeared below. Fisher felt his grip slipping and tried to swing his body toward what he thought was the thicker part of the roof as he fell. He misjudged both his direction and the distance, crashing down four or five feet from the gutter. But the mistake was fortuitous: He hit between two rafters, and the metal absorbed a good deal of the shock as he rolled down against the surface. His pistol flew away, spinning wildly before sliding into the gutter, its long nose pointing skyward. Fisher threw himself out after it, sliding hands-first down the slope.

Howe grabbed at the thug's weapon, shoving his shoulder into the goon's midsection. The world narrowed to a blue-smoke oblong, a thick hard rectangle in the middle of his eye, the middle of his head. Everything around him blackened, became a void. He felt the warmth of the metal on his fingers, then nothing; ice froze his eyes and chest and hand. He found himself revolving, then floating, then on the ground.

The gun sat a few feet away. Something clawed at him, a wild animal, a lion. A howl shook his ears. Howe threw himself in the direction of the screech, then flew toward the L-shaped metal, the Beretta in the gravel. Something stomped on the back of his head, and the black void squeezed the side of his face. Howe pushed forward, determined to get the gun now, determined to get it and beat the blackness back.

Fisher couldn't stop his momentum as he hit the end of the roof. He grabbed at the gutter but the metal wasn't tightly fastened; the lightweight aluminum shot out from the building and then immediately bent downward under the FBI agent's weight. Fisher tried swinging his legs up and over as he fell, but he could only get them halfway before the other end of the gutter gave way. He tried to get his feet down to hit the ground in a reasonable manner, but instead slapped against the building and then crashed into the pile of barrels, which fortunately broke most of his fall as he hit the ground. He rolled in the middle of them, head spinning so badly that he had trouble reaching for the small gun in the holster on his leg.

Howe realized he had the gun in his hand and scraped against the pavement, his skin tearing away as he tried to get up. He jerked around, saw his captor running back toward the car.

Where was Alice?

"Alice!"

Where was Alice?

Fisher struggled to his feet, both hands on the hideaway Glock and ears ringing loudly. He fired twice, winging the man who'd started to run to the car and sending him to the pavement. Fisher saw Howe on his right, just getting up; the girl must be inside the building.

There was a window on the side of the building behind him. Fisher took a step backward toward it. Howe yelled something.

"Yo, Colonel, cover those assholes near the car until the cops come," Fisher said, shouting over the banging that had taken over his head. Then he went to the window and smashed it open with a metal shovel that lay in the grass and jumped through.

Or at least tried to jump through. A piece of glass snagged his trousers and then his shoe, ripping them and sending him crashing to the floor off balance.

"My third-best pair of brown pants," he complained, pulling himself against the wall and looking at his exposed calf and sock. "Now I'm pissed."

Howe leaped through the open door, throwing himself to the ground. Something crashed on the far side of the building; he cringed, expecting bullets to slash through him.

Still cringing, shaking now with fear, he got to his knees. He had the gun in his hand.

Where was she?

He was in a large, empty room. There were two doors twenty feet across from him, hallways into the back. Howe got up and started for them, his knees stiffening. He got to the wall and leaned against it, listening.

Fisher saw something move in the filtered light across the open space.

"FBI. Give it up," he yelled.

"I'll kill her!"

"That'd be really stupid," said Fisher.

The man replied by firing three times in Fisher's direction. The FBI agent hit the deck, crawling around the back of what appeared to be a desk.

"Give it up, I'm telling you," he yelled.

"Screw yourself."

Two more shots, one of which splintered the desk.

"Maybe we can make a deal," yelled Fisher.

"Fuck off."

Two more shots, both so close that splinters sailed just

over Fisher's head. He sprawled out on the floor, pushing himself to a second desk.

"I know you want to give up," said Fisher. "And I'm the guy you want to talk to."

Only one bullet this time, and back at the other desk. The gunman was about halfway through his magazine—unless, of course, he had another mag or two with him.

"Look, we can work a deal," said Fisher. "Why'd you want Howe? Who hired you?"

This time the bullets sailed within inches of Fisher's head. He heard a muffled sound, then footsteps; Fisher started to get up then threw himself down, another bullet flying in his direction.

Howe saw her and flew up toward her. As he leaped he saw the other hand, then the face of the man who held her. But he was already launched, already sailing into them. He crashed against their bodies and rolled downward, a siren sounding in his ear, the floor rattling as if by gunfire or thunder. He grappled for the man, threw a punch and then another punch, felt something smash against his face hard. He punched back harder and harder, furious now, his fists compressing against the hard bone of a skull.

And then something lifted him from the floor and pushed him to the side, gently yet with a good amount of force.

"Take it easy, Colonel," said Andy Fisher. "You scramble his brains and I'm not going to be able to trust what he says."

CHAPTER

18

By the time Tyler and his people were ready to lift the UAV, the backup units had arrived. Two large gunships circled overhead as a company's worth of soldiers scoured the hills, looking for more attackers. The unit commander was excited because they'd heard reports that there were stragglers in the area but had not been able to hunt them down; the incident represented an opportunity to put one more nail in the coffin of the old regime.

Tyler's stomach knotted tighter as the Pave Low moved forward. Somebody shouted something and he winced; he whirled around, found himself staring into Somers's face, then turned back, cringing: He knew, just knew, he would see the helicopter keeling over, in flames, gunfire erupting all over again.

But nothing like that happened. Sling attached and taut, the helicopter lifted upward and ahead, taking the North Korean robot aircraft under it as easily as a man might pluck a piece of paper from the floor. Tyler watched as the helicopter flew toward the well-secured air base to the south.

"You all right?" asked Somers after the Pave Low disappeared.

"Yeah," said Tyler.

"That was a damn brave thing, getting those guys out of the helicopter."

Tyler looked at Somers. "You keep saying that."

"You've seen a lot of action, haven't you, Major?"

"Not really."

Tyler knew many, many people in the Army who had seen much more combat. And certainly when viewed against the long history of conflicts—wars that extended years rather than weeks—he had seen almost none.

"Getting to you?" asked Somers.

The question caught Tyler off guard. He liked the historian: He was a smart guy, insightful, and easy to like. But there was a line.

"It's not getting to me," said Tyler, turning away and walking toward the Chinook that had brought the reinforcements.

Somers caught up with him as he neared the door to the massive helicopter.

"I didn't mean to offend you," said the older man.

Tyler looked at him. He didn't know how to explain what he felt and what he had done; he couldn't describe how fear had crept beneath what just a few weeks ago had been easy conviction, how second-guessing had wrapped itself around his determination. Everything he did now he questioned. Everything he did was wrong. And he was always afraid.

To the people on the outside, it wasn't there. Somers saw only him jumping into the chopper.

Why had he done it? Not because it was the right thing to do or the brave thing to do, but because it was the *only* thing to do. He had been scared—damn scared.

"It was nothing," Tyler told Somers, then climbed aboard the chopper.

CHAPTER

19

Fisher leaned forward against the back of the chair, watching through the one-way glass as the two local detectives continued the interview. He'd found some safety pins to clip his torn pants together with, and had washed his face and hands. As soon as they brought his coffee he'd feel good as new.

"Got no idea who hired us," said the man the detectives were interviewing. He'd been the one back by the car when Fisher arrived and Fisher assumed he was the driver. As a general rule, drivers didn't know all that much about the operation they were involved in, but the two detectives apparently hadn't learned that from NYPD reruns. They kept circling around and taking fresh starts at the same question, and the suspect kept coming back with essentially the same answer: Damned if I know.

The other two goons were in the hospital. The one Howe had wrestled with was in pretty serious condition, with internal bleeding and a concussion. Fisher thought that was a waste: If he was going to beat him senseless, he might just as well have killed the guy and saved the county some dough.

"Like I been telling you, I got no idea," said the suspect one more time.

One of the detectives made a big show of disgust, slapping his hands down on the table and walking out, playing the first strains of the time-honored good-cop–bad-cop routine. Fisher watched the suspect twitch nervously for a few seconds, then got up from his chair. He met the policewoman who'd gone for coffee at the door.

"Just in time," he told her.

"I'm sorry. I had to clean the cup."

"Shouldn't have bothered," said Fisher. "Scum adds flavor."

Fisher took the coffee and went into the interrogation room, where the other detective was speaking in the low, confidential tones that were considered de rigueur for the nice-guy part in the play.

Fisher had never been much of a fan of good-cop–bad-cop. It seemed to him that anyone stupid enough to fall for it wasn't much of a source to begin with. Sure, it had worked for Eliot Ness, but Fisher suspected the brass knuckles Ness's sidekick got to use in the back room were more responsible for success than the crumpled cigarette Ness stuck in a suspect's mouth.

But you had to go with what you had. Fisher tossed a pack of cigarettes on the table, along with some matches.

The man looked up at him. "I don't smoke."

Fisher pushed out the chair and sat down, thinking they just didn't make goons the way they used to.

"You're with the Genovese family, right?"

"Huh?" said the man.

"Genovese. He's trying to muscle into the D.C. area," said Fisher, pulling over the cigarettes. He punched one out of the pack.

"What do you mean?"

"What I said. You're on DiCarlo's crew, right? You guys clipped some poor fuck by the river two weeks ago."

"I had nothing to do with that," said the man. "And I'm not with the Genovese family."

"They don't call it Genovese anymore, right? Those New York guys—that would be like calling it *omertà* or Our Thing or something, right? I mean, even the word *mob*, that's no good."

"I ain't with fuckin' Genovese, right? I'm not from New York. I ain't with those guys."

"Word is, you are."

"What word?"

"Word I hear," said Fisher. He took a long pull from the cigarette, held it a tick, then let it out. "Word that's going around the street. And the jail."

"Hey, screw you. Who are you?"

"Andy Fisher. FBI. I was doing some checking inside. You're with Genovese."

"I'm with Sammy Gorodino."

"Sammy the Seal?" said Fisher. "No way."

"Hey, bullshit on you, asshole."

"So, what's the story on Howe? He owes your boss money?"

The goon glanced at the Virginia detective, then back at Fisher. "You for real?"

Fisher shrugged.

"I just do what I'm told. Sammy tells me what to do and I do it."

"Sammy's where?" said Fisher.

"Oh, fuck you. I'm not telling you that."

Fisher took a sip of his coffee. It occurred to him again that it might have been much better if the cup hadn't been washed.

"I can find Sammy," said the detective next to him. "He owns a restaurant in a strip mall out near Circleville."

The goon's face twitched ever so slightly.

Fisher pulled out his satellite phone and slid it across the table.

"Call him," he told the goon. "And tell him you're going to be released on your own recognizance this afternoon. Tell him there are some rumors going around that he ought to know about, rumors that you were talking about his auto parts business. False rumors, and you don't want him getting upset. Because you told that asshole FBI agent nothing, and the raid that's coming had nothing to do with any sort of information you gave out. And you're being let go free was just some sort of trick by this jerk Andy Fisher."

The man looked at Fisher, then at the detective, then at the phone.

"There's a bowling alley," he said. "It's over by Kird-wood Park."

CHAPTER
20

Alice looked much younger asleep. She had pulled her hair back and tied it so the doctors could treat the small cut on the right side of her mouth. The strands at the top of her forehead looked like the fine threads at the edge of a scarf.

Howe gazed at the down in front of her ear, a shade lighter than the trio of freckles beneath it. Her lips were a soft pink, loosely pressed together; her body moved upward gently with her breathing.

"Who were they?" she said without opening her eyes.

Howe stooped down. "Alice?"

"Who were they?"

Her left lid opened slowly.

"I'm not sure," said Howe. "They were after me. I'm sorry they hurt you."

Fisher had told Howe that the goons had probably started following him sometime the day before and seen where Alice lived. They probably had left someone there to watch her as a backup.

"They thought I was your girlfriend." Alice pushed her legs off the bed and sat up.

In the hallway Howe heard the footsteps of the detective and FBI agent who'd been waiting to see her.

"You going to be okay?" Howe asked.

"I'm okay." She was still in her jeans and the T-shirt she'd been wearing earlier. Aside from a bruise where one of the thugs had squeezed her arm, she was unhurt.

One of the investigators pushed back the curtain behind him. "Uh, Colonel Howe," said the woman. "Excuse us, but we'd prefer if you didn't talk with Ms. Kauss until we've had a chance to interview her."

"Protocol," said the other detective.

"Yeah, I'm sorry," said Howe. He looked at Alice as he spoke. "I just wanted to make sure she was okay."

"I'm okay," she told him.

"I guess we have to reschedule," he said.

"Call my office."

"I will." He nodded. He couldn't tell how angry she was with him, though he figured she must be very angry. "Okay," he said, leaving.

21

Fisher had never quite gotten the point of bowling. Maybe it made sense as a metaphysical exercise, the round sphere of the life force laying low the solid pins of orthodoxy, but the people who played it regularly didn't seem to be the metaphysical type. Most of them seemed to be in some sort of pain: They unleashed the ball, stared as it rolled down the alley, then cringed as it toppled its targets. A few did odd dances, as if calling on the gods of thunder to be merciful, and even those who emerged from the process with smiles on their faces set off immediately to handle the paperwork.

Not much sense in it that he could see.

Fisher walked through the alley, turned past the shoe rental register—another activity he didn't understand—and through the double doors that led to the lounge. He went to the bar and pulled open his coat, removing his Magnum to the wide-eyed stare of two rather large men standing a few feet away.

"There's six bullets in that, and I'm counting them when I leave," he said, placing the long-barreled gun down. He walked over to the table where Sammy the Seal was sitting with a few of his bodyguards.

Sammy was only thirty-three, but Fisher's sources on the local organized-crime task force had him pegged as an old-line mob type too dull to make the transition to semi-legal activities like the movies or stock market. He relied on muscle and wits to keep afloat, which meant he'd be a prime candidate for the federal Witness Security Program in a few months. Fisher appreciated this, actually: There was something admirable about a man too dumb to be successfully dishonest.

Fisher sat down and tossed the thin wallet with his Bureau credentials on the table.

"FBI," he told Sammy. He glanced up at the two bodyguards clutching their chests behind him. "Don't have heart attacks, guys. I'm here to talk. And not about auto parts, prostitution, or the movies. Though I might mention that the coffee you serve in your pizza parlors is class A heartburn material, a plus in my book."

"Who the hell are you?" said Sammy.

"Andy Fisher. I picked up a couple of your people earlier today. They should've called by now."

"I don't have people."

"Well, I didn't bother to run DNA tests on them," said Fisher, taking out a cigarette, "but they looked human. Walked and talked."

Sammy looked at his cigarette.

"Mind if I smoke?" Fisher asked.

"I do mind, yeah. It's against the law in this county."

Fisher lit up anyway. "Maybe you can use the charge for a plea bargain."

"Why are you here?"

"Somebody hired you to freeze William Howe. Problem is, they didn't tell you Howe was a national hero."

"He's no hero," said Sammy, making a face.

"You look at his résumé?"

Belatedly realizing he had said far too much, Sammy shut up.

Fisher leaned forward. "All I want to know is who hired you? Between you and me."

"You think I'd screw a client like that?"

"I hope so," said Fisher.

Sammy laughed. "Get out before I throw you out."

"Flip on the news," said Fisher. "Put on CNN. See what kind of shit you're in."

A dim light began to shine somewhere in Sammy's brain. He called over to the bartender and told him to turn on the television.

"And bring a round of drinks. What are you having?"

"Coffee," said Fisher.

"Coffee's old."

"Can't be any worse than the crap they have over at police headquarters."

Sammy frowned. The station came back from a commercial. A picture of Howe flashed on the screen. Sammy stared at the television, doing a rather convincing impression of Paul on the road to Damascus. If his jaw hadn't been attached, it would have been part of the rug.

"Guy told us what hotel he was in, had a name, that was it. We didn't know, I swear to God," said Sammy. "I swear. Off the record. 'Cause you ain't read me my rights or anything, and you can't use this."

"Oh, yeah, way off the record," said Fisher. "So, who hired you?"

"A Chink," said Sammy. "Guy named Sin Ru Chow. We do some deals sometimes. He's who you want to talk to."

"That's the best you can do?" Fisher.

Sammy was too distracted to answer, absorbed in the television broadcast. Every one of his limited brain cells was now devoted to trying to figure out how to extricate himself from this very serious mess.

"If you happen to think of something," said Fisher, pushing a card to the middle of the table, "call that number."

He picked up his credentials and took his gun from the bar. Outside, the SWAT team was just getting into place for the raid.

"Short guy with the dumbstruck look on his face in the lounge," Fisher told the commander. "You can't miss him."

22 "Howe."

"Colonel, stand by for Dr. Blitz."

Howe held the cell phone away from his body. He was sitting at the side of a desk in a large room that filled most of the second story of the Circleville police station, going over the incident with one of the detectives for the third time.

"I have to take this, and it's kind of private," he told the man.

"My part is wrapped up just about anyway," said the detective amiably. "I'm going to go get a Coke. When you're off the phone, we'll go talk to my boss, okay? Back in room two downstairs?"

"Yeah, okay," said Howe as the detective got up.

"Colonel, I hope you're okay," said Blitz over the cell phone.

"I'm fine," said Howe.

"I understand the FBI caught some of the people involved."

"Yes."

"I have some other news." The national security advisor paused for a moment; Howe could hear him murmuring something to one of his assistants before coming back on the line. "Your clearance has been restored. The CIA people made a mistake."

"Okay."

"I'm wondering if you could come over to my office and look at some photos we have. We want to confirm they're the UAVs you saw in Korea."

"All right. It may take a while. I'm at the police station, making a statement," said Howe.

"Understood. But the sooner the better."

"Yes, sir."

CHAPTER

23

Sin Ru Chow, whose status as lowlife was attested to by all and sundry, had vanished, and not even the experts on lowlifes at the Washington, D.C., Police Department could locate him. Fisher told the detective he talked to there that they could remove the underworld thug's photo from their rogue's gallery; it was a good bet that the next time he was seen, it would be on a mortuary slab.

With the safety pins holding his pants together beginning to chafe, Fisher returned to his apartment for a fresh suit. The phone rang as he was coming through the door; he answered it, hoping it was someone trying to sell him vinyl siding.

"Andy, where are you?" asked Cindy Malone, Jack Hunter's secretary. "Jack's been trying to get ahold of you all day."

"Shouldn't cost more than a few thousand to repair," Fisher.

"A few thousand for what?"

"Which?"

"Don't be smart, Andy."

"That's what they pay me for, isn't it?"

"What did you break this time?"

"I'm not telling you until the bill comes in," said Fisher. He'd been thinking of the warehouse roof; the repair bill for the bullet holes in the helicopter would undoubtedly hit five figures if not six.

"Jack is having a press conference first thing in the morning and he wants you there," said Malone. "Since you rescued Howe."

"No, thanks. I have to get up to New York. Listen, if you want my advice, tell him not to hold a press conference."

"Why not?"

"We haven't broken the case yet."

"But Howe's okay. The press wants a hero."

"Or a goat," said Fisher. "Tell Hunter to hold off."

"But, Andrew, *please*."

He hated it when she said *please*.

"I'm telling you, Cindy, we haven't figured it all out yet." He glanced at his watch. "What are you still doing in the office? It's after eight. You're missing your *Wheel of Fortune* reruns."

"I had to stay until I got you."

"Well, now you can go."

"Please. The press conference is already scheduled. It'll make Jack very happy. And problems with your expenses are much easier to smooth over when he's happy," she said. "Tell you what: You do this, and I'll get him to sign some blank vouchers right when he's smiling for pictures. How's that?"

"I have more important things to do than press conferences," Fisher told her.

"Like what?"

"Like putting on my pants," he said, hanging up.

PART FIVE

Grasping at Straws

CHAPTER

1

Fisher stood at the window of the Scramdale-on-Hudson train station, gazing out at the parking lot as it filled with morning commuters. There were more luxury SUVs per square inch in Scramdale-on-Hudson than anywhere in the universe. This was no doubt a function of the difficult terrain, where investment bankers and entertainment lawyers daily negotiated such dangers as overfertilized lawns and exotic clematis.

The parade of Mercedes and BMWs up to the station was broken every so often by a Volvo wagon, undoubtedly driven by renegade hippies struggling to get by on trust fund money. It was a good bet their nannies lugged D. H. Lawrence in their diaper bags rather than the de rigueur Shakespeare to read aloud at naptime.

Fisher lit a cigarette as a Crown Vic appeared in the parade. The car was stopped twice by the lot attendants, trying to enforce local regulations against riffraff. Fisher ambled down the steps as the car finally pulled up. He tossed his cigarette to the curb and got in.

"You better pick up the butt or they may give you a

ticket for littering," said Macklin, who was behind the wheel.

"If you drive out to the end of the lot you can cut over the dirt and get onto the highway."

"That'll get us going back toward the city," said Macklin.

"That's where we want to go."

"Why?"

"I want to talk to Mrs. DeGarmo again."

"Faud's landlady?"

"Yeah. She's the only woman in Queens who knows how to make a good cup of coffee. The stuff they have at the station is atrocious."

Mrs. DeGarmo remembered Fisher a little too well.

"It's about time you come back," she said, laying on the bad grammar and Italian accent for effect when he and Macklin rang the bell. "The leak, she still leaks."

"I was afraid of that," said Fisher. "This is my assistant," he added, gesturing to Macklin. "He's an expert in leaks."

"Where's your tools?" asked Mrs. DeGarmo.

"We investigate, then we get the proper tools," said Fisher. "Is that coffee I smell?"

She eyed Macklin suspiciously.

"I brought more doughnuts," said Fisher, holding up the bag.

"All right, you come in," she told Fisher. Then she turned back to Macklin. "You, I don't know about."

"Mrs. DeGarmo, we've met before," said Macklin. "I'm with Homeland Security. Remember?"

She squinted at the ID card he produced.

"Oh, okay, come in," she said, waving her hand. "If Andy says."

"He's good with a flashlight," said Fisher, who was already in the hallway.

Fisher went into the bathroom, taking off the top to the toilet tank.

"It's already been searched, Andy," said Macklin, coming in. "I keep telling you. Faud Daraghmeh's probably back in Egypt."

"He's from Yemen."

"Whatever."

Fisher searched the bathroom carefully, discovering that Mrs. DeGarmo had changed her denture cream. He asked her for the key to Faud Daraghmeh's apartment, which had not yet been rented out.

"Why search again?" asked Macklin when he came back downstairs. By now Mrs. DeGarmo's "stories" were on and she was in the front room, watching them.

"Best place to hide something now," explained Fisher, helping himself to some coffee. "Come back after it's been searched."

"No way," said Macklin.

Fisher sipped the coffee, which was ever more bitter than he remembered. He wondered if maybe he should go into the plumbing business so he'd have a legitimate excuse to visit Mrs. DeGarmo when the case ended.

"You're grasping at straws, Andy," added Macklin. "You know this case is closed."

Fisher said nothing, examining the list of items seized during the earlier search. Faud's computer had checked out clean; besides his schoolbooks, the only papers he had in his apartment had been junk mail. He had two pairs of "battered dress shoes," three red button-down shirts, assorted T-shirts, one pair of polyester pants, two pairs of dress pants, and one pair of jeans.

No suitcase? No backpack?

No underwear or socks.

Fisher took a long sip of coffee. The grains from the bottom of the cup settled on his tongue.

Heaven. But he had no time to linger.

"All right," he told Macklin. "Let's get going."

"Where?"

"Library."

*   *   *

According to the want ads, there had been more than a dozen vacant apartments in the immediate area the week before. Ruling out ones still advertised this week, Fisher found eight possibilities. He also got a list of apartment brokers.

"You have your people go to each one with the description of Faud Daraghmeh," Fisher told Macklin, giving him the list. "It's probable that he'd take an apartment within ten or so blocks of the train, something easy to walk."

"Why don't you think they already had a place set up somewhere else?" said Macklin.

"I do. But we haven't found it, and this is the grasping-at-straws phase of the case," said Fisher. "So we have some serious grasping to do."

"Andy, the case is closed," said Macklin. "It's done. Don't you think?"

"No," said Fisher. "And I'll tell you something else: The fact that we can't find this guy makes me worry. A lot."

"You're worrying? Really?"

"That's my point," said Fisher.

Fisher made his way into Manhattan and up to Washington Heights, where he went not to the apartment that had been raided but to the shoe repair shop across the street. The proprietor stood at his workbench behind the front counter, looking exactly as he had when Fisher had last been there. The only sign that he had moved in the interim was the fact that there were no cobwebs or dust on him.

"You've come for the other heel," said the man when Fisher walked in.

"I'm always looking for other heels," said Fisher. "You remember me?"

"I fixed your right heel the other day." The man pointed to a book of tickets. "You're number 657A92. You take a D width. Wide foot."

"Wide foot, big brain," said Fisher. He slipped off his left shoe. "How much?"

"Ehh. Ten dollars. Two minutes."

Fisher reached for his wallet.

"No, you pay when it's finished." The cobbler reached over to the side of his bench and pulled over a thick book of customer tickets. "Here. Fill this out."

"What? Another one?"

"Every job gets a new receipt," said the man. "Everyone comes into the shop—new ticket."

"Everyone?"

"*Sí.* I have this shop for fifty years. Every customer gets a receipt. You know how many shoes I lose? None. Because they have a receipt. That is the secret to a fine business. Receipts."

"Even for ten minutes?"

"Every customer has to have a ticket," the man assured Fisher. "Every one. Address and phone number. Those are the rules. You think I stay in business for fifty years without a system? You make one exception, you know what you get?"

"Tennis shoes," said Fisher.

The proprietor nodded grimly.

"Your helpers do that too? Fill out receipts."

"My helpers? Of course." The cobbler frowned. "Someone comes in, they make out a ticket."

"Just to talk?"

"No talking. Work only." The man's frown deepened. "Maybe that's why they quit, eh? They don't even have the respect to tell me to my face. I have to guess when I don't see them. These people."

"They spend a lot of time talking to people when they worked here? Friends or anything?"

"No talk. I pay good money to work. Work only. No friends. None."

"No one?"

"Everyone who comes in: shoes and a ticket. You want

to talk, you go to Joe's down the street." He gestured in the direction of a barber. "He talks. Aiyeee, he talks. Numbers too."

"Did they know any customers?"

The cobbler rubbed his chin with his little tack hammer. "Well, customers. They bring a few. That's good for business."

"They filled out a ticket?"

"All the time. Those are the rules."

The tickets were discarded once the book was filled, but by then the important customer information had been added to the owner's permanent records. Each night after closing, the cobbler copied the day's ticket stub information into a black-and-white marble notebook of the sort schoolchildren once used before the days of PDAs.

"See, is guaranteed," explained the cobbler. "A sole, guaranteed for the life of the shoe. What if you come in next year, you say I have given you a sole, when all I did was the heel? Ehhh." He waved his hand as if he were smacking an imaginary cheater.

"You don't remember your work?" said Fisher.

"Oh, I remember, but this way, I put it on paper, the customer just nods. I learn in the early days. Believe me, people cheat you."

"I'll bet," said Fisher.

After Fisher's heel was fixed and paid for, they sat together going over the notebooks from the past six months. Fisher jotted down addresses of people the cobbler didn't recognize as being longtime residents of the area.

It amounted to only three entries. Each name was Arabic, though that was hardly telling in New York.

Fisher found a cab that had somehow strayed uptown in error and went to check out the addresses. One was over on Amsterdam Avenue, a few blocks away in a large apartment complex; the second was up in Inwood, the very northern tip of the island. And the third one didn't exist.

Which naturally made it the most interesting of all.

CHAPTER

2

The bomb had already been made for him. All Faud had to do was put the wiring in and set it in the hallway. He had been warned to follow the directions very carefully or face catastrophe. He worried now as he stood with the wire over the connector: Had he followed the steps precisely right?

Surely he had, he told himself. It was a devil again distracting him. The imam had warned him of this.

Seeing the imam had been a surprise and a great consolation. He was prepared now. He had told himself before that he was prepared, but now he truly felt it.

The truck would be waiting. He would take the canister he had prepared and then drive to the station. So long as he went in at precisely two A.M., no one would see him. Once past the gate—he had practiced jimmying the lock already—no one would stop him or even ask about the bags he carried.

He could open them if asked. The gear inside looked as if it came from the fire department.

If all went well, he would be in his spot by four o'clock. And then he would simply have to wait.

Pray and wait. Things he was used to doing.

Faud's fingers shook as he brought the wire near the connector on the bomb he was setting. Worry seized him.

What if the imam had lied? What if this bomb was not a diversion in case he was found, but a way of killing him?

The top was covered with a mesh bag of nails. His body would be torn to shreds.

He was unprepared and would not enter paradise if he died today. His hand jittered again.

No, he told the empty apartment. *I trust the imam and I trust God.* He closed his eyes and pushed the wire around the post, screwing it down as he caught his breath.

3

Dr. Blitz frowned in the direction of the tuna fish sandwich Mozelle had brought, then turned his attention back to the draft report on the Korean government situation, studying the language the State Department had recommended the President use in his speech to the UN next Monday. The speech would call for a plebiscite on reunification, though the wording being recommended was so guarded even Blitz wasn't sure that's what it said.

Certainly there was a need to be diplomatic: Anything the President said might be interpreted as pressure and be used by Korean critics to stir up resentment not just in the North but in the South as well. Still, it had to be clear that the U.S. was not only in favor of the vote but would help Korea—all of Korea—work toward overcoming its divided and tumultuous past.

It would be an expensive commitment. Treasury had sent over a memo claiming that simply keeping the North from starvation would cost twice what the U.S. had spent on Iraq, and there were no oil reserves to defray the costs. Peace was an expensive proposition.

Blitz wasn't generally one to worry about the costs of things; the bean counters would always complain, in his opinion. But Congress would undoubtedly use the money issue to throw up roadblocks.

An issue for tomorrow. Right now he had to get the speech right. Blitz brought up his word processor and began preparing a few changes. He was just getting into the flow when Mozelle buzzed in

"You wanted to talk to Major Tyler in Korea?" she asked. "He's on line three. It's pretty late over there."

"Thanks."

Blitz turned around to the phone.

"Tyler?" he asked after punching in the line.

"Dr. Blitz?"

"I heard you had a bit of trouble out there," said Blitz.

"Yes, sir. No serious casualties. Pilot broke his leg, some concussions. That was the worst of it."

"God was with you."

"Yes, sir."

"What can you tell me about the UAVs?"

"Nothing beyond what was in the interim report," said Tyler. "They look like mini-airplanes to me, or even something closer to spaceships. The radio control gear and the engines were missing. The design itself I guess was interesting, but I'm not an expert."

"So you're sure there were no engines?"

"Yes, sir. No engines there. Or the control apparatus they would need to fly."

"Good," said Blitz. He'd thought of having the President mention the weapons in his speech as an example of the North Korean threat—evidence that they were much more advanced than the intelligence community gave them credit for being—but now it seemed unwise. The project was obviously just another boondoggle. It would be interesting to see where the design had come from: Russia was the leading candidate, but it would be months if not years before it was tracked down.

"Tell me about North Korea. What's the situation on the ground there?" asked Blitz. He listened as the Army major told him more or less what he had expected: The people for the most part were anxious and hungry. There were still bands of resisters, as his experience at the airfield attested. And there was a great deal of animosity between North and South, making for friction.

"Putting the two halves together won't be easy," Blitz said when Tyler finished.

"No, sir."

"Has to be done, though."

"Yes, sir."

"Do you mind if I mention what you've told me to the President?"

"No, sir. I, uh, I'd be flattered."

"He was asking about you," said Blitz. "He knows you did a hell of a job."

"Thank you."

"You sound tired, Major. I'm sorry for interrupting your sleep."

"Thank you, sir."

"I hope to see you soon," added Blitz as he hung up.

CHAPTER 4

Howe spent all of the morning and a good deal of the afternoon recounting the kidnapping for investigators. They were spare with their own details, but it was clear from their questions that they connected it with the Korean operation, an attempt by the Korean he had rescued to tie up loose ends.

Howe asked one of the investigators—a DIA officer named Kowalski—point-blank why they'd bother. Kowalski blinked a few times and then shrugged.

A long queue of messages awaited him both at the motel and on his cell phone's voice mail when he was finally done with the interviews. He sat in the motel lobby systematically listening and recording the numbers and callers on a pad. Before he decided who to call back, however, he phoned his mother for the second time that day, just to reassure her that he was all right.

"Jimmy called you," she said, mentioning his friend. "He's hoping you're all right."

"Yeah, he called my cell phone too," he told her.

"Well, people worry."

"I'm okay, Ma." It occurred to Howe that he had been having some variation of this conversation for forty years.

"He has tickets for a football game."

"NCAAs, Mom. It's basketball. In New York. I already left a message telling him I can't go."

"He's very excited."

Howe laughed. "He's always excited about something."

"Just so you know." His mother paused, changing the subject. "I'm going to bingo tonight with Gabby Thomas. I suppose my ears will be red for days."

"I guess," said Howe. He listened to his mother tell him something about the neighbors, then told her he had to get going.

"Well, of course you do. I will talk to you when I talk to you," she said.

"Love you."

He didn't usually say that, and it took his mother a half-second to respond.

"I love you, too, Billy."

Among the callers on his voice mail were three members of the NADT board, along with Delano, who was belatedly expressing surprise at the security snafu and sympathy about the "incident." Howe decided that firing the vice president would be the first thing he did; one thing he didn't need was a phony.

Howard McIntyre was the one person he wanted to talk to who *hadn't* called. As Howe went through the cell menu to find his number, the cell phone rang; it was Alice.

"Hi," he said.

"I wasn't sure I'd get you," she said. "I thought I'd just leave a message."

"It's me in the flesh," he said. He winced, overly self-conscious but unable to do anything about it.

"Well . . ." she started.

"Well, what?"

"I, um . . . I'm sorry."

"Sorry?"

Howe felt a pain in his ribs, a physical pain: She was dumping him.

Not dumping him exactly, since they weren't a couple

or anything like that, but she was going to tell him they couldn't be.

The pain was like a hard cramp, the sort that might come from sudden depressurization.

He loved her, and he wasn't going to let her walk away.

"I was rude yesterday," she said.

"Rude?" The word croaked from his mouth. "You weren't rude."

"I should have thanked you for saving my life. But I didn't."

"If it weren't for me, you wouldn't have been there. So I apologize. *I'm* the one who should apologize."

What else is it? he thought to himself. *Go ahead and tell me.*

Go ahead.

"Why don't we argue about it over dinner?" he told her.

"Argue?"

"I'm joking. Want to have dinner with me?"

She hesitated. If she said no, he would ask, straight out, if she was seeing someone else.

Then he'd pull out all the stops. Though he wasn't exactly sure what that would mean.

"Where do you want to eat?" Alice said finally.

CHAPTER

5

Macklin put a surveillance team on the real addresses but couldn't come up with enough people to canvas the area of the phony address, which would have been across from Madison Square Garden if it had existed. Fisher decided to walk it himself, checking variations of the address on the theory that the real address would turn out to be some variation of the false one. He found a pizza parlor, an Israeli restaurant, and a junk shop proclaiming that it sold Manhattan's finest selec-

tion of antiques, but no safe house or reasonable fac-
simile.

"What'd you find out?" asked Macklin when he called
in to see if anything was new.

"Scalpers are getting five hundred bucks for decent
seats to the NCAA play-offs this weekend," said Fisher.

"Five hundred, huh? Cheap."

"Yeah, I bought two and charged it to your task force."

"You're shitting me."

"I am," said Fisher.

"God, you just about gave me a heart attack," said
Macklin.

"You search those two apartments?"

"Jesus, Andy, there's no way in the world I can get a
search warrant based on an address in a shoemaker's
ledger. You know that."

"You have to be creative, Macklin. Come on. You're dis-
appointing me."

"Look, if it helps, the Amsterdam Avenue place is vacant."

"Sure that helps," said Fisher. "That's probably the
place."

"I don't think so. The building was torn down two
weeks ago."

"Maybe we should sift the rubble."

"You're kidding, right?"

"We're grasping at straws, Macklin. You have to get into
the spirit of things," said Fisher, though he, too, doubted
that sifting the ruins would actually turn up anything.

"I put it under surveillance. Somebody's watching it."

"What about the other one—up in Inwood, right? Let's
get a search warrant."

"If we see anything suspicious, then we can move."

"He's a terrorist and a fugitive, Kevin. You put that on
the legal papers, the judge pounds his gavel, and we go in."

"Come on, Andy. This is New York. I couldn't get a
search warrant here to raid Lee Harvey Oswald's house."

"That's because he didn't do it," said Fisher.

Macklin, no conspiracy buff, changed the subject. "Kowalski has a phone conference set up for five."

"That's nice."

"Come on, Andy. I have a number for you to call in to. You can do it with your sat phone. He's been in D.C. talking to Howe and getting some other background. He really thinks the case is wrapped up," Macklin added, "but if you want to present your arguments to him—"

"Listen, I'll make you a deal: I don't scalp the tickets and I miss the phone conference, okay?"

"Andy. Look, I'll call you, okay? Just leave your line open."

"What kind of seats you want? On the aisle?"

Macklin hung up. Fisher walked around some more, hoping to be struck by inspiration; the only thing that came close was a bike messenger crossing against the light. Finally, Fisher decided he might just as well head back up to Scramdale; with any luck he'd be on the train when Macklin tried to connect for the conference call.

His wanderings had taken him over to Seventh Avenue, where there was an entrance to the subway. Unsure whether the lines that stopped here went to the Grand Central train station, Fisher did something native New Yorkers are loath to do in public: He stopped and consulted one of the large subway maps near the gates.

The trains in question were the 1, 2, 3, and 9, and are known collectively as the Broadway Line, taking their name from the fact that they follow the street. They did not, in fact, go to Grand Central, though it was possible to get there via a shuttle at Times Square.

Much more interestingly, Fisher realized that, not only was it the same line that went to Washington Heights, but the train ran north to Inwood—and its last stop in Manhattan was within two blocks of the address he'd found earlier.

A straw, surely, but one to be seized.

* * *

"Last natural forest in New York," said one of the detectives Macklin had sent to watch the Inwood address. He jerked his hand behind him, gesturing toward the expanse of trees rising to the northwest. "You know, Peter Minuit bought Manhattan on a spot over there."

"I'll take the tour later," said Fisher. "We have a suspect or what?"

"Basement apartment, halfway down Nagle," said the detective. "Separate entrance. Looks vacant."

Nagle mixed small food markets with check cashing shops with travel agencies; some of the signs were in Spanish but the graffiti betrayed a much wider mix of ethnic slurs. The man playing tour guide was named Witt. He was a state trooper whose enthusiasm made it clear he was not a native. Fisher and Witt sat in the front seat of a Jimmy SUV; Witt's partner was in the back, nursing a 7-Up. They had a clear view of the apartment's entrance, which sat between two travel stores. The entrance to the upper portion of the building was near the end of the block. Fisher noted that there were plenty of pay phones along the street.

"You interview the subject?" Fisher asked.

"Our orders were to watch the place," said Witt. "Nobody's come in or out."

"You mean nobody's used that entrance."

"It's the only way into the apartment."

"Where were you born?"

"Long Island. Why?"

There was almost surely another entrance to the building from the apartment itself; the unit would have been set up originally either for a superintendent or else was a utility area for a furnace. In any event, there was no sense making a federal case out of it.

"Drive around the block a bit. I want to see what it looks like."

"If we leave, we're not going to know if anybody comes in or out."

"Yeah," said Fisher.

The trooper put the truck in gear. They drove past the 207th Street train yard, then back around toward Baker Field and Inwood Hill Park. It was a very mixed neighborhood, a little lower in the pecking order than Astoria, maybe, but probably a notch or two above the place in Washington Heights.

Witt pointed out some rocks he said had been disturbed by the "glaciers."

"Very historical area," said the trooper as they swung past the Dyckman House, which had been built just after the Revolutionary War and, by some colossal municipal oversight, had actually been preserved by the City.

"I'm thinking our guys don't care too much for history—or glaciers," said Fisher. "Park the car and let's go talk to Mr. Brown."

Fisher had the others go around from upstairs, covering the back entrance.

"You sure you want both of us there?" asked Witt. "What if he shoots you or something?"

"I doubt we'll be that lucky," said Fisher.

He gave the others a minute to get into position, then went down the stairs and rapped loudly on the door. He had to try twice before he heard shuffling inside.

"Yes?"

"Mr. Brown?"

"Yes?"

"FBI. I'd like to talk to you for a second."

"FBI?"

"You probably hear that all the time, right?" said Fisher. He had his wallet out and held it up against the window near the door. "Here, take a look. I want to ask you a couple of questions."

"FBI?"

"Yeah."

"J. Edgar Hoover?"

"His illegitimate son."

Locks began turning. Fisher held his creds out as the door opened.

There was no need to. Brown was blind.

"You're with the FBI?" asked the man, who was about sixty-five. He had an ebony face with short but full gray hair, and walked with a slight stoop.

Fisher glanced at his feet. He was wearing sneakers.

"I wanted to ask you about some shoes," Fisher told Brown. "You have some dress shoes fixed a while ago?"

"Dress shoes? Me?"

"Mind if I come in?" said Fisher.

"Come along."

The apartment had a mildew odor and the white walls had weathered gray. There wasn't much furniture: a sofa and easy chair in the living room, a bed and wardrobe in the bedroom, table and chairs in the kitchen.

"What does the FBI want with shoes?"

"We're very into heels," said Fisher. "Mind if I look at yours?"

"Look away," said Mr. Brown.

Fisher followed him to the closet. Mr. Brown's dress shoes were worn at the heels and hadn't been repaired since they'd been bought, let alone within the past six months. Fisher looked around the closet and under the bed without finding any other shoes—or sarin gas, or E-bombs, or anything except a little dust. He went with the man into the kitchen, telling him about the shoemaker but being purposely vague about what sort of case he was working on. Mr. Brown had lived in the Inwood area for more than thirty years, though he'd only had this apartment for about five. He had not been to Washington Heights in more than three decades, not since his friend Jimmy Fleming had died; they used to talk baseball and drink beer in Jimmy's kitchen on St. Nicholas Avenue.

"Used to cheat," said Brown. "I know he did. But he was a good sort otherwise, so I let him. And he was free with the beer."

St. Nicholas was a block away from the apartment the three suspects had been in, but it was obviously just a coincidence.

But what about Brown's name and address? Fisher's theory was that the terrorists had used it as a way of passing along the address either of a drop or a meeting place. But if Brown had lived here for all that time, it couldn't be either.

Just another coincidence, then?

That was the worst part of the grasping-at-straws stage: The straws inevitably came up short, bent, and twisted.

"Someone's in the hall out there," said Mr. Brown. He jerked his hand toward a door at the far end of the kitchen.

"Just my guys backing me up," Fisher told him. "Lot of people come down that hallway?"

"Nah. Door's been stuck for a year."

Fisher got up and looked at it. It had at least a dozen coats of white paint and several varieties of locks, including one keyed dead bolt about six feet from the ground.

Higher, he thought, than Mr. Brown could reach.

"Mind if I try it?" asked Fisher.

"Suit yourself."

"You got the keys?"

"Don't need keys from the inside."

"When was the last time the apartment was painted?" Fisher asked.

"Oh, God, before I moved in. The landlord's offered to spruce things up, but it's fine with me."

"Maybe you should try the door," suggested Fisher.

Brown got up and went to it, opening all of the locks—except the dead bolt.

"See?" said Brown.

Macklin was unsympathetic when Fisher called him from the stakeout car.

"Let me get this straight," said Macklin. "You want a

warrant to search the apartment of a blind man because there's a lock on the door he can't reach?"

"Pretty much."

"With nothing to link the blind man to the terrorists."

"That's right. He's not involved."

"You know, Fisher, I used to think you were a genius," said Macklin. "Now I think you're a crank."

"Since when are those mutually exclusive?"

"You missed the phone conference. Kowalski was asking for you."

"And?"

"DIA wants to close down the task force."

"Why?"

"Because it's finished."

"You haven't found out who bought the sarin gas or where they were going to use it, or how. You don't have Faud. And then there's the E-bomb."

"The E-bomb was a red herring," said Macklin. "Like your door lock. Look, we got a good bust on the sarin warehouse. We're still interviewing those guys we picked up in Washington Heights—"

"Who don't know anything," said Fisher.

"Who claim they don't know anything. Meanwhile, this Daud Faraghmeh—"

"Faud Daraghmeh."

"Whatever. He's gone. He hopped a plane out of Kennedy, I guarantee. He'll turn up twelve months from now in some CIA report on Egypt."

"Yemen."

"Whatever. Listen, in these days of budget cuts, we all have limited resources—"

"You been talking to Jack Hunter?" Fisher asked.

"As a matter of fact, he was in on the conference call, and he agreed that the task force is no longer necessary. We need to shift our resources around, especially with the President coming to town. The locals can take over the investigation and fill in the holes for the prosecutors. Hunter was mentioning a corruption case that he wanted you to—"

"We must be going through a tunnel," said Fisher. "You're breaking up."

"I thought you were still with the surveillance team."

"Can't hear a word you're saying." Fisher hit the End button, then turned to Witt, who had a bemused expression on his face.

"Zone sergeant would dock your pay if you tried that as a uniformed trooper," said the detective.

"Fortunately, Macklin's not a sergeant," said Fisher, "though he is often zoned. Let's go get something to eat. Bag the surveillance."

"Bag it completely?"

"Until Wednesday. That's when his home aide comes to take him shopping."

CHAPTER

6

Alice didn't look quite as beautiful as Howe remembered when he met her at the restaurant.

Somehow that made him feel even better about her. He took her hands and then leaned forward over the table to kiss her as she rose; she held back a moment before kissing him, her lips soft and wet with the wine she'd been sipping.

Howe ordered a beer, then began looking at the menu.

"How's their spaghetti?" he asked.

"You're having beer with spaghetti?" said Alice.

"That's not good?"

"I'm sure it's fine."

"I'm not really a fancy guy," said Howe. "I think that's why I didn't get all that excited about the house the other day. To me, you know, a house is just a house."

"It's more than that."

"For some people, sure." He saw by the look on her face that she'd taken that as an insult. He tried to change the subject by apologizing for the kidnapping.

"Well, *you* didn't kidnap me," she said.

"I'm sorry that you got involved, I mean. . . ."

The waiter appeared with his beer, then took their orders. Alice chose a special; Howe stuck with the spaghetti.

"Can we start all over?" he asked as the waiter left.

"Why?"

"Because we're kind of on the wrong foot here," he said. "I mean, we're different and—"

"Being different bothers you?"

"No," he said, shaking his head. He took a sip of the beer.

This was all a mistake, he thought to himself. But he was stuck now, and she was stuck too. She tried making conversation and he tried not stumbling. Their salads came. Howe had never been very good at small talk but tried some now, asking about the difference between romaine and iceberg lettuce. She told him the leaves were different.

"Why'd you want to have dinner with me?" he asked finally.

Alice put down her fork. "*You* wanted to have dinner with *me*," she said, taking her napkin off her lap.

She put it on the table and pushed her chair back.

"Wait," he said reaching for her arm. "The food's just coming. We might as well eat."

"Thanks anyway," said Alice, taking her hand back and walking away.

CHAPTER

7

"You want Syracuse over Kentucky?"

"I don't want anything over anything," Fisher told Macklin. "I don't bet."

"You don't bet? Go on. You have every other vice possible. You're telling me you don't gamble?"

"A man has to draw the line somewhere," said Fisher. He continued scrolling through the notes on the computer, where the case information was compiled.

" 'Final Four, first time in New York City,' " said Macklin, obviously parroting a commercial Fisher hadn't heard. " 'Games this weekend, with the championship next Monday. Come on. Join the pool. You have a one-out-of-four chance of winning.' "

"And a three-out-of-four chance of losing my money."

"All right, Fisher. Just don't pout on Tuesday when we're splitting the winnings."

"I'll do my best."

"Listen, the Secret Service is asking for a little cooperation running down some leads. . . ."

"I don't have time to talk to every nut in New York City, Michael."

"It's not every nut. Just the violently psychotic ones."

"Yeah, well, I don't have time." Fisher got up from the computer.

"Where are you going?"

"Grab a smoke."

Fisher hadn't lied exactly: He did have a cigarette immediately upon going outside the house.

It's just that he had that cigarette in one of the task force vehicles, which he drove to FBI headquarters in Virginia. Six hours and countless cigarettes later, he corralled his quarry, Martha Friedrickberg, an expert on identity theft who had investigated the credit card ring that was selling IDs to the terrorists.

Martha worked in an office that could have passed for a surgical scrub room. The whitewashed walls had nothing on them, her metal desk was bare, and even her computer was immaculate. The distinct odor of Listerine filled the air as Fisher entered the room.

Friedrickberg looked up from her computer. "Andy Fisher. Oh, Gawd."

"Happy to see you, too, Martha. How's the germs?"

"In stasis until you arrived."

"Stasis is good or bad?"

"Neither. That's the point: balance." Friedrickberg pulled a spray bottle out from a bottom drawer and placed it at her elbow. "What do you want, Andy?"

"I need some information on that credit card ring."

"Which one?"

Fisher started to explain.

"You could have just called on the phone," said Friedrickberg, turning to her computer.

"You would have taken the call?"

"Of course not."

"Yes, well, you're an exception in many ways."

She pulled up a list of numbers and pointed to it. Fisher leaned over the desk to look at it; Friedrickberg wheeled her chair backward.

"Just a lot of numbers, right?" said Fisher.

"And streptococcus is just another bacterium."

Fisher straightened. "I'm guessing it's not."

"Have you had your sinuses flushed lately?" Friedrickberg wheeled herself back behind the desk, closer to her bottle. "You'd be surprised what lurks in your septum."

"What about those numbers?"

"Fifty-three point six percent are from Asia, primarily Japan. We've tracked a significant subset to American tourists and businessmen."

"And this has something to do with strep throat?"

"I despair sometimes, Andy. I truly do."

Fisher instinctively reached for his pack of cigarettes. Friedrickberg was quicker on the draw, however: She had the bottle squared and ready to fire before he took the pack from his pocket.

"No smoking in the building," she intoned.

"Yeah, I know that," said Fisher. He twirled the pack between his fingers.

"I'm warning you, Andy. There's ammonia in here."

"So the significance of the card numbers is what?"

"There's an Asian connection. As a matter of fact, some of us think the real masterminds *are* Asian. They found these poor immigrants from Nigeria, knew they'd be willing to make some easy money, and set them up. Every few weeks they supply fresh data: credit card numbers, social security, date of birth, et cetera. The Nigerians go out and start creating a file, usually by applying for cell phones. They get it going, then sell off the cards. Sell a card for two hundred dollars, you've made more than a hundred percent profit."

"That's all they make?"

"The cards don't stay active for all that long. The credit card companies tend to figure out what's going on relatively quickly, since they're looking for this. What you want to do is use the card to set up new accounts, keep turning everything over. A few hundred dollars a shot, ten of them a week—not a bad income."

"Have you figured out the others yet?" asked Fisher.

"We're working on it."

"They work with real cards?"

"There's always a real card at the root, if you can trace it back far enough. They probably steal the cards from the same source, then divvy them up. Probably they throw some of the new cards back once they set up accounts, rather than taking in cash, because the amounts are small."

"Can I get an updated list of cards?"

"It's hard to come by."

"You're telling me you don't trust me?"

"We have different goals. You want to close your case. I want to close mine."

"Mine's more important."

"That's like saying one form of *E. coli* is more dangerous than another," she said. "It depends on your perspective."

Fisher patted the end of his cigarette pack against his palm. Friedrickberg threatened with her spray.

Then, completely out of character, she put it down.

"The problem with our investigation is getting access to records," she said. "As soon as most people see false charges on there, they report it and the credit card company gets involved. The people who have the cards stop using them. They're afraid of the mess involved in untangling their credit records."

"That's tough?"

"It's a real pain in the ass, especially once these people get involved. They do dozens of cards with all sorts of aliases and accounts. Just tracking them is difficult. We've tried using phony cards," added Martha. "But we think someone inside the credit card companies must be involved, because the phonies never go anywhere. If we just had the right circumstances, we could set up a sting and unravel this thing."

"I'm too busy to go to Japan right now," Fisher said.

"You don't have to. Just your credit cards."

Reluctantly, Fisher reached for his wallet.

8

The new chairman of the board of NADT's board of directors was a former vice president of the United States, now semiretired but still a major player inside the Beltway. Richard Nelson had a strong handshake and a confident manner, and he put Howe completely at ease when they finally met to discuss the job. Nelson had an office on K Street. There was a private club on the second floor of the building. He led Howe there via a private elevator; they sequestered themselves in a corner of the large room, alone except for Nelson's bodyguard, who stood a respectful distance away across the room.

"It's a ridiculously important job," said Nelson. "It's the equivalent of an undersecretary of defense, at the very least. And you're the best man for it."

"I hope so," said Howe.

"Well, I'm sure of it. So is the board of directors."

"I was told there might be questions about what happened in Korea," said Howe. McIntyre had advised him to take the problem head-on, a strategy Howe himself favored.

"None. The CIA and the FBI were the ones who were flummoxed, not you. The attempt on your life the other day proves it. Was your lady friend hurt?"

"She's not, uh, my girlfriend," said Howe. He winced a little. "She was just a real estate agent who had been showing me houses. The thugs got the wrong idea."

Nelson shook his head. "Thank God nothing happened to her."

"So what happens now? The board takes a vote?"

"They've already voted," said Nelson. "It was unanimous. You have the job—assuming you and I can come to terms."

On Wednesday morning, Mr. Brown's home aide showed up bright-eyed if not bushy-tailed at precisely nine A.M. The two state troopers had been reassigned to help the Secret Service on the psycho beat for the President's visit next week, so Fisher took the surveillance himself, huddling in a peeper-type raincoat on the corner opposite the main entrance. He had a paper bag around a beer can for camouflage; he'd poured out the beer and replaced it with coffee. This made it a little sweeter than he liked, but then, surveillance was all about weathering discomforts.

Fisher had put motion detectors with wireless alerts in the hallways so he could move around a bit and not have to stare at the place the whole time. He could see the stairway down to Mr. Brown's apartment with the help of a curved mirror in the lobby, but he had to stand directly across from the doorway to see it through the glass.

An hour passed, then two. Fisher went and bought another beer and another coffee at the store.

"Your liver's not going to know if it's coming or going," said the clerk in Spanish.

"It doesn't now," answered Fisher.

Mr. Brown and his aide returned a little past one. With no other lead, Fisher followed the aide to a bar two blocks away, where the young man had a Bud Lite before reporting to another assignment. Since the city council had not yet gotten around to outlawing lite beer, Fisher had to leave him be.

He was heading back toward Mr. Brown's when his sat phone rang. Worried that it was Macklin trying to hook him into the psycho watch, he checked the number before answering.

"Hey, Martha, how's my credit card doing?" he said, hitting the Talk button.

"Looks like you just bought a couch in Peoria."

"Great," said Fisher.

"It's a start, Andy," said Friedrickberg. "You'll move on to big-screen TVs by the end of the day, I promise."

"Bureau's going to reimburse me, right?"

"Oh, I wouldn't worry about it. You can always declare bankruptcy."

"Sounds promising."

"Listen, I did a little checking on your behalf, into your case."

"And?"

"I have a list of the regular customers. They're just mailing addresses for the most part: boxes. I can send it, but only to you."

"Let's save some time," said Fisher. "Which one is in Inwood? Nagle Avenue?"

"Jesus, Andy, how did you know?"

It was in Mr. Brown's building, two floors up.

Despite the fact that Fisher warned them the apartment would be empty, Macklin and the U.S. attorney who had obtained the search warrant insisted on joining Fisher, the two NYPD plainclothes detectives, the six uniform patrolmen, and the postal inspector on the raid. It was the postal inspector Fisher really wanted, since he figured the apartment was being used primarily as a mail drop. There was an oversize box in the lobby; the mailman said it usually accumulated nearly a month's worth of junk mail before being emptied.

Today it held only a week's worth, judging from the dates on the circulars and the thin community newspaper. There were no credit cards, a fact that bothered the federal attorney greatly since they had relied heavily on the cards for the search warrant.

The second-floor apartment itself was completely empty, without even furniture; if Faud Daraghmeh had stayed there, he had removed all traces of himself.

"I'll give him one thing," said Macklin. "He's a tidy son of a bitch. Assuming he was here."

"Let's talk to Mr. Brown and see if he'll let us look in his place," said Fisher.

"On what grounds?" asked the attorney.

"On the grounds that he's a nice guy with nothing to hide."

"You're really stretching it," said Macklin.

Brown *was* a nice guy, but the search of his apartment turned up nothing. When Fisher suggested chemical detection gear, the U.S. attorney left the apartment shaking his head. Macklin sighed and followed, as did the policemen. Fisher sat down with Mr. Brown and had a beer, which tasted a little funny without coffee in it.

"Tough day, huh?" asked the blind man.

"They're all tough."

"Tell me about it. But at least you got that door unstuck for me. I appreciate it."

"You're welcome," said Fisher. "Here's a question for you: Why would someone who lived in Inwood want a copy of a community newspaper from Chelsea?"

"See how the other half lives," said Brown. He found this funny and laughed.

Fisher sipped his beer.

"Or he used to live there," said Brown.

Fisher jumped up. "Thanks for the beer."

"You leavin'?"

"Gotta go find the newspaper office," said Fisher.

10

Three of the apartments listed in the *Gazette* had been rented, one by a woman and the other two by young men. Fisher concentrated on the men first, spending a good deal of Thursday and much of Friday morning ruling them out as Faud Daraghmeh.

This would have been relatively easy had he been able to see them at any point; the first renter turned out to be a six six weight lifter from Wisconsin seeking fame and fortune as an actor in New York. The other was a Buddhist monk, shaved head and all.

Which left, at least as far as this straw was concerned, the woman. The landlord hadn't given Fisher a name, and in fact had just rudely hung up when Fisher tried to get more details. Fisher went over to the apartment two blocks south of the Fashion Institute and realized that he should have come here first: The name taped on the mailbox was Fama Ahmed Ali. The apartment was on the third floor of a large building; there was no way for one person to watch it without camping directly outside the door, where he could be seen.

"No stakeout," said Macklin. "We don't have the personnel."

"You can't get NYPD to do it?"

"They have their hands full. Not only do they have the Final Four, but there's a big session going on at the UN right through the weekend. The President's coming up Monday. This is huge, even for New York."

"Get me a search warrant, then."

"A search warrant?"

"If I go knocking on the door and it is Faud Daraghmeh or his sister or whatever, they'll start flushing the evidence as soon as I leave."

"We're not even close to reasonable grounds here, Andy."

"You're telling me in all New York City, there's not one judge who'd give you a search warrant?"

"Jeez."

"What if we got an anonymous tip that Fama Ahmed Ali was plotting to kill the President."

"You can't do that, Andy! Christ."

"Just asking a theoretical question."

"I'll see if I can get a warrant. Don't call in a threat. Don't. Don't."

"Now, would I do that?"

A set of stairs sat at the end of the hallway on the third floor. Fisher had propped open one of the heavy glass and wrought-iron doors, which let him hear but not see what was happening in the hallway; he came down the steps a few times as the elevator stopped on the floor, but in the three hours he spent there, no one went in or out of the apartment. Finally, Macklin called: He'd managed to get the search warrant and even two NYPD officers to help in the search.

"Just two?" said Fisher, leaning back on the staircase. The steps were made of marble, though at some point someone had painted them with a very thick paint, then recoated them for good measure. The paint had peeled back to the sides of the steps but was still fairly thick on the risers. This seemed to be some object lesson in fashion, pretension, and perhaps utility, though Fisher couldn't quite figure what it was.

"Is there someone inside the apartment?" Macklin asked.

"I don't know," said Fisher. He glanced at his watch; it was nearly five. "Not much use hanging around, though. Let's hit the place now."

Macklin couldn't get into the city until seven, and so they set up the raid for seven forty-five.

Raid was a bit of an overstatement. With the two cops guarding the fire escape and Macklin and another Homeland Security agent behind him, Fisher banged on the door and told the occupants to open up. When no one answered, he used the key supplied by the landlord's rental agent, pushing the door open.

He jumped back just in time: A homemade bomb exploded in the interior of the hallway, sending shrapnel flying through the apartment.

CHAPTER

11

"I need to find a place to live," Howe told her.

"There are hundreds of real estate agents in this area."

"Yeah, but you already know what I want."

"Do I?"

"Yeah."

She sat back in her seat, then pulled the keys from the corner of her desk.

Howe followed her out to the lot. He pulled his seat belt on, watching her silently.

"There's a good condo development two miles from the highway. It's solid, not too fancy."

"Show me that house again, the one you liked."

Her faced reddened but she said nothing. As she pulled up near it, he saw there were two cars in the driveway; another Realtor was showing the place.

"So, why did you get mad at me the other night?" he asked as she turned off the car.

"I wasn't mad. At first. Then I got mad."

"Because I drink beer with spaghetti."

"No. Because . . . I don't know. You took it for granted."

"What?"

"Kissing me like that."

"Kissing you? I thought after what we'd been through that—"

"That what?"

What had he thought? That he liked her, that he owed her, that he wanted her.

But he seemed unable to say any of those things.

"I didn't mean it as a bad thing," Howe told her.

She put her car in gear and pulled away from the curb.

"Where are you going?"

"This isn't your kind of house. You think it's too fancy."

"Yeah, but *you* like it."

"You're the one who's buying. Or renting. Which one is it?"

"I can buy," said Howe. "They made a ridiculous offer and I took the job yesterday."

"You don't think you deserve it, do you?"

"No, I don't," he said.

"Well, you do."

"How do you know?"

"You just do." She turned the car around the circle at the end of the cul-de-sac. As they started back up the hill, the people were coming out of the house.

"Let's go take a look again," said Howe. "What the hell? You like showing it, and I'm not doing anything."

She didn't smile, but the way she turned her head told him somehow she would stop.

CHAPTER

12

Fisher sat with the bomb squad people as they sent a small robot rover into the apartment to look for more bombs. The rover looked a bit like a Martian lander, and the photos it sent back to the laptop were every bit as sketchy. The herringbone-pattern linoleum drove the automated video controls nuts, and the operators had a hard time making sure there were no more trip wires or similar devices in place. But at least the man at the laptop was free with his Camels.

The bomb squad moved in with full-gear even after the

rover's search came up empty. Fisher gave them a few minutes, then went inside.

"You shouldn't be in here," said one of the officers in a mattress suit near the door.

"If it hasn't gone boom yet, it's not going to," said Fisher, squatting down to examine the doorway. At the bottom was a set of connectors similar to those used in a simple burglar alarm system. Opening the door had broken the connection and set off the bomb. Fisher followed the wire down the scarred hallway to where the bomb had exploded.

"How did you know there was a bomb in there?" asked the NYPD expert who was taking measurements with a laser ruler in the hall.

"I didn't. I saw the connector thing and I jumped back," said Fisher.

"You're lucky the guy was an amateur: Somebody who knew what they were doing would have set it to explode closer to the door or even out in the lobby. Between the heavy door and the shape of the hall, most of the explosion was channeled away from you. Otherwise you would have been nailed."

He meant that literally: 10d nails had been packed over the weapon as shrapnel.

"You see this kind of bomb before?" Fisher asked.

"Oh, sure. Amateurs. Or someone trying to convince us they're amateurs."

"Most people who are stupid are just stupid," said Fisher.

"Can't argue with that. Were they trying to kill you specifically, or just anyone?"

"Don't know yet," said Fisher. He squatted down to examine a large piece of the exploded bomb, which lay partly embedded in the wall. "Probably just anyone. How would you turn this off?"

"You mean disarm it? Probably some sort of bypass switch at the door."

"There isn't one," said Fisher, rising.

"Remote control or something. It wouldn't be hard."

"Yeah, except that's not part of a remote control unit, right?" Fisher pointed to the piece. "It's just a metal piece where the explosives were."

"Might've disintegrated. Crime scene guys will go over it pretty well."

Fisher walked to the far end of the hallway. The window had been blown out, but the locks in the frame were still secure. The bathroom to the right had an open window, but it was too small for anyone but a thin child to climb through. He went into the room on the left. There was no furniture or clothes, no sign that the room had been occupied. The window had a simple lock at the top, but it was not engaged. Fisher checked the casement for another trip wire, then opened the window. The fire escape was to the right.

He leaned out, got his foot on it, then climbed over.

"Fisher, what the hell are you doing?" shouted Macklin, coming into the room just as he swung out.

The FBI agent leaned back over. "You wouldn't want to do this every day, would you?" he said, climbing in. He scraped his shoe against the side of the building, but the height was a powerful incentive and he kept his momentum going forward. He got into the building.

"What the hell are you doing?" Macklin asked again.

"Trying to figure out how Faud got in and out. And whether he was planning on coming back."

"He won't be coming back now, that's for sure," said Macklin.

"Guy's going to run out of places to stay eventually." Fisher walked to the bathroom. There was soap and toilet paper but nothing else. Fisher leaned over and sniffed the soap. "Ivory," he declared.

"Yeah?" asked Macklin.

"Same stuff he used at DeGarmo's."

"That'll close the case."

"Just what I'm thinking," said Fisher.

"Want to dust it for prints?"

"You're starting to get the hang of the sarcasm thing, Macklin. Keep it up and in a couple of years you'll actually say something biting."

Fisher decided that the bomb had been left for the same reason some people slid hairs in door cracks and dusted the floor with powder: It would clearly and emphatically demonstrate that the apartment had been discovered. That didn't mean collateral damage wasn't welcome, only that it wasn't first on the priority list.

"I think he'd have some sort of vantage point to watch from, or be nearby when the bomb blew," Macklin told Fisher. "What if we search every apartment the fire escape connects to?"

"That's twenty-one apartments," said Fisher.

"We should at least make sure he's not living in another one here, and that this is just a decoy."

The bomb had gotten NYPD somewhat more interested in what was going on, and Macklin now had the manpower to do the interviews. On the other hand, the explosion had alerted the other occupants of the building, and Fisher figured anyone dumb enough be a terrorist or hide one would be smart enough to lie about it or, smarter still, to have fled. Still, there was always the chance that someone might remember something about a cross-dressing neighbor with five o'clock shadow. Besides, they were still mired in the straw-grasping phase of the investigation, and so Fisher didn't object—as long as he didn't have to do any of the interviews.

"What are you going to do?" Macklin asked.

"Climb the fire escape."

"It's getting pretty dark."

"It is, isn't it," said Fisher, going to the blown-out window and stepping through the frame.

*   *   *

A pair of mangled beach chairs sat folded at one side of the roof, but otherwise it was empty. The small door at the top of the stairway locked from the inside. Fisher jiggled it but it wouldn't give. Picking the lock was no good; Fisher had to go all the way down and then trudge up the stairs to see if there was a bag or other hideaway.

A simple dead bolt secured the door to the roof; there were no bags or keys hidden anywhere that he could see, and his second search of the roof failed to turn up anything except a fifty-cent coin near the edge of the roof. A ladder led from the back of the building to the adjacent roof. Fisher climbed over it and continued his search, still without results. A third roof sat adjacent to this one, eight feet lower and across a narrow alley.

The sun had gone down quite a while ago, but the lights from a building across the street made it possible to see, though not particularly well.

Which was why he wasn't sure whether the long narrow object near the front of the roof was a ladder or not.

The easiest way to find out was to jump across. Fisher did so, rolling onto the flat surface and bumping into a large can of roofing tar. Fortunately, its top remained intact; Fisher was already down to his last reasonably clean suit.

The object he'd seen was a long two-by-four with three shorter pieces of wood nailed to it. Fisher took it to the side and hooked it over the brick lip on the adjacent building. The board made it possible to get up to the other side without too much trouble, though it creaked under his weight.

So the guy who used it was a little shorter and at least as skinny, Fisher thought.

The FBI agent picked up the edge of the board and flipped it back to the other roof, then jumped back to examine the roof. There was no stairway down; the roof was accessed through a flat trapdoor that was not only locked but chained.

A small bag was wedged in a crack in the low wall at the front of the roof. Fisher held it up and saw that it was marijuana, or at least something herbal. He stuffed it back in place and continued his search in the shadows. As he did, his stomach began to growl. Wondering if he could hunt up a midnight hot dog vendor, he went back to the ladder board and hooked it into place. He was just reaching across when he saw the tar bucket he'd knocked into earlier.

The thing was, the tar on the roof was dry—very, very dry.

And who tarred a roof in March?

Old can, probably used as a seat.

Or a hiding place. Fisher pried it open.

The remnants of tar had congealed long ago. Newspapers had been stuffed into the top, and in the middle of the newspapers sat a small knapsack. There was a shirt inside, along with a gas mask, an autoinjector similar to the one he'd found at Mrs. DeGarmo's, and a set of night goggles.

CHAPTER 13

"Hey, Colonel, how are you doing?" said the voice on the cell phone when Howe answered.

A very recognizable, if inconvenient, voice.

"I'm very busy right now, Fisher."

"That wasn't my question."

"It was my answer," said Howe.

"Listen, I need some advice."

"This is a real bad time, Fisher. I've had a tough few days and I'd like to relax."

"Tell me about it. I just missed getting blown up by a nail bomb in New York City."

"What do you need advice for?"

"If you had an E-bomb, how would you drop it? Would you rent a plane?"

"How do you know it's going to be dropped?"

"I don't. That was what the experts said when we were talking about it. You would use it over a set of transformers or a big switching yard, someplace where you can have a big impact. So I'm figuring airplane."

"Or a cruise missile," said Howe. "Or a UAV."

"What's a UAV?"

"Fisher, where are you?"

"At the moment I'm standing in a hallway of a prewar apartment in Chelsea, watching some crime scene guys pull nails out of the wall."

"Can you get to a secure phone?"

"If I have to. Take me an hour and a half, though."

"Call me back on this line with your sat phone, then I'll call you."

Howe killed the cell phone. There was a secure phone at NADT he could use, but of course that meant leaving Alice.

She was in the kitchen, clearing the dishes from dinner.

"I'm going to have to go," he said.

"Now?"

"In a few minutes, yeah. It's, um . . . it's important."

"And you can't talk about it."

He shook his head.

"Is it related to the other day?" she asked.

"No." His answer was honest—he didn't think it was at first—but as he thought about it he decided it might be. It was too late to take it back, but the realization made him feel guilty, as if he'd deliberately lied.

"Very mysterious," she said, closing the dishwasher. Alice walked to him, sliding her arms around his waist to his back, pulling him down to her lips. "When did you have to leave?"

14

Howe's story about the UAVs gave Fisher a tenuous connection with the Koreans, but the agent had already used up his quota of tenuous connections on the case.

"You have any evidence there were other UAVs?" Fisher asked as they discussed it over the secure connection. Fisher was using Macklin's office; he pushed back in the seat and gazed up at his reflection in the overhead mirror.

The man looking down at him frowned. Fisher decided mirrors were overrated.

"No evidence at all," said Howe.

"How about the CIA or somebody. Would they know?"

"The CIA didn't even know they existed until I saw them," said Howe. "One of them was just recovered a few days ago. It's being shipped back for inspection. One of my guys is going to be on the team looking at it. I mean, one of NADT's guys."

"Could they have smuggled one of these UAV things out of the country?"

"If they could get an E-bomb out, sure. They're pretty small. The North Koreans exported all sorts of weapons, Fisher. They used to sell Scud missiles all over the world. We could've stopped them, but we didn't."

"Mistake, huh?"

"You have any serious questions?"

"If you had one of these E-bombs, you could drop it from a UAV?" asked Fisher.

"You could. Or you could just fly the UAV to a specific point and altitude, then detonate it. There's a problem, though, from what I've heard. The UAV they found has no engine in it."

"You can't just slap a motor in the sucker, huh?"

"It's harder than you think. Has to be pretty small."

"Who makes small engines?"

"There are a couple of manufacturers. U.S."

"Can I get a list?"

"Sure. There's another problem. You have to control it somehow. Controlling an aircraft over many miles can be pretty tricky. Even something like the Predator—"

"Why do you have to control it?" asked Fisher. "Can't you just program the course in, if you're going to blow it up anyway?"

"You could, I think," he said.

"Who would know?"

"I can find somebody at NADT for you."

"What's his number?"

"I'll have him call you. Won't be until Monday."

"Sooner the better."

"Monday."

Fisher prodded a cigarette from his pack. He was out of matches and his lighter had no more fluid. He started rifling Macklin's drawers, but all he found were a few old *Playboy*s.

Left by the drug dealers, no doubt.

"What about a sarin bomb?" asked Fisher.

"Sarin? The nerve gas?"

"Yeah. Could you put that on a UAV?"

"Sure, but there'd be no point," Howe told him.

"Why not?"

"Has to be used in a closed area if it's going to be effective."

While that wasn't precisely true, it would be much more effective if that was the case. And besides, the canisters they'd found on Staten Island were rigged for high pressure—the experts thought they would attach to a sophisticated dispersion system—but not shaped into bombs.

"Tell you what, Colonel: See if you can hunt down that expert for me before the weekend. If you can, call me. If you can't, no big de—"

"I can't," said Howe before Fisher could finish.

"No big deal unless I call back and say it *is* a big deal."

Howe hesitated. Fisher smiled at the face he'd be making. "All right."

"You're a good man, Colonel. Even if you don't smoke," said Fisher, hanging up.

CHAPTER

15

Clarissa Moore, the CIA officer heading the special study group, was waiting for Tyler when he and the others got back to South Korea. Tyler shuffled his feet across the macadam toward her Hummer, his legs so tired they felt as if there were lead weights strapped to his thighs.

"Hey," he said, climbing into the truck.

"Hey yourself," said Moore. "Good job up there. I heard about the UAV."

"Saved a couple of lives in that helicopter," said Somers, sliding in behind him.

Tyler leaned back against the seat, half-listening as Somers told the story. He recognized bits of the account, but it seemed foreign, as if he hadn't been there but had only heard the story before.

Moore twisted around to look at him. "You okay?"

"I just need a little sleep," he said.

"That's it?"

No, thought Tyler. *I need to escape. I need ...*

... Angel's wings.

"Yeah, I'm beat tired," he said, forcing as much enthusiasm into his voice as he could, trying to make it sound as if he were laughing at himself.

16

Blitz squeezed his eyes together, trying to get them to focus. He was used to operating on very little rest, but even for him the past few days had been a real drain. He had worked over the entire weekend, with maybe a total of four hours' sleep; it was now Monday morning and he was due to leave in an hour to fly up to New York City with the President. The latest draft of the President's UN speech sat on his desk; Blitz hadn't even had a chance to look at it.

Mozelle came in with a fresh cup of coffee. Blitz blinked at the coffee, then reached for it.

"Colonel Howe is outside, with one of his technical people from NADT. He says he has information about the Korean UAV."

Blitz looked at his watch.

"Send him in. But buzz me in ten minutes if they're not out."

"I was going to give you five."

Blitz took a sip of the coffee and rose, willing his body into alertness.

"Colonel, congratulations," he said as Howe entered. "I understand you and Dick Nelson reached an agreement last Thursday. I'm sorry I haven't had a chance to get to you since then, it's been a zoo here. Has the NADT board voted yet?"

"They gave Mr. Nelson the go-ahead before he spoke to me," said Howe.

"Congratulations." Blitz came out from around the desk and shook Howe's hand.

"That's not why I'm here."

Howe introduced Dalton; Blitz had undoubtedly met the scientist before but couldn't quite place him. He listened for about thirty seconds as Howe went over the UAV's capabilities, hypothesizing that it could be used to launch an E-bomb.

While there weren't any "hard connections"—he meant real evidence—the juxtaposition of the two technologies represented a real threat.

"Well, certainly," said Blitz.

"So what are we going to do?" asked Howe.

"First thing, alert the task force investigating the E-bomb," said Blitz.

"The FBI agent is on that task force," said Howe. "They're on it."

"Good."

"These UAVs would be very difficult to find by conventional radar systems," explained Dalton. "We have a solution: Our integrated radar and sensor viewer could be tuned to pick them up."

"I'm not sure I'm following," said Blitz.

"We want to make the system available," said Howe. "We have two."

"We're getting way ahead of ourselves here," said Blitz. "They didn't find power plants with those UAVs—or control systems."

"There are a dozen engines that could be used," said Dalton. "And the flight could be preprogrammed in."

"Contracts with NADT have to go through a certain procedure," said Blitz, pained that he had to explain this to Howe.

"This isn't about contracts or money," said Howe. "These units—we'll give them to the government free. We're concerned about the threat."

Mozelle opened the door.

"I'll tell you what, Colonel: Get with Teri Packard to discuss it," Blitz said. Packard was an NSC aide who handled terrorism. "She'll be in touch with the working group. She can talk to the military people. This way, if we need that capability, we'll have it."

"The Pentagon is on line two," said Mozelle, pointing.

"I'm sorry," said Blitz. "Things are hectic this morning

because we're flying up to New York with the President to address the UN. I'm afraid I have to go."

Howe knew a blow-off when he experienced one. Still, he followed through dutifully, going over and briefing Packard on the UAV's potential.

"DIA is pretty sure the E-bomb was just a hoax," said Packard. "They're pulling people back from the task force. So is Homeland Security. FBI has only one person still assigned, and his boss wants him back as well."

"These things are a threat," said Howe. "They could be shipped into the country in pieces, assembled, then flown off any local airstrip—even a deserted highway in the middle of the night."

"Granted. But there's no evidence that they're here."

Howe folded his arms.

"But we can get an alert out and have you tied into the review of the UAV's capabilities," added Packard, trying to seem conciliatory. "It would be good to have your expertise involved."

"Great," said Howe, getting up.

CHAPTER 17

Fisher spent Saturday and Sunday chasing leads from the credit card accounts. The closest he came to anything interesting was a farm run by former hippies in far northern New Jersey; the cows looked as though they were being fed hashish in the barn. Unsure whether that would be a matter for the DEA or the Future Farmers of America, he decided to look the other way.

The visit to Faud's apartment and the subsequent adventure with the hand grenade had prevented Fisher from following up on Harry Spageas, the man who worked at the florist near Faud's apartment. With Macklin and the NYPD continuing their interview of the neighbors—and with nothing definitive yet from the crime people checking out the bomb—Fisher headed over to Steve's Florist on Monday morning to see the store owner and get Spageas's address. The fact that the owner's first name was Rose raised certain questions about predestination and parental premonition, but Fisher never got to raise them, for as he walked through the front door he found the proprietor being questioned by a uniformed NYPD officer. Rose had filed a complaint because both of her delivery vans had been stolen the night before.

"One is bad enough," Rose complained. "But both? It shuts me down."

Rose was the sort of woman who had begun tinting her black hair blond thirty years before and still did it now that the roots were coming in gray. She had a naturally indignant chin, and though she came up to about Fisher's chest, she had shoulders a linebacker would spend thousands on supplements to get.

Fisher let the officer continue the interview. Rose thought that the vans must have been stolen by a competitor and gave the men a half-dozen leads.

"I didn't realize the flower business was so cutthroat," said Fisher when the cop was done.

"You'd be surprised," said Rose.

"So they were here last night and they're missing this morning," said Fisher. "You're sure they were here last night?"

"Mira said so, yes. She's the manager."

"I met her. You have an employee named Harry Spageas, right?"

"A damn good question," said Rose. "He didn't show up Friday."

"Where does Harry live?" asked Fisher.

Harry *Spaneas*—not *Spageas*, but Greek enough—lived four blocks away from the florist shop on the bottom floor of a three-story row house across from the entrance ramp to the Triborough Bridge.

He didn't answer his door, or his phone, which Fisher tried from his cell phone. Fisher leaned on the other bells, hoping they would bring some little old busybody out who would know exactly where Harry was. But no one appeared.

"Let's go look in the windows," Fisher told the patrolman. "Guy lives on the ground floor, right?"

The ground floor was actually about six feet above street level, and Fisher found it necessary to borrow a garbage can to look through the windows.

"I don't know about this, if it's kosher," said the patrolman. "I better check with my sergeant."

"Tell him there's a guy lying on the floor in the hallway that looks a lot like the subject," said Fisher, pressing his face against the glass. "Tell him there's a pool of blood around his head."

"Are you kidding?"

"I only wish I was," said Fisher, jumping down from the garbage can.

Harry Spaneas had been killed either by a pair of .22-caliber bullets to the face or a similar bullet fired point-blank into his skull from behind. Given that he was lying facedown when they found him, Fisher figured that the bullet in the back of the head had been for insurance or good luck, but he'd leave it to the medical examiner to make the final call.

"Does this connect to Faud or not?" asked Macklin when Fisher called him from Spaneas's kitchen to tell him what he'd found.

"I don't know," said Fisher. "NYPD's going through the apartment now."

"How cold was he?"

"Yesterday's coffee cold," said Fisher. "But not much of an odor. I'm figuring he was killed sometime yesterday, before the florist trucks disappeared. But maybe not."

"So they stole the trucks?"

"Could be."

"Come on, Andy. Of course they stole the trucks, right?"

"Michael, if you already know the answer, don't ask the question."

"I don't. I'm asking. You're connecting the murder with the trucks?"

"Why not?"

"Well, lack of evidence, for one."

"He had a spare set of keys, which are not around anywhere," said Fisher.

Macklin chewed on it for a second, processing the information slowly. "Well, let's get some bulletins out on them," he said finally.

"NYPD already has," said Fisher. "You find anything from the neighbors of that apartment?"

"Nothing."

Fisher pushed back in the chair. He'd already checked Spaneas's name against the database of possible terrorists and come up blank, but that wasn't definitive proof of anything. He wondered if it was possible that Spaneas had let Faud stay with him. There was no evidence that he had: A single coffee cup sat on the washboard, along with one knife and fork and plate. But anyone who took the time to think about what they were doing could set that up to make it look as if only one person, Spaneas, had been there.

E-bombs, night goggles, and nail bombs. Hired killers. Flower trucks.

Kind of a jumble, actually. One half of the operation was very sophisticated; the other half, not so much.

Which argued that he was looking at two different operations.

"Hey, Fisher, are you there or what?" said Macklin.

"I'm here," he told Macklin. "Is the Washington Heights apartment still sealed?"

"Yeah."

"Can you get somebody to let me in?"

"Why?"

"I'm running out of straws," said Fisher.

18

When Howe told McIntyre what had happened, his new vice president for government affairs told him he sounded as if he were making a sales pitch for the Advanced Military Vision radar. And his offer to lend the device and the aircraft that were currently outfitted with it made it seem even worse.

"Why?" Howe asked him.

"Because nobody does anything for nothing in this town," said McIntyre. "Probably not in the whole country."

"Isn't it our duty to do something?" asked Howe.

McIntyre sighed. "I like you, Colonel, and I owe you a lot, but boy, do you have a lot to learn."

"Other people have a lot to learn," said Howe.

McIntyre looked as though he were about to launch into an extended lecture about the facts of life when the telephone cut him off. It was from Nelson; Howe told McIntyre to wait and then picked up the phone.

"Colonel, what are we doing with this UAV business?" asked Nelson as soon as he got on the phone.

Howe explained the situation briefly. Nelson was already well informed enough to point out the NSC objection: The UAVs they'd found in Korea had no engines.

"An engine could be supplied," said Howe.

"Just follow channels on it," urged Nelson. "All right?"

"Yes, sir," said Howe. He hung up.

"Nelson gave you flak?" said McIntyre.

"More or less."

"Well, this isn't the military," said McIntyre. "You don't work for him."

"He's head of the board."

McIntyre shrugged. "The person you have to worry about is the President. Besides, right now they need you a heck of a lot more than you need them."

"So they all think I'm trying to sell the AMV radar system?" said Howe.

"Yeah."

"But I'm not."

"You have to take a step back." McIntyre's hand jangled a little, a twitch Howe had never noticed before. "People are a little scared of you."

"What do you mean?"

"Yeah. It'd be like a four-star general calling up out of the blue and saying, 'Hey, this a problem.' "

"A general would have his calls returned."

"You'd be surprised," said McIntyre.

"So I should just sit here and do nothing?"

"Yup."

"I can't, Mac. It's way too threatening."

"Then you have your staff do it," said McIntyre. "Have them talk to the military people, government agencies. They get the ball rolling."

"That will take way the hell too long," said Howe. "I can't just hang back."

"Sometimes you have to if you want to get things done," said McIntyre.

CHAPTER

19

"So, what did it mean that the three slimebag terrorists who'd live in the Washington Heights apartment had actually lived there, with stuff and everything, unlike the apartment Faud had blown up?"

"Jesus, Andy, that's a real question?" asked Macklin as Fisher sat down on the couch in the living room. "It means they lived here."

"So Faud must have another place to stay? Besides his apartment."

"That a question or a conclusion?"

"Both."

"Maybe you should talk to them yourself. They're at the new Special Prisoner Holding Area on Plum Island."

"What are they going to tell me?"

"Jeez, if I knew that, you wouldn't have to talk to them."

Fisher got up and went to the kitchen, where Macklin had left the inventory of the items they'd removed. The DIA techies had managed to retrieve most of the files from the hard drive; the inventory included a rundown. It appeared that the three students were running a term-paper Internet site from the apartment. It brought in about six or seven hundred bucks a week, barely enough to support the rent and other expenses.

"What sort of tickets did they have?" Fisher asked Macklin, looking at the inventory. "Parking tickets? They have a car?"

"No. Bastards had tickets to the NCAAs. They even have four tickets to tonight's finals. Four of 'em. Those suckers are so valuable, I had to take custody of them myself."

Fisher gave him an odd look.

"I'm just kidding, Andy."

"Where are they being held?" asked Fisher, grabbing his coat.

The Special Prisoner Holding Area had been constructed off the shore of a secure testing area controlled by Homeland Security at the tip of Long Island. It consisted of two large barges that had once been leased by New York City as temporary jail facilities. The water around the barges was filled with coiled razor wire; there were two posts with machine guns on land and a pair of small patrol craft, also armed with machine guns, patrolling in the water. Fisher had to run a gamut of high-tech sensors to get onto the barge where the three men were held; he was wanded twice and had to turn over his cell phone, all of his weapons, and most importantly his cigarettes before being allowed inside. Even Macklin, who was head of the task force and had been there several times before, was carefully searched before being cleared. The doors were all operated by remote control; none of the guards had keys of any kind.

The first man had given his name as Ali Muhammad, which was a little like calling himself James Smith. Immigration had just identified him as an Egyptian student named Ali al Saad, which was also probably an alias, though Fisher was not particularly interested in his specific identity and said nothing when Macklin quizzed him on it.

"Syracuse or Kentucky?" Fisher asked the prisoner.

Ali gave him a blank stare.

"Thanks," said Fisher.

"That's it?" said Macklin.

"That's it," said Fisher. "Bring in the next one."

CHAPTER
20

Howe tried to follow McIntyre's advice and hang back, but when one of the generals he'd contacted earlier got back to him and offered to forward the preliminary report, Howe couldn't stop himself from saying yes. The report wasn't much more than what he'd already seen—it was a field briefing forwarded from the scene to a CIA reviewing team—but it did include a set of digital photographs. The shots were a bit grainy, but one thing that caught Howe's attention were two large arrangements of tubes at one corner. At the center of each one was a large, elongated tube that looked like the cans used on dairy farms to collect milk. Around them were clusters of smaller cans or pipes, like coffee cans soldered on. They looked somewhat like rocket motors, though Dalton pointed out they were too large to fit in the rear of the UAVs.

"Besides, if they're rockets—and I'm not saying they are—they'd be solid fuel boosters," added the scientist. "If you used them to propel the plane, you couldn't shut it off. You'd have the rocket ignite, boost you to altitude maybe, then glide back?"

"Why not?" asked Howe.

Dalton shrugged. He leaned over, trying to get a better look at the photos. "Not enough detail to know what's going on."

"I know the guy who took the photos and wrote the report," said Howe. "Maybe he can tell us something more."

"Can't hurt."

It took Howe's secretary only a half hour to run down Major Tyler in Korea—one more measure of the power and reach of NADT. It was a little past midnight there, and Tyler sounded as if he'd dragged himself from bed.

Which, he told Howe, was the case.

"Only for you, Colonel."

"I appreciate it. I'm looking at some pictures you took at the UAV base. There's some tubes and things on the side of the hangar. Would you mind if one of my technical people went over it with you?"

"Tell you the truth, Colonel, I haven't a clue what any of that stuff is. I took a whole set of pictures just because of that. I'm lucky I knew which one was the UAV."

"There are only three pictures attached here, and only one of the hangar."

"Yeah, probably all they forwarded because of the bandwidth. I have the flash card."

"Can we get it?"

"I think we can e-mail it over a secure network."

"Let me see about the arrangements."

An hour later Dalton went over the images with Howe.

"My guess is that it's some sort of booster system. This here, this is definitely part of a solid fuel rocket system: The design looks pretty basic, something you'd see around 1960, 1965, but it looks sound."

Dalton slapped the keys, bringing up a photo of the underside of the robot plane. "It would elevate the aircraft: It would be like something you'd use for a takeoff. I'm not a propulsion expert, but I know rocket-assist packs have been used to help heavy bombers off airfields. This might be something similar, except that my feeling is this aircraft could take off from a really short field as it is."

"So why would you need them for a UAV?" said Howe.

"I don't think that you would. Maybe for a really quick takeoff, but this can use a short field as it is." Dalton shrugged. "Until we have that UAV here, it's impossible to say if they're related."

"How much of an airstrip would those aircraft need to take off?" asked Howe.

"Have to have the engineers do the numbers once they have the aircraft and can model it, but I'd guess not much. Any military field in North Korea would have been more than adequate. I think they could come off a road. Maybe even my driveway."

"Could the boosters lift them straight up?"

"Not straight up. You'd need a bit of an open area to climb out and get altitude, but not much. I don't see why you'd need it, to be honest. You have the airfield, so this is a lot of trouble for nothing."

"I'm guessing there's a reason," said Howe. "We just haven't figured it out yet."

CHAPTER
21

Dr. Blitz eased away from the Philippine ambassador, squeezing into the press of UN delegates in the center of the reception. The President's speech had gone reasonably well, though a final assessment on audience reaction wouldn't be possible until later in the day, after the delegates began cabling home with their true reactions.

A new era for Asia. Or more precisely, the *foundation* of a new era for Asia.

Japan could now safely remain on the pacifist course America had steered for it at the end of World War II. That in turn reduced the pressure on China to expand its military capacity, at least in the short term. Naturally the President had not put it so baldly, speaking only of peace and economic opportunity.

Those were the ultimate goals, and they were achievable as long as America retained its power in the region. There were many in this hall—too many—who did not understand or fully appreciate that; they looked at America's military and economic might as potentially evil things. They did not completely understand the U.S, its historic perspective and foundation. But then, they could hardly be blamed for that: Many of the people in Congress didn't understand it.

History wasn't taught in the schools anymore, Blitz lamented to himself as he smiled his way past several African delegates. Kids didn't even know the dates of the American Revolution, let alone the Korean War.

A waitress passed nearby, offering a plate of Thai shrimp. Blitz declined: Spicy food at receptions always gave him heartburn.

A buzz at the other end of the hall indicated that the President had changed his mind and decided to attend after all. Blitz took a step toward him but found his way blocked by the Chinese representative to the UN. Xi

Hiang was too important to duck; Blitz bowed his head and greeted the man properly.

"Peace, then?" asked Xi.

"Peace, yes," said Blitz.

"Korea is an interesting country," said Xi, still speaking like a sphinx. Much like Blitz, Xi had an academic as well as government background, and the national security advisor waited for the lecture about history or at least a remark in that direction. But Xi said nothing else, and Blitz was moved to ask if his country was afraid of peace, aware that he was being provocative.

"Afraid?" Xi spoke English as well as Blitz but he said the word as if he did not understand the meaning.

"Afraid of the future?" prompted Blitz, trimming back the question slightly. "The uncertainty."

"One should never be afraid of the future," said Xi. "For it comes of its own. As for peace . . ."

An aide tapped the UN representative on the arm, and Xi turned before finishing. Blitz, too, was interrupted: France's UN representative told him she thought the President had done very well.

"I'm going to stay in New York this afternoon and into the evening," the President told Blitz a few minutes later. "We can sneak over to the NCAA championships."

"Presidents can't sneak anywhere."

"Relax, Doc. The IBM box has already been reserved, and we have Secret Service people flanking it. You just don't want to see Syracuse win," added the President. "Come over with us. Take the night off."

"I have a pile of work."

"State will be there. And I think Claussen from the CIA."

The President was teasing him: He often joked that if he wanted Blitz somewhere, all he had to do was invite his rivals. Obviously the President was feeling good about the speech and Korea—and maybe even the basketball game.

"Oh, I suppose I can go back later with you," said the national security advisor.

"Who says there's room on the plane?" said the President before turning away.

CHAPTER

22
Fisher left the interrogation room as quickly as he could, striding down the caged hallway to the small observation area. Identity confirmed, he was searched again before being allowed out.

Fisher checked his cigarette pack when the guard handed it back to him with his weapons: You just never knew about the ethics of people connected with the prison system.

"It's going to be tonight," said Fisher as he counted.

"What?"

"It'll be at the basketball game. The championship."

"What is?"

"Whatever they're planning."

"How do you know they're planning anything?"

"Because they know less about college basketball than you do." His cigarettes counted, Fisher put one in his mouth and lit up. "Call off the game."

"Oh, yeah, right. You're talking about the NCAA championships here, Andy. New York worked for years to get this, to bring them to the Garden. You're out of your mind."

"Faud left the bomb. That tells us two things: One, he's not back in Yemen; two, time is running out. I thought it was an early-warning system, but I'm wrong: It's a diversion." Fisher took a long drag on the cigarette, striding out to the gangplank that led back to land. It was a gorgeous New York day—sun high in the sky, the odor of dead fish on the wind—but he didn't stop to notice.

"We got their sarin," protested Macklin.

"Maybe we didn't get it all. I'm telling you, you have to stop that game."

"The security tonight is going to be crazy," said Macklin. "Half of New York will be locked down. They'll never get close."

"The E-bomb," said Fisher.

"They have it?"

"I don't know."

Fisher thought about that as they reached the car. "We have to get the police to stop and search every flower truck in Manhattan. Anything that looks like the ones taken from Pete's Florist."

"Man, you're reaching."

"I have a thing for roses," said Fisher, sliding into the car and taking out his sat phone.

Howe was just thinking of leaving the office early when his secretary buzzed him to say he had a call.

"I think I'll deal with it tomorrow," he told her.

"It's somebody named Andy Fisher," said the secretary. "He said it was important."

Howe punched the button on his phone.

"I figured it out," Fisher said. "They're going to set the E-bomb off in New York tonight."

"What?"

"Somewhere around eight o'clock. Maybe a little after. By my watch that's four hours. I have this theory, but it doesn't have a lot of proof."

"Share it," said Howe.

"The Korean is pissed about us beating the crap out of him, so he hooks up with these crazies here. I don't know whether he sells them a bomb or is going to set it off himself, but it's hooked into this terrorist cell of assholes with sarin gas. Maybe they got the sarin from him, too, I don't know."

"How do you know there's an E-bomb?" asked Howe.

"Because one of my suspects, the one I can't find, has night-vision goggles and an injector to ward off the effects of sarin gas. The only thing I don't have totally worked out is how the bomb goes off, because the tech people I talked to say it's got to explode in the air. Or that's the best thing or something; I forget the details."

"The UAV?"

"Yeah, that's what I was thinking."

Howe stood up from his seat. *You could use the rocket pack to launch the UAV like a missile. Once launched, the engines would take over.*

"You sure about all of this?" Howe asked Fisher.

"Of course not. Listen, we have to keep air traffic away from New York, and we have to look for a UAV. I have to talk to a million people, and most of them think I'm a pain in the ass, so it's going to take a while."

"Have you talked to the Air National Guard?"

"My task force guy will, but I don't know how serious they're going to take him. *I* don't even take him seriously," said Fisher. "But you've got a ton of pull, right?"

"I'll do what I can," said Howe.

"I'm counting on that," said Fisher.

Howe pressed the button to talk to his secretary. "I need to get ahold of the unit responsible for air traffic over New York," he told her. "I want to talk to the commander personally, right away. And then I need to have one of our planes at Andrews readied for a flight: Iron Hawk. You can get me the numbers I need, right?"

"Yes, sir, but—"

"But?"

"It's almost five."

"We'll pay you overtime," snapped Howe.

"I meant you better let me call over to Andrews right away," said the secretary. "Because otherwise the ground people may go home before you get to them."

PART SIX
The Final Four

CHAPTER

1

Madison Square Garden was neither near Madison Avenue nor appreciably square, and the last time anything approaching a garden had been on the spot, the local Indians were unloading swampland on the Dutch.

Which made it the quintessential New York landmark, if not the essence of New York itself.

"You're being kind of hard on the place, Andy," said Macklin as they walked across Eighth Avenue. Ordinarily that would have been suicidal, but the area had been blocked off for the game. Traffic snarled through the rest of the city, but the streets around Madison Square Garden were a veritable island of peace and tranquillity.

Except, of course, for the troop trucks, Humvees, Stinger antiaircraft missile batteries, two tanks, and upward of five thousand National Guardsmen, soldiers, and police officers.

"You'd think they'd've let a pretzel guy inside the barricades," said Fisher.

"Well, well, Cassandra showed up in person," said a voice from behind a phalanx of approaching soldiers.

"Kowalski, it's about time you got here," said Fisher. "Did you find the UAV yet?"

"I have half the damn Air Force flying overhead, Fisher. You sure as hell better be right."

"Only half, Kowalski? I thought you had pull."

"Yeah, yeah, wiseass. Real funny. How are they getting the gas into the place, anyway? Did you think about that?"

"I thought about it, but I couldn't figure it out," admitted Fisher.

"We have the ventilation system guarded," said Macklin. "And the backup generators. Everything's been checked and rechecked. Power goes off, we'll have it back on in a jiff."

"Unless they blow up the bomb overhead, right?" said Fisher.

"Well, yeah."

"Or within five miles."

"Or more, depending on how good the bomb is," said Macklin. "But if they don't, we're fine."

"That's what I like about you, Michael: You're always looking on the brighter side of things."

"Maybe I should get more batteries," said Macklin.

"Nothing's going to happen," said Kowalski. "I think this is all just the product of Fisher's wild imagination. Even the maestro of conspiracy falters once in a while."

"Don't lie, Kowalski," said Fisher, taking out his cigarettes. "I get it wrong *all* the time. Want one?"

"I wish I did smoke," said Kowalski, shaking his head. "What a fuckin' nightmare. I don't know whether to hope you're right or wrong."

"Wrong's better," said Fisher. "What's the latest on the florist trucks?"

"NYPD's got a good handle on it," said Macklin. "They have an exclusion area and they've already searched beyond it. There are no vans within ten blocks."

"Oh," said Fisher.

"Oh?"

"Stop the trains."

"Which trains?"

"Anything that goes anywhere near Penn Station." He threw his cigarette away and began running toward the nearest police command post. "Amtrak, LIRR, New Jersey, subways—everything."

"Andy?" yelled Macklin.

"Just do it!"

CHAPTER

2

Faud huddled near the end of the passage, sipping the last of his bottles of water. He did not know exactly when the time would be. He knew only that he was to wait until the lights blinked off.

The journey across the tracks had been an ordeal—a train had come just as he opened the panel—but it was past. The rest now was easy.

When the lights went off, he would put on the heavy coat and the hat, pull up the two tanks that looked like an oxygen pack. He would need the goggles to see. He had a light, but it was better to use the goggles: The light would give him away.

Faud would carry the pistol in his hand.

Several times he had thought of dressing and being ready, but the weight of the gear dissuaded him. He also had been instructed to keep the tanks in their insulated case for as long as possible.

The air tube where he could insert the gas was only a few feet from the shaft he had to climb. He had a small drill to make the hole. Once the nozzle was inserted, he would set the unit down and turn the wheel at the base of the tanks, activating the pressure feed. The gas itself was under very high pressure and would probably fill the ventilation system itself so long as it remained hot, but there was no way of knowing whether the loss of power would permanently disrupt the forced-air system, and the mechanism was designed to cover that contingency. The room above the insertion point had steam pipes that would make the system considerably hotter than the seventy degrees necessary for the sarin to remain a gas. If the auxiliary power came on, the gas would be forcefully pulled into the building, killing everyone within seconds; but even if it didn't, the flow of air through the system and the difference in pressure would bring the gas up into the building.

As long as Faud managed to find the right duct line. There were three; he had to tap the one farthest to his right as he climbed from the shaft.

That was what he had been told. He knew a great deal about the gas, but nothing about the shafts.

If all else failed, he had already decided on an alternate plan: He would pass the ventilation shaft and walk to the end of the room, where the stairs led to a hallway behind a concession area. He would simply turn on the gas and walk through the stuffy building. Those who did not die of the gas would die from the panic as they tried to escape.

His place in Paradise would be guaranteed no matter what else happened.

The imam had insisted on giving him a plan to escape after he placed the gas, and told him it was his duty to follow it.

Was it, though? The imam had been wrong on many things; perhaps he was wrong on this as well.

Was it sacrilegious to ask such a question?

Faud finished the water. He should not think of it anymore. His path now was clear. He had only to wait for the dim light at the far end of the shaft fifty feet away to go out.

3

The lights on the coast shone like the diamonds of a woman's necklace, glittering against the blackness of the nearby water. A yellow string of jewels circled the shore, the lights of cars on the Belt Parkway.

A 747 had just taken off from Kennedy Airport; Howe could see it climbing off to his right. Air traffic in the region had been strictly curtailed, and the few flights allowed into the New York metropolitan area had to follow instructions to the millimeter. Two Air National Guard F-16s circled over Manhattan, ready to pounce. Another pair was standing by on the ground in nearby New Jersey.

Howe's aircraft, the Iron Hawk, was not equipped with offensive weapons, but its AMV radar provided a finer detection net than the F-16s' APG-68. So far all he'd spotted were a few birds. The radar popped them on the screen momentarily, briefly tracking them before its program decided for sure that they were birds, not a cleverly designed aircraft whose radar profile mimicked a seagull.

If Fisher was wrong, Howe would look like a fool. He could already hear Nelson's voice and see Blitz's disapproving stare. But he had decided he didn't care. He had to do what he thought was right, which meant risking looking like a fool.

No, it meant he *would* look like a fool sometimes. But it was worse to *feel* like a fool.

Howe checked his fuel and the rest of his instruments, then began a turn as he banked over New Jersey. Patrolling like this was surprisingly difficult; it was so boring that the natural temptation was to wish something would happen. That he didn't want: Among the eight million people down there in the city was his friend Jimmy, who'd scalped tickets to the basketball game Fisher thought was the target. Howe had tried calling him but gotten only his machine.

The F-16 pilots were jumpy despite the cool and laconic snaps of their communications. When an Airbus heading in from Chicago failed to acknowledge a ground communication, the lead pilot jumped on the air so quickly that the airliner's captain apologized three or four times for what was, at worst, a moment's inattention.

"Iron Hawk, this is Falcon One," said the F-16 flight leader as they worked through their patrol pattern.

"Iron Hawk," said Howe, acknowledging.

"Viper Flight is about to take off," said the pilot, informing Howe that a second group of F-16s was coming up to spell the first group. Falcon One and Two would head back once their replacements were on station. Another pair of F-16s would take their turn below on standby, providing blanket coverage of the airspace.

Howe started to acknowledge when a ground controller from an FAA station to the north came onto the line with a warning: A light plane was straying off its flight plan toward the restricted area north of Manhattan and, thus far, had failed to answer hails.

The pilot in Falcon One opted to check it out himself, instructing his wingman to remain in the patrol area until he was relieved. Even as he was giving the instructions, the F-16 pilot was changing course and lining up an intercept on the small plane, which was just heading over the Hudson River south of the Tappan Zee Bridge.

"It is what they say it is," Howe told Falcon One, checking the contact with the AMV radar. He was too far to see if there was a bomb aboard. "Nothing else there."

"Falcon One."

Howe checked his position, orienting himself in the night sky as he flew westward, tracking over New Jersey as he flew toward the light plane. The police had already been alerted to check all of the airports in the area that might be used to launch the UAV. Vehicle-based installations of Stinger missiles were guarding the main power plants in the area, and a separate F-16 flight was over Indian Point, the nuclear power station along the Hudson up near Peekskill, fifty-something miles north of New York City.

Everything was covered. Except what they didn't expect.

And what would that be?

A light plane reconfigured to hold a bomb?

The civilian pilot was answering the F-16's radio call.

If Howe had the UAV, he'd set it up in a barn somewhere north of the city, one that had an open field for it to climb through after the rocket engines ignited. When the time came, he'd pull open the big doors and fire away.

Something flashed in the sky ahead. Howe's breath caught in his chest as his brain tried to make sense of what his eyes had just seen.

CHAPTER

4

Fisher stood on the A train platform, hands on hips. Six National Guardsmen with M16s and bulletproof vests watched from the stairs behind him; another knot of men patrolled both sides of the long platform, which sat between the north- and southbound tracks.

NYPD had already considered the problem of trains coming into Penn Station, which sat below the Madison Square Garden area, and posted details to search the trains before they got to the station. The job was not as difficult as might be imagined: Relatively few trains were inbound to the station at this time of day, and their progress could be easily tracked.

The subway was a somewhat different matter, though here, too, the police seemed to have corralled the problem. The stations on Thirty-fourth street—not just at Eighth and Seventh Avenues but Herald Square on Sixth as well—were closed. Trains were permitted to run through on the lines but there was no stopping.

"What's going to happen?" Kowalski asked Fisher, joining him on the platform. "They pack the train with the gas, then arrange to set off the E-bomb when it's in the station?"

Fisher didn't answer. A light lit the tunnel at the far end. The platform vibrated with a low rumble as the A train approached. The noise of the train's steel wheels grinding against the rails crescendoed into a loud smack of rolling thunder as the train sped through the station. Fisher saw that there were armed policemen and Guardsmen in each car.

"Maybe we should have them just shut down the trains," said Kowalski after the train passed. "You think? We can. We've arranged it."

"Not necessary," said Fisher. He went over to the edge of the tracks. "Okay."

"Okay what? Stop the trains?"

"Nah. That'll tip them off."

"But—"

Fisher jumped down onto the tracks.

"Jesus, Andy, are you out of your mind?" yelled Kowalski. "That's a live track. You touch that third rail and you fry."

"You coming?"

"No fucking way."

"Your call. Tell Macklin to meet me inside Madison Square Garden."

"Inside where?"

"If I knew, I wouldn't have to go this way, right?"

5

There was no reading on the radar. The flash had come from the ground well in the distance. Howe hit the magnifier command, confirmed that it was clean, and then went quickly to the infrared screen, even though the computer should have already used the sensor to compile its "read."

Nothing.

So what had he seen?

He nudged his left wing down, sliding the Iron Hawk into an orbit over the spot where he had seen the spark of light. All he could think of was the flash of a rocket—or the UAV—taking off.

The F-16 pilots were talking about the light plane. Howe ignored them, pushing against his restraints. He had to find the stinking thing: He had to see it so he could shoot it down.

Or, rather, tell the others to shoot it down.

"Iron Hawk, this is Falcon Two."

Was that it, the blur at the right side of his windscreen?

The smudge disintegrated into a shadow. Howe started tacking south and then saw lights on the ground, red lights. . . .

A fire?

With that much of a spark?

He eased back even more on the throttle. The Iron Hawk practically walked over the spot: The gear said the plane was doing only 120 knots at 3,000 feet.

A fire truck. Several fire trucks.

Something shot into the sky.

A gas station was on fire.

He was surprised to realize he was a little disappointed. He had no right to be: No doubt the men fighting the blaze down there were in every bit as much danger as he would have been, if not more. He pulled back gently on the stick, starting to recover.

"Iron Hawk, Falcon One is escorting this aircraft out of the restricted zone. Pilot appears lost," said the F-16's pilot.

Howe acknowledged. He switched the radar back to its standard settings; the F-16 and the private plane were at the top of the scan area, heading to the northwest and a small airfield where a squad's worth of regular Army soldiers would be waiting along with local police and a federal marshal. The small plane's pilot was about to spend several of the most uncomfortable hours of his life.

Howe cut back east, heading in the direction of Connecticut. The replacement F-16s were now on station. Howe checked in with the new pilots, one of whom he thought he knew from a temporary assignment in Alaska nearly a decade before.

Before he could ask, a civilian ground controller broke into the circuit.

"We have a landline threat, a phone call," said the man, his words rushing together in his excitement. "A hijacking on Qual-Air Flight 111 out of Boston!"

The Viper commander acknowledged the communication calmly, then checked with his military ground controller. The Qual-Air flight was legitimate, a charter plane that had just taken off. The civilian controllers were still in the process of contacting the pilot to see what was going on, but there was no indication that the plane had been hijacked.

A hijacking?

More likely, a ruse intended to cover the real attack, thought Howe.

The airspace over the corridor was effectively locked down; controllers began holding takeoffs and diverting anything that might come even remotely close. The two F-16s on the ground in New Jersey took off. Viper flight began tracking north, one airplane on a direct intercept with the other hanging back in reserve.

Howe tracked southward over the Hudson River, certain that this was a trick. But where would the real attack come from?

The west, he thought, where there were plenty of places to launch the UAV. He banked ten thousand feet over the George Washington Bridge, turning in that direction. As he did, the radar buzzed with a contact forty miles beyond the clutter of the land. It was low, close to the water. Howe stared at the display, where the red triangle for the unidentified object glowed like a pinpoint in the long-range scan.

Probably another bird, he thought.

He waited for it to disappear from the screen.

It didn't.

CHAPTER
6

Blitz nearly jumped when the phone rang. He glanced across the room at the President, then picked it up.

"Nothing new," said Brott, the NSC military aide who was monitoring the situation from the Pentagon. "Civilian plane, false alarm."

"Right," said Blitz.

The Secret Service had asked—demanded, really—that the President leave the city when the alert came through three hours before. The President had folded his arms across his chest, listened patiently to their arguments, and looked at Blitz.

"I think you should go," Blitz had told him. Even as the words left his mouth, he knew D'Amici wouldn't.

"With due respect, gentlemen, fuck yourselves," said the President. It was the only time in his life that Blitz could remember the President using that particular profanity, at least since he had been elected to office. "The people of the United States did not elect me to run away and hide from terrorists," continued the President. "And if something horrible does happen here, then this will be exactly where I should be."

He was a stubborn son of a bitch. That's what it came down to. It wasn't the fact that he thought his place was here; it wasn't that he thought the political ramifications of running from a rumor of danger were immense. The real reason he was staying was that he wouldn't back down from any confrontation. In his heart of hearts, he probably wanted to go down on the streets and work with the details trying to catch these jerks.

Blitz admired that instinct, even as he questioned the wisdom of it.

"Keep me informed," he told Brott.

"Yes, sir. Mozelle wanted to talk to you."

Blitz pushed down the button on the receiver and called his aide at the White House.

"You okay up there?" she asked as soon as she heard his voice.

"Not a problem here," he said.

"Lot of calls. One in particular I thought you'd want to know about," said Mozelle. "Your friend Kevin Smith called. He was mad that you didn't tell him you were coming into the city."

Smith was an old friend; they often got together when Blitz was in New York or he was in D.C., but security and the press of business had prevented him from calling this time. Blitz made a mental note to call Smith later on and tell him he was sorry.

"He said he had tickets to the NCAA championship game tonight," Mozelle continued, "and he would have taken you instead of his brother-in-law."

"Oh," said Blitz softly.

Tempted as he was to call Smith's cell phone—he knew the number by heart—he realized he couldn't. Instead he hung up and rose, looking out the nearby window at the brilliantly lit Manhattan skyline.

"I hope you're okay, Kevin," he told the glass. "I hope to God we're all okay."

CHAPTER

7

Fisher walked up along the track about a hundred yards, slowing as the light from the station faded behind him. The problem wasn't the darkness; he could see fairly well. But the schematic of the tunnel system he'd seen earlier had shown a passage here to his left, and he couldn't find it now.

Fisher took another two steps. There should be a little work light along the narrow walkway that flanked the tracks here somewhere.

As he stared at the wall, the light appeared about ten yards to his right. But it was dark. The socket was empty.

Fisher glanced down the tracks. The light bulb had been unscrewed and thrown on the tracks. He could see the glass shards quite clearly.

Which was a problem, actually. All of a sudden there was plenty of light flooding into the dark tunnel: A train was approaching.

Rather quickly too.

The door he was looking for stood next to the light. He made it with something like three seconds to spare, pulling himself up onto the ledge as the train's brakes squealed and the tunnel shook.

When the train passed, Fisher took his pistol from its holster and opened the door.

CHAPTER

8

Howe steadied Iron Hawk on its course toward the contact, riding over the rooftops of Bergen County, New Jersey. He had the UAV now, the computer boxing it in the upper right corner of his screen.

"Zoom on Unidentified 1-3-1," Howe told the computer, using its tag for the contact. The image blossomed in his screen. It was as if Howe were hovering just in front of its nose. The UAV was moving at just over three hundred knots, skimming above the waves at about eight feet roughly forty miles from the tip of Manhattan, across Brooklyn in the Atlantic due south of Long Beach, Long Island.

"Viper Two to Iron Hawk. Colonel, is this it?" asked the pilot in the second F-16. He was approximately twenty miles beyond the Statue of Liberty, just about ready for an intercept. Viper One was north, escorting Qual-Air back to Boston because of the earlier threat.

"Affirmative, I have the target on my screen," said Howe. He read off the UAV's location, heading, and speed, pulling back on the magnification level so he could better direct the F-16.

The fighters that had just taken off checked in. One peeled off to back up Viper Two; the other took up a patrol position in case this, too, was a ruse.

It wasn't. Howe felt his heart beating steady now, the rhythm familiar. His fingers felt heavy, his eyes almost hollow.

He'd flown in combat before, but this time it was different: This time there were people he knew on the ground, in harm's way. This time his own people were in the crosshairs.

The contact tucked left, adjusting its course. There were thirty-five miles between it and New York.

As Viper Two approached, it quickly became apparent

that he would have to get very close to the UAV to shoot it down. The UAV's extremely small radar profile protected it against a longer range shot by the AMRAAM missiles; the pilot's best bet would be to choose either heat seekers or his cannon. Howe could see him sizing up his strategy and preparing for it: He had a parallel track to the UAV's course that would allow him to turn and get on its tail as it approached; the F-16's superior speed would make the terrorist craft an easy target.

Not easy, exactly. Viper Two still had no idea where it was. In the dark night, moving at hundreds of miles an hour, the world was a flashing blur. The airplane and its target moved through four dimensions—three spatial, one of time—in a complicated dance. It was man against machine, and the jock at the stick of the F-16 was now in a confrontation where the slightest error, the wrong twitch at the wrong moment, might mean disaster. The pilot had trained for countless hours, but no simulation, no drill, could come close to duplicating what he was flying against now.

Howe had been there himself. You reached down at that moment and found what you had.

He watched the display. Viper Two couldn't find the UAV, even as he closed.

"Turn," snapped Howe. "Now."

The F-16 stuttered in the display. Then it moved downward toward the water, pirouetting on its wing, 18,000 pounds of metal and machinery transformed into a graceful ballerina. The wings straightened and the dancer became a linebacker blitzing unmolested toward the fleeing quarterback.

"Range is five miles," said Howe. "You're dead on. Dead on and steady."

"Roger that."

Howe told the computer system to zoom in on the target. The screen blinked—and then went back to the large-area scan.

He started to curse, then saw the change was not due to a malfunction: A second contact had been spotted, this one behind him, only five miles south of the Statue of Liberty.

CHAPTER

9

The only person in the room whose face wasn't a mask of worry was the President's. Blitz watched him from the other end of the suite, still working the phone as he talked to congressional leaders about an amendment to the Medicare Prescription Bill. Each call began the same way: *Senator, how are you? Did you catch my speech? We need your support on this legislation.*

It was impossible to tell from the President's reaction whether the man or woman on the other line was for or against the proposal. Only when the call ended and he signaled one of his aides with a thumbs-up or -down could one judge the success of the call.

Meanwhile, the Secret Service detail, chief of staff, and military aides were walking back and forth, trying to appear calm. They had formulated and reformulated and formulated once again plans in case the alert proved real. They had flashlights, night-vision goggles, flak vests—everything they needed, Blitz thought, which only made the situation seem even more impossible.

The President finally put down the phone and got up from his chair.

"So, what do you think, Professor?" he asked. "Should we head over to the Garden?"

The Secret Service people began to protest en masse. The President raised his hand to shush them.

"What do you say, Doc? We getting over there or what?" asked the President.

"I wouldn't want to get in the way of the professionals while they were doing their work," said Blitz.

"Neither would I," answered the President. "Come on. We're not cowering in a hotel room."

"Sir . . ." started the head of the Secret Service detail. "With all due respect, your safety—"

"My safety isn't the question," said the President. "The question is, who's going to win this stinking basketball game? Syracuse or Kentucky? I have Syracuse. My national security advisor takes Kentucky. Now, let's get our act together so we don't hold up too much traffic, all right?"

CHAPTER

10

Three people tried to speak over the same radio frequency at once. Howe sifted through the cacophony, eyes glued on the new triangle on the right side of the display.

How the hell had the system missed the contact earlier?

Maybe it hadn't. Maybe this was just an anomaly, a screwup.

Or maybe it had been lost in the clutter until now.

Howe yanked at his stick, snapping back in the direction of the UAV. The Iron Hawk pulled nearly 9 g's, testing the limits of his flight suit and its wing structure as it jerked onto the new course. A pair of fists smashed against Howe's temples, gravity angry that he had dared to fight it. Momentum slammed against his chest, drove down against his groin; Howe fought through it, his brain swimming hard to keep up with the superbly engineered plane as she shrugged off the awesome forces trying to pull her back.

The aircraft won. Iron Hawk began accelerating.

Howe blinked his eyes and saw his target on the screen seven miles away, flying to his right now as he leaned on the throttle and strained against the stick.

Lady Liberty stood proud in the harbor, her arm holding a beacon to the oppressed of the world.

"Splash Target One!" reported the F-16 pilot. "Splash that motherfucker!"

"I have a new target," reported Howe, belatedly realizing he had forgotten to alert the others. "Tracking.

The UAV dipped right. There was a Navy destroyer ahead, near the mouth of the harbor.

Someone was hailing him.

The Navy people couldn't see the target, but they could see him: The targeting radars on their ship-to-air missiles were locking on him, ready to fire.

"Iron Hawk acknowledges," said Howe, slapping at his Talk button. "I am in pursuit of an unidentified aircraft, probably one of our targets."

The black shadow flew toward the center of the statue ahead.

Those bastards are going to blow up the Statue of Liberty, Howe thought to himself. *And there isn't anything I can do about it.*

CHAPTER
11

The corridor was a utility passage that connected to another set of tracks and opened directly across from a passage way below the Garden. The only way across was through a set of girders and then over the tracks; unlike the other tunnel, there was no walkway on the side.

According to the plans, the access had been closed off. Pretty much a dead giveaway, as far as Fisher was concerned.

He climbed down between the girders, trying to judge

whether the rumble he felt was coming in his direction or not. Finally he decided to take his chances; with all these tracks down here, the odds were that it wasn't.

But it was. Fisher was just reaching the metal plate that covered the opening when the yellowish-white light crept across the wall.

He pulled down against the plate, trying to get it to open. It didn't budge.

Fisher took a step back. Ordinarily he would have reached for a cigarette so that he could fully contemplate the implications of the panel being secured in place. But the approaching train made such contemplation a difficult venture. The FBI agent kicked at the bottom of the metal with his foot.

It still didn't move. The tunnel now practically quaked with the thunder of the approaching subway cars, the rattle moving the ground in a motion not unlike the steady, comforting *perk-perk-perk* of an old-fashioned coffeemaker.

The light filled the space, casting him in shadow. Fisher glanced to the left, admiring his growing length. . . .

And finally spotting a second panel, six feet away.

He stepped over to it and saw that it was propped up at the side of the opening. The FBI agent slid in feetfirst, and found himself in a dank, water-filled hole.

CHAPTER

12

Howe watched the UAV pass under the Verrazano-Narrows Bridge like a rifle bullet moving at just over 275 knots. It nudged right slightly, its faceted beak aimed directly for the Statue of Liberty. Howe was flying more than a hundred miles an hour faster than the UAV, but even with that advantage he couldn't close the distance between him and the UAV before it slammed into the statue.

And even if he did, he had no weapons aboard.

But he couldn't simply pull off. He stayed on his course.

And then the UAV made a course correct, turning not right, which would have taken it over Manhattan, but left, flying toward northern New Jersey.

Howe didn't understand for a moment. It seemed to him that the enemy plane—an unthinking missile—had had a change of heart, warned off by the glare of the statue herself.

Then he realized that it had never been programmed to strike the statue.

An E-bomb would be targeted for a power yard or a transformer station to have maximum effect on the power grid. It was possible to shield some devices against the weapon itself, but a close-range hit on a weak link could not be defended against. Even if the weapon proved not as powerful as its designers intended, a jolt directly over a concentration of power lines would fry the Northeast grid for months.

There were plenty of choices in northeastern New Jersey. Hit the right one and the power grid would come down. You didn't have to hit Manhattan at all.

"Iron Hawk, this is Viper One. I need vectors to the target. Iron Hawk? Iron Hawk?"

Howe responded with the course and location, even though he knew the F-16 was too far off. It would take it at least three minutes to close the gap. By then the UAV would be over its target.

The UAV began to rise. That must mean it was getting ready to ignite its bomb.

He had it in his screen now, less than two miles ahead. If he had a cannon, he could easily shoot it down.

He could run the damn thing down, collide with it.

I don't want to die.

The idea shot into his head, the errant firing of a cramping muscle.

It was just ahead of his left wing now, eight hundred meters, seven hundred. The AMV showed it clearly in the display—the bomb was lashed to the body—but he wasn't watching the screen; he was looking at it in his windscreen.

He'd have only one chance. Howe eased his grip on the stick, trying to avoid the tendency to overcorrect.

As Howe came up, something about the night reminded him of the dim computer screen he'd fiddled with in the Smithsonian, the simulation of the Hurricanes taking on the V-1s in the air over the Channel.

He could do that now.

Tip the wing right, get the UAV to tumble into the water.

Was he chickening out?

There was no more time to think. Howe pushed the stick, threw his body with it, came back.

A long tunnel opened behind him, the rushing howl of the engine rising two octaves into a shrill hiss. He felt his right arm cramp into a rock.

The Iron Hawk stumbled but held solid, following its pilot's command.

The wings of the two aircraft smacked against each other. The UAV tumbled, its gull wings spinning. The craft's tail turned over once, twice, three times. The plane's internal guidance system started to correct but it was too late: It was far too low to recover from the spin. Gravity had too firm a grip for the craft to shake off; it spun once more, then hit the water about ten yards from shore, disappearing in a volcanic burst of steam.

Iron Hawk rolled awkwardly but recovered, the modifications designed to ensure her survivability in combat proving her salvation now. Howe steadied the craft, eyes on the AMV screen, hardly breathing. He was lost, unsure where he was in the sky—unsure even if he hadn't blown himself up.

He blinked, and he had it all back.

He was rising over the Hudson River, turning eastward

now, New York City a bright mélange of lights. The UAV hit the water below.

He'd saved the damn place, he and the F-16 pilots, and Fisher, and a million other people, doing their jobs and putting their necks on the line.

He'd saved the whole damn place. Manhattan sparkled like a fistful of diamonds, her bright lights blazing in the dark night. New York, New York, brighter than ever.

And then every light in the city flashed out.

CHAPTER 13

Now. It was time. Faud pulled on the goggles and fumbled with the pack, removing the coat.

Was this what God wanted?

To even ask the question was blasphemy.

Faud felt his body tremble as he hoisted the oxygen pack to his back. His hands were so slippery that the pistol fell to the cement, clattering on the floor. As he stooped down to grab at the gun, the blood rushed to his head. Faud felt himself loosing his balance. He tightened his hand around the weapon and straightened slowly.

He must not fail, he told himself.

CHAPTER 14

Fisher waded through the water, reaching a set of concrete steps as the lights snapped off.

Damn it, he thought to himself, *I'm always running late in this stinking city.*

He stepped up to the top of the stairs. A long stretch of pipes ran to the right, splitting the passage in two. He heard something move ahead.

"Yo. Give it up," yelled Fisher.

There was no answer.

"You're not going to make it to the ventilation system. You have to climb all the way up the shaft. I'll shoot you before you make it halfway up. A couple of times."

No answer. Fisher sighed and reached to touch the wall with his left hand, walking gingerly along it. The bottom of a service elevator shaft opened about fifty feet ahead.

"You see me, Faud?"

The terrorist answered by firing a gun.

"Dinky little twenty-two, I bet," said Fisher.

The gun flashed again, this time giving Fisher an idea of where it was. He fired three of his .44's six bullets, and all smacked hard against a pipe at the far end.

The terrorist shot again. He, too, missed, though Fisher noted that the ricochet was a bit closer.

"All right, let's get this part out of the way," yelled the FBI agent. "You have the right to remain silent. Anything you say can and will be used against you in a court of law. You have a right to an attorney—"

A succession of bullets flew through the air. Fisher fired again. When he heard Faud dropping his gear, he realized he'd missed again.

"Hey!" shouted someone from above. Macklin was in the elevator shaft. "Hey!"

More gunfire. More smoke. Fisher tried to remember what the technical people had told him a few weeks earlier about sarin's ability to spread.

Just as well he couldn't remember, he thought.

"Stop him!" yelled a voice as the subbasement once more echoed with the roar of gunfire.

Fisher dropped to his knee.

So, where was the terrorist? And did he have friends?

Fisher realized where he was too late to beat him back to the passage. He fired a shot, then yelled to Macklin to grab the canisters.

"Where are they?" shouted Macklin.

"I haven't a clue," yelled Fisher. "But they'll look out of place, even down here, don't you think?"

Fisher stopped, listening near the opening. Faud was out on the track somewhere.

"Firemen," said Fisher aloud.

"Firemen?"

"Who would you let into a building in a blackout? A fireman," said Fisher, answering his own question. "Jeez, what a dummy. I've been thinking Con Ed. Look for a fire-man's oxygen tank," he shouted to Macklin.

"Really?"

"Macklin, if you're going to ask me questions all day, we're never going to catch this scumbag," said Fisher.

He stuck his hand through the opening, then pulled back just as a fusillade of bullets hit the wall. He got down on his stomach and slid beneath the pipes to the entrance Faud had used. But it was still pitch-black and he couldn't see.

Cursing, Fisher reached back and pulled off his shoe, then slid around so he could throw it in front of the other opening. When Faud started firing, Fisher pulled himself out, fired once, and tumbled down onto the tracks.

Faud stood in the darkness a few feet away. Fisher brought his gun up to fire. As he did, Faud aimed first and pulled the trigger.

Empty.

"Who says today's not my lucky day?" asked Fisher, rising slowly.

He, too, was out of bullets, though he wasn't about to share that bit of news.

"You heard your rights, right?" Fisher asked.

The terrorist threw down the gun. Fisher saw him pull something from his pocket—not a weapon, but some sort of canister.

"Let me just guess: sarin gas, right? Going to kill us both?" Fisher took a step. Faud took two backward.

"Except you took the antidote, right? I did," lied Fisher.

They'd offered him a shot but he hated needles.

"Give it up," said Fisher. "You're only going to kill yourself. The antidote might not work."

"You'll die too," growled the man.

"Hey, let's say you're right. Where's the thrill in that?"

Fisher took an awkward step forward with his shoeless foot. The terrorist had taken off or lost his night vision goggles. They were twelve feet apart.

"Better watch where you're going," said the agent as Faud edged down the tunnel. "Lights are going to come on and you're going to fry yourself."

Faud took a step backward, then another.

"Mrs. DeGarmo says hi," said Fisher.

Faud didn't answer.

"I didn't think that was going to work," said Fisher. "But seriously, now, you better watch where you're going. Power comes on, this tunnel's a death trap. Come out with me and we'll talk."

"The power won't be on for months."

"I wouldn't count on it. Con Ed's not nearly as inefficient as everyone thinks."

"Go to hell."

"I appreciate the sentiment. And I'm not kidding about the rail. Really."

Fisher saw the man move his hands. He dropped down, grabbing for the backup Glock he had in a holster on his calf. Before he could fire, a flash of light blinded him.

Then there was an awful sound, something like a scream that twisted in half. The tunnel filled with acrid smoke, the scent of burnt flesh permeating the dank space.

"Told you the lights were coming back on," said Fisher. "You didn't think I could keep them off forever, did you? The paperwork alone is ridiculous."

He holstered his pistol. Faud lay slumped against the third rail, still frying. The can of gas lay in the middle of the tracks, unopened.

"Andy! Andy Fisher!" yelled Macklin.

"Where the hell have you been, Macklin?" asked Fisher, turning back.

"He hit the third rail?"

"Guess he didn't believe me about the power." Fisher pulled out his cigarette pack. "You stopped the trains, right?"

"Like you said."

Fisher lit up. "Good. Only damn place in New York City you can smoke in peace anymore."

PART SEVEN

Home Again

CHAPTER

1

They left it up to the President.

The terrorist was dead, his canisters of sarin gas secured. A thorough search had turned up nothing, there were guards all over the place, and the crowd outside was as patient as New Yorkers could be.

Which wasn't very.

"I say let's move on with it," said the President. "The hell with these terrorist scumbags."

"You shouldn't say *scumbags*," said one of his advisors.

"You want me to say what I really think of them?"

The man shut his mouth.

The tip-off started at ten P.M., a delay of only an hour and a half. As an added bonus, the network agreed to cut the number of commercials and show the game as it was meant to be played, without interference.

Dr. Blitz left the President just before the end of first half of the game, walking outside with the Secret Service bodyguard to the task force trailer. There he was briefed personally by the Homeland Security agent who had coordinated the operation, Michael Macklin. Macklin, his clothes soiled with dirt and sweat, looked as if had crawled through the sewer to get there.

"We don't know yet if the man who died down there worked alone or not," Macklin told him. "He didn't have an accomplice on the scene that we've found, which was one reason we were able to fool him with the temporary blackout. That was supposed to be his signal to begin."

"Who figured that out?" asked Blitz.

"Andy Fisher," said DIA agent Kowalski, standing nearby. He had a pained expression on his face. *"The* Andy Fisher."

"So Fisher and Colonel Howe were right: It was connected to the UAV and the E-bomb," said Blitz. "Which means the Korean is still at large somewhere."

"Or he sold the thing to them before he escaped."

Blitz turned around. A tall, bedraggled man in a rumbled brown suit stood before him. He was missing a shoe.

"Agent Fisher, how are you?"

"Actually, that's Special Agent Fisher." Fisher took a puff on his cigarette. "They screwed up the paperwork somewhere a few years ago and promoted me by mistake."

Blitz shook his head. As the President said, a real pistol.

"So, where is this Korean?" Blitz asked.

Fisher shrugged. "Not my case."

"Maybe it ought to be," said Howe.

"Take it up with the boss," said Fisher, drawing on his cigarette. "Meantime, I thought I'd go watch the end of this basketball game."

CHAPTER

2

When dawn broke, Kuong's ship was several hundred miles from the American coast, well on its way to Africa. Once there, Kuong would make his way to Nigeria, where he would board the first of several airplanes for the flight to Peru. How long it would take to accomplish that journey, he did not know; it would be many days if not weeks, considerably longer than the trip he had taken to board the *Beneficent Goddess*. But this was necessary, and because it was necessary, he did not mind it.

He had watched CNN via the satellite dish during the night. By the time the clock passed ten and there was no announcement, Kuong knew there would be none. His plan had failed.

He had been reluctant to turn the set off, hoping still that the stories would come. He longed to watch the casualty lists and footage of looters rampaging the city. He wanted to see the parade of ambulances and the somber faces. He would have laughed at their tears.

It was not to be—not now. Revenge would have to be sought far in the future.

Some men would conclude optimistically that failure would make his future success that much more delicious. But Kuong did not believe such lies. Bitterness could never really be washed away. He stood at the bow of the ship, staring at the pink light pushing back the gray of the ocean.

CHAPTER

3

Howe swung the door open. "Home!" he yelled.

He heard his mother talking in the kitchen, muttering about the food or maybe complaining that he was late.

"Hey," he said, coming through the small dining room.

"Well, about time." His mother turned from the stove and kissed him. Howe saw she hadn't been talking to herself but to his friend Jimmy's wife. They'd just arrived for dinner. "Hey, Deb," he said to her.

"Hey yourself. And you're Alice?"

Alice stood in the doorway, a bashful smile on her face.

Whether it was the light or the smile or something else, she looked more beautiful than ever.

"How'd you get hooked up with this character?" Deb asked.

"I tried to rent him an apartment."

As his mother introduced herself, Howe slid toward the back of the kitchen and helped himself to beer. A few minutes later, with the women showing no sign of needing him or even noticing that he was still there, he slipped out the side door and went to find Jimmy. He found him hauling out some brush in the side yard.

"Working for your supper?" he asked his friend.

"I figured I'd at least earn a beer."

Howe handed him his.

"Don't mind if I wipe the bottle," said Jimmy.

"I would if I were you."

"So? They catch the bastard?"

Howe shook his head. He trusted his friend more than just about anyone in the world, but he still had to be careful what he said. After the first flush of stories, the news reports had been very vague about what had happened, saying there seemed to be a Korean connection but not really explaining. And of course they didn't know about Howe's role in it all.

It was clear that the UAVs had been launched at sea. Dalton said the booster would have made it possible. The Navy had several candidates, but thus far the ships they had checked had turned up clean.

More than likely, the man Howe had rescued had been involved in the attack. They knew who he was now: a high-ranking relative of Kim Jong Il who'd commanded a military unit as well as a development facility. He'd been too well known to sneak out of the country on his own—or maybe too cunning to miss the chance of turning his escape into a gesture of defiance against the Americans. It was just a matter of time before they found him, Howe thought.

But it might also be just a matter of time before he struck again.

It wasn't his job to worry about it. He'd been thanked for getting involved—but also subtly reminded that it wasn't his job.

Screw that, he'd told them all. Except the President.

"Don't drink it all," said Howe, reaching for the bottle.

"Get your own," laughed Jimmy. "You can afford it."

"It's not the money, it's the principle," said Howe. But he let his friend keep his beer.